Requited Unrequited Love

Mina Ramzy

CONTENTS

To all the women who feel suppressed by their culture.
I hear you.
I am with you.

Content Warnings

The following content may contain elements that are not suitable for some audiences. Reader discretion is advised.

- Mention and depiction of sexism

- Mention of drunk driving and car accidents

- Mention of queerphobia

- Mention of mental/personality disorders (eating disorder, addiction, psychopathy)

- Mention of suicidal thoughts, suicidality and suicide

- Depiction and mention of self-injurious behavior (self-harm)

- Depiction and mention of death

- Depiction of excessive or gratuitous violence

- Depiction and mention of blood

- Abuse (physical, mental, emotional, verbal)

- Child abuse

- Rape and sexual assault

- Depiction and mention of cancer

- Use of profanity / Cursing and vulgar language

- Explicit and graphic sexual content

DISCLAIMER
Some passages in this book might be considered more non-fiction. These parts aim to raise awareness of mental health and cultural suppression.

PLAYLIST

Prisoner - The Weeknd, Lana Del Rey
Pretty When You Cry - Lana Del Rey
Daddy Issues - The Neighbourhood
Consideration - Rihanna, SZA
For Whom The Bell Tolls - J. Cole
Take Me To Church - Hozier
Fuck Love (feat. Trippie Redd) - XXXTENTACION, Trippie Redd
I Can't Handle Change - Roar
Bad Girls - M.I.A.
Pretending (feat. Jessie Reyez) - A Boogie Wit da Hoodie, Jessie Reyez
I Wanna Be Yours - Arctic Monkeys
Another Love - Tom Odell
Romantic Homicide - d4vd
Scars - Michael Malarkey
Lose My Cool - Amber Mark
Losers - The Weeknd, Labrinth

Dear Yessie - Jessie Reyez
L$D - A$AP Rocky
All The Time - Jeremih, Lil Wayne, Natasha Mosley
Habits of My Heart - Jaymes Young
Tether Me - Galleaux
Jocelyn Flores - XXXTENTACION
Song Cry - August Alsina
Bloodstream - Stateless
SMTS - Jeremih
Broken - Lund
Exorcism - Clairity
Darija Freestyle - Dounia
If Only - BRIDGE
Don't Go - Reece
All Mine - PLAZA
Queen Tings - Masego, Tiffany Gouché
Keda - Sherine
Moeiteloos - Fresku, Shadi

CHAPTER ONE

I'm in need of change. And I don't mean changing my sheets—although I also need to do that. I mean, life-changing *change*.

As I'm sitting in a coffee shop, sipping on a latte, with my notebook full of bucket lists and lists, I skim through them, and I realize there are a lot of things on them I can't cross off. I might never be able to. The things being extreme is not the reason. For some, these might be yearly or even daily activities. It's because I'm not allowed to.

I'm Egyptian, which means I grew up with double standards. Where men are at the top of the pyramid and women, well, they are certainly not standing beside them.

In my culture, men can go where they want, when they want, with whom they want, explaining themselves *if* they want. Women, however, cannot. It is as simple as that. If you want to go somewhere, you either go with your family or with your new family. In other words, going on field trips, vacation with friends or something like exploring yourself while studying abroad will never happen. Women can go on trips with their husbands, and women can explore themselves when they're married—in their new kitchen. After all, there's a way out for everything as long as it can prevent women from going away.

I failed to benefit from many opportunities abroad because of this. Of course, I used to wonder why. Well, the answer I've always been given is, "Someone can do something to you!" or, "It's just the way our culture is ..."

Thus, it all boils down to this: men can do what they want, which means women can be in danger; ergo, keep the women behind closed doors until there's a man who wants to protect them. From men. From themselves? God, I despise men. It might not be all men, but there is no way to distinguish them. All of them show beautiful colors before showing their true ones, so it's best to stay wary of them all.

There is a saying in Arabic that goes: *Ely etls3 mn el shorba, ynfo5 fel zbady.* Literally translated, it means the person who got burned by soup will even blow on yogurt. Figuratively translated, it means when someone betrays you once, you will never trust again. Not even the people you know can be trusted and have no intention of betraying you.

As I said before, my bucket list items are not extreme; they're pretty mundane. And if they aren't, I tend to make them so.

I wanted to write a prisoner. We would become pen pals and exchange letters. But I realized I wouldn't exactly be able to handle that ... Instead of writing a prisoner, I decided to have a pen pal. It's via an app, and you get matched based on interests and proximity. I have talked to some people through the app, and they're all very friendly, but there's one particular person I speak to daily. His name is Adam—well, it's not his real name since everyone is anonymous. But Adam is nice.

Another earthly item is for me to watch the sunrise at the beach. This would mean that I have to be outside at four a.m. My curfew is set at eight p.m. And I don't know if something like a not-being-allowed-to-leave-the-house-before-a-specific-time *time* exists, but I highly doubt that mine is set before four a.m. I've already tried asking my brother or mother to accompany me, as it is the only way, but of course, I always get an *inshallah*, which basically means *no* but with more letters.

So, if I don't get married—and I'm definitely not planning on it—I will never see the sunrise. Or sleep over at my friend's house, or go on vacation alone or with someone other than my family, or live on my own with decor that is to my taste. For some, these might be common activities, while for me, they are bucket-list material. It feels as if my culture is holding me back from living a life

I should be able to live. Because of it, I have lost opportunities, friendships, and my sanity.

I just turned twenty-five, and I realize now that change doesn't come to you with age; you have to go after it. Or rather, make it happen. I'm not trying to get disowned, but seeing as my life won't wait for me to make that change, it seems I shouldn't either. I have to start sooner rather than later, or before I know it, I will be forty-five with a curfew at nine—hopefully. And without ever having seen the sunrise.

It also seems I'm not the only one who needs change. An old friend of mine has been having trouble paying his accountancy fees, and his accountant happens to be from Egypt too. He asked me to go over there and try to smooth things over, thinking the accountant might be more lenient if I went in his stead.

I totally get it. Egyptians are the worst when it comes to meeting other Egyptians. Before greeting each other properly, invitations to their children's weddings have already been given out. And, no, they're not even in the womb yet.

Once I finish my latte, I gather my long beige trench coat and notebook, which has a black velvet cover with *Memento Mori* written on it in gold. Latin for death being inevitable.

The way I see it, there are two types of people in this world. The first type is the *carpe diem* people. They seize the day, live in the present, have no regard for the future, and enjoy the small things life has to offer every day. The second type is the *memento mori* people. They remind themselves that life is temporary and the afterlife is infinite. This doesn't mean they sit on their asses all day, waiting for the other shoe to drop. They know their time might be limited, but it's also a generous amount if luck is on their side. If used wisely, great things can be achieved.

I'm a *memento mori* person—with good reason. Tomorrow is never promised, and yet we find ourselves taking it for granted because it has been promised to us up until now. And it's exactly because we're well aware of this that we preoccupy ourselves with our goals per diem.

I walk over to a trash can in all-black leather pumps, skinny jeans, and a long-sleeved turtleneck bodysuit. The outfit might be basic, which is what I was going for. I don't want the accountant to think I'm there to seduce him. Though it certainly wouldn't be a problem if it happened subconsciously. That's actually where the black pumps and the trench coat come in. If I wanted to let him know I was, in fact, trying to seduce him, I would have worn a little black dress without stockings. This way, I look modest yet provocative by showing my curves. Not that there is much to show. I'm so flat that I could cross-dress without needing a binder—which is kind of awesome, if you ask me.

In this fashion, the accountant won't think much of it—consciously. He will probably assume he has it all figured out because I didn't go for the obvious route, and he will treat me as someone who wasn't trying to manipulate him. And since it's human nature not to want to give someone something when you know you are being manipulated into giving it, all of this will lead to him giving in and giving me exactly what I want—while being manipulated to do so.

Being a psychology major does this to you sometimes, and yet I've never strayed away from my goal as a therapist; I am helping someone. Is it ethical? Probably not, but God is the only one who can hold me accountable, and I think he's busy doing other things.

I throw away the cup and leave the coffee shop, which is next to the accountant's office. I arrived earlier than expected, so I drank a latte to kill precious time.

All I know is that his name is A. Elias. I'm assuming I should address him as Mr. Elias.

I enter the building, and the receptionist tells me the directions to the waiting area. I take a seat on a black leather couch. A couple of minutes pass by, and all I can hear and see is a ticking clock, indicating that. Until I hear a man calling for me. "Ms. Armanious?"

I turn my head to the direction his voice came from. "Yes?"

He extends his hand for me to shake. "Good afternoon. My name is Virat. I'm Mr. Elias's assistant. It's nice to meet you."

Even if he's wearing a very notable navy-blue suit, I immediately notice his fluffy, dark hair. It's so fluffy that I want to jump up from my seat and run my fingers through it without greeting him back. But I probably shouldn't act on my intrusive thoughts.

I jump up from my seat and shake his hand in one stroke so as not to give my fingers a chance to do the ruffling as well. "Hi. Nice meeting you too!" I say, smiling, trying very hard to hide that I was thinking about assaulting him.

"Mr. Elias will see you now. Follow me, please."

As I follow him through some corridors, we finally reach a door.

He holds out his hand to it. "This is his office."

"Thank you for leading me here."

"My pleasure, Ms. Armanious." He then disappears into the corridors we just walked through.

In front of me is a white door, entirely covered in squares of glass, and in them, I see my reflection. My soft, angled eyebrows and brown eyes, the few freckles covering my face. The side-parted light-brown curls, reaching all the way to my hips.

I tilt my head to the left, examining myself some more until there's nothing to examine anymore. The door flies open, and shivers fly down my spine. A tall man materializes before my eyes. He is so tall that I only see his collarbones sticking out of two undone buttons of a white shirt.

I pause for a second before tilting my head back. And that is when I see his face. He has wavy, slicked-back, pitch-black hair with some strands covering his forehead. A pair of flat, filled black eyebrows accompany a pair of blinding green eyes. Topping it all off with a trimmed beard and a set of full lips.

We're both finding the toe caps of our shoes resting on the sill of the door. Making us stand so close that it feels as if we are touching each other. As if his body heat were melting from him to me, making all my muscles solidify and unable to even unsheathe myself from him.

We keep staring at each other, and then he breaks the silence. "Were you planning on standing there forever if I hadn't opened the door?" he says with a gruff voice, holding on to the door handle, the one I was supposed to hold to open the door.

Even when his eyes are blinding mine, they widen. "You could see me?!"

"I could see you since it's one-way glass."

"Meaning ..." Meaning I totally just made a fool of myself by checking myself out, as if using the mirror in my bathroom, adding to my always-sucky first impressions.

"Meaning the inside of the door is transparent and the outside of the door is reflective."

As he repeats what I already registered, I can't help but feel embarrassed, letting my body heat take over my cheeks.

I finally avert my gaze down to his shoes. To end up not finding the toe caps of derby shoes—what is to be expected of men in an office setting—but of black leather loafers, the good kind, and black slacks with his shirt tucked inside of them. I stop myself from studying the rest of his clothes since I can do that from my short-term memory, which lets me realize that I only saw his collarbones, no tie. His shirt is even unbuttoned, and he isn't wearing a suit jacket either. Would this still even be considered a suit? His assistant even had a pocket square.

He breaks out of my fashion handcuffs by breaking the silence again. "However, the outside of the door is not meant to be used as a mirror."

I see; he could not let that go. Of course, he had to break that to me, making me want to break him in half.

I take a deep breath to redeem myself. "I was a little distracted. My apologies."

"Then, don't be. I don't have time for that," he says while looking at me, dead serious.

I beg your fucking pardon?

I want to scratch open his perfect face and do more. How dare he talk to me this way?! But I'm here to achieve something, and I can't achieve it if I show *my* true colors. Men are dogs, right?

So, fine, Mr. *Kelb*, while you show leading behavior, I'll answer you in submissive behavior, leading us to engage in together behavior. I want to stay away from us utilizing opposed behavior since it will ultimately lead to aggression. Verbally. And physically, since I still stand by wanting to scratch open your face.

Thank you, Timothy Leary, for providing us with the *Rose of Leary* to understand the impact of behavior on others. I will use it well—ish.

The heads of my eyebrows raise and pull together. "I truly am sorry. You probably have a packed schedule, and I was just daydreaming. God, I'm so embarrassed. Should we maybe reschedule so you can see your next clients and not run late because of me?"

He will now assume I must feel guilty—not really; screw his schedule—and will start letting me off the hook. Then, it is back to my scheme.

He frowns at me. "That would be another hassle. Since you're already here, come in."

Another hassle? Is he calling me the first hassle? Oh—

Keep your cool, Kristina. You're about to do business.

As I walk past him into his office, I can't help but smirk a little. Until creaking reaches my ears, and I catch on to the fact that he's closing the door, making my smirk disappear in the blink of an eye and making me shriek instead.

"Don't!" I lower my voice. "I mean, don't close the door ... please."

I keep facing his desk, so I can't tell what kind of expression he's making. After a few moments, creaking reaches me again, indicating that the door is wide open. Then I hear footsteps approaching.

There are two chairs, and I sit on the right chair, facing his directly, with my legs crossed, one arm on the armrest of the chair and the other arm extended on his desk.

He walks toward his chair, pulls his pants legs up from his thighs, and sits down. He then entangles his hands in front of him on his desk.

"How may I help you?" he asks.

He really was dead serious about not having time. He went straight to business.

If I suddenly bring up that we're both Egyptian, I'd be contradicting everything I just said. How can I turn this around? I discreetly start scanning through his office. There're a lot of bookshelves with the book spines facing inward. There's some art on the wall, plants, and a coffee station.

Wait a second. He didn't even offer me something to drink. How rude.

When I scan his desk, I see my savior in a frame. It's a picture of him and a girl. I'm assuming it's his sister, girlfriend, or wife—a very wide variety of possibilities. He has his arm around her, and behind them is one of the Pyramids of Giza.

"The pyramids, I see," I say, looking at the picture while smiling.

He looks at my hand that's resting on his desk. "I already know you're from Egypt, and I know that you know I am as well."

An immediate heatwave—one I'm supposed to only experience in Egypt—comes crashing down through me as I realize I've been caught red-handed.

"H-how do you know so much?" I ask. No, really. He one-lined everything I'd wished he *hadn't* known.

"Your surname somewhat betrayed you, Ms. Armanious."

Damn it. I hoped he would be an airhead. Now, the entirety of my plan is in shambles.

"Not to mention, I know what brought you to me as well," he brags.

Great, he knows even more. *No need to brag about it, though, Mr. fucking Elias.*

He untangles his fingers and grabs a file from his desk. He slides it in front of me and sits up straight again.

I take the file and see the name João Salvador—the name of my friend in question. "How did you—"

But before I can even finish asking, he interrupts me. "The how is not important. Sending an Egyptian woman isn't going to help his case."

As he says that, I rise to my feet, resting both my hands on his desk. "That's not the reason I was sent here!"

He scoffs. "Then what is the reason you're here, Ms. Armanious?"

That is a good question, Mr. Elias. Because you are, in fact, correct. I was sent here for that exact reason. For being both Egyptian and a woman. But you were not supposed to be this conscious of that fact. Denying it would be unproductive, so I will tell you the truth—by omission—since nothing is more believable than the truth.

After calculating what formula I will use to solve this new problem, I take my seat again, clear my throat, and answer him. "Well, you're not completely wrong, Mr. Elias. The reason I'm here is only because I'm Egyptian too. It was never about me being a woman." That's a lie. "If João knew any men who were Egyptian," I say, which is another lie, as João, in fact, knows my brother, Delano, "I'm sure he would have asked them." A third lie since he deliberately didn't ask Delano.

The corner of my mouth quirks up. "Would you have preferred a man?"

He breathes out through his nose. It might have been a chuckle. "If this is your MO of asking me about my preference, then, no, I don't like men."

By all means, know Latin too. Why am I no longer amazed by his abundance of knowledge?

"A big loss for men." This is my MO for telling him he's attractive. My MO of letting him still give me what I'm after.

"If you say so."

"I do say so."

We keep staring at each other in silence again, and I decide that, this time, I'll be the one to break it. "So, why have I never seen you at church? Do you go on Sundays?" I'm still desperately trying to break the ice—or more like his thick skull.

"I do." Only his index finger lifts from his desk, pointing at me briefly. "You don't."

"I don't indeed. I go on Fridays."

He tilts his head at me. "How come?"

I take a time-out in the second round of our staring contest. "It just better fits my schedule if I go on Fridays." The fourth lie. I'm on a streak.

I don't go on Sundays because everyone goes on Sundays. Truth be told, I'm not that fond of Egyptians. The only thing they can do is judge, gossip, and act all holy and mighty. I used to go when I was younger, but my mother was against me wearing certain attire and behaving in certain ways. She cares a lot about their opinions, and the reputations of her children are very important to her. So, when I reached the point where I was just sick of it all, I decided I wasn't going anymore. If people don't know me, then they can't exactly judge me. I just made sure I was always busy on Sundays with schoolwork. It took a lot of persuading and convincing to make it a regular thing for me to go alone on a weekday, but now my mother knows how I truly feel about Egyptians. And when people ask her why I'm never with her, she tells them I'm busy.

The only exception to my dislike is my best friend, Alex. She's like an emulsifier, able to mingle with both water—me, Adam's ale; nice to meet you—and oil—them since I find them greasy and they tend to smear people. Yet she has been unsuccessful in doing what an emulsifier is meant for—encouraging a union. Even though she has been using force—more like forcing me—to make it happen.

She also goes on Sundays, so there's a good chance they already know each other. I decide to use that to keep this conversation flowing in the right direction.

"Do you happen to know Alex Basalious? She goes on Sundays as well. She's a friend of mine." Not only do I love Alex because she's Alex, but also for being here in spirit and saving my skin.

"I know who she is. We have a mutual friend. I don't know her personally though."

"A small world," I say, trying very hard to digest the awkwardness that's cooking up inside my stomach. With her protection being short-lived, my heroine even leaves in spirit for me to fend for myself again.

He nods. "So it seems."

The small talk has been going on for a very long time. It's quite obvious we're both thinking it. I guess it's time for me to actually get down to business—something I might have been dreading, worrying about not being able to help João because of this unforeseen ambush, being Mr. freaking Elias's knowledge.

"I'm going to cut to the chase and not waste any more of your time," I say. "João has it tight right now, and I was wondering if he could—well, if *I* could negotiate a delayed payment. He will pay everything that has to be paid in two months' time."

He leans back in his chair, throws his head back, and exhales sharply. I'm very confused as to why.

Then, he sits up properly again with all his facial muscles relaxing. "That is what he told you to ask me?"

I frown, still not understanding his reactions, and answer him—more like ask him my answer. "Yes?"

"What else did he tell you, Ms. Armanious?"

"He just told me he needs more time because he'll receive the money, which he lent, in two months."

"That true?"

He gets up to stand behind the chair I'm sitting on. He then bows down and closes me in by putting the tips of his fingers next to my hand on his desk, and with his other hand, he opens the file in front of me to the first page.

"Read it," says his urging voice from behind me.

I slightly turn my head to try to catch a glimpse of him, only to descry both our shoulders. I turn back to the file and read it. It says that João has already missed two months' worth of payments.

"Did he tell you this?" he asks, exposing the shell of my ear to a tingling sensation.

"He didn't." I take my eyes off the file to roll them at my lack of knowledge.

He grabs the file and settles down again. "Perhaps he shouldn't lend money he needs himself."

A scowl charges into the cells of my face. "It was for something important. Someone was in need."

"Which resulted in me still doing what is expected from me without getting what I expect in return."

That makes me understand his frustrations. He didn't owe João anything, and he still did him a favor by continuing to do whatever an accountant does for a client.

"For someone to end up barging into my office, being a nuisance and demanding things without knowing all the facts," he grumbles.

A refractory period. My wires stopped firing; they blew out. Except my eyes. They blow open, blinking rapidly as I try to process the words he just uttered.

He said what? *Barging* in? Being a nuisance?

To not be taken seriously by my family? I've somewhat accepted that. But to not be taken seriously by some stranger at that? Crossing. The. Line.

I'm done censoring my thoughts. I'm turning off the inhibitory control of my prefrontal cortex. I'm about to go haywire on this man.

I laugh a little and get up on my feet. I take my time buttoning up my trench coat and say nothing while thinking about how I'm going to go about switching between personas. He looks bewildered as he examines me, not understanding what I'm doing.

Once I button up my coat and tie the belt around me, I put my hands in my pockets and look him straight in the eyes with the dead-serious expression he happens to be so familiar with.

"It's liberating to drop facades, don't you think? See, I wanted you to think that you were dominant. I even wanted you to think I would polish your shoes if you asked me to," I say. "But none of it is going to work if you already have knowledge I wasn't counting on you having, so there's no point in pretending anymore."

He leans back in his chair, too amused. "You are finally showing your true colors."

"I finally am. And all my colors despise you. From the moment I walked into your office, I've thought you were an arrogant dick."

"You thought you could manipulate me? That doesn't work with me."

So I've noticed. "And I no longer need it to work. You will get your money. Mr. Elias, may I give you some advice?"

"I'm all ears."

I put my hands on his desk and lean forward to level my face with his. "When you receive the money, maybe you should invest it in something called a soul." I straighten my back.

He looks up at me with his smug face. "Mm-hmm. I will definitely consider it."

As I turn around and walk toward the door, he calls for me. "Oh, and, Ms. Armanious?"

I halt and turn around again.

"Since we're giving each other unsolicited advice, I would advise you to come prepared when you decide to make a case."

He steps toward me, probably wanting to see me out. But there is no way in hell I'm leaving before giving him an actual piece of my mind after he said that.

"Oh? You fucking—" I, unfortunately, don't get to finish my sentence because his assistant steps into his office.

"Pardon me for interrupting you, but there simply isn't time for you to finish what you were about to start, as his next appointment is in the waiting room …" His assistant trails off.

"It's fine. We were already done here," Mr. fucking *Kelb* says.

Before he can say anything else, I look at him with my lips pushed upward and leave. I don't say anything to him or his assistant, which he doesn't deserve.

While winding my way to the entrance of the building through the corridors, I see a frame with pictures. And there he is, the arrogant dick. I immediately feel rage washing over me again. There is a picture of his smug face with his smug smile. And then I see his name—Augustine Elias. Now, I know what the A stands for. Awful. Aggravating. Atrocious.

Once outside, I call João, and he picks up. "Krissie, how did it go?"

"João, it was a complete disaster. He had me figured out the minute he saw me, when I couldn't even see him. Even before seeing me."

"Too bad. It was a long shot, but it was worth trying. Thanks anyway."

"Why didn't you tell me about the two months you still have to pay for? If you had, I could've been better prepared for what was coming." As I say this, I realize that Mr. *Kelb* was right, and I hate it.

"I don't know. I thought it would be unnecessary if you guys hit it off. But it's okay. I can still borrow money from someone and then give it back to them in two months. I was just hoping to end the whole lending-and-borrowing-money cycle that had caused me trouble in the first place."

"I understand. I'm still sorry for not being able to help you the way we hoped I could."

"No, really, it's okay, *miga*. Let's meet up soon, okay? Talk to you later."

"Yes, see you." I hang up.

I'm so pissed off. Augustine. Doesn't that mean he's supposed to be some kind of saint? Instead, he was a rude, arrogant, ill-mannered demon. When he called me a nuisance, I completely lost it. Or when he told me he doesn't have time for me to be distracted—who even says that to someone they have just met in an office setting? So fucking unprofessional. He is so—

No. I won't give in to the stream of thoughts that was about to flow inside of me. It's not worth it. *He* is not worth it.

I'm not going to waste my precious time hating on some stranger I will never see again.

CHAPTER TWO

As I'm still very annoyed by yesterday's events, I decide to do the thing that always brings me happiness—talking to my pen pal, Adam. I have no idea who Adam is, what he looks like, how old he is, or what he does. All I know is that he's funny, he understands me, and we click. For me, that's enough. I don't need more than that.

I'm sitting angled on the black velvet L-shaped couch in my living room with a pillow behind me and my legs bent. I grab my phone and start texting him.

Eve: Adam. How is this day treating you?

It's a funny story, how Adam and I started talking. When I was setting up an account on the app, I had to come up with a pseudonym. I named myself Eve after the first woman on Earth. Eve doomed all of humanity with her actions, and I guess you could say that I, too, have had to endure some bad outcomes because of my actions. It was befitting, so I went for it.

Then, I came across Adam's account, and I found it ironic that someone else out there also had a reason to name themselves after the first man on Earth. So, I decided to message him with: "As I have been created out of your rib, it would only seem natural to befriend you."

To bond with him and his rib cage again, for old times' sake.

Ever since, there has never been a dull moment while talking to Adam.

My phone chimes with a specific sound, indicating that I have a notification from the app.

Adam: Even though the day has barely started, I would say anything is better than the day I had yesterday. Therefore, today is very good to me. How is today to you, Eve? I hope you refrained from eating any apples. The last time you did that ... let us just say no one was ecstatic about it.

As I mentioned, Adam has exactly the sense of humor I so enjoy.

Eve: Oh, I hear you. My yesterday sucked too. I guess that is just who yesterday decided to be. But I'm glad to hear that today is treating you with the utmost respect, as I seemed to not have done that when I took you down with me all those thousands of years ago. Did I ever properly apologize?

Adam: I would have to agree about yesterday being, well, yesterday. And you haven't, Eve, though even if you had, it would quite literally not have changed anything. I would still have had to leave behind the beautiful garden we were living in.

Eve: In my defense, you didn't have to accept the apple I gave you. You could have refused it and let me be the only bad girl. You could have stayed in the garden you oh-so love.

I don't know why, but Adam has mentioned several times that he loves the Garden of Eden and that he wishes he could have stayed there. I wonder why.

Adam: And let my wife team up with Satan alone? Not a prayer. I had to protect you.

Eve: You wanted to protect me? From Satan? Oh, Adam, I think you were supposed to protect yourself from me.

Adam: I was inexperienced back then. Cut me some slack, will you? You have done quite enough, Eve. You know, dooming humanity, for instance.

Eve: No fair, Adam. We were Bonnie and Clyde before they even were a thing. We did this together.

Adam: I suppose you are right in a sense.

Eve: I'm always right, except when I choose what to eat. Then, I'm wrong—*very* wrong.

As I smile at my screen, I see my brother walking over to sit next to me. I toss my phone to my feet out of reflex. It's not as if he would look at my screen, but still.

"Delano, how is this day treating you?" I say, still smiling.

Delano is the blessed one of us two. He has an undercut with curly brown hair, full eyebrows, and to top it all off, he has blue eyes. He got his eyes from our father, who sadly passed away in a car accident when I was only three years old. I don't remember my father, but I feel like I know him through the stories Mama shares with us, the picture albums, and looking at Delano. Almost every day, Mama grabs Delano by the cheeks to take a good look at him, and her gaze into his eyes *screams* that she reminisces about her husband and that she misses him deeply.

And sometimes, she says what we observe. "Oh Delano, *habibi*, you are the exact copy of your father."

It makes me glad that, in a way—even against all the odds of Delano having those eyes—something of his still lives on. That, in a way, *Baba* lives on in Delano.

And sometimes, I wonder, if he were still alive, would certain things have turned out to be different? Better?

"Treating me? How can a day treat me? That makes no sense, Kristina. What are you on about? A day is not a person," Delano snarls.

Delano, however, doesn't understand me like Adam does. It's not because of an age gap. Delano is only two years older than me, and we get along just fine. It's just that we have different ... personalities.

"It's a figure of speech, *ya homar*." I push him away from me and grab my phone again to check if Adam has responded, but unfortunately, he hasn't.

Delano scooches back next to me. "What are you up to on this impossible-to-treat-you day?"

I can't seem to argue with that because now, he's right. What I'm up to today is not a treat at all.

"You know how Alex just loves Egyptians? She's dragging me to go hang out with a few of her friends she hangs out with on Sundays." I sigh. "Delano, include me in your day, so I don't have to torture myself with fake smiles and bonding over Egypt, please?"

Who am I to go against chemistry? I wanted Alex to reach her full potential as an emulsifier, to reach a suspension. An emulsion—a mixture of my sweat and tears.

"No way. I'm meeting up with Farah today. If you don't want to go, just tell her. I'm sure she'll understand."

Tell her I don't want to? Understand? I'm not sure we're talking about the same Alex.

"I already did all of that for months, and today, she has decided that if I say no one more time, she'll barge into our house and drag me—even if I'm still in my pajamas—to go hang out with them. And you know how Mama is; she would love nothing more than for me to befriend all those people and go on Sundays. She even allowed me to go on such short notice. The notice being an hour ago."

"Yeah, that does sound more like Alex." He chuckles. "I genuinely think that you would meet a lot of great people if you go on Sundays. I mean, I go, and I enjoy it," he says, looking at me with sympathy.

That might be, but I also know Augustine goes on Sundays, and there's nothing great about him. In fact, he's trash. No, calling him trash would be an insult to trash. He's not worthy of any words. Or anything, really. I have badmouthed this man in my head so much in the past twenty-four hours that it makes me glad no one can read my mind. It's barbarous, to say the least.

And we have anything *but* chemistry. Although, I guess you could say I'm hydrophilic since I'm Adam's ale and that he's hydrophobic. We don't go well with each other at all. And I don't want to since I'm also *augustinophobic*.

"Mweh, maybe never," I say, shrugging my shoulders.

I go to my room to get ready. I don't want to meet judgy Egyptians in my pajamas for the first time, and I know Alex wasn't joking when she said she would be here in an hour to drag me out of the house.

I take a shower and decide to put my hair in a high, slicked-back bun. I suck at doing makeup, so all I use is some mascara and highlighter. And yet I still manage to look like an absolute clown. Makeup is an art form, and not everyone is an artist.

I also decide not to wear heels today. Instead, I wear flat black ankle boots. Which means I will be downgrading from five feet seven to five feet two.

But I don't want to pass on the only characteristic people define me by. My signature style. It's basically half of my personality at this point—Kristina with the long trench coat.

I have so many; it's getting ridiculous. A clothing rack full of them. I have trench coats in black, white, and gray. I have them in all shades of nude—in all the neutral colors really. Not only that, but I also have trench coats in both white and gray, or brown and olive green. No, seriously. One side is one color, and the other side is the other color. And the cherry on top? A trench coat that is nude with a leather back—my newest prized possession. Now, I would be lying if I said that I'm done buying trench coats. Even if my clothing rack can't handle the coats, I will make it handle them. It might be starting to become a problem though. Maybe I'm the problem?

After a lot of overthinking about the outfit, I go for light-colored straight jeans, a black turtleneck sweater, and a white trench coat. I wanted to wear all black because that's basically the other half of my personality, but I guess adding more color to my outfit somehow means I have my life together and am not, in fact, miserable—although that notion is debatable. Stereotypes are a curse, and yet even when we're aware of them, they're hard to ignore, let alone change when they're rooted so deeply in our subconscious.

I walk out of my room and already see Alex sitting on the couch with Mama. Alex has dark brown eyes, and her black hair reaches down to her shoulders. Her hair might be straight, but she totally isn't. This is the joke she always cracks, and I find humor makes up half of her personality.

The moment I stand in front of them, their conversation halts. I know I was the subject of it, but they didn't even try to fool me by changing it.

"Mama, aren't you a little too old to be gossiping?" I say while crossing my arms and cocking a brow.

"I'm not gossiping. I was just talking about you."

Sometimes, I can only laugh at how my mother contradicts herself within the same sentence.

My mother has brown eyes and curly shoulder-length hair—we had to get it from someone. She always straightens it, though, which I think is a shame because her hair is beautiful when she wears it naturally. You could say I'm the exact copy of her.

I hug Alex. "I thought we were meeting downstairs. You didn't even give me a chance to prove to you that dragging me out wouldn't be necessary."

"Oh, babes, it was never about taking you with me by force—that I can handle. I thought you would take it a step further and escape by jumping out of your window."

"What? I would never jump out of a window just to avoid confrontation."

"Yeah, well, I never know with you. Sometimes, I think you have yet to be diagnosed with Egyptian-people phobia," she mocks.

"*Yalahwi*? That is a thing?" My mother looks at Alex, concerned.

She realizes we aren't alone and sits down again to hold my mother by the shoulders. "Oh, *tant* Diana, don't worry; that's not a real thing." She giggles. "But Egyptophobia is, and that is the fear of spending the rest of your life in Egypt."

"Are you diagnosing me right now?" I ask.

"Am I wrong, Miss Therapist?" She winks at me.

I roll my eyes at her. "I only fear spending the rest of my life there because I always get sick there. Imagine being sick the rest of your life and then you just die? That's an awful fate."

"You have to face your fears head-on!" Alex cheers.

"Well, I would say I'm about to, wouldn't you?"

"Yeah, finally."

I take a seat next to my mother and face her. "Mama, as you probably already know"—I shoot Alex a poker face since I'm fairly certain she's responsible for my mother allowing it on such short notice—"I'm going to meet up with Alex's friends she hangs out with on Sundays in a restaurant not too far from here. I have already sent you the location."

My mother looks at me, happy—a little too happy. "Okay, *habibti*, have fun!" Alex is already at the door. I realize that my mother hasn't said anything about my curfew. I'm almost at the door, and she still says nothing.

I. Am. So. Going. To use this to my advantage. Egyptians are a free pass to go outside till whenever? I might actually start to love them; what a beautiful bunch. This is wild. I need to celebrate this new discovery. Is this the change I have been longing for?

As I'm far ahead in planning my new life, I'm interrupted by reality. "Oh, Kristina? Send me the phone numbers of the people you will be with and be back at eight," my mother says.

Dreams really do shatter within a matter of seconds. I can quite literally hear glass breaking. Of course, the curfew still stands. Life can't be that beautiful. We can't win them all.

I turn around, trying to put up my sincerest smile. "Will do, if I get them myself in the first place." And I wasn't planning on getting them in the first place.

This will be the first and last time I will hang out with this bunch. I'm only giving it a shot for Alex's sake.

Alex and I leave my house and walk to the pub. Now, I know I said I was going to a restaurant, but a pub is essentially a restaurant that serves a great variety of alcoholic drinks. So, I was telling the truth. With an omission. That is kind of my thing.

"Alex, do these people know you have a girlfriend?" I ask while linking our arms together.

"No, not all of them, but I'm just going to say it the minute it comes up."

I give her a worrisome look. "But what if they judge you?"

She turns away for a second and then faces me again. "Well then, I'll show them how perfectly amazing I am, and then they won't be able to."

I laugh. "You truly are amazing, you know." I lean my head against her shoulder—my way of hugging her as we walk.

"So are you, and I'm proud that you decided to come with me today. It will be fun, I promise."

"Fine, I'll take your word for it. But, Alex"—I stop walking, and she comes to a stop too—"if I even have the slightest inkling that anyone has anything to say about you, I will scratch open their faces right then and there."

She first stares at me with wide eyes and then laughs. "My own personal guard cat? You should have brought Lady along to assist you in your little scratch party."

Lady is my cat, but to me, she's my daughter. I guess I can be considered a full-fledged cat mom instead of an adult. She's a Bengal cat, and she's gorgeous.

"Don't worry; I will scratch and hiss for the both of us."

"Well, I'm glad since I can't scratch anyone. My nails are too short because you know—"

I interrupt her and hold up my hand to her. "I already know, and I don't want to know more about you topping your girlfriend."

"Kris ... I was about to say that my nails are too short because I have stress and bite them all the time." She looks at the ground and sulks.

"Oh, that was so uncalled for. I'm sorry." I feel like such an asshole for assuming that she wanted to make a perverted joke out of it.

She looks at me with her mischievous grin. "But you aren't wrong; it's so much more comfortable with shorter nails when—"

I interrupt her again. The shame I feel disappears as fast as the new life I envisioned for myself. "Oh my God, no. I knew it. I hate you!"

I try to suppress my chuckle by pursing my lips and closing my eyes, but we both end up laughing out loud.

We arrive in front of the pub, and Alex stops me from entering. "Now, remember, Kristina, don't run away the minute you feel like you want to. Give it and them a fair chance, *mashi*?"

"Don't worry, Mom. I won't run away!"

"Good girl! Let's go in."

We enter, and I follow her. She is making her way toward a round table with five people already sitting around it. Alex walks up to one girl, and she stands up. They hug, and I stand next to them with my head turned toward them to avoid looking at the others at the table.

I might dislike Egyptians, but that doesn't mean I don't feel shy and awkward around them. They're in a pack, and I'm a lone wolf.

Once Alex is done hugging her friend, she introduces me. "Everyone, meet Kristina. Kristina, meet everyone," she says, delighted, holding out her hand.

I face the table, scanning the people from the left and then around the round table. Until I sense someone getting up right from me, I immediately avert my attention entirely to the right side of the table.

My eyes go round, and my mouth goes even rounder. I'm genuinely caught off guard because before me materializes the man I thought I would never have to see again.

"You have got to be fucking kidding me?" I snarl as our eyes lock.

Everyone at the table starts to murmur. And I realize what I was thinking was put out into the world. I also realize that I didn't even greet these people before snarling my first sentence. God, my first impressions always suck. I know I said I wouldn't run away, but don't I deserve a free pass right about now?

"Do ... you two know each other already?" Alex questions, baffled.

With our eyes still locked, I decide that I'm not going to look away first because I don't back away from a challenge. Even if it is an unsolicited one. "No, and I would like to keep it that way," I mutter.

Of course, the only seat that is still available is the one next to him. Alex sits to the right of her friend, with the seat to the right of Alex available. Next to it, *he* is seated.

This is just great! I pout and sit down.

The guy sitting to his right whispers in his ear, "Augustine, do you know her?"

He turns left to look at me, which makes me turn right. He tilts his head and holds it there for a couple of moments. Then turns back to the guy sitting next to him and shrugs. "It seems that I don't."

I face the ceiling. *God, if this is your way of punishing me—because I wanted to use Egyptians as a means to escape my curfew—then I would rather choose actual hell.*

Alex tries to distract everyone from what just went down. "Did you guys already order any drinks?"

"No, we were waiting for you, but we can order now," her friend says.

We order drinks, and the waiter brings them to us. I ordered a glass of red wine. I hadn't planned on drinking today, but since I can't physically escape, I'm going to escape—a tad—mentally. I chug the wine and put the empty glass in front of me.

"Since not everyone knows each other, I think it would be good if we had a round of introductions, wouldn't you all agree?" Alex's friend suggests.

"Yes! That sounds like a great plan," Alex agrees.

"Okay, great. I will go first, then Alex and so forth," her friend says. "So, I'm Sarah. I'm twenty-three years old, and I'm in law school. Also, I'm engaged to that fellow over there, next to Augustine, Tony."

The guy next to Augustine waves.

Engaged at twenty-three? That's relatively young, if you ask me. What's the rush? I'm going to have to conceal this fact from my mother because if she were to find out, there's no doubt that she would tell me I'm already expired goods.

"Well, I'm Alex, I'm twenty-six, and I'm in law school too. Also, I'm queer."

I turn my head to her, blinking, but as soon as I see her confident smile, I can't help but be proud and smile as well. Although that smile is short-lived.

"Queer? What does that even mean?" the guy next to Tony asks.

I frown, and when I'm about to open my mouth, I feel Alex holding my hand under the table, caressing it with her thumb. Her way of telling me I should keep my cool and *not* lose it.

Augustine looks at our hands, then lifts his head to the guy next to Tony. He also puts his entangled hands on the table, giving me flashbacks, as he did the same thing with his hands in his office.

"Being queer means that you are part of the LGBTQ+ community, however, without labeling yourself. Your orientation might go beyond the labels given, you maybe haven't completely figured it out yet, or you just simply don't want

24

to label yourself." He turns his head to Alex. "Correct me if I'm wrong, please."

Both Alex and I look flabbergasted. She, probably because someone you would expect to be against it due to their religion and culture, is educated on the matter. I, however, because I realize that he might have a soul after all.

She gives him a proud look. "No, that's exactly it, actually!"

"Which pronouns do you prefer?" he asks her.

"She/her are fine. Thank you for asking. I really appreciate it."

He gives her a sincere smile. Now, I'm no expert in the broad spectrum of smiles, but I sure as hell didn't get one yesterday. He was so rude to me. I'm not jealous, not at all. This just fuels my vendetta against him.

"So, does that mean you have a girlfriend?" the same guy asks.

"I do actually. She's lovely," Alex answers.

"So, is she Egyptian too?" he asks as a follow-up question.

God, since when did this become an interview?

"No, she isn't. Her parents are from Eritrea."

"Oh, that's cool. So, different cultures?"

"I mean, in a way, but she's Orthodox too, she just goes to a different church. So, I would say that religion-wise, only the language is really different."

Hence, thus, and so. I'm not sure if he's truly interested or if this is his way of judging her. This whole thing is too confusing. I want to go home, cuddle with Lady, and talk with Adam.

As I daydream about a better now, I register that people are looking at me because it's my turn to introduce myself. I didn't say anything the entire time, hoping they would forget about the only thing I said since I have been here.

"Oh, well, I'm Kristina Armanious." Fuck, no one said their surname. I hate it here. But it's fine. I have to remind myself of the spotlight effect. I'm overestimating that anyone noticed that I did. No one probably noticed.

"I'm twenty-five years old and study psychology because I would like to help people. Also, I'm straight, single, and satisfied." Alliteration at its finest.

While I was saying the last word, I briefly looked at Sarah. So what if that last part was meant for Miss Engaged? She didn't attack me, and yet I felt as if I had to defend myself. How pathetic.

Sarah chortles. "I like how you added those last three words."

Before I answer her, I feel the wine making its entrance into my brain. Feeling my inhibitory control losing control and my filter getting filtered out. "I thought adding 'also,' followed by your love life status, was part of it. My bad."

Wait, did I just say that out loud? Not soon after, I get confirmation I did.

Sarah, Alex, and the third girl laugh, and I can feel Augustine's gaze on me.

Where is the rule book for hanging out with Egyptians? I need it right about now. I have embarrassed myself enough as it is.

Augustine starts introducing himself, making me shift my eyes to my lap. "My name is Augustine Elias. I'm thirty-three. I'm an accountant, and I want to help others too. Also, the alliteration that was just made? Same."

Okay, first of all, did he just say his surname to spite me? Screw the spotlight effect. It obviously was noticed. Furthermore, I didn't know he was *that* old. In addition, no, not same. There is nothing the same about us. The nerve this man has to associate me with him and the nerve he has to be adding to *my* alliteration.

I notice I haven't thought about the *and finally* part because I'm blurting it out, "More like making their lives miserable."

He ignores it.

"I guess it's my turn. I'm Tony, twenty-eight years young, and I'm an accountant too. Also, that's my beautiful fiancée."

This time, Sarah waves.

The guy next to Tony starts talking. "I'm George, thirty years old. I work in HR. Also, this is my wife, Mariam." He grabs the girl next to him by her shoulders.

She chuckles. "I'm Mariam, twenty-four, and a nurse. Also, George."

Mea culpa. Married? At twenty-four? Now, I'm definitely expired goods. Miss Engaged, I take it all back. I should have been shooting daggers at Miss Married instead. Or should I say, Mrs. Married? It's people like these that remind me of my commitment issues. And that age gap—six years? That's way too big. I would never marry someone that much older than me. Hell, I would never marry, period.

I excuse myself to go to the restroom. I don't need to go; I just need a break. I'm glad my brain didn't decide to run with, *Mea culpa, I need a break. You guys are mentally draining me, and I have wanted to escape the minute I saw you all, especially him.*

I lean with my shoulder against the wall across from the restrooms, my back facing the corridor entrance where they are located. I grab my phone and decide to text João.

Kristina: You will never fucking guess who I had the displeasure of meeting again. But, like, guess.

As I type the sentence, I hear footsteps approaching and stopping right behind me.

Then Augustine's familiar raspy voice reaches me, which causes me to stiffen entirely. "Notifying your lover of all the latest deets, are we?"

What? I literally just introduced myself as single, and he even retweeted it in real life. What is he on about?

I don't turn around yet. I roll my eyes and hit Send. "It's rude to spy on people, you know."

"I'm not spying. I announced myself to be right behind you. Also, I'm not to blame for you being so little."

That makes me turn around, and it makes me angry. He managed to push the wrong buttons yet again.

He's leaning with his shoulder against the wall, arms folded. He is mirroring me.

But before I can get the anger out of my system, he says more. "You being little doesn't mean you have to act childish too, now does it?"

Oh? Also thinking little of me, are you? I. Am. Fuming.

"Excuse me?" I finally snap.

"I'm insinuating that we aren't alone, so the least you can do is act civilized."

"Oh, how delighted I am that we're alone now!" I scoff. "I don't like you all that much. In fact, I loathe you." I'm not delighted. I don't like being alone with him at all.

"The feeling is mutual." He leans his back against the wall now.

"I'm not going to pretend to like you if I don't," I hiss. Lady, I wish you were here to show this stupid man what real hissing is all about. But don't worry; I will never let this awful man lay his eyes on your beautiful fur.

"It's not about pretending; it's about not causing a ruckus in front of others who clearly have nothing to do with the matter. It's being mature."

"Oh? You're calling yourself mature?"

Look at me while I'm talking to you, damn it.

I walk to stand in front of him. I notice now that he's wearing a suit today. He even has a tie on, which makes me take a step closer.

"You're unnecessarily tall." I grab his tie and pull his face toward mine. "Level with me for a sec."

He looks startled. Good.

"Being tall doesn't equal being mature. My behavior is caused by you. So, no, I won't refrain from displaying it. If you have a problem with it, go deal with it."

He glares at me and grabs my hand that's holding his tie tightly.

"Childish," he grits out, jaw twitching.

Oh, how mature of you. Aren't you, like, forty?

"Let go of my hand," I order.

"Let go of my tie."

But then I feel his touch to be suffocating. Instead of being enraged, I become more frightened.

"I—I can't let go if you're holding my hand so tightly," I stammer.

"Perhaps you should have anticipated this before grabbing my tie." His eyes pierce through me. "It's the consequences of your own actions."

My eyes dilate with the realization of the words he just uttered. I have heard those words before, in a dark time that has taken me many years to forget about. I'm in awe. I avert my eyes from his to look at our hands, and then I look back up at him, feeling my eyes well up before tears flow down my cheeks. Hesitantly,

I bring the fingers of my other hand to my cheek and feel the tears with my fingertips. And I feel more coming.

He looks alarmed but doesn't say a word. Instead, he immediately lets go of my hand, and I slowly let go of his tie. I face the ground, turn around, and rush to the back door, leaving the pub.

I keep walking until I come across an abandoned park. I sit on a bench and grab my phone to text Alex.

Kristina: I'm fine. Don't come looking for me, please. I need time.

I turn off my phone and put my hands on the insides of my thighs to squeeze them as hard as I possibly can, and then I tilt my head back to stare into the sky.

I learned something new today. I learned I am not over what happened all those years ago. Not even close.

One reminder—that is all it takes to relive something again.

As I sit there, I let myself sob until there are no tears left.

CHAPTER THREE

Adam: Eve, here is a burning question for you. Why do humans weep?

Eve: Adam. They weep when they are sad or suffering but also when they are proud or overjoyed. It's a way to describe emotions when they are too intense to be put into words. That is why they weep, Adam.

A couple of weeks have passed since that day I hung out with Alex's friends. I also haven't been going to church since then. The thought of me being in the building two days prior to them being in that same building is too much of an embarrassment. As I have had the time to properly process everything that went down, I'm painfully aware of how awkward the whole thing was. The first time I opened my mouth, I cursed, and I was kind of being a brat. And Augustine being there might not be an excuse, but it completely ruined my mood.

I quite literally ran away after I clearly said I wouldn't. And the worst part was, I started tearing up like the little child he had said I was.

Oh well. All's well that ends well. And for me, it ending well is that I never have to encounter them again. If I avoid Sundays, like I always have, I can soon put this nightmare behind me. There's no way there will be more surprise encounters. That would just be absurd.

I told Alex I wasn't ready to talk about it, so we haven't yet. That's one of the things I love most about her—she always respects boundaries and never pressures someone. Even if we have good intentions of wanting to comfort someone, their saying no should always be respected. In any situation, should that two-letter word *be respected.*

She's coming over today, and I'm okay-ish now, so I'll briefly explain what went down. In return, she can tell me what went down after I left. I bet they thought, *What kind of nutjob runs off in the middle of being with people?* Me. I'm that nutjob. She's me, and I'm her. We're one and the same.

The doorbell rings, and I open the door. I let Alex in, walk toward the couch, sit, and put my feet up on the edge of the couch. Alex takes off her coat and shoes and sits next to me.

"Is anyone else home?" she asks.

"No, just us, so we can talk freely."

She kisses her palm and extends her arm to touch mine. I touch her palm with mine and put it against my cheek. This is our way of showing each other affection, and it has been our way of showing it for as long as I can remember.

"Are ... you ready to talk now?" she asks me.

I nod. "I am."

"What happened after you went to the restroom?"

I breathe out. "Remember when I told you I had to help my friend João with something regarding his fees?"

"Yeah, I remember. What about it?"

"Turns out that the person he had trouble with was Egyptian, and that person was Augustine."

She scowls. "No way?"

"Yes way, and the day before we went to the pub, I was in his office. And let's just say that it wasn't at all sunshine and rainbows." I sigh. "More like thunder and lightning."

"You guys fought in his office?!"

"When things started to get heated, his assistant interrupted us by saying that there wasn't time for what I was about to start, so not entirely."

"So, that's how you already knew him! I was so confused, but I didn't want to make a fuss about it in front of the others." She rubs her temple. "When you left to go to the restroom, I was looking at him, and his eyes followed you until you weren't in sight anymore. Not ten seconds later, he excused himself as well."

"He gave me a piece of his mind, saying that I was acting like a child." I roll my eyes. "And I told him I'm not going to pretend to like him if I don't."

Alex nods. "Then, what happened?"

"We kept going back and forth for a while." I pause and then continue with uneasiness in my voice, "Let's just say he said something that made the past make its way to the present."

Alex winces and leans in to hug me. "I understand. I'm so sorry."

I hug her back tightly and feel my eyes getting wet, but I'm able to shield the tears from falling. We hug each other for a while, until I feel like I can let go.

Alex clears her throat. "When he came back, he told everyone that you'd told him to tell us you unfortunately had to leave because of an emergency. I thought you'd left because you were done with being there," she says. "Then, I saw him grabbing his own coat, and at that moment, I read your text. He wanted to go after you. He was about to excuse himself, and I interrupted him," she points out.

I lift my eyebrows. "What?"

"Yes. And when I interrupted him, he saw me holding up my phone while looking at him. He understood I realized he wanted to go after you and listened to me by putting his coat back and sitting down again."

"So, no one thought I was a nutjob?" I say in disbelief.

"Well, you did say good afternoon by saying—and I quote—'You have got to be fucking kidding me.' But other than that? I think you're in the clear."

I laugh. "God, don't remind me. You are never going to let me live that one down, are you?"

"Definitely not. It's just so you. I love it!"

I didn't expect him to cover for me in front of everyone. For weeks, I thought he had told them what really went down, how I had basically assaulted him, scolded him, cried, and then just ran away. He could have, but he'd chosen not to, even if he had every right to put me in a bad light. It's not like I didn't deserve it.

But what I really didn't expect was him wanting to run after me. And even if he had, what would he have wanted to do? Comfort me? The person who caused you to cry, wanting to comfort you. How ironic. The one who hurt you cannot heal you. *Ever.*

As we sit on the couch, Lady jumps on my lap. I pet her head, and then she walks to Alex's lap.

She pets her. "Hello, gorgeous. You totally missed out on the scratch party Kris was organizing."

"I practically hissed at Augustine, channeling my inner Lady," I say.

"No! You did not?" She giggles while rubbing Lady's belly.

"I sure did." Now, after the fact, it's not something I'm entirely proud of.

I tried to let what happened go, but I can't. "Alex, did anyone say anything about me after I left or in the last couple of weeks?"

She shifts her attention to the ceiling. "I don't know about Augustine,

George, or Mariam. It was the first time I actually talked to them. I did talk to Sarah though. She just thought you were funny."

"To laugh at?" I pout.

"To laugh because of." She reassures me by petting my head with her other hand. "Maybe hanging out with so many for the first time wasn't my brightest idea, but maybe we could hang out with only Sarah, if you're up for it?"

I go poker-faced. "Yeah ... I think I've had enough hanging out with Egyptians for the next five years. Let's maybe discuss this again sometime in the future."

She squints her eyes at me and tries to suppress her smile. "I won't force you, but who knows? Maybe somewhere in the near future, you'll change your mind about things."

Change. Yes, I would love nothing more than change. Changing my mind? That is not going to happen anytime soon. But changing my life? It would be great if that happened sooner rather than later.

"By the way, Kris, your mom told me on Sunday that you haven't gone to church in a couple of weeks. Why?"

"Did she seriously tell you to ask me this?"

"Well, no ... but yes?" she says, squinting her eyes again.

I squint my eyes back at her and click my tongue. "I'm going tomorrow, so you can tell her that. You can also tell her that if she wants to know something, she can ask me instead. Also, ask her what's for dinner since she likes telling you things that are meant for me."

"She means well."

"That might be, but having good intentions shouldn't always excuse certain actions."

We talk for a while about everything and nothing. Eventually, Alex leaves.

And I have koshari for dinner. It's an Egyptian dish with rice, pasta, and tomato sauce, topped off with dried chickpeas and dried unions. It's good—so good.

After eating dinner, I take a shower, get into bed, cuddle with Lady, and fall asleep.

It's Friday morning. Which means it's time to stop avoiding going to church. Besides, I never stay long. After the service, I usually sit at a table by my lonesome, eat something quickly, and immediately go home.

Today, I'm putting my hair in a low bun because I wear a headscarf in church. I'm covered in black, from coat and sweater to pants and boots.

I take the subway, get out at my stop, and arrive in front of the building. I always enter from the back door. That way, I can just sit on a bench in the back. To not stand out. The service usually takes about two hours.

The service ends, and I go to the front, where people can light candles and pray. As I light up a candle, I close my eyes to pray. I pray for my family, Alex, and people in need. And then I pray for what I truly want. Freedom. I pray for the change I long for, which is getting harder and harder to subdue. Every day, I am faced with the fact that marriage is the only option. And every day, I catch myself thinking, *Will I only be able to* live *once my mother* dies?

When that thought resurfaces, I feel conflicted. It's awful to think such a thing. I have already lost a parent. I don't want to go through that again, especially since I would be losing both a mother and a father, as she's tried to fill in both roles for as long as I can remember.

And then there's the other side of the coin. The side that rings to remind me that every day I don't experience change is a day closer to it being too late. I didn't choose this upbringing. I didn't choose to be part of this culture. I was put in this world with this ideology forced upon me.

Don't get me wrong; I don't repel religion. In fact, I think it's a beautiful thing. To believe in a higher power, to have rules you follow to avoid sinning, to be *good*. But you don't necessarily have to be religious in order to be good. There are people who are atheists and are the purest souls out there. At the same time, there are religious people who have the darkest places in hell reserved for them. In the end, what defines whether you're good is not your ethnicity, skin color, culture, religion, gender, sexual orientation, or someone else. But *you.* You define it by your intentions and actions.

I do, however, repel culture. And the problem is that ever since we were little, we were brought up with the idea that the fine line between the two is nonexistent. Religion has been made into culture. If I were to ask anyone to point out to me where in the Bible it says that women aren't allowed to live on their own, not a single soul could show me that verse. There simply isn't a verse that says, *Women, thee shalt not liveth on thy owneth unless thou art wedded.* Now, I'm no expert in Shakespearean language, but I am an expert in knowing that verse doesn't exist. There also isn't a verse saying that women can't travel on their own. All those restrictions that we women deal with daily are cultural norms. And yet we grow up with the notion that all those things are like lying and cursing—*sinning.* This is what I mean when I say that the fine line is nonexistent.

To me, Egyptians are a constant reminder of the culture I oh-so loathe. The thing that confines me. Not only that but most of them are also allowed to do the things I just mentioned. Because not every parent confuses religion and culture with each other. There are just some unlucky women out there, and I happen to be one of them. But those Egyptians being allowed more than me—even if we're supposed to be the same—makes me enraged beyond words. Jealousy is a disease, and mine translates into hating those who have what I desire.

For years, I have shown *learned helplessness,* and I still do, in a way.

I thought I could never escape the culture. I always thought I was put in it, was a victim of it, and had no control over it. So, I did what any person eventually would: I stopped trying and accepted my fate. And even if there were opportunities presented to try again, the *learned helplessness* prevents you from using those opportunities. You don't even bother trying anymore.

It's a cycle and a hard one to break. But nothing is impossible—even the word itself says that. *I'm possible*. Possible to transform something once the awareness of transformation needed arises. Right, Audrey Hepburn?

As I'm deep, *deep* in thought, I feel someone standing next to me, touching my right shoulder with theirs. At first, I think it's by accident, then I hope the person will pray quickly and leave. So, I keep my eyes shut. But seconds become a minute, and I still feel the sensation of someone's shoulder against mine. Pressure. Uncomfortable.

I open my eyes and direct my face to the right, only for recognition to dawn. Because before me is none other than Augustine Elias. The man who has been my nemesis before I even met him.

I scoff. "You have got to be f—" I don't finish the sentence. I quite literally shut myself up by slapping my hand over my mouth. And I'm glad I did.

If I had finished that sentence, I would have been advocating for the pub events to repeat themselves again. I definitely don't want that. Also, I'm in church. I can't curse in church. But I do have to admit, God, what a great way to trick me into thinking I would never have to face that face again. Good one. Isn't this like the second time, though? I would say that it's quite enough right about now.

I clear my throat and go again in a way that corresponds with what I originally wanted to say and is actually allowed to be said. "Holy moly," I say. "Good heavens."

We're still touching shoulders, but our heads are turned to one another.

"You sure do have a way with words," he says.

"I would say you do too, as you just made use of alliteration."

"You're the blueprint."

I don't know what to say to that, so I avert my eyes from his to the candles. Meanwhile, he lights up a candle. He's wearing a black shirt—two undone buttons yet again—tucked inside gray slacks and black leather loafers. I have to admit, he does have a sense of fashion.

"Stalking me now, are you?" I say while lighting a candle as well.

"Oh, no. I can assure you, this just happened to better fit my schedule. I also happen to have better things to do than stalk someone I don't know."

Fridays fitting better in one's schedule? Please, that's the lie I invented, and now, he wants to use it against me?

I see a *tant* who also always goes on Fridays, and she walks toward us.

"Hi, *tant* Samia. How are you?" I turn around a little to give her a hug and three kisses on her cheeks.

"Hey, *habibti*. I'm good, *alhamdulillah*. How are you?" She holds me by the shoulder that's free from Augustine.

I grin. "I'm fine. *Noshkor rabena.*"

"Are you sure? I haven't seen you in the past couple of weeks."

"Yeah, I was just a little busy." *Yeah, right. Busy being embarrassed.*

As I talk to her, I notice Augustine is still standing next to me. Why isn't he leaving? Can't he see I'm in the middle of a conversation with someone?

"Have you already met my son, Augustinus?" She grabs Augustine's arm to pull him toward her.

I'm shocked to my very core. It's even stiffened. "Your what? Son?"

They don't look alike at all. She has short, straight brown hair and brown eyes. I have known her for the longest time. I sometimes even have breakfast with her. And now, I find out that same woman is his mother? The better question would be, *Why am I not leaving?*

"Yes. He always goes on Sundays, but the past couple of weeks, he's somehow also wanted to go on Fridays," she points out.

I look at him mockingly. "Oh, has he now?"

He avoids me by fixing his gaze on the floor. Mothers tend to blow our covers sometimes by speaking the honest truth.

Someone calls for his mother.

"Oh, I have to go. It was nice seeing you again, Kristina. Hopefully, I will see you again next week." She kisses me goodbye.

"Yes, *inshallah ya tant!*"

She then shifts to Augustine. "*habibi*, I will meet you at the car, okay? I need to take care of something first."

He nods, and she leaves.

"Lying in church now, are we?" I ridicule. I only realize now that his actual name is not Augustine, but Augustinus in Arabic.

He finally lifts his face. "I didn't want to leave things unresolved."

"You were worried because liquid was rolling down my face?"

He looks at me, concerned.

I sigh. "It had nothing to do with you. There was something in my eye."

"In both your eyes?" he questions while frowning.

That's a good point.

I blink several times. "There were some *things* in my eyes."

"Who is lying now?" he says as he crosses his arms.

I shrug my shoulders. "Then, I guess we're both liars."

He holds out his hand to me. It's big and veiny, and his fingers are thick and long. "For what it's worth, I'm sorry for causing some things to be in your eyes. Truce?"

I keep staring at his hand for a while and then look up at him. I simply can't act like everything is suddenly all okay now because the last couple of weeks were hard. So, I won't. I never pretend.

"Sorry. I don't want to shake your hand. You might hold my hand tightly again and tell me it's the consequence of the action of shaking your hand." I turn around to walk away from him, but then I'm brought to a halt because he grabs my hand instead.

I twirl, look at his hand holding mine, and glare at him. "I'm sorry, but are you seriously holding my hand right now? This has to be some sick joke. If I don't give you something, it doesn't mean you can just take it instead."

He slides his hand from mine up to my wrist and holds it. Then his jaw tightens. "Why do you keep running away from me?"

"Because I don't particularly like you, and I don't want to waste my time talking to you."

He studies my face. "Yes, we have already established that we're not that fond of each other."

"Good. The feeling remains mutual. Don't you want to stop wasting your time as well?"

"I don't want to leave things unresolved, even given our circumstances."

I peer at him. "A truce is not needed. We won't be seeing each other again, so that's a resolve in itself. Let's make it sooner rather than later."

His lips purse.

"You can let go now," I say, glancing down at his hand still holding my wrist.

He does as well and slowly slides his hand from my wrist to my hand, all the way to the tips of my fingers, and finally, lets go.

I look back up at him. "There. It's resolved. Goodbye." I turn around, winding my way to the back door. Leaving him standing by the candles.

Maybe it was unnecessary not to accept his truce, but it won't matter in the long run. We might have crossed paths a couple of times now, but all those times were mere coincidences. And I know how the saying goes—*Once is chance, twice is coincidence, and a third time's a pattern.* But sayings are averages, and individually, we can deviate from those averages.

As I leave the building, I decide to keep my headscarf on.

I realize it has been a long time since I visited my father's grave. So, I decide to do just that. I go to the nearest flower shop because I always buy the same bouquet when I visit him—a bouquet of nine blue roses. There is a good reason behind it. Blue represents both his eyes and him being mysterious and unattainable to me. Nine roses represent eternal love, wishing you spend the rest of your life with someone. Well, in my case, it's wishing that I *could* have spent the rest of my life with him. To have had the pleasure of getting to know him. To have had him within my reach, holding his hand and he mine.

But even if I didn't have those things, I feel like I want to talk to him. Even though I don't remember meeting him, I feel like I know him through and through, through stories and memories of others. I know that he didn't have a favorite color because he used to say he only had a favorite *bow* of colors. When asked why, he would always say that it brought him comfort, knowing that after darker times, better times always await us. And that rainbows are there to remind us that everything does *brighten* up again.

I think I understand what he meant by his metaphor. Everything is temporary, which makes it a blessing and a curse. Our suffering is temporary, but so is our joy. When we are at our lowest, we know that better times are coming, which lets us keep going. When we are at our highest, we know it won't last, and that saddens us, and sometimes, we even act on that sadness. This is reality. Reality is, in fact, a beautiful yet cruel thing. The only thing that has been granted equally to all is this reality.

You sound like you were such a beautiful and pure soul. Does a part of you live on in me too? Is that why I don't need context to understand what you meant by saying certain things? If it does, I'm glad to still always have you with me in a way.

As the poet Andrew Marvell has written to his coy mistress, *Had we but world enough and time.*

On his tombstone, it says, *Husband and Father*, and right under that, it says, *Sleep on now, and take your rest. —Matthew 26:45.*

I kneel down and rest on my lower legs. I put the bouquet next to his tombstone and grab the wilted one to put next to me.

No one has ever bought me flowers. I hoped you would be the first one, Baba. But I guess I was the one who gave flowers to you first. To put on your grave.

I stare at the tombstone. Take your rest. Is that really what death brings you? I won't deny that I thought it did. That death brings you peace. But there is also a good chance that it doesn't, that it could bring more suffering, more than we already experience. There is no way of confirming unless you cross over, and then there is no turning back. You will have the answer, and you will be stuck with that answer.

You have the answer, Dad. You tell me if it's better than being alive, waiting for the moment that you aren't anymore. And if living is essentially waiting for the inevitable, is there really any value to it?

To be, or not to be; that is the question. Isn't it, Hamlet?

I miss you. Can you miss someone you don't remember? Do I miss you, or do I miss the idea of you?

In my life, I miss being cared for and loved by a man, a father figure. A man who would let me stand on his feet to dance and twirl me around like a princess. A man who would treat me like a princess, showing me what the standard is and that I should never settle for less.

I just know that is the kind of father you would have been. But I didn't get to experience those things. You didn't get to live long enough to define that standard for me.

Your leaving wasn't a natural cause. It was because of a mistake. A mistake of someone that could have been avoided had that person been responsible, had that person not been drinking. I wonder what your last thoughts were. Were you scared, scared of dying? Or were you just sad—sad that you didn't get to say certain things to certain people, sad that you wouldn't get to experience your children's milestones? Or were you hopeful? Hopeful that, out of all the people who had experienced a car accident, you, too, would survive it. Honestly, I hope you weren't thinking anything at all. I hope you couldn't process what was happening, that it was a quick, painless death.

This shows that even strangers can dictate your life. A stranger can give you the happiest life, yet that same stranger could also end your life.

When I wasn't provided with what the standard should be, I went looking for it myself. I went looking for someone who could fill in your role. Male validation. And unfortunately, I looked for it in the wrong place.

It made me the person I am today. Disgusted by men, repulsed by love, and, above all, easily frightened.

But I wonder, Baba, if you had been here, do you think I would have been different around men? If I had seen your marriage right before my eyes, would I have loved love? Or would it not matter because my experiences with love would have channeled the person I am either way?

It must have been lonely for Mama. You left behind two half-versions of yourself, a constant reminder that once you were with her, but it being nothing but a memory now. And I know it caused her to be overprotective because she feels as though she needs to give love, care, and worry twice as much. Fulfilling your role.

I want to see you. I take a picture out of my wallet. It's a picture of him holding me when I was just a newborn. *Instead of a picture of you holding me in your arms, it should have been a picture in which I'm embracing you back.* The realization hits harder than it did before.

Rain starts pouring down. I'm glad. This way, no one will notice if you cry. And I tend to do that a lot. Tears and droplets, they become one and the same. As the rain droplets fall, my tears finally do as well. In sync, both I and the sky weep.

She's shielding me, and I embrace her, and we find comfort in one another.

CHAPTER FOUR

Eve: Adam. This time, I have a burning question for you. Have you ever had to say goodbye forevermore?

Adam: Eve, I would say I have. To both people I loved dearly and people I hardly knew.

Eve: Then, I wonder, Adam, would you say goodbyes are supposed to be easier when you didn't bond with those people?

Adam: No, I wouldn't. In fact, I imagine partings to always be tough, in a sense, whoever it is with.

Eve: How come?

Adam: It's because of what those people could have become. By parting with them, you will never find out whether that person would have been your soul mate or someone who would have shattered your very soul. That is why they are all tough, Eve.

I have a bachelor's degree in psychology, specifically a bachelor of science. I'm working toward my master's degree. The next step would be to apply for licensure. In order to do that, it is required to have had about two years of supervised experience. I'm already doing an internship under the supervision of a therapist. I get to help treat people with different disorders. But I want to have more experience in the field. I have had offers to go abroad, but unfortunately, that has never been in the cards. I don't have to explain why, because before I know it, I'll be cursing at my ancestors again.

So, I have been searching for opportunities here instead, and I've finally found something I'm passionate about. I found a crisis counselor position at a suicide prevention lifeline. Some people who experience suicidal thoughts consider calling the suicide prevention lifeline as a last resort. And a crisis counselor is the one on the other end of the line. During the call, it's important to actively talk about suicidality, to let it be known that people aren't alone in experiencing those thoughts. But the most important thing is to listen to what they have to say and to show them genuine empathy, to be genuinely empathic.

The goal is not to tell them that life is beautiful and worth living. The goal is that *they* truly believe that living life is worth it. And when they are searching for a reason to keep on living, I want to assist them in finding that reason, even when they feel that life has given them enough reasons not to.

Let's face it; we all have thought about it at some point in our lives. That life itself has no meaning and thus is not worth living. The philosopher Albert Camus has said, *Life is meaningless, but worth living, provided you recognize it's meaningless.*

Albert Camus's take on it is that life indeed is meaningless, and we can't make it meaningful either. Humans always need meaning, and when it isn't there, they try searching for it, which ultimately ends up in discontent. But understanding the notion that life is absurd is, in fact, the first step to being truly alive. Meaningless doesn't mean that it can't be enjoyed. So, he urges you to embrace the meaningless, accept the absurdness, and enjoy life as it has been given to you. To embrace the absurd while smiling.

To me, Camus is the child *carpe diem* and *memento mori* would have birthed. Whether we are rich and have it all or are poor and have it *mal*, everyone will eventually end up ending. Life itself might not have been equal for all, and how it ends won't either, but there is one thing we all have in common, and that is the ending itself. Death. Doesn't. Distinguish.

So, if we're all going to evaporate anyway and we will be dead forever, why not take everything life has to offer? *That* realization is what I want to share. I want to help people live the life they are meant to live.

Arguably, I could be acting out of selfishness. Maybe I want to see people live a life *I* wish I could live. Does true altruism even exist?

In the tale of Abraham Lincoln, Lincoln was traveling and saved pigs from being stuck in the mud. A fellow traveler told him that his act was genuinely altruistic. Lincoln denied this, and the fellow traveler asked him where the selfishness lays in his act. Lincoln responded that his act was the essence of selfishness. He explained that even if he saved the pigs at his own expense, he did it to avoid feeling guilty and have peace of mind.

Using deduction, I would deny true altruism. But the philosopher Joel Feinberg argues that feeling good after a good deed should be considered a byproduct as long as the intention was to do good. Only then is it an altruistic act.

True altruism might be debatable, but my intentions aren't. I know my intentions to be pure, and to me, that is all that matters.

There is only one problem, and that is the working hours. Working at a suicide prevention lifeline is not some typical nine-to-five job; people might need support at any given time. That might be in the morning, in the afternoon, but especially at night.

The problem lies in my curfew. If I have to be home before eight p.m., I can't exactly have a shift that starts after eight p.m.

That is why, today, I'm going to have a talk with my mother about this matter even if she never wants to listen to me. I have sacrificed a lot because of her rules and whatnot, and I simply won't let her take this away from me. This is work, but above all, it is helping people in need, help that I know I can and *want* to provide.

I leave my room and walk toward the living room while carrying Lady in my arms. My mother and Delano are already sitting on the couch. I put Lady next to them and walk around the coffee table to face them. The couch is my audience, and the floor behind the coffee table is my stage.

"Mama, we are going to have a talk. Now." As Delano tries to stand up to leave, I stop him. "Delano, I would like you to be a part of this talk, so stay seated, please."

He hesitates but sits down again. "Uh, okay ..."

My mother first looks at Delano and then up to me. "*Naa3m ya* Kristina?"

"Mama, as you already know, I need a lot of experience before I can apply for licensure. I'm already doing an internship, but I want more experience, and I've found something that means a lot to me."

"*Tayeb helw,* what is it?" she asks.

My expression troubles.

She directs her chin to her shoulder. "*Fe eh?*"

"The matter, Mama, is that it's being a crisis counselor at a suicide prevention lifeline, which means that the working hours are also at night."

Her face hardens. This is it. This is what I was afraid of. This is all I know. "Kristina, you know you aren't allowed to be outside after your curfew."

I finally snap, "Why?"

"What do you mean, why?" she says as deep furrows take over her forehead.

"What is up with that curfew? Why am I not allowed to be outside after eight?"

I have always obeyed, but not anymore. I won't. I won't accept anything anymore without proper reasoning. I'm not a child who will accept the reason *because I say so.* I'm an adult now with a mind of my own. Things change, people need to adapt. And so does she.

She sighs. "You know this already. You're not allowed to be outside after your curfew because it's dark and late."

Circle reasoning. *Not good enough, Mama. Not anymore.*

"Delano is allowed to be outside at night though. He comes home at, what? Around four? And just for the hell of it." I glower at him. "Don't you, Lano?"

He looks at me with uneasiness. "Uh. Yeah … sometimes."

She exhales, frustrated. "Delano is—"

I interrupt her. "A man? So what? Allowing men to be outside is the exact reason you disallow women to be."

"What are you implying?" he asks.

"God, it's not about you. I'm talking about men in general."

"It's just the way it is, Kristina. I can't make more of it. If you want to get more experience, you will have to search for something else. I don't want to talk anymore," she concludes. As she always does.

I feel a lump in my throat, as if I were wearing a collar of thorns. I want to give in to screaming and crying because it's unfair. It's unfair that I started this conversation, knowing it would ultimately end up in defeat. But I won't accept it. Not fucking anymore. "Yeah? Well, you know what? The hell with double standards and the hell with this culture."

"*Ya bet!*" she screams angrily.

I let her and ignore it. I grab Lady from next to them, glare at Delano, and go to my room. I lie on my stomach and bury my face in my pillow. I don't scream but groan into it and soak it by crying. I let myself for a while.

There is a reason I'm this upset. All of it is rooted so much deeper.

I shall present my life in a nutshell. When I want to go somewhere, not only do I have a curfew, but I also have to basically give a presentation on the event I want to go to. First, I have to mention where the event is going to take place. I even have to prove this fact by using a reliable source—my live location.

Furthermore, I must let it be known with whom I'll be. This translates into my creating personality profiles. I also have to add their favorite color and what their first word was as a baby. Kidding, but I do have to mention their name, age, what they do, where they're from, where I know them from, and more. So, isn't it the same? If not worse?

Even further than more, I have to explain in approximately one hundred fifty words—with a ten percent margin—why I want to attend this event. Is my being there necessary to reach a representative sample? If not, then I don't contribute to the validity of the research. Therefore, I'm an unnecessary presence. Statistical noise, if you may.

And even with all this information given, she won't hesitate to text or call me multiple times during the event. She even tells me not to be late when I haven't even arrived at the event.

And, of course, there is a deadline for this presentation—days prior to me going to the event. When I present this before the deadline, I have to wait and see whether I have passed or not. It's the time she's grading me in. The time she's going to use to consider it. To me, passing equals permission. If I pass, then I might go to the event. At short notice? Don't know her. And the professor, who's my mother, doesn't accept late submissions.

It wouldn't even shock me anymore if she were to ask for a PowerPoint presentation. I can't seem to escape academics, not even in my personal life. Although she doesn't have to ask for it, since I once made one of my own accord. When I wanted to adopt a cat, I wasn't allowed to do that either, of course. I mean, what's new? I created a PowerPoint presentation, explaining why getting a cat would be a wise choice. I even based all my facts on reliable and valid research, for instance, stating that cats are good for our cardiovascular and mental health.

There is another thing worth mentioning. Responsibility is something I have never experienced in my life. When I have an appointment—whether it be medical or something else—my mother tags along. If I want to do something—for example, take care of something for her—I get refused by, "Maybe next time," every time. How am I supposed to prove myself if I don't even get a chance to do it? I almost wasn't allowed to do the internship I'm doing either. Just because it's required for me to do, she allowed it. If it wasn't for this internship, I would probably still not have my own debit card.

She knows everything there is to know about me—apart from one thing.

So, privacy? Don't know her either. My mother is someone who tries to read my screen when I'm on my phone and just comes into my room whenever she pleases. And when I tell her that there is something called privacy, she tells me that we don't have any secrets. In her eyes, it makes her behavior somehow acceptable, which it clearly isn't. But I have always accepted it, and by doing that, I have given her a free pass to keep doing what she wants to do. Old habits really do die hard.

Since I'm in it, I might have my own room, but it doesn't feel like it. All the furniture was not chosen by me. It was chosen for me by my mother. And when I say that I don't like it, I'm being childish. I might be childish, but isn't your room supposed to be your safe haven? The place that is *yours*, according to your standards, to make it feel like *your* true home? I'm not allowed to live on my own, so I have to accept it or get married. The only choices I have are both ones I don't want. I will never have a space of my own. I will never be able to explore myself, to explore my own routine, to be wholly independent. To buy things I like and throw away things I don't.

It's so mundane, but to me? To me, it's *everything*.

Regardless of everything, I have managed. Strict parents create the sneakiest kids, after all. We lie. A lot. Like, a lot, a lot. So lot that it might be considered pathological at this point.

To sum up the nutshell, I'm a twenty-five-year-old child until I leave this household.

Don't get me wrong; I love the woman. I do, but I'm just sick of it all. This is how she was raised. She doesn't know any better. She might have been raised this way in Egypt, but we aren't there. And yet she doesn't seem to consider that in my upbringing. I might be complaining, but this? This isn't me just being her daughter anymore. This is me being controlled. And if she accepted that when she was younger, it doesn't mean that I have to too.

Surely, she has noticed that going from zero responsibility to being married and having your own household is a step that requires transportation by a vehicle. Because I sure as hell would not be able to survive the real world in these conditions.

God, I know J. K. Rowling created Dementors to suck the joy out of people's souls, but did she really have to create my mother among them? Sorry, but not entirely.

I sit up straight on my bed with my back against the wall. Lady is sitting on my lap, and I pet her as I stare at the clock on the wall across from me.

It's so quiet that I can hear the clock ticking loudly. It's maddening. I keep staring at it some more. *Ticktock.* It's nerve-racking. All I can think about is breaking its hands.

And I act on that intrusive thought. My eyes don't avert from the clock. I slowly put Lady on the bed, walk toward the clock, and grab it from the wall. I put the clock on my bed and rip out its hands. Having its hands in my own, I break them in half. *Click.* To stop them from moving while I can't seem to. To stop them from killing me slowly.

I wear my black hoodie, joggers, and a coat and put on a black beanie while wearing my hair down. I look in the mirror and see my puffy eyes. I look numb. But I couldn't care less because it's exactly how I feel. Numb. I'm feeling too much all at once, which makes me feel nothing at all.

I kiss Lady's paw. "I'll be back."

She squints her eyes at me. God, I love her.

"Kristina, where do you think you're going? You are not allowed to leave the house," my mother says.

"Out. With Alex. Her home. Will be back at eight," I say while putting on my sneakers.

"Kristina?! I didn't say—"

Delano cuts in on her. "Mama, let her go."

She looks at him, disappointed for his interfering, and then looks at me, disappointed for ... well, me being me, I guess.

I look at them, facial muscles relaxed, and leave the house.

I'm walking down the street toward the pub I went to with Alex and her friends. I already knew the place before meeting them there. It's the place I always go when I feel angry, annoyed, or addled. It might be the prime reason why I agreed to meet them in the first place. I knew the place would bring me comfort if the people didn't.

Fuck, I can't believe I have to lie to be alone. I have always wanted to take myself on dates; go to a hotel room to enjoy myself, reading a book in silence; or go to the cinema to watch a movie. To enjoy my own company. But that is somehow unbelievable to my mother because when I tell her I want to go somewhere alone, she automatically assumes I'm lying and that I'm going to hook up with some guy. She thinks having a curfew and being with other people prevents things like that from happening.

Well, sorry to be truthful, Mom, but there is something called actually lying, and I tend to do that a lot. You're even the reason for me to go beyond a lot. Also, two people hooking up doesn't only happen at night. It also occurs in broad daylight, in a car parked in an abandoned parking lot. Not that I would know, of course. I just wanted to park it out there.

I arrive at the pub and sit on a stool at the bar. The bartender must be new because I've never seen her before. She looks young. I'm guessing she's a student working part-time. She has long, straight black hair and brown eyes. She's very pretty.

"Hey! What would you like to drink?" she asks.

"Could I please have two glasses of the wine of your recommendation, filled until they basically overflow?"

She chuckles. "That's basically a bottle."

"A bottle it is. Can I have a bottle then?"

She looks hesitant.

I sigh. "I'm kind of having a bad day ... a bad life, even."

She grabs a bottle and opens it. "Do you want to talk about it?" she says while getting a glass and putting it next to the bottle.

I take off my coat and put it on the stool to the left of me. "No need to dirty the glass. I will finish it anyway."

I take the bottle, take a big sip, and put it down again without letting go of it. I'm holding on to it for dear life. That's how much I need this right now.

"Bartenders really are part-time therapists, aren't they?" I ask her.

She grins. "Oh, totally. I think they should add it to the job description at this point."

"Right?" I say. "What's your name?"

"Ji-hye. Yours?"

"Kristina. Are you a student?"

"Yeah, an English lit major. I work here part-time. You?"

English lit? That's freaking amazing. I considered majoring in that, too, but my mother said literature is an avocation, not an occupation. So, I obeyed. How illiterate of me. I was controlled.

"That's so awesome! I'm a psychology major."

"So, you're the real therapist," she says, smiling.

"Well, I aspire to be." I gulp more of the bottle down.

Sometimes, I have to escape reality. And there seems to be only one way I can—intoxicating liquor. I do drink, but I never get drunk. It would feel as if I were betraying my father by getting that. So, I never let myself escape entirely. I know my limits to prevent that from happening.

I'm leaning with my elbow on the bar, supporting my temple with my palm. I keep drinking from the bottle until about half of it is consumed. I can feel the effects of it.

My thoughts wander to what went down at home, and the realization of it all saddens me. That I have been refused to do something yet again. My eyes are teary, but I don't cry. I'm just sad and so very tired.

It all just hurts so damn much.

From the corner of my eye, I sense someone sitting beside me. I don't pay it too much attention at first, but now, Ji-hye is frowning at the person next to me. While still supporting my temple, I turn my head to the right to look at them. And, of course, it's him. The one who always pops up so randomly. This time in a black turtleneck and beige slacks. He stares at me.

"Ha, Gustav. What's the big idea?" I say sarcastically.

"It's Augustine."

"Who cares?"

"Well, my mother, for one."

I exhale sharply. "So much for goodbye."

Once, twice, thrice. There's nothing supposed to come after that sequence, yet here you are. What brings you here? What is the fourth time considered? Maybe fate.

"I respected the goodbye. I refrained from going on Fridays. This is just a mere coincidence."

Or not. I nod at him and avert my face from his to stare at the bottles behind the bar. I put my hand on the bar, and with my other hand, I bring the bottle back to my lips.

He stares at my hand holding the bottle. Once I put it down, he starts talking again. "Penny for your thoughts?"

Meanwhile, he points at his glass and gestures for two, please, with his hands to Ji-hye. She smiles, pours down two glasses of whiskey, and puts them in front of him. He slides one toward me.

I look at the glass, grab it, and pour its insides in his.

He nods a few times, pressing his lips. "Surely, you can accept a drink from me?"

My eyebrows lower. "Surely, I won't."

I don't like whiskey. Also, I don't want to accept anything from him. What? All of a sudden, we're drinking buddies now? No way. No whiskey for my thoughts.

He glances at me. "Who caused things to be in your eyes this time?"

My eyes widen at what he said. It's like when you have been trying so hard not to look sad or cry and someone asks you whether you're fine, you just break. Because you were pretending to be fine, and when someone sees through you, well, then there is no need to try to hide anymore, as all is in sight. Their realization makes you realize how not fine you are.

Apparently, no whiskey for my thoughts, indeed, since I'm about to pour them out. I'm going to vent to the man, after all. I'm not sober enough to use reason as to why I shouldn't confide in him anyway.

I breathe out heavily. "The double standards of our culture are quite literally preventing me from living my life."

"Elaborate, please." He takes a sip from his glass, which contains the contents of two glasses since I poured mine into his.

"I wanted to work somewhere, but I can't because of my curfew, which is set at eight p.m. And the only way to escape my curfew is to get married to some man who's supposed to allow me to go outside instead."

I realize how dumb the whole thing is. What's the difference supposed to be between an unmarried woman and a married woman when it comes to being outside at night? It's not like it's going to be less dangerous. It's not like wearing a ring is protection. It doesn't mean men will leave you alone. For some, it makes it even more exciting that you're taken, and they get to put their hands all over you. It makes me sick.

"So, your only solution is marriage?" he asks.

"Basically. I don't see my mother changing her mind anytime soon. She might never change her mind. She told me that once I get married, my husband is supposed to set the rules."

"And you don't want to get married?"

I scoff. "No."

He frowns at me. "Why don't you want to get married?"

"I ... I have my reasons."

It's quiet for quite some time. I take another sip from my bottle and face Ji-hye. We smile at each other.

He stares at the ceiling for a while and then turns his head to me to break the silence in the most unnatural way. "Then, marry me."

I nearly choke while sipping on the wine. "E-excuse me?" I utter in disbelief.

Never in my life did I think that someone would ever propose to me, and then it just happens. Just like that.

Ji-hye and I look at each other, shocked. Then, we both look at Augustine.

"Mr. Elias, with all due disrespect, I think you're drunk," I say.

At this point, Ji-hye has poured herself a glass of whiskey and is just standing there, listening to us.

He looks at me with that dead serious expression of his. "I'm not drunk."

"That is exactly what a drunk person would say."

"I want to get married."

Now, I frown at him. "Why do you want to get married?"

"I have my reasons."

Of course, he uses an altered version of my words against me.

"You must be out of your mind," I tell him.

"On the contrary. You want freedom, don't you? I can grant you that."

Tempting. Very tempting. So tempting that I want to get married right now and apply for the position after the ceremony—still wearing the wedding dress. But it's him—the only person I have met I can say that I absolutely loathe. I can't marry my nemesis.

But I'm not sober either, so I can't help but give in a little. I'm a whore for freedom—that's the reality of it all.

I can feel my face getting flushed. "How would that even work?"

"We would get married, pretend to love each other in front of others, and live our separate lives, keeping our distance from one another when no one is watching," he explains.

"So, it would be strictly business?"

"Indeed. I would even set up a contract, if you preferred. No one would find out about it either. It'd be between you, me"—he turns his head to Ji-hye, which makes her flinch—"and her since she's quite literally a witness."

I glance at him. Not saying anything because I have to process what is going on and also because I think he's messing with me by using my sorrows against me. That is what people who are not fond of each other do, right?

"So? What do you say, Miss Armanious, will you be my faux wife from this day onward?" he asks.

"Well, it's tempting—I can at least give you that. But I need to be sober to make a decision like that. I think. I think that I think that. Is what I would think if I were sober." *Did that even make sense? I don't think so.*

"You want to have this conversation sober? Understandable. Your free time tomorrow, give it to me."

I obey. I don't know if it's the wine or a sign to go through with this. I shrug my shoulders. "I'm free after three."

"Good. You can come by my office to discuss this further."

Oh, no. If there is one thing I'm never doing again, it's going inside his office. "Yeah, no. Believe it or not, I dislike both you and your office. I would like to go to a coffee shop. There is one next to it if you want to be in proximity to the office you oh-so love."

Coffee shops are also crowded, which is good. I like crowded places.

"Oh, I believe it. Fine, coffee shop it is. At what time can you be there?"

"I can be there at four."

"Then I will see you at four."

He stands up and puts on his coat. "Let's leave."

"Excuse me? Why?"

He points at the clock behind the bar. "It's almost time for your curfew."

I look at the clock, which says 7:48. I roll my eyes and stand up. I might break the hands of that clock as well. Maybe all the clocks in the world.

He grabs my coat from the barstool next to me, making me look confused at him, and then he stands behind me and puts my coat on for me. Once my coat is on, he holds my shoulders from behind and whispers in my ear, "If you accept, you will just have to hold on a little longer."

I turn around to face him, and we look into each other's eyes. Both of us wearing no expression. Processing. It feels as if by accepting, I'll be making a deal with the devil.

"Can I pay for the whiskeys and everything she had, please?" he asks Ji-hye.

My nose wrinkles. "What do you think you're doing?"

"I'm paying."

"Yeah, no shit, Sherlock. I mean, don't. I'm going to pay for it myself," I tell him, annoyed.

"Don't be ridiculous."

"No, you don't be ridiculous. Did you even listen to anything I just said? I hate double standards, and I hate men paying for women because it's the manly thing to do."

He looks at me, offended. *Be offended, Augustine. It was meant to be offensive.*

"Can I please pay for the bottle?" I ask Ji-hye while giving her my card.

She shifts her attention between Augustine and me a couple of times and then slowly reaches for my card.

He exhales. "You are really difficult, Miss Armanious."

"Well, you'd better get used to it, Mr. Elias. Do you think you can handle living with me?"

"I can handle you."

He pays for the glasses of whiskey, and we say goodbye to Ji-hye and leave the pub.

"Well, I'm going to walk home. See you, I guess." I wave once and slightly turn around.

He interrupts me from turning around completely. "May I walk you home?"

"No." I finally get to turn around and even take a first step.

But he grabs my hand to stop me. "Perhaps I should have phrased that differently. I am walking you home."

Honestly, I'm too tired to go against him right now. There is always going to be tomorrow to do that. So, I will let him today. "Fine, only if you let go of my hand."

He glances at his hand holding mine and retracts it immediately, as if surprised himself that he was holding my hand.

We walk together, and the silence is killing me. Thank God I don't live far from the place.

"You were alone?" I ask.

"I was, and so were you."

"Well, you know what they say. If you're both alone, then you're together," I announce sarcastically.

"Together in solitude?"

I look up at him for the first time since we started walking. I don't know why his answer made me look up. Maybe because that answer exactly describes how I feel about the phrase. Since I have always perceived everyone to be one of the seven billion lonely souls out there, it resonated with me. But it somehow also reminds me of Adam, it being something he would say.

"Yeah ..."

We arrive in front of my house and stare at each other again. It's uncomfortable, and yet I can't seem to withdraw. It's as if his deep emerald-green eyes are set on drawing me in to the core.

"I don't know how you got here, but don't drive while you aren't completely sober," I urge him.

"I would never do that."

He probably thinks I'm saying this because I somehow worry about him. I mean, don't get me wrong; I might dislike him, but I don't want the man to die. Although knowing Augustine—as he has shown me multiple times that he's much smarter than I give him credit for—he would suspect another reason for me to say that.

"Good," I say.

"Good night, Miss Armanious."

"Night ... Mr. Elias."

He leaves, and I enter my house. I toss my sneakers and run from the front door to my room to avoid everyone. But when I open the door, I see Delano sitting on the edge of my bed with Lady next to him. Holding the clock and its broken hands in his.

"Can we talk?" he asks.

I realize now that I was being a dick to him before leaving. I took my frustrations out on him. I grab Lady and sit where she was lying. I put her on my lap and face him. "Delano, I shouldn't have dragged you into it. I'm sorry."

He puts the clock next to him and his hand on my shoulder. "Kristina, I'm sorry. I know you have been struggling, and I'm so sorry that I'm allowed to do more. I can't imagine how much it sucks, what you go through ... but I don't want you to hate me because of it."

I grab the hand that he put on my shoulder and hold it with both hands. "Lano? I could never hate you."

His eyes glisten. "But still, you—"

"I envy you."

I hold his hand tighter. "You have your own life, independent from Mama and independent from me. I, however, don't. Everything is known about me. You do as you please, and I can't. It's not about you being older because when you were my age, you already did all of those things.

"The only reason you're still living here is because you choose to be here. If you want to leave, you can. But why would you when you're basically living on your own, just not paying rent? You get responsibility, and by getting that, you gain independence." I take a deep breath. "It's not hate, Lano. It's jealousy. I'm jealous of you."

Delano is definitely an exception to my *hating those who have what I desire* rule. I can't believe I made him feel that way. I hate that.

He squeezes my hand briefly to let me know that he heard me. "I have tried talking with her about you multiple times, but she just won't budge."

"I know, and she will never budge."

"So, what will you do?"

As he asks me this question, the wavelength called green radiates inside of me since nothing else has been processed yet. It makes me say something bright.

I smile at him. "There seems to be a light at the end of this tunnel."

CHAPTER FIVE

Adam: Eve, what motivated you to choose to do something that wasn't allowed?

Eve: Adam. I thought we could put the past behind us, but alas, you can't seem to let it go.

Adam: We can never truly put the past behind us when we are confronted with it in the present.

Eve: Fair. I will share the honest truth with you. It all comes down to this: it's precisely because I wasn't allowed something that I wanted to do it so hopelessly.

Adam: After the fact, don't you regret it?

Eve: Dooming humanity shouldn't be taken lightly, of course, so, yes, I would say that I do. But in general, aren't some rules meant to be broken?

Adam: Which rules are meant to be broken, Eve?

Eve: The ones that limit you in reaching your full potential, Adam.

And with that being said, I, too, have a choice to make today. Since God has granted us free will—to not be robots, programmed to behave in the ideal way—we have a choice. But having a choice introduces, by default, both good and evil. Eve knows best.

Even though existentialism denies the existence of a god, its assumptions go hand in hand with God's principles. The challenge every individual faces is to use their freedom to give their existence meaning every day, by means of every little thing. Albert Camus is basically the founding father of this philosophical belief.

There is more to it, though. Humans have been put in this world without having asked for it, which ultimately makes them victims of the circumstances. Humans might be victims, but they are free. From the minute they are born to the second they die, they are responsible for their own deeds and destiny. God chooses not to influence that. He might know what you will choose since it's *maktub,* but something being written doesn't automatically mean that it was chosen for you. It's important to be aware of that fact.

So, humans are supposed to give their life meaning by making choices. But the choices made involuntarily influence the lives of others, which hold us accountable.

And regarding others, communicating with them is experienced as problematic. People are estranged from one another, which makes them existentially lonely. You can't wholly be united with another, let alone rely on them. When it comes down to it, egoism is a mechanism of survival. When a situation calls for it, humans won't hesitate to save themselves at the expense of another human being.

All the choices we have made up to the present have led us to be the person we are at present. And the past, which is unreformable, will always influence both the present and the future.

It's deep, it's dark, but it's life. Life as we know it, life as we live it.

After having this epiphany, I know what I should choose. I should use my free will to reach my freedom. I'm a victim of a culture I sure as hell didn't ask for, but I'm responsible for my destiny. And since I can't even communicate with my mother, well, it seems that egoism is, in fact, something I'm not hesitating to use. If the choice I make today will either give me the future I long for or give me a future I loathe, then there is no need to fret now, is there?

Today, I'm working at the clinic where I do my internship. At this clinic, people with a lot of different disorders get treated. For instance, people with anxiety, phobias, mood disorders, eating disorders, psychotic disorders, and addictive disorders.

Most people in this field choose to specialize in one disorder to know everything there is to know about it, which is understandable. Just like surgeons have one specialty, therapists have that preference too.

I, however, have always thought there to be one thing people with a disorder have in common, which is feeling different and sometimes even divergent.

Disorders aren't dichotomous, yet people tend to treat them as such—either you have it or you don't. But science has proven that not to be the case; it's a spectrum. Every mental disorder is displayed on a spectrum. People society considers normal are in the inner tails of the spectrum, having no symptoms. The people who find themselves in the middle of the spectrum might experience some symptoms but are not considered to have a disorder. And then there are the people in the outer tails of the spectrum, which society considers abnormal.

As stated before, usage of the terminology *normal* and *abnormal* is incorrect since there aren't two spectrums. It's about being in different places within the same spectrum.

But being able to be anywhere on the spectrum makes even a disorder unique and that much more complex. That's what's called homogeneity. Two people might have the same disorder but experience completely different symptoms. Labels are too simple, and sometimes, I think it would be better to stray away from them.

A person is not their disorder; it's something they have. It might seem silly to some, but there is a big difference between the phrases *I am a disorder* and *I have a disorder*. The disorder doesn't define you as a person; it's something apart from you.

A person is not their disorder. They didn't choose it; it happened to them. For some, this might make all the difference in not being ashamed of it and even accepting it as something they have to work with and on.

There's another thing people with a disorder have in common. Deviating from the "norm" often gets accompanied with suffering. Human beings are social animals. Since the beginning of time, they have traveled and survived in groups. They have the need to belong. It's evolution. It's practically in our DNA.

And the symptoms those people experience are a suffering in itself. And suffering is something people want to end. And what is the first method people consider? Ending it *all*.

That is why suicide prevention is so important to me. People with different disorders might experience a variety of symptoms, but the suicidal thoughts, those are the same—they're actually fighting two battles. And, of course, people in crises experience those thoughts as well. And even more people, who suffer in other ways—there are many, after all. It's a diverse group with similar thoughts.

I want to help everyone. Let them live another day, fight another battle and, most importantly, be stronger than their suffering. And even when it won't always be easy, to enjoy life as much as they can.

Today, I'm having a last session with Thomas. Thomas has suffered from anorexia nervosa, but it transitioned into bulimia nervosa.

Having anorexia means having a limited food intake, resulting in significantly lower body weight. They eat less than their body needs. The reason they do this might be because of a fear of gaining body weight. They experience a disrupted body image as well, which directly reinforces the need to uphold being underweight. Most of the time, it's also about having control, and eating less is a sense of control because it leads to losing weight.

By being underweight, you have a starved brain, which can cause people to get repetitive and even compulsive in their behavior, which only reinforces the disorder.

Anorexia is hard to keep up, which is why it often transitions into bulimia, causing people to develop binge eating—a food intake that is significantly bigger than average.

Everyone has experienced binge eating in one way or another, for example, finishing an entire bag of chips on movie night. But when a person genuinely thinks they can't stop and feels guilty after—so guilty that they're a poor excuse for a human being and decide to skip breakfast as punishment or work out to make up for it—then those are symptoms related to bulimia. Bulimia is also characterized by purging the food that they've binged. The feeling of losing control is experienced as very unpleasant, and they try to gain control by skipping meals and working out. Their self-image is inversely proportional to their weight, so they are convinced they're less of a person if they're heavier or curvier.

Thomas has finished his treatment, and we're having a debriefing.

I'm sitting in an office and hear someone knock on the door. "Come in."

Thomas peeks from behind the door, smiles at me, and walks toward the chair across from me to sit. "Hey, Kristina. How've you been?"

"Hi, Thomas. I've been good. How have you been?"

"I've been great! Thanks for asking."

"Last day, huh?" I say, smiling with raised eyebrows.

He brings the palms of his hands together. "I can't believe it, but, yes, it is," he says ecstatically.

I get up from my chair. "Well, since it's your last day, how about we celebrate it by going outside in this beautiful weather?"

"I would love to! But is that even allowed?"

I shrug my shoulders. "Well, therapy in nature is a thing."

"But don't you have to write everything down?"

"Don't worry; I always listen first before writing it down." I grab my long gray coat from behind the chair.

"But won't you forget?" He gets up as well.

I stop putting on my coat and look at him while smiling. "No. Not when something matters."

He returns my smile with a soft one and goes to the door. "Nature, here we come!"

We reach a park covered in the color of the eyes of the man I might start tolerating soon. The color green tickles my olfactory bulbs. And it's quiet, so much so that you can hear birds chirping.

"So, tell me, Thomas, how were the last couple of weeks?"

"So, about two weeks ago, I was released out of a clinic. In the clinic, every day for a month, we would get a list with six dishes being served at specific times, and when we ate them, we would get a stamp. So, in that way, I felt I had control somehow."

I nod at him, showing him that I'm listening and inviting him to continue.

"I also liked that there was a group, so I made friends—people who exactly understand what I go through and would never judge me. It was also a comfort, knowing that I'm not alone in something, that there are others who experience what I experience," he says. "But it was also hard because I had to do the thing I fear most six times a day. Instead of once or twice, if lucky. So, sometimes, I would cry because I was just so scared."

Back when I was a first-year student, I could never quite grasp the fear of eating. My professor told me it's okay not to understand something when you haven't experienced it, that it's only natural even. But she also told me we can try to understand if we imagine something we have experienced.

She told me, "Kristina, I want you to imagine your worst fear. Whether it's a phobia or something you just fear in general. What do we do when we're frightened or scared of something?"

I answered her, "We avoid it at all costs."

She nodded at me. "People with eating disorders, they're afraid of eating, just like you're afraid of that thing you just imagined." She continued, "Yet eating is something that can't be avoided for too long because it would end up in death. They experience fear on a daily basis." She said, "Kristina, imagine having to deal with your fear on a daily basis. How would that make you feel?"

I answered her, "It would be exhausting to be on high alert all the time."
She nodded at me again. "Exactly."

Since that moment, I have tried to understand people by imagining anything that causes me to feel something that's in line with what they feel. Of course, I will never truly understand, even thinking that would invalidate someone's feelings. But I try to understand and be empathic to help them better.

He resumes, "There was also a focus on body image. So, instead of associating feelings with how we perceive our bodies, we got to the root of our feelings. Usually, I would not be having a good day, and then I would think to myself, *I feel like this because I'm too fat*. It's like not thinking anything about your weight, and then all of a sudden, you do, but your weight didn't change in a matter of seconds—that's impossible. That actually taught me how to get to the core of what I'm feeling, and then I don't associate it with my weight anymore."

"That is so good, Thomas! Would you say that you're also convinced that your feelings and body image are not associated with each other?"

"I mean, I would say yes. For instance, at first, I would feel shitty, then I would perceive myself as fat, and then I would feel even shittier. And sometimes, the feeling would get accompanied with thoughts like, *Shitty people don't deserve to live*. I was genuinely convinced of that, which scared me a lot. But now, when I feel shitty, I just think, *Why do I feel shitty?* Most of the time, it's because of an inconvenience that happened that day. Then, I think to myself, *Something happened today that made me upset, hence why I'm feeling like this*."

"Yes! That is what they call relabeling," I say.

"Yeah? I didn't know that, but I know that it has really helped me a lot."

I put my hand on my chest. "I'm so glad."

"So, I'm still using the method of eating six times a day with a list and crossing off my meals. At first, it was hard because at the clinic, there was supervision and I was with others," he says. "But then I made it a routine, and one day, something happened to me, something I'd thought I would never get to experience again."

My eyes dilate. "And what is that?"

He looks at me, his eyes welling up with tears. "For the first time in the longest time, I experienced hunger again. True, genuine hunger. My stomach even made the sound of hunger! It made me happy. Words cannot describe how happy. Happy that my body was capable of experiencing it. I had missed the feeling of it so much. I felt included, human even! But above all, I didn't feel guilty that I was hungry. I didn't even feel the need to compensate for it by throwing up."

He titters as tears roll down his face. He wipes them away. "I'm sorry for crying, but even thinking about that moment makes me so emotional. It's a very important moment for me. To me, it represents recovering."

Oh, Adam, I wish I could show you this side of weeping. Weeping because you have overcome something. Weeping because you have finally made it.

I'm fighting back my tears, but these tears, Adam, are tears of being overjoyed and so proud.

I don't win the fight, as I always lose against my tears. They run down my cheeks. "Thomas, I cannot put into words how grateful I am for you sharing something so important with me. I'm overjoyed, truly."

He sniffles. "I can see that."

We both laugh.

"You played a big role in all of this, and I'm so grateful to have had you supporting me. Is it okay ... to hug?" he asks.

"Yes, of course!"

We hug, cry some more, and laugh again because we find ourselves sniffling in sync.

When we both have calmed down a little, I let go to hold him by his shoulders. "I have something for you." I let go of his shoulders and grab a small box from the pocket of my coat.

"Are you proposing to me? I don't think that's professional at all!" he jokes.

I snort. "Well, no, but yes?" I open the box and hold it out to him. "This is what they call an anxiety ring. The beads are shaped like periods and commas, representing semicolons. They can move all over the ring and be rotated. I have one too." I show him my ring.

He takes the box out of my hand and wears the ring. He plays with the beads for a moment and then faces me with glossy eyes.

"I hope this ring will serve as a constant reminder of our time together, which was all about getting better and never giving up," I tell him.

He smiles at the ring on his finger and then looks back up again.

"When you have the feeling that things are getting tough again or you find yourself relapsing, I hope this ring symbolizes that you should keep on going. That I will be here for you for as many times as you need. Just never give up fighting, please, because you're strong, Thomas, and you have proven that by winning this battle. You are more than capable of seeing anything through." I put my hand on his shoulder. "Keep paddling against the tide to not get dragged backward anymore."

He breathes out. "Kristina, how can I possibly ever thank you?"

I shake my head at him. "There is no greater thank-you than having me accompany you on your journey and you trusting me enough to be there."

He grabs my hand that's resting on his shoulder and holds it tightly. I squeeze his hand back.

"*Ik waardeer jou enorm,*" he says.

"What does that mean?"

"It means, *I really appreciate you* in Dutch."

"How do you say *thank you, I appreciate you too* in Dutch?"

"*Dank je, ik waardeer jou ook.*"

I try repeating it, but my accent is so off that it makes him laugh out loud.

We walk back to the building.

"Kristina, I think I finally understand what your tattoo on your forearm means. Can I see it one more time?"

I take off my coat and show it to him. It's the psi symbol, the twenty-third letter of the modern Greek alphabet. It symbolizes psychology. But the straight line of the symbol is a little different on my arm. Instead of a straight line, it's a wonky dashed line between a period and comma.

"It's a rocky journey to go from wanting to end it all to wanting to give everything another chance and to keep on going. Which makes it a semicolon.

And it's the psi symbol because of mental health awareness," he says.

"Yes, that is exactly what it symbolizes to me too. I told you that you would understand sooner rather than later."

"I'm awesome. I just deciphered something on my own."

"Well, I wouldn't say you did. The ring was practically a decryption tool."

He looks at the ring and pouts. "Let's just ignore that fact and continue to believe I'm awesome."

I chuckle. "You are awesome, Thomas. Always have been, always will be."

It's men like Thomas who make me reconsider my whole *be wary of all men* notion. Thomas is the epitome of a good man, a genuine soul. And I'm grateful to him for proving to me that overgeneralizing people is unfair to pearls like him.

After saying our goodbyes, he leaves. I look at the clock, and it says three o'clock. Which means my day at work is over, but my day as Kristina the prisoner is about to start. Although negotiations about ending my life sentence might start as well.

I go to the restroom to look in the mirror. I notice that I'm looking quite puffy because of all the crying I did with Thomas, so I put on red lipstick. It's so showy that I'm sure no one will pay attention to my eyes.

I take notes of the session with Thomas, chat with my colleagues for a while, and once I see the clock strike three thirty, I leave to take the subway to the coffee shop where I'm supposed to meet Augustine.

Honestly, I know how it'll go. He will tell me he was drunk after all and that he didn't mean anything he said yesterday. Or that all of it was some joke because seeing me suffer and then be hopelessly hopeful was somehow entertaining. I wouldn't blame him if that's what he's going to say—since the whole thing is utterly insane—but I won't deny that I think it's unfortunate. It would have solved many of my problems in life.

I'm in front of the coffee shop, and it's three fifty.

So, I'm early, is what I think, but as I peek inside, I see Augustine is already sitting at a table with something that appears to be a notebook. Or maybe it's a planner. I can't see it yet. And, of course, he's wearing something elegant yet again. Does this man even own sweats? He's wearing gray slacks this time and a white button-up shirt with the first two buttons undone—a tendency.

My phone rings, and it's my mother. "Mama?"

"Kristina, where are you? Aren't you supposed to be done with your internship?"

"Yes, I am. I'm just meeting Alex for coffee real quick, and then I'll go home."

"You didn't say you would go."

"Yes, I'm sorry. I forgot. I won't make it long."

"You get an hour, *salam.*"

She hangs up, and I squeeze my phone. This woman is unbelievable sometimes.

I enter the coffee shop. Once I'm standing next to his table, he stands up and parts his lips to speak, but I beat him to it by pouring out my frustrations on him. "Before you say anything, I know you'll tell me it was all a joke, and that's fine; I really don't blame you. I mean, it's rude. Very rude. You're rude. But it's fine." It's a notebook and planner in one. No, seriously, the left page is for planning, and the right page is for note-taking. I love it. I want it. If there is one thing I'm good at, it's wanting notebooks and stationery and then not using them. Exactly like how collecting books and reading books are two *completely* different hobbies.

One corner of his mouth lifts, and he puts his hands in his pockets. "I already had a hunch that this would happen."

"About what happening?" I say, confused.

He gestures for me to take a seat across from him, sits down again, and grabs a small package from his coat to hold out to me.

He stares at my lips. "I know it's not the real thing, but after the fact, I understand how not serious you must have thought I was. Here's my way of saying that I was, in fact, dead serious."

It's a candy ring. The ring is black, and the red candy is shaped like a diamond, strawberry-flavored—my favorite.

"Don't worry; I don't mean anything by it," he adds.

I laugh out loud.

"It seems I've missed the part where I was amusing you." He frowns and puts the small box between us on the table.

"Don't worry; you could never. It's just that I gave someone a ring today as well." At the end of the day, you reap what you sow. Literally.

"You rejected my proposal by proposing to someone else?" He points with his index finger at my eyes, shifting between them. "And is being rejected the reason you had things in your eyes again?"

I can't believe he realized I had cried. I thought the lipstick would do the trick.

I ignore his remark. "No, it wasn't a proposal, and I didn't reject yours either. In fact, you have piqued my interest, Mr. Elias, so much so that I'm willing to accept your offer."

He looks at me in disbelief. "You are?"

"Yes. I am. I made a cost-benefit analysis, and it appears that it would benefit me more than it would cost me," I tell him. "But there are some points we need to be clear on before I make a definite decision."

"Understandable. Let's discuss those points over coffee."

We walk toward the counter.

The barista greets us. "Good afternoon. What can I get started for you?"

"I would like a coffee, please, black," Augustine says.

A chuckle instantly leaves my lips. "Black, like your soul?" I murmur.

"I thought I didn't have a soul?"

Damn it, he's right; I did say that. "I—I assumed you would have bought one by now."

The barista faces me. "And for you, miss?"

"Can I have a latte, please?"

"Coming right up. You can take a seat. I will bring it to you," she says.

We both thank her and go back to the table we were seated at. Not two minutes later, the barista comes and serves us our coffee.

We each take a sip, and then he starts talking again. "So, tell me, which points are those?"

I take out my small notebook from the pocket of my coat that I'm still wearing. At my break today, I made a list of things we need to discuss—or rather my requirements if, by some miracle, he was serious. And by some miracle, he is.

I begin listing the points. "Here are the ground rules. First of all, no one can ever know about it. Only you, me, and the bartender. You won't tell a single soul, not even your best friend, if you have one, which I doubt because who would want—" No, more negotiating, less insulting. "And I won't tell mine."

He rolls his eyes at me. "Which I already stated the first time I proposed this to you, but fine. What else?"

I glare at him. "Also, it's an arrangement, strictly business. There won't be falling in love—ever. I'm serious. This is not some story where mere exposure is going to do the trick. I have no desire to be involved with you. Never have, never will. Not now, not ever."

He scoffs. "That is the last thing you have to worry about. As I have also stated before, we will live our separate lives, keeping our distance from one another when we're alone."

"Good. That brings me to my third talking point. Don't interfere with my life, and I won't interfere with yours."

"Music to my ears," he says. "Miss Armanious, are you just going to keep repeating what I have already said before?"

God, I want to strangle him to death. Or more like until he faints because that's legal, right? Right?

"Hush, Mr. Elias. I'm not done with my talking points. No PDA, only if it's really necessary to make it believable. Otherwise, no physical contact ever," I threaten.

"Needless to say, I have no desire to touch you."

Yeah, right. Then, mansplain me why you always end up grabbing my hand or wrist.

"Good. I don't want you to," I maintain.

"Good."

"Great."

We stare at each other.

"Which brings me to the next talking point. If you do, however, want to touch someone or be touched by someone, don't do it in the space we share. Go to a hotel."

He ignores it. "What else?"

"What else ... Regarding the space we share, we can share the living room and kitchen, but we don't have to be there at the same time. We would treat each other like roommates would."

"Sounds more than good to me. Anything else?"

"My cat will be living with us. You'll probably see her from time to time, but she'll mainly be in my room, of course." I will try to prevent it as much as possible though. I promised Lady that he would never lay his eyes on her beautiful fur. I can't break a promise I made to Lady? That'd be beastly!

He tangles his hands in each other, puts them on the table, and tilts his head a little. "What if I told you I'm allergic to cats?"

"I don't see how that's my problem."

He shakes his head, pressing his lips together. "I'm glad I'm not actually allergic to cats."

"Then why would you say that?"

"To see how you would react."

"Well, I don't care about you."

"I know."

"To me, you're nothing but a means to an end."

"Let's keep it that way."

"Only now do I agree with you."

He nods. "More to add to your litany?"

"We have to come up with a story. I guess we could say that we fell hopelessly in love at first sight."

He shakes his head again. "Wouldn't work."

"Why not?"

"The second time we met, the people we were with heard you muttering that you would like to keep not knowing me."

"You mean, the Egyptian ensemble," I say while closing my eyes and rubbing my temples.

"I do mean that one."

I hate that one. I want to go inside my medial temporal lobe, grab my hippocampus, and throw it away just to forget about that one. I take a sip of my latte, and he takes a sip of his coffee. He's mirroring me.

I nod at him. "Right. I guess we can say that it was love at *third* sight."

"Fair enough. Anything else?"

I write down that it was love at third sight on the note I made before. I already wrote this note with carbon paper underneath, so everything I have written down so far, a copy of has been made.

"That's all I have to say. Do you maybe have anything to add?"

"Not right now," he says. "So? Are you satisfied, Miss Armanious? Will you accept the offer of my last name?"

I frown at him. "I would never take your last name. But if you don't have a problem with these conditions, then, yes, I accept the offer of being your faux wife after all."

"Terrific."

I turn my notebook and slide it on the table to him. "I want this signed and stamped, stat."

He signs the note and slides my notebook back to me. I sign it as well and realize that I don't have a stamp. On impulse, I kiss my version of the contract on the upper-left corner of the page, leaving a red mark of my lips. I rip the page behind the carbon paper and slide it to his side of the table.

He looks at my version of the contract and then at his. "Where is my stamp?"

"Excuse you?"

"You have to stamp the edge of every page of a contract."

He's enjoying putting me on the spot. But I won't let him.

"How could I forget?" I say sarcastically.

I hesitate at first but decide to go through with it. I grab his version of the contract, kiss the upper-right corner, and slide it back to him.

He looks at the mark and smirks. "Careful. There's no turning back now." He then raises his chin and holds it there. "You okay with that?"

"I don't want to turn back. I want to move forward."

"Marriage isn't supposed to be taken lightly. Once we do this, there really is no turning back. Divorce is unacceptable in our religion or culture without proper reason," he points out.

I hold my ground. "As long as we stick to the contract we made, there's nothing to worry about."

"Yes. But if you ever fall in love with someone, you do understand that by doing this"—he gestures between us—"you will never have a future with them. You won't be able to get married again. Is that something you're okay with?"

"No need to worry. I don't fall in love."

He studies my face as I shoot daggers at him, imagining doing exactly that.

Augustine holds up his hands to drop the subject. "I won't contest you."

I slowly nod at him and look outside the window.

"Perhaps it's time to exchange contact information. I don't think that the coincidences will allow a fifth time of us running into each other," he suggests.

I look at him mockingly. "You mean, a fourth time. No need to deny you were actively looking for me when you started going on Fridays. Your mother blew your cover."

He raises one eyebrow defensively. "I wasn't planning on denying it. I was looking for you."

"Yet you lied about it at first." I take a sip of my latte, making a slurping sound on purpose just to spite him.

"So I did. I didn't want to discomfort you by admitting to that." He takes a sip of his coffee. "But so did you—lie, that is."

He's talking about me telling him he didn't make me cry. I really need to stop reminding myself of things I want to forget.

I click my tongue at him and give him my phone. He gives me his, and we put our numbers in each other's phones.

When we return each other's phones, I save him under the name Nemesis with Benefits. I think it's befitting. I don't know what name he's saving me under, but I doubt it's under Kristina, since we somehow don't address each other by our first names.

"So, what happens now?" I ask him.

"What happens now is that I pay a visit to your house to ask for your hand in marriage." He looks at me while drinking his coffee.

I lean forward, wide-eyed. "What? Just take it. You have been doing just that," I say, shaking my hand.

"I might have your permission, but I need your family's as well. Even more so."

No. That's too much. Too awkward even. Too unbelievable? How did I go from cursing the culture and despising men to being in love with one—from that very culture—enough to want to get married? But he's not wrong. The reason I'm doing this in the first place is that it's the only way my mother would ever approve of me moving out.

I sigh. "Fine, but don't tell me you're going to bring your family as well and that we'll have to sit awkwardly while drinking tea and have them all ask a million questions, ones that we quite literally don't have answers to."

"Unfortunately, yes, though it's kind of how that works."

The costs are getting heavier by the second. But I want the benefits more than anything.

I glance at him, put my notebook and the candy ring in my pocket, and go to the counter to pay.

"Can I pay for a black coffee and a latte, please?"

"Yes, one second, please," the barista answers.

I hear Augustine's harsh voice from behind me. "What are you doing?"

"Paying?" I pull out my card.

He grabs the wrist of my hand holding the card. "No kidding, Sherlock."

I swear to God, if this man touches my hand, wrist, or any other body part of mine one more time, I'm going to go berserk.

I turn around to glower at him. "Copycat."

"You told me I couldn't pay for you last time. How is this any different?"

"This is different, Mr. Elias, since I'm the one who asked you here, so I'm paying. That's how things like this work. The one who asks is the one who pays."

He looks at me, stunned. As if it were the first time someone has offered to pay for him.

"Now, can you please let go? There's a queue, and I have to go," I tell him.

He lets go of my wrist. "Go where?"

"Apparently, my new curfew is set at five." I hand my card to the barista and pay for the drinks.

We leave the coffee shop and stand in front of it, facing each other.

"So, when do you want to ask for my hand?" I ask.

"As soon as possible. Once I do that, we'll be engaged, since there's no such thing called having a relationship in our culture."

And he's not wrong yet again. I don't know how, but women are expected to just get engaged to some stranger because they can't date to get to know someone. I mean, come on, really? It's the twenty-first century. But now—*now*—it works to my advantage that that's the norm. The sooner we get engaged and married, the better.

"Yeah, okay. I guess, let me know whenever you're ready to propose?"

And they say romance is dead.

"Will do."

"Cool. Later."

"Take care, Miss Armanious."

He walks to his office, and I walk to the station to catch the subway, which are in opposite directions.

No one hates Egyptian men more than Egyptian women. And no one hates Egyptian women more than Egyptian men. Yet we all end up getting married to one another. It's a never-ending paradox. If that's not the embodiment of cognitive dissonance, I don't know what is. It has to be extremely uncomfortable marrying someone you hate. Although some would argue that there is a thin line between love and hate.

That might be. I mean, I've read plenty of books with the enemies-to-lovers trope, and I know they all end the same way—as lovers, obviously. But this is real life, so it won't end like that because enemies don't actually turn into lovers. Only if at least one of them already loves the other secretly or unconsciously. And that's not the case here.

Besides, real enemies don't want to be near each other, just like I hate the thought of the forced proximity of living with him. It's going to be tedious to see his face every day, but I have much bigger fish to fry—being free like one.

The way tropes progress doesn't happen in real life, but the tropes themselves can inspire us.

So, yeah, marrying someone I don't love might be unorthodox—something the Orthodox Church definitely would disapprove of. This might be the end of my villain origin story. By doing this, I will truly be a villain.

I'm going to do all the things you wanted to prevent me from doing, Mama, while living in a lie. You made me do this. This is on you. Ironic, but you left me no choice. I was a ticking time bomb, and you knew I would explode any minute now. Yet you turned a blind eye, not dismantling me.

We could have compromised. But compromising means settling a dispute by mutual concessions. And if one party automatically gets what they want by not accepting the compromise, well, then it wasn't fair, to begin with, now was it? And what to do when someone doesn't want to compromise? You go behind their back and do everything exactly the way you've always wanted to.

Ignorance is bliss, Mama. Remember that.

CHAPTER SIX

Eve: Adam. We have discussed making choices before. Do you believe we decide our fate with our choices?

Adam: Eve, in essence, absolutely. Be that as it may, we are limited in deciding our fate because of several factors we simply have no control over. Be it the choices of others or the way our world functions.

Eve: Doesn't that mean you aren't in control at all?

Adam: No, I wouldn't say that. You control what you can and let go of what you can't. That is how you maximize your control without losing your sanity in the process.

Adam is, as always, right. When I started studying psychology, I made a list of all the things I worried about. Then, I went over each and every worry of mine, contemplated whether it was something I had any influence over whatsoever, and if I didn't, I crossed it off and never looked at it twice. For the things that were not crossed off, I wrote next to them how I could influence them and what actions would bring me the most desirable results. It has helped me a lot.

But once I got older, the line between what I could control and what I couldn't control blurred. I knew that the things I couldn't control could be controlled if I opposed. It was confusing, to say the least, so I stopped using the method altogether. Because, at first, I could cross something off without thinking about it twice, but then I had to debate to which extent I could cross something off.

But now, I don't have to cross things off anymore since I made the choice to oppose. Did I make the right choice? I don't know yet. I guess only time will answer that dichotomous question.

Today, Alex is coming over. I have to tell her that somehow, in a matter of weeks, I fell in love with someone I told her I hated. This is going to be tricky because Alex always sees through me—to her, I'm like transparent glass. I want to tell her the truth—I do—but I know she's going to talk me out of it. And she'd be entirely right because what I'm about to do is insane. Absolutely. Fucking. Insane.

But I need freedom. From my family, from my past. I have always been behind closed doors, where no one can see. No one can see what is happening to me. No one can see that I'm sad and afraid. In return, it makes me not be able to see outdoors. It's not one-way glass; both sides are reflective. It's quite ironic that I will search for freedom now in a new, enclosed environment. But it will be on my terms, and that is change.

And yet I fear being alone with Augustine in one house. I fear being alone with him anywhere.

Here's the thing about fears though. You will be confronted with your fears in life; it's inevitable. But it will be all right, and if not, at least it will be over.

Because everything is temporary, and that's a comfort in itself. It means you get through it if you push through it.

But I'm going to ignore my fears for a second. I'm going to think about what brings me joy and what makes me feel alive. And I immediately feel stronger already. That is my anchor, the thing that lets me hold my ground. The thing that's worth the suffering.

The end goal—I can picture it. A parallel universe? A version of me who's free and isn't easily frightened anymore? I want to reach that. And if I have to travel this bumpy road to get there, so be it. Because it must be so liberating not to be afraid anymore.

I wish telling Alex was my only concern. But, unfortunately, I also have to tell my family. How does one even start?

Oh yeah, by the way, some guy is going to come over, and he wants to take me off your hands by asking for mine.

I never used to think about these things because the plan always was not to get married. But now, I regret not thinking about these things because I have no clue how to even go about them.

I hear someone softly knock on the door of my room. There's no doubt it's Alex since my mother never knocks while I'm here, and Delano never enters while I'm here.

"You may enter, Miss Alex Basalious."

She opens the door with a lopsided grin and bows so elegantly. "I have graced you with my presence. Be honored."

"How could one not be?"

I walk toward her, kiss the tips of my fingers, and put them on hers. She puts her fingertips on her cheek, and we smile at each other.

We lie next to each other on my bed, staring at the ceiling.

Her arms are resting at her sides. "What did I miss?"

I sigh. "The usual. My mother refused to allow me to work as a crisis counselor because of the working hours being at night." I put my hands, tangled in each other, on my stomach. "God, I fucking hate this culture."

"I hear you, babes," she says.

I turn my head to her. "Riddle me this, Alex. Where in the Bible does it say I can't be outside after eight?"

She faces me. "It's a mystery."

"That woman is getting on my nerves," I say.

"There're a lot of things we don't choose, like our sexuality or family. That choice has been made for us."

I nod at her.

"We choose our friends, though, so when they are being toxic, we can also choose to end friendships. People even encourage us to. But when family members are being toxic, it feels as if the choice has been made for us yet again." She pauses. "You're stuck with them, whether you like it or not."

"It's unfair," I tell her.

"That's family for you. Family is, even when it's at your own expense, something you have to respect."

I bite the inside of my cheek. She's right, and I hate that it has to be that way.

She continues with her voice breaking, "So, what happens when two things that were chosen for you don't go together? They clash. Hard. And you're in the middle, being crushed by it."

Alex covers her face with her hands. I sit up straight and grab her shoulders to let her sit up as well. Then I hold her hands and slowly remove them from her face. Her eyes are wet and red.

"Alex ... what happened?"

She sniffles. "This culture, our religion. My identity."

I grab some tissues from my nightstand and hand them to her. She takes them and blows her nose.

"Being queer might be a sin in the Bible, but the Bible also says that we should love and accept each other, no matter what." She takes a deep breath. "Lying is a sin; cursing is a sin. Every sin is supposed to be equal, yet this one is put next to murder."

"People interpret things in a way that's in line with their actions to avoid cognitive dissonance. And they do this by projecting what could be their negative traits onto others," I try to explain.

I sense her attention shifting from me when she looks at the ceiling, trying desperately to hold back the tears and being deep in thought.

"Penny for your thoughts?" I ask.

She finally faces me again, tears falling down. "I can't wrap my head around what makes people so disgusted by two people of the same gender falling in love ... to detest *love*."

I pull her into my embrace, feeling how much this hurts her because she's shaking uncontrollably as I hold her.

I place my cheek against hers. "Only ignorant people have a problem with that, Alex. People who have a problem with that are conformists."

She nods against my cheek and embraces me back. We hug until I feel she has calmed down.

I hold her shoulders. "Now, woman up, or how else will you face your Eve, Eve?"

"Two Eves?" she asks while wiping away her tears.

I let go of her shoulders. "Two Eves, two Adams, one Eve, one Adam, and one very bad decision on what to eat—you name it."

She blinks several times. "Kristina, did you just insinuate a threesome?"

"What? No. Why would you think—oh."

She laughs out loud, and I'm glad. If there's one thing that hurts me, it's seeing her bright smile disappear behind her pursing lips as she tries to hold herself together.

"What about your Adam?" she asks.

"What about him?"

"Do you guys still talk on a daily basis?"

"Yes, we do actually."

Talking to Adam might just be the highlight of my day. I rarely smile at my phone, but when I talk to Adam, I apparently do because my mother gets nosier and asks me why I'm smiling. I always lie and tell her that Alex sent me something funny. Which she does and I also always smile because of that. It's kind of the *truth by omission* again.

"And you're sure you're not in love?" Alex questions.

My eyebrows shoot up. "What? Of course, I'm sure. I don't even know who he is."

"So?"

"So? So, I can't exactly fall in love with someone I don't know."

"Believe me, you can. It's how I fell in love with Senait. Love can be blind."

That might be, but I'm not capable of falling in love—haven't been for eight years now. And now, I have to convince her that I somehow have. This is going to backfire—tremendously.

"Yes, but you and Senait are the definition of soul mates," I say. "How is she, by the way?"

Alex sighs. "Swamped in schoolwork, so I don't get to see her all that much. But once I do, let's hang out together."

I smile. "I would love that."

My phone chimes, but it's not the notification sound of the app I use to talk to Adam; it's a normal text message. I grab my phone to read it.

Nemesis with Benefits: Can we come by today?

My eyes widen as I read the text. I haven't even prepared for this mentally, let alone physically, by actually preparing and telling my mother. But there's no time to lose. I don't want to postpone this any longer because I've already been patient for many years. The last mile is the longest—and the hardest.

I text him back, confirming that they can and send my exact address along with it since he only saw the building I live in and not the actual apartment when he walked me home.

I get up from my bed and face Alex. "Alex, I hereby invite you to be in the audience for my newest intervention."

Her forehead creases. "Your what?"

I grab her hand, guide her to the living room, and then I softly push her to sit on the couch.

I go to Delano's room, knock quickly, and open the door. He's sitting at his desk. I grab his hand as well and bring him to sit next to Alex.

"What's happening right now?" he asks.

She shrugs her shoulders. "Her newest intervention."

He narrows his eyes at her and then shrugs his shoulders as well.

I search for my mother and see her standing at the stove, boiling water. I turn off the stove and grab her hand, guiding her to the couch and letting her sit next to Delano.

"*Fe eh?*" she asks with a cocked head.

In sync, Alex and Delano answer, "Her newest intervention."

She frowns. "*Eda?*"

They both shrug their shoulders at her.

Meanwhile, I'm searching for my last spectator. She's sitting under a chair at the dining table. I grab Lady and put her on Alex's lap. She starts petting her.

Now that the crowd has gathered, I take my place on my stage. I've done this so many times that there's even a print of my feet on the carpet behind the coffee table.

I want to tell Alex with them present because she won't be able to interrogate me now, which is exactly what I need because I won't be able to lie myself out of this one. Not to her.

I commence my speech. "Dear family members, thank you for gracing me with your presence yet again. I have gathered you here today for a long-awaited announcement."

I hold out my hand. "Unravel this mystery, please. Always the bridesmaid, never the ... ?"

All of them squint their eyes at me, even Lady.

"Never the groomsman!" Delano shouts confidently.

Alex gives Delano a slight push with her elbow, disagreeing with him. "Never the center of attention, obviously."

"*Ana mish fahma haga,*" my mother confesses.

Alex leans forward to face my mother. "*Tant* Diana, you have to finish the phrase."

My mother leans forward to face her as well. "*Leh*?"

Delano bows, turning his head several times to look at them both. "Because it's a riddle."

"Okay, have any of you even seen *Corpse Bride*?" I ask to interrupt their rambling.

Delano grimaces. "How can a corpse be a bride? Wouldn't the corpse be in a casket, not at a wedding?"

Alex snaps her fingers and points at me. "Oh! The movie?"

"Corpse *meen*?" my mother wonders.

"I wish I were in a casket right about now," I mutter.

"What?" all three of them ask.

I blow out air. "Nothing. Can you all just listen for a second without uttering all your thoughts right away?" I continue, "The saying goes as follows: *always the bridesmaid, never the bride.*"

"So, she isn't a corpse bride, but a bridesmaid. Who's alive?" Delano concludes.

Alex gasps. "It means that you aren't married!"

"*Meen el* bride?" my mother asks.

I slap my forehead with the palm of my hand. I can't believe they can't figure it out. I don't want to be direct about it either. But I don't have time for this, so it seems I have no choice but to utter the biggest lie in history. I'd better brace myself. "I am in love."

They stop chattering almost immediately and look at me wide-eyed. Lady doesn't though; she's still squinting. I think she forgot to listen to the rest of the conversation. Honestly, I don't blame her; it was getting confusing.

"In love," my mother acknowledges.

"In love?" Delano questions.

"In love?!" Alex yells. "With who?!"

"With Aug—" I sigh. "With Augustine Elias." I avoid eye contact by fixing my gaze on the ground.

Suddenly, Delano and Alex shoot up, which causes Lady to jump from Alex's lap. It startles me, so I immediately face them again.

"I thought you hated him?" Alex asks.

"How do you even know him?" Delano follows up.

My mother averts her eyes from them to me. "That's wonderful, *habibti*!" she cheers with a bright smile.

"Yeah, totes wonderful!" That's a lie. I want to run away from this situation. But he's also the means to me running away. It's all getting too confusing.

"Oh, and he's also coming over here today to ask for this." I hold up my hand to them.

Delano and Alex look at each other, shocked.

My mother seems shocked, too, but for a different reason. "*Yalahwi*? Today? We have to clean the living room!"

"Delano, Alex, help me clean. Kristina, go wear something that isn't sweats, black, or both," she orders.

Alex gestures a salute. "Yes, ma'am!"

Delano walks toward the kitchen to grab cleaning supplies.

I watch them hysterically move around the house until my mother practically shoos me away to my room.

So, no sweats, black, or both. How about a suit that isn't black? I rummage through my closet and find a gray suit and a white turtleneck. I can work with this. I then grab my black pumps from under my clothing rack, wear everything, and put my hair in a tight, low bun, parting it to the right.

I look in the mirror, only to realize that it looks more like I'm the one doing the proposing instead of being proposed to. Or like I'm on my way to a job interview. I mean, I am in, a way—with his mother being the manager and Augustine being the position.

The living room has undergone a transformation as well. It's neat and tidy. My mother has even pulled out the kahk—popular Egyptian cookies, entirely covered in a layer of powdered sugar—and has put them on the coffee table.

As I'm walking toward the coffee table to take one, I hear the doorbell ring, feeling my heart rate and blood pressure climbing up *way too fast*.

My mother, who's wearing a dress now, opens the door to welcome our guests. Alex and Delano leave the couch to welcome them as well. However, I am still standing at the coffee table since I want to eat a cookie. But I guess I shouldn't. I can't greet my future in-laws with a full mouth and exhale powdered sugar on them. My first impressions always suck, but at least I know how to prevent this one from totally sucking—because it's going to suck, no matter what I do.

The door opens, and first, I see two women—his mother and the girl in the picture with him in his office, who turns out to be his sister after all. She looks exactly like him up close. She has short, wavy black hair, thick eyebrows, and green eyes.

Behind them is Augustine, wearing a gray suit with a white shirt—buttoned up and everything. I'm cringing—hard. Now, they're all going to assume we wanted to match. But there's one difference between us. He's also holding a bouquet of white flowers.

"Come in!" my mother exclaims.

Delano and Alex take their coats and hang them up in the hallway. His mother and sister then follow my mother to the couch.

Delano and Alex follow them and close the door that separates the hallway from the living room.

Augustine hands me the bouquet. "Here, for you."

I'm speechless. I've never received flowers—*ever*. Which might be normal for some, but I adore flowers. So, to me, it's a big deal. And him giving them to me now? I can't help but feel ... grateful.

I slowly extend my arm to take the bouquet from him and put it against my nose to inhale the scent. It's tickling my nose, and it smells like lemons at the exact moment you cut it in half, pungent yet sweet at the same time.

My head tilts up. "Thank you."

I hold the bouquet with one hand and extend the other to him. "Here, give me your coat."

"No need." He hangs up his coat and then looks at me from head to toe. More like from toe to head since he starts by looking at my pumps, making his way to my face.

One of his eyebrows pulls upward. "Copycat?"

"You're the blueprint. You're even copying me calling you a copycat."

I hope he doesn't notice that my calling him the blueprint means I'm copying what he said to me at church. How am I so stupid to contradict myself like that?

He ignores it and studies my suit some more. "Am I the one proposing, or are you?"

I mean, he's not wrong. I thought the same thing. But I would never admit that to him.

"Attire has no gender," I say.

I open the door that leads to the living room, and he follows me.

Augustine greets my mother by giving her three kisses on her cheeks—well, not really, more like putting his cheek against hers to make smooch sounds. I don't know why, but greeting people like that is an actual thing.

Then he walks toward Delano and Alex to greet them as well. He even hugs Delano. It seems they were already friends, which makes this all even weirder than it already was.

I walk toward his mother and greet her the same way he greeted mine, and then I face his sister.

I place my cheek against hers. "Hi. I'm Kristina Armanious."

"Hi. I'm Marina Elias."

"I guess that would make us the *ina* sisters. Miss Basalious over there"—I point at Alex, and she waves—"and I are the *ious* sisters."

Marina chuckles. "I like that."

Ever since we were little, Alex and I have always assumed that no mother could handle us both, that we're sisters who are bound to each other by the last part of our last names. We were young and stupid. But now that we're older, we're somehow still stupid.

I put the bouquet in a vase on the kitchen counter.

Seated from left to right are Alex, Delano, my mother, Augustine's mother, and Marina. Across from them, behind the coffee table, are Augustine and I, sitting on chairs. It feels as if we're about to be interrogated by the police. It doesn't only feel like it, that's exactly what's about to go down. And frankly, Augustine and I don't have our stories straight regarding our crime.

"So, how did you two meet?" my mother asks.

So, the real answer, Mama, is that I went to his office intending to manipulate him, but he had already caught on, which resulted in us fighting. But I can't exactly tell you that since I told you I was meeting Alex that day. Also, I just can't tell you that.

But since Alex is here, she'll probably be confused for a second, then figure out how we met and understand that I can't say that. But then Alex is going to want to interrogate me since she'll also realize that she doesn't know when, how, or why I fell in love. But if I avoid her for now—until I have prepared the version of the story I'll sell her—then it should be all right. Right? Right ...

I can only deal with one person at a time, and I'm starting with the woman who gave birth to me. Which is only natural, of course. She gave me my beginning, so it's only fair to give her one as well.

I secretly tug at his belt loop.

Sending a signal to let me answer the question.

Signal received because he doesn't answer the question.

"Oh, the first time I saw him was in a coffee shop. I was waiting for Alex. We started talking and found out that we go to the same church and then just hit it off."

Both Alex and Augustine look at me with creased foreheads. But only for a second because they both now realize how we first met and understand why I said that. I can't believe I predicted this.

"When was this?" his mother asks.

He answers her, "About a couple of months ago."

His mother continues, "But if you had already hit it off, why did you all of a sudden stop wanting to go on Fridays?"

"Yes, Augustinus *habibi*, I always see you on Sundays. How did you meet after that if she goes on Fridays?" my mother wonders.

Alex, Delano, and Marina look at each other, puzzled. But none of them interferes, which is only natural since they're clueless as well.

I can't lie to save my life. My lies aren't lying enough. *What is happening to me? What is even happening right now?*

"I mean, the who, what, where, when, why, which, and how aren't that important, are they?" I propose with a sheepish grin.

Our mothers face each other, their faces saying that something isn't adding up.

I quickly interrupt them from putting two and two together. "Can we just get married? Please?"

Not only do I give speeches, but apparently, I do theater as well. Playing the character who's desperately in love, like Juliet. Maybe I should start considering changing my major.

"She means, do we have your blessing?" Augustine says.

My mother scans him. "You want to marry her?"

"Oh, absolutely. I would love nothing more than to be her husband." He grabs my hand and holds it.

Gross. And I hate it when he holds my hand, but I can't exactly retract it. So, I try to put on a sincere smile to hide the discomfort I'm in at this moment.

They gradually shift their attention from us to each other and chatter away.

While maintaining the smile, I lean in to whisper in his ear, "I swear to God, if you don't let go of my hand right this second—"

He turns to me, causing me to lean back a little because his face is very close to mine. "It won't be believable if we don't do anything. Be glad I'm not kissing it," he says. "Besides, the contract states PDA if necessary to make it believable. You made that clause."

I get up and release my hand from his. "Can I offer you all some tea?"

Alex gets up as well. "I'll help her!"

No. Oh God, no. This is her way of interrogating me. *Alex, your time has yet to come.*

"No need. He's going to help me!" I tug at the end of Augustine's sleeve.

Alex gasps and looks at me with her jaw almost hitting the floor. I know she feels betrayed.

Augustine rises and walks with me to the kitchen. "Why am I helping you?"

"Why not?"

"Because you hate me, and if a chance ever arises to not spend a second with me, you never hesitate to take it."

"Good. So, you do know that."

He shakes his head and clicks his tongue.

"Because she wanted to interrogate me since she knows about me hating you. And I don't know what to say to make it believable that I don't anymore because I still do," I explain.

I put the kettle on the stove and grab the box with tea bags.

"Can you grab the cups from there?" I point at the cabinet above me.

I can grab them myself, but in order to do that, I would have to climb on the counter because I'm too short. To do that now would not be very ladylike of me.

He stands behind me and opens the cabinet, closing me in. But he doesn't make physical contact. Then, he grabs seven cups and puts them in front of me on the counter. He's so damn tall, like a titan; it's insane. I'm even wearing heels right now.

"May we use this?" he asks.

I lean back to look at the cabinet—touching his collarbone with my head—and see him holding a tray. I lean forward and nod.

He takes the tray, closes the cabinet, and puts it in front of me. He then moves away from behind me to stand next to me again. I don't understand why he felt the need to move behind me in the first place. He could have easily grabbed everything from this position.

The kettle whistles, and I turn off the stove. I fill all the cups, and Augustine puts them on the tray. I hand him some spoons, and he puts them on the tray as well.

I'm holding the box with the tea bags, two jars with sugar and powdered milk, and Augustine's holding the tray. We wind our way back to the living room.

We put everything on the coffee table, and everyone starts making their tea how they like it.

As I reach for the strawberry-flavored tea bag, Augustine does as well. It's the last one.

I suck in my lips.

He whispers, "May I like strawberries too, Miss Armanious?"

That's not why I'm annoyed right now. I'm annoyed because he somehow always ends up touching my hand. And I don't like to be touched, especially by him.

"You may, Mr. Elias, and because of that, I won't like strawberries today. You can have the last tea bag."

"Don't be ridiculous. We can share it." He puts the tea bag in my cup, and it reaches a deep red color. "Is this enough strawberry for you?"

I nod. "Yes, you may extract the tea bag. It has extracted quite enough."

He takes it out and puts it in his cup.

"How sweet!" my mother says.

"*Awy!*" his mother adds.

I completely forgot we aren't alone for a second. I guess you could mistake tormenting for teasing if you have no context. Teasing is cute, in a way.

We both smile at them and sip on our tea.

Lady starts using Augustine's leg as a scratching post.

"Lady, don't!" I urge her, but she doesn't listen.

Augustine grabs Lady and puts her on his lap. "Hello, Lady."

He scratches her chin, and she purrs.

What? I feel deeply betrayed. Lady never warms up this fast to anyone. And it took him like, what? Ten seconds? What if she likes him more than me? What if she would rather spend time with him when we live together? That's my new worst nightmare.

But I'm glad he doesn't dislike her. His disliking cats would automatically be a deal-breaker for me. I mean, how can someone even dislike cats?

I can't help but smile at them. I pet her head while he continues to give her chin scratches.

After drinking tea and chattering for a while, our mothers sit on one end of the couch. They already knew each other because his mother not only goes on Fridays but also on Sundays.

Delano and Augustine come to sit on the chairs where Augustine and I first sat. Alex, Marina, and I now find ourselves on the other end of the couch. I'm sitting between them.

I see Augustine talking with Delano—more like Augustine whispering and Delano nodding with crossed arms. I have no idea what they're talking about, but since they were already friends, it's only natural, I guess.

Everyone already knew each other because they all went on Sundays. I'm the only oddball here.

"How old are you, Marina?" I ask her.

"Twenty-eight."

"Marina is like the older sister we never had," Alex tells me.

"Right? About time," I say.

Marina beams at me. "I would love to have you as my sister-in-law."

She's so sweet. It makes me feel *that* much worse about this whole facade. But becoming friends with her? I would like that since I'm very lacking in the friends department. My only friends are Alex and João. And Lady. And Delano.

I beam at her as well. "I feel the same way."

"Marina, I hereby declare you *not* on Kristina's Egyptians blacklist," Alex determines.

"Alex!" I practically yell.

Marina laughs out loud. "Well, I'm honored, but I totally understand you, Kristina. Egyptians are not an easy bunch."

I gasp at her words and hold both her hands. "You believe so?"

"Yes, in fact, I even understand why you would prefer Fridays over Sundays.

If I didn't have work on Friday, I would probably consider going then as well."

I bow down, placing my forehead on her hands as I hold them. "Angel, where have you been all this time?"

Marina bows to face me. "I guess waiting for you to take my annoying brother as your husband. About time he moves out. He's way too old to still be living at home."

"Wait, Marina, you just got engaged yourself, didn't you?" Alex asks.

"Yeah, I did." She holds up her hand to show us her ring.

I only notice it now. It has a very big, round diamond. It's gleaming, and it looks so elegant on her.

I avert my eyes from her ring to her again. "Congratulations!"

"Thank you, sweetheart."

As we're all sitting and each of us is deep in conversation, I realize their father isn't with them. He might no longer be here, just like mine. Or there might be another reason for it. But I don't want to pry. It's a way to maintain the distance we have to keep from each other in order for this to work flawlessly.

After a while, I gesture with my head to Augustine for him to follow me to the balcony. He excuses himself and does.

"What is it, Miss Armanious? Tired of acting all coy with me when you would rather strangle me to death?"

I lean over the railing a little and groan. "It's exhausting, to say the least."

"Make-believe?"

I nod without facing him.

"You'd better get used to it because this is how it'll be. We will have to gather exactly like today from time to time," he says.

"I mean, I like your mother and sister, so I'm not entirely opposed."

"I already had a hunch you did."

"So, what happens now?" I ask.

"Now, we go on dates."

I turn to him. "Do we actually have to? Can't we just lie and say we did?"

He's holding the railing with both hands, spread out, turned to me. "Oh, definitely. We're not actually going on dates." He pauses. "Perhaps just once."

"I can do once. What else?"

"We start wedding planning."

"I mean, we don't *need* to have a wedding. We can just sign whatever has to be signed and let the priest pray whatever has to be prayed."

He scoffs. "Miss Armanious, and I say this with all due respect, but if anyone ever finds out about our little pact, you'll be the reason."

My eyes shrink. "What makes you say that?"

"Two people who are supposedly hopelessly in love, to the extent that they want to get married right away, are deciding not to have a wedding? It's like you're asking them to catch you red-handed."

Okay, fine, maybe he's right. Okay, fine, he's right. I'm not thinking rationally about this at all. All I can think about is getting it all over with. "That's fair."

Augustine's mother calls for us from the living room. We go back, and I see her, Marina, and Alex already wearing their coats.

"*Yalla habibi*, it's late. Everyone has work tomorrow. If you want to spend time together, you can go on dates now," his mother says.

That's the funny thing about this culture. They think that two people don't date before meeting each other's parents. They probably assume that the first words exchanged between them when meeting each other for the first time is an address and someone's father's availability.

"We will," Augustine confirms.

We will, unfortunately.

Augustine wears his coat. Delano, my mother, and I say goodbye to them—for a while since Egyptians say goodbye to each other longer than actually sitting with each other. Believe me, it's a thing.

Eventually, they all leave. Alex leaves with them, so she doesn't have time to interrogate me. Which is a good thing.

I take a shower and lie in bed.

And suddenly, it all hits me.

From this day onward, we are officially engaged to be married.

CHAPTER SEVEN

Adam: Eve, here's a vexed question for you. Is the line between love and hate thin, thick, or nonexistent?

Eve: Adam. Isn't this a trick question rather than a vexed one? If so, then the answer is all of the above, depending on who you have in mind, of course.

Adam: Can you elaborate on that?

Eve: For you, anything. The line is thin for siblings. The line is thick for God and Satan. And for us, the line is nonexistent.

Adam: Are you suggesting you hate me?

Eve: Not at all! It simply means that even though I gave you all the reasons to hate me, you still loved me regardless. Love and hate, they are both directed toward a person you somehow always find yourself thinking about.

Adam: I've never hated you, Eve.

Eve: The feeling is mutual. I have never hated you either, Adam.

It's Sunday. And instead of sleeping in, I somehow find myself getting ready. Now that I'm "engaged," it's only natural for me to want to go to church to see my fiancé. This is not what I think. My mother said this as she practically dragged me out of bed this morning.

I will have to find something so I won't be able to go on Sundays because I will *not* be making this a regular thing. Over my dead body. Not even then.

Since I'm not planning on staying there, I'm wearing a simple all-black outfit. I wear my nude trench coat, grab my boots from the rack at the front door, and put them on.

Delano and my mother also put on their shoes, and we leave the house to drive to church.

Delano always drives. Both my mother and I have a license, but we don't particularly like driving.

I don't like driving because the thought of me being responsible for someone's death makes me sick to my stomach. I'm also scared of driving in itself. My father's death has significantly impacted me regarding driving and cars. It's also the reason I always prefer public transportation over cabs.

We arrive at church, and the service is about to begin. Delano goes to the men's side and stands next to Augustine, who's also wearing entirely black. Now, I really have to keep on my coat because our outfit matching is getting ridiculous.

I stand beside my mother on the women's side.

The men's side consists of two rows of benches on the left side of the church, and the women's side consists of two rows of benches on the right side.

The service ends, and I see Alex already approaching me.

She hugs me. "I can't believe my eyes. Is this astral projection? Or are you really here?" She pinches my shoulder to make sure.

"*Ay!*" I whisper-shout, rubbing my shoulder. "I'm here in body, I'm afraid."

"Good, because we have to talk," she says sternly.

Shit. I totally forgot about that. I look around and see Augustine alone at the candles—ironic.

"We totally will. Let's talk at my house soon!" I slowly start shuffling away.

"Fine, but where are you going right now?"

"To him." I point in Augustine's direction.

She puts on her playful expression. "You have it that bad for him?"

"No? I mean, yes, obviously, but no?"

She laughs out loud. "Fine, go. I'll see you later."

I kiss my hand and touch hers. She puts it on her cheek. She then walks a little with me toward Augustine, pushes me against him, causing me to bump into his back, and leaves.

"Sorry," I say while rubbing my forehead now.

He turns around. "Miss Armanious? Careful now or else I'll start thinking you're the one stalking me."

"Believe me, that's the last thing I would do."

He puts the candle down and faces me again. "What brings you here?"

"My mother thinks I'm so hungry for you that I have to grab every chance I can get to see you."

"Are you?"

"Am I what?"

"Hungry."

What is he talking about here? Emotional or physical hunger? It doesn't matter. I'm hungry for neither. "No."

"Perhaps you'll be hungry tomorrow."

"What?"

"Dine with me."

"But I don't want to dine with you, no offense."

"Taken," he says. "I've already made reservations. It's what engaged people do; they have dinner together."

I blink several times. "You made reservations without consulting me first?"

"I already had a hunch you would be here today. Had my hunch turned out to be incorrect, I would have contacted you."

I realize now that my being "busy" is not a good enough reason for my mother not to go and see him on Sundays. Because even he expected me to be here, which means my mother intends to drag me out of bed every Sunday morning. So, I try the only thing I can think of, not to let that happen. "Say, Mr. Elias, why don't you come on Fridays from now on? You did it to stalk me, no? Can you make stalking me, like, a regular thing?"

He sighs. "I didn't, and I can't."

I click my tongue. "Why not?"

"I work on Fridays."

"But you came here several Fridays."

"I did—by calling in sick, using my vacation days, and miraculously having all my medical appointments scheduled to be on Fridays."

Oh, wow, he went all out to apologize to me. But I see, this won't be the solution.

I continue our previous conversation. "What if I refuse to have dinner together tomorrow?"

"Then, you refuse; however, you'll just be postponing the inevitable."

I frown at him. "The inevitable?"

"You said you can do one date. I'm here to collect."

This man is unbelievable. How is having dinner together keeping our distance from each other? But he isn't wrong; I did say that. I hate how he always remembers my exact words and how he always uses them against me.

"Fine. Then, I'll be *famished* tomorrow," I tell him oddly gently.

"Terrific. I'll send you the details," he says. "Have a good day, Miss Armanious."

"Yeah ... you have a"—I scowl because I sure as hell—heaven—am not about to say good—"day," I say after a long pause.

He presses his lips together to suppress his smile and leaves, this time leaving me standing at the candles.

Tomorrow is going to be hard. First, I have work, and then I have him. And sooner rather than later, I have Alex. I'm going to need the rest of the day to mentally prepare myself.

I walk downstairs to the canteen and see my mother having breakfast with Augustine's mother. I greet them.

"Mama, I'm going home," I say.

She cocks her head. "Why?"

"Kristina *habibti*, did you see Augustinus?" his mother asks.

"Yes, *tant*, I did."

"Good, *ya sokar*."

"Why don't you want to stay to be with him?" my mother asks.

"He left, and I'm seeing him tomorrow, so I have some things to take care of. Can I go now?"

"*Hader*." She hands me the keys.

She has to hand them to me because I don't have my own set. That's how much responsibility I have been given—none.

I take the subway and arrive home. Then, I change into sweats and grab my notebooks full of my bucket lists and lists.

I need some encouragement to see tomorrow through, and I need to come up with the story I'm going to sell Alex.

My bucket lists give me courage. Seeing things crossed off and crossing them off instantly brings me this fuzzy feeling. No, scratch—cross that. It gives me a *kick*. I love it so much that when I have already achieved or done something that wasn't on one of my lists, I put it on them just for the sake of crossing it off again. It might be a waste of ink, but not a waste of kicks.

As I open my notebook, I hear my phone beep—unfortunately, a normal text. I grab it to read it.

Nemesis with Benefits: Can I come pick you up at 5:45 p.m. tomorrow?

Pick me up? No, I would rather not be picked up. I won't be able to survive a car ride with him. I can already taste the awkwardness on the tip of my tongue. I dislike its taste.

I text him that I would rather meet him there and to send me the name of the restaurant.

Nemesis with Benefits: As you wish. It's called Seafood & Champagne.

Can you be there at six?

I confirm that I can and grab my laptop to search the restaurant.

As I scroll through the website, I immediately realize three things: it's elegant, expensive, and I feel *excluded*. I don't belong there at all. I wanted to wear something simple, but as I scroll some more, I see everyone looking sophisticated—*too* sophisticated.

Damn you, Augustine, what are you playing at here?

If I just wear a suit again, I can avoid wearing a dress. Which is good because I don't like wearing dresses, especially short ones. I simply can't wear those.

But I don't want to wear the same color as him again. *Think, Kristina.*

The instrument I'm using to predict the outcome of another measure is my previous experiences regarding Augustine's clothing. The other measure being Augustine's clothing choice for tomorrow.

So, if Augustine wore gray the last time I saw him and black today, he'll probably wear beige or white. Since I haven't seen other colors on him except for those neutral colors.

I think for a while.

Okay, I've made up my mind. It has to be beige. Which means I have to avoid all my nude trench coats. I have a dark brown suit. If I wear that with a black bodysuit and a black coat—just in case he wears white after all—I think it'll be elegant enough for the place. Right? Right …

I hope my previous experiences regarding his clothing have enough criterion validity for me to be right about this prediction.

I take the suit out of my closet and make my way to the living room to iron it.

My mother has just arrived home.

She points at the suit in my hands. "Kristina? Are you planning on wearing that tomorrow?"

"Well, yes?"

"*La,* you wore a suit when he was here, and I didn't like that one bit. It's time you wore a dress. Or are you planning on wearing a suit on your wedding day as well?"

I mean, if it's allowed, why not? I don't see the problem with that. I actually love that idea. "I mean, if it's—"

She interrupts me. "Kristina, go find a dress. You have plenty, and you never wear them."

I groan quietly and return to my room to hang the suit in my closet. I just need to obey a little longer. The finish line is in sight.

I rummage through my closet and find a black satin dress. I try it on. It's long—so long that I can't even see my feet anymore. I grab shorts and wear them underneath. I think I can work with this.

I go to my mother, and she nods in approval. I go back to my room to change into sweats again.

Then, I sit on my bed with my notebooks. I open one to my bucket list called Activities At A.M.—by that, I mean things I want to do at night.

At the top of the list: *Watch the sunrise*. Right under it: *Go to a bar at night*.

The first thing I'm going to do the minute I'm married to that wretched man is watching the sunrise. I won't even wait another day to do that because I. Simply. Can't. Wait.

This gives me the courage I need. Now, it's time to fabricate the story I'm selling Alex.

So, she knows I hated him because of our first two meetings. But I didn't tell her about our meeting at church, so calling it love at third sight will be believable. If I say he came to apologize, which really did happen, and that we talked everything out and have hit it off ever since, which really hasn't happened, that would be believable.

And if she asks me what changed—since I've been swearing off men for eight years now—I'll just say that Augustine somehow makes me feel comfortable, which he really doesn't. She'll probably be too over the moon for me to ask any more questions, and then that will be that.

It's Monday. I just got off work and am making my way home to get ready and meet up with Augustine. I mean, I had better plans in mind for my evening, but fine.

I know I keep repeating that I hate Augustine. I do, but I might say it more than I actually do. He might not be as arrogant anymore, but the way he spoke to me the first time we met and what went down at the pub are things I can't just gloss over, glamorizing them and hiding they happened.

Besides, holding my ground that I hate him and reminding him of that fact will only ensure we keep our distance and respect the contract we made. Who would want to get close to someone who greets them with, *Hi, I hate your guts,* every time they meet? No one.

I put on the shorts I found yesterday and a bra that transforms my pancakes into fluffy ones. I usually don't care much about my Dutch mini pancakes, but the dress I'm wearing shows cleavage, so I kind of have to turn them into American ones.

I put on the dress, wear my hair down, and apply some red lipstick and mascara. Then, I grab my heeled sandals and black coat.

I enter the living room. "Mama, I'm leaving. I'll be back before eight."

"Oh, *habibti,* Augustinus already called me and asked for my permission to make it a little later than eight and said that he'll bring you home."

What the actual fuck? First of all, how does he have her number? When did he even call her? When was *my* permission asked to do that? Second, he just had to ask, and almost instantly, my curfew is lifted? I've been asking for *years.* You have got to be fucking kidding me right now.

I form a fist, pressing my sharp nails into the palm of my hand. "Oh."

She pats my shoulder. "Have fun, *habibti.*"

"Yeah, thanks, Mama. Will do." Will *not* do. I wasn't planning on it, but I'm definitely not going to have it now.

This is infuriating. Even Delano has asked her several times to push my curfew to at least nine, and she wouldn't budge. And suddenly, Augustine waltzes into my life and can make the impossible possible. And the worst part is, I'm going to have to endure a car ride with him after all.

I leave the house and walk to the station. Thank God it's not far from here. I only have to ride four stops and walk five minutes to be there at six.

It has been a very long time since I dressed up like this. I can't even remember the last time I wore a dress. I won't deny that it is fun, though, having an occasion to dress up for. I never had one of those—until now.

As I'm sitting in the subway, we go into a tunnel. I look out the window and see my reflection clear as day in the darkness filling the silent subway. As if looking in the mirror and being the only one here. That image disappears as fast as it came when the subway gets out of the tunnel, and noise takes over again. I can sense all the skyscrapers, streets, and vehicles. Outside.

That is what Augustine symbolizes. From being in an enclosed environment my whole life, just like that, I get to see outside and everything it has to offer.

I didn't have the chance to take a good look at myself in the mirror today before leaving. But seeing myself all dolled up like that, even if it was only for a split second, I won't forget that image of myself.

I'm in front of the restaurant, and it's even fancier in real life than in the pictures. The doors are made of glass, and the name Seafood & Champagne is above them in big white LED lights. It's so bright that it makes me close my eyes a little.

I go inside and see a small counter with a hostess behind it.

"Good evening. How may I assist you?" she asks me.

"Hi there. I think the reservation is under the name Elias, but I'm not sure if he's here already ..." My voice trails off.

"Oh! You must be Ms. Armanious. He's already seated in the back. I will take you to him."

"Oh, yeah. Thank you so much!"

She walks to the back of the restaurant, and I follow her. We reach the back, and I can already see Augustine sitting at a table for two. He's wearing black. A black suit—an entire suit—with his black shirt buttoned up.

I mean, even if my prediction was very off, it wouldn't have mattered because the plan was to wear dark brown. But my mother had other plans for me, as she always does.

So, we're matching—yet again.

But I also see some color at his fingertips. Red. A bouquet of red tulips. Flowers.

"Flowers. For me?" I ask him.

He stands up from his chair. "For you," he says as he hands them to me.

I inhale their smell. They smell sweet, like honey.

The hostess extends her hands to me. "Ms. Armanious, you can give your coat to me."

"Oh, thank you so much."

As I try to put the bouquet on the table, Augustine beats me to it by reaching for them and holding them instead. I take off my coat and hand it to the hostess.

She leaves, and while I move my chair backward, I ask him, "So, why did you invite me to this specific too-fancy restaurant?"

He sits down again. "I was wondering what you would look like in a dress. I wanted to see you in one."

He's eyeing my dress all the way to the floor. I'm guessing he meant a *short* one.

And why would he even say that? If I didn't know better, I would say he's flirting with me.

I sit across from him at the table, and he hands me the bouquet again. I put them on the windowsill next to me.

I look up at him. "Are you going to keep buying me flowers?" I won't deny that I love it. This is the second time I have ever received flowers, and frankly, I can't get enough.

"Do you want me to?"

"Yes," I blurt out. "I-I mean, no?"

"Duly noted."

I support my elbows on the table and put my fingers into each other to support my chin. "How about you tell me why you didn't ask permission to talk to my mother."

"I assumed I wouldn't need permission since it would've been granted automatically."

I tilt my head to the right a bit. "What makes you say that?"

He mirrors me by letting his fingers support his chin. "This is what snippets of freedom taste like. Do you like its taste?" He tilts his head now as well. "If you do, I can give you even more. A whole meal at that."

I love it, Augustine, so much that I would like to have this for breakfast, lunch, and dinner every day for the rest of my life. "I do."

"Good. Then let me serve it to you." He hands me the menu. I take it from him and open it to look through the dishes. And the first thing I notice is the ridiculous prices because one meal here might be the same price as three meals for a week straight anywhere else.

As I read through the menu, I feel him staring at me. I look up at him and follow his eyes. He's staring at my left collarbone—*or cleavage?*—my left forearm and right wrist, shifting his attention between them.

He points at them. "You have tattoos."

"I do," I say, still looking at them.

My mother doesn't—definitely doesn't approve. But when I got them, I just did it. Because I needed them, and since they're permanent, there wasn't much she could do besides giving me the silent treatment for months. I have more, but they're not all visible, so she doesn't know about them. No one knows about them.

The one on my collarbone is the name Kyrollos Armanious, written in Arabic—my father's name. And the one on my wrist is a cross made of flowers.

"Do you?" I ask him.

"I do too."

I study him. "Where?"

"Upper body."

"Interesting."

A waiter approaches our table. "Good evening. Would you like to order?"

Augustine faces him. "May I have the mixed seafood grill and boiled potatoes with butter, please?" Then, he faces me. "Do you like champagne?"

"I do."

He faces the waiter again. "And a bottle of Dom Pérignon Brut, please."

Too expensive. What is he even doing right now?

"Yes, absolutely." The waiter writes it down on his tablet. "And for your beautiful girlfriend?"

I wave my hand at the waiter. "Oh, no, we're not—" Why bother? It won't matter if I explain it. I get why he would make that assumption. Might as well practice. "Could I have the same, please?"

"Yes, coming right up!" The waiter writes it down, takes the menus, and leaves.

Augustine smirks at me. "Copycat."

I roll my eyes at him. "Oh, please," I say. "There's something we need to discuss."

He runs his fingers through his hair, causing more strands to cover his forehead. "Do tell."

"Regarding living together, we obviously have to have separate rooms, so when can we go house-hunting?"

"I already found a house. It has separate rooms, as you wish. It's going under renovations as we speak." He pauses and nods once. "Literally."

What? This man is unbelievable.

I close my eyes and rub my temple. "Mr. Elias, do you need to be reminded of the fact that I'll be living there with you, ergo, I should have a say in things?"

"You do have a say in things."

"*Eda?* Well, you're not showing it clearly." I exhale. "What's the rent? How much is it?"

If we split it, hopefully, it'll be affordable. Since I'm not the richest. Actually, I'm not rich at all. I'm pretty broke at the moment.

"Don't worry about it," he says, gesturing with his hand.

My nose wrinkles. "Excuse me? What do you mean, don't worry about it? I don't want to be some parasite living off you."

As I say this, his eyes widen, and his mouth hangs open loosely. He's dazed, and he looks ... grateful even.

"Two mixed seafood grills, boiled potatoes with butter, and a bottle of Dom Pérignon Brut!" the waiter sings.

He puts the plates on the table and fills the glasses with champagne. We thank him, and he leaves.

Augustine only takes a small sip of the champagne and then slides it to the side of the table.

I give him a questioning look.

"I'm driving, so I won't be drinking even if it's just champagne," he says. "Enjoy your meal, Miss Armanious."

I grab my glass of champagne and chug almost half of it down. "Yeah, you too."

We eat but don't talk—at all. It makes me question what the whole point was of us having dinner together in the first place. But the food is good. I'm trying really hard not to use my hands. When I'm eating seafood at less fancy restaurants—as one does—I go all in. And by that, I mean that my whole face gets covered in all the fish's liquids.

Augustine seems to be a natural at dining at fancy restaurants. He's not struggling at all. He even knows how to use the tools to crack open the lobster.

I stare at my lobster, which isn't cracked open. I love lobster, but I can only crack it open if I battle with it using my claws and teeth. No tools. We always fight fair and square. I always end up winning all three matches too. But I guess that today, I'm going to be a sore loser after all.

At last, you win, lobster. You win.

"Do you need some help with that?" he asks.

I shift my attention to him. "What?"

He points at the lobster on my plate with his fork.

My cheeks turn the color of the cooked lobsters staring up at me. "How did you—"

"You were looking quite disappointed at it."

He grabs my plate, cracks open the lobster, and dissects it completely, retrieving its meat from its tail, small and thin legs, knuckles, and large claws. He does it so flawlessly.

We are complete opposites.

Once we finish our plates, the waiter picks them up. I'm now finishing the bottle of champagne.

Augustine clears his throat. "I propose an apology in advance."

I wipe my mouth with a napkin. "For what?" I ask, muffled.

And before I know it, he gets up, stands beside the table, and goes down on one knee while holding up a box from Tiffany & Co. with a big emerald-shaped diamond ring in it. I shift in my seat for my knees to face his and put the napkin down. I don't say anything because I'm truly speechless.

What does one even say right now?

Stupid man, who's somehow still bigger than me, even when on the floor, groveling at my feet.

I hear gasps and people murmuring. Oh, now he's done it.

I force on a smile for the audience we now have and bow down, bringing our faces inches from each other while holding on to that smile for dear life. "What the hell are you doing?"

He frowns at me. "Proposing?"

"Really, Sherlock? I mean, why the hell are you doing this?"

"You deserve to experience this at least once in your life."

I turn to face our audience. They've stopped eating and are now cheering and squealing. And filming.

"Miss Armanious, will you do me the honor of being the bride to my groom?" he says, delighted, as if he'd been waiting his entire life to do this.

I laugh tensely. "I'll be your bride."

The sounds of loud clapping and whistling reach my ears.

As he's putting the ring on my finger, I whisper, "Faux bride."

He locks eyes with me. "I'm aware. You don't have to use every opportunity to remind me of that fact."

"Good. Keep it that way because your actions are telling me completely different things."

After a short while, the commotion finally ends, and Augustine sits down again.

The waiter approaches us with chocolate mousse cake, topped off with strawberries and blackberries. "It's on the house for the beautiful lovebirds!"

We thank him, and he leaves again.

I take a piece of the cake, including all the strawberries, and leave all the blackberries on the plate for him.

"It seems I do have to use every opportunity to remind you of the fact that I like strawberries just as much," Augustine says.

"Oh, no. I'm aware. It's just your punishment for not discussing things with me before you do them."

As I devour the cake and strawberries, I look at the ring, troubled. I'm no expert, but once, I was so bored out of my mind that it resulted in me watching a YouTube tutorial on how to know what makes a ring expensive. They called it the four *c*'s—carat, clarity, color, and cut. And as I assess this ring according to the four *c*'s—with my knowledge on the subject for dummies—the outcome is that it's expensive. Very expensive. And just as beautiful ...

He sees me looking at the ring. "You don't have to actually wear it, only in front of our families and friends."

"Why would you buy me such an expensive ring?"

"I just told you, taking this away from you as well would be cruel. I'm already ruining your life as it is."

Deep lines appear between my eyebrows. "Ruining my life?"

What is he even talking about? He's giving me everything I want by marrying me. If anything, it's me ruining his life. I don't even understand what he's getting out of this.

"Taking away your chance at love," he clarifies.

I exhale heavily. "I already told you, I don't care about that, and I don't need your pity."

"It's not pity; it's remorse."

Oh, I see. It's not flirting at all. He's not doing this because he wants to do this, but because he thinks *I* want him to do this, that *I* want this. Or to make himself feel better. Either way, I don't want his remorse.

Even so, he doesn't understand that his buying me such an expensive ring—when it's pointless—makes me feel guilty. Because it's a waste. I know he has to play the part in front of others, but he's taking it way too seriously when it's just us. And we agreed that there's no need to pretend when we're alone.

"If you'll excuse me for a second, I need to use the restroom," I say as I get to my feet.

I walk toward the restroom, and when I see him grab his phone and be distracted, I change course and tiptoe to the counter.

"Hi. Can I pay for the table over there, please?" I point at Augustine.

The hostess searches for our table in the register, and suddenly, her eyes go bigger. "The whole bill?"

I lean back a little. "Yes ... Why? How much is it? Why did you say it like that?"

She doesn't answer me. Instead, she turns the register for me to see what she saw. It says about four hundred dollars, if I tip them correctly.

I look at her. "What? I'm sorry. I know the food was good and all, but did the oysters get served along with the pearls without me being aware of it or something?"

She laughs. "It's the bottle. It's the most expensive one."

Damn you, Augustine. I could have eaten seafood at a local restaurant, bought a bottle of champagne from Target, and enjoyed it just as much, paying only twenty dollars.

We're not even by a long shot, but this is a start, right? A very rough start at that because now, I'm officially broke.

I pout and slowly give her my card, as if I could retract it at any second.

She places her hand on her mouth to hide her laughter and takes my card. "I'm sorry, sweetheart, but I love the fact that you're paying. Fuck the patriarchy."

"I agree. Fuck the patriarchy."

We smile at each other, and she hands me back my card.

I make my way back and sit at the table again.

"Are you ready to leave?" Augustine asks.

"Yes, gladly."

He holds up his hand for the waiter to come. "May I have the bill, please?"

The waiter scrolls through his tablet. "There is no need for that since it has already been paid."

"What?" he grits out, then faces me with a creased forehead.

I immediately look out the window to avoid him. *Oh, look at outside being so beautiful! Nature sure is pretty,* even though it's too dark to see nature, and I only see my reflection.

"I think this is my cue to leave," the waiter says, and he acts on that cue because he leaves.

"What did you do?" Augustine asks.

I'm still facing the window. "Paid."

He sighs. "Is that a fact, Sherlock? You're confusing me. I asked you here. Following your logic, I'm the one who's supposed to pay."

Stop copying me, you annoyingly huge man. Doesn't he understand that mirroring someone is only cute if you do it implicitly? He doesn't even try to hide it.

I turn to look at him. "Yes, and I would have agreed, but you bought me a very expensive ring. Paying for dinner is literally the least I could do." I add, "And you're confusing me more!"

He puts his palms on his forehead, his fingers tangling in his hair, and groans. "You are driving me insane."

"You'd better get used to it. But could you be the one driving now though?

Driving me home, that is. It's getting late."

He gets up from his chair, and I do too. The hostess comes with our coats, and we wear them. Then, I grab the bouquet, and we leave the restaurant.

A valet brings his car around to the front of the restaurant. He gets out and hands the keys to Augustine. It's a black Range Rover Sport SUV—I know because Delano is obsessed with cars and likes to ramble on about them.

Augustine opens the door for me, and I get in. He then gets in himself and starts driving.

I look around and study the interior of his car. It's spotless. Everything is covered in black leather. It even smells like leather. The smell of a car that was just bought—that's what my olfactory bulbs are signaling.

"A nice car you've got here," I tell him.

He glances at me. "Well, thank you."

"Did you just purchase it?" I lean forward to put my index finger on the dashboard, where the airbag is stored, and rub the surface to see if there's any dust. There isn't.

"No, I didn't. I try to keep it clean."

From the corners of my eyes, I see how he makes a left turn by resting his right palm on the steering wheel and sliding it upward to make the turn single-handedly.

I turn to him. "By the way, could you tell me the address of the house?"

He nods. "I will text it to you."

"Thanks."

There's a reason I didn't want him to pick me up; it's just so awkward. I don't even know what to talk about other than his car.

"Did you enjoy the food?" he asks.

And he doesn't seem to know either.

"It was good."

"I'm glad to hear it."

I keep looking out the window until I'm not because my attention shifts to the dashboard—specifically, to the clock on the dashboard. It says 8:49 p.m.

And I immediately feel an adrenaline rush just by seeing those numbers in that specific order.

We arrive in front of my apartment building. As I reach for the door handle, he presses the button that locks all the doors. The sound of the doors locking—four clicks simultaneously—hammers into me.

What the hell?

I narrow my eyes at him.

He unlocks the doors, gets out of the car, walks around it from the front, and opens the passenger door. He then holds out his hand to me.

I click my tongue. "I don't want to hold your—"

"Look at your window. Be discreet about it."

I do as he says and see my mother gawking at us. *Is this woman seriously watching us right now?*

I put my hand on his, and he helps me get out of the car. He then links my arm in his and walks me to my front door. My mother opens the door before we even get to ring the bell.

"*Shokran ya* Augustinus," she says.

He gives her a soft smile. "It was nothing, *Tant.*"

He unlinks our arms and places his hand on my cheek, cupping it. "Until the next time, love," he says in a soothing tone.

Pretending is hard. My facial expressions can't seem to pretend along. It's taking me everything in my power not to make a weirded-out expression right now. "Yes, *inshallah.*"

My mother holds her cheeks in her hands. "How sweet!" she squeals.

Augustine says goodbye to her and leaves.

As I try to get inside myself, my mother stops me. "Let me see the ring!"

I hold up my hand to her. "You knew about it?"

"Of course we knew. How else would he have known your ring size?" she says. "It's also the reason I didn't want you to wear the suit. He asked us to make sure you wore a dress."

That bastard. He planned everything behind my back. He's probably also the reason I was dragged to church yesterday. Easy to have a hunch if you plan something to have the hunch in the first place. I was already wondering how he could've possibly known that I like the emerald-shaped diamond above all. It was Delano and my mother. But I need to make sure. "Who picked out the ring?"

"He did. He only asked Delano what your preferences are when he was here with his family, but he chose it himself."

So, that's why they were whispering.

"That's sweet ..." I tell her.

"Too sweet!" She enters the living room.

I take off my heeled sandals and coat and leave them in the hallway. I enter the living room as well, put the bouquet in a vase on the kitchen counter, and flop down on the couch in exhaustion.

Since he has collected his first—and last—"date," that will be it for now.

Thank God, I survived it—my bank account, however, not so much.

CHAPTER EIGHT

Eve: Adam. I have been thinking, and I realize now that a lot of people do things behind other people's backs.

Adam: Eve, I happen to be guilty of that myself. Would you consider it a bad thing?

Eve: I would consider it a very bad thing if it turned out you had gone behind my back, eaten the apple first, and made me the bad girl in our little tale.

Adam: What makes you think I did?

Eve: It's called an Adam's apple for a reason, and the only logical thing I can think of is it being your apple, which you ate first.

Adam: I understand. Nonetheless, I can assure you, Eve, I might have been the first person on Earth, but I was the second person to eat. Perhaps we should call it Eve's apple.

Eve: I like that. I like it when fruit becomes mine and mine alone.

As I'm sitting at my desk, working on my résumé, I hear someone knock on my door. I think it's Alex at first, but she won't come until later.

I turn around and see Delano's face peeping from the cracked open door. This is a first because he rarely enters my room while I'm in it. Which makes me realize he enters it when I'm not in it, since he had to steal a ring of mine and return it again.

I gesture with my hand but say it as well. "Come in."

He walks toward me and sits at the foot of my bed. My desk is right in front of it, so I swivel my chair one hundred eighty degrees to face him.

He snickers. "Oh, how the tables have turned."

"You mean, the chair." Since he doesn't always roll with figures of speech.

He points at the ring boxes on my desk. One being the candy ring and the other being the actual engagement ring. "No, the tables. Now, I'm the one who's jealous of you."

I frown. "Why?"

"You get to marry the person you love. I don't have that luxury."

Delano is in love with Farah and has been for years now. But it isn't just a silly crush. No. It's unfair, heart-wrenching, and complicated. Farah is Egyptian, too, but she's also Muslim. This means that Delano and Farah can't be together because their religions are in the way of it ever happening.

And the worst part? I'm going to do what he has been fantasizing about for years. He wants to be able to hold Farah, kiss her, propose to her, and live with her. I have never seen someone love another like Delano loves her, with every fiber of his being.

And him thinking that I'm fortunate to do it with the one I truly love makes my heart ache for him more than it already did because I'm nothing but a phony.

He rests his hands on my bed and leans back to look up at the ceiling. "You know what fucks with my head even more? It would have been possible if the roles were reversed, if I were Muslim and she Christian."

I shake my head. "It wouldn't have been, Delano. You might have been able to marry her, but she wouldn't have been able to marry you."

"Maybe, but at least it would have been one step in the right direction of it ever happening."

Converting isn't a solution either. It doesn't matter who converts; converting for love and not God is just plain wrong. They know this. They even discussed it.

Their whole situation was doomed from the very start. And it has been for many years now.

He breaks the silence. "It just doesn't make sense to me."

"What doesn't?"

"We might believe in different gods, but doesn't it all boil down to the same thing? To not sin and be good. Yeah, sure, the details differ, but the bigger picture is the same. Isn't that what actually matters?" he says. "We're supposed to *love* everyone, and yet we're not allowed to be *in love* with just anyone."

I agree with him. That has never made sense to me either. But me admitting that right now won't help his case. Nothing I say will help his case.

He resumes, "I've heard so many stories where people had to let each other go and they lived miserable lives just because they couldn't go after what they genuinely wanted. Doesn't that make you pity those people, Kris? Not being able to be with whom they genuinely want to be with, so they settle for less and live an unhappy life."

I do, so much that it hurts me physically.

I say the only thing I can come up with. "You know what they say, Lano. We won't be tempted beyond what we're able, and temptations come with escapes so that we can bear it."

His brows knit together. "What kind of test is that?" Then, he murmurs, "If he really does exist."

My eyes flare open, and I whisper, "Delano! What makes you say that?"

"Because I don't think a god would be this cruel, just to challenge me."

I shift my gaze to his feet. "I-I don't know what to say ..."

"I know you don't, and you don't have to because the bottom line will never change."

I tilt my head at him.

His whole face relaxes. "*Deen* over *Dunya,* right?"

Which means the afterlife over our temporal life with its concerns and possessions. It's the embodiment of *memento mori.*

He blinks away the liquid that was starting to take over his eyes. "I just love her. I don't know what will happen to us, but all I know, and have known for as long as I can remember, is that I love her. So damn much."

I nod at him while pressing my lips together. "I know."

We both move our attention to the door when someone knocks. It's Alex.

She slowly opens the door and stands there, making motion-like gestures with her hands. "What's with the vibes here? They're off."

Delano sighs. "Just me feeling miserable."

She sits next to him at the foot of my bed. "About?" She looks at me, asking me with her face what he means.

I raise my chin, pointing it at Delano, telling her he'll tell her himself.

"About what you're miserable over too. How we don't choose who we fall in love with, whether it's someone of the same gender or someone with another religion."

Alex screeches and takes off her cardigan. "Oh, don't even get me started, Delano. It's a living hell on a daily basis, wouldn't you agree?"

He leans back and groans. "I just want to be with her, not having to hide and go on a proper date for once. To get to know each other even better."

"I hear you. I just want to kiss my girlfriend whenever I feel like it without worrying about the possibility of a *tant* seeing us or getting cursed at in the streets," Alex says. "Even when we love like others—I would say even more, since we face extra hurdles and we choose not to give up—our relationships aren't valid."

Delano pushes his underlip against his upper lip and nods, disgusted by the truth of what she said.

He looks at me. "At least you have someone you can love in public and actually be with, Kris. That's why I'm the one who's jealous of you now."

Alex nods. "I would kill to be able to marry Senait. *Kill.*"

God, I feel like such a fucking asshole. Because what I have is what they would die for, and yet it's not sincere at all. I'm even using it for selfish reasons. I'm the fucking worst, and I don't deserve to succeed in what I'm doing.

Not only that, but also this is the reality for a lot of people. People who don't even love each other can be together and are, and people who truly love each other can't. The unfairness of it all—I hate it. And I hate participating in it even more.

So, I decide to suggest the thing that might somehow take away some of my guilt—but probably not. "Would you guys like to go on a double date?"

They look at each other, confused, and then at me.

"What do you mean?" Delano asks.

I lean forward to close the distance between them and me, grab one of their hands and hold it. "I want you"—I direct my face to Delano—"and you"—I direct my face to Alex now—"to bring Farah and Senait to the wedding as your dates."

Delano's eyes shimmer. "No way. Really?"

He then looks at Alex with a smile that reaches his ears, and she returns it.

And I can't help but smile as well because seeing them happy makes me the happiest. "Yes, I would love nothing more."

Alex interrupts us. "Don't get me wrong; I'm stoked—really. But what about your mom?"

I shrug my shoulders. "It's supposed to be my wedding, right? I get to decide who comes, and I want them there," I say. "Besides, I'll just tell her it's only natural to bring a plus-one to a wedding."

"What about your fiancé? Would *he* be okay with it?" she asks.

Oh, him. I completely forgot he'll be there, too, and that it is his wedding just as much as it is mine.

"No doubt. He even set his own friend straight about what it means to be queer. Someone who wouldn't be okay with it would not have done that," I tell her.

Alex giggles. "Love how you used the word *straight* to say that. But, yeah, no doubt. Now that you mention it, he even asked about my pronouns, not mockingly, but with genuine respect."

"Augustine is the best. He even knows about Farah and has always told me he feels sorry for me. No doubt he would be okay with us bringing them," Delano adds.

Sometimes, I still can't believe that Augustine and Delano already knew each other.

I laugh nervously. "That's Augustine for ya."

"Thank you, Kris. I'm going to ask her if she's up for it," Delano says.

"She has no choice. Her name literally means wedding and happiness."

All three of us laugh.

Alex faces Delano with her mischievous look. "So, double date?"

"Double date!" he exclaims.

At least, this way, there will be love when we celebrate it that day.

Delano leaves, and I'm now alone with Alex, which means that interrogation time is about to start. I change my seat and sit next to her at the foot of my bed.

"At first, I was confused about how you went from hating him to loving him, but now, I'm just so happy for you that you've found someone," Alex tells me while holding my hand.

Wait. That's it? But I even took the time to plan out what I would tell her. I've put in the work, so I'm going to present my findings. "Yeah ... well, he went to church on a Friday to apologize, and then it just happened from there."

She pets my head. "Well, I'm glad."

I force my lips into a firm line. "Thank you, Alex."

I wish it didn't have to go like this. Me lying to her. Her being the best and being happy for me that, after all these years, I have somehow fallen in love. I want to tell her everything, come clean, let her talk me out of it. But I can't. Because I'm selfish.

Too selfish.

Since I have the address of the house, I've made an appointment with the realtor, and I'm going to view it today. Behind Augustine's back. Since he does things behind my back, it's only fair if I do the same. But the real reason I'm going to view it is that I need to know the cost of the house. And since Augustine doesn't talk in numbers but in don't-worry-about-its, I need the help of a realtor who won't spare my feelings and will tell me how much it is.

And if I find out it's out of my budget, I will demand that we find another place. I don't need much, just my own room.

It's not that far from my house. I just need to ride about five stops with the first subway, change subways, and ride a few stops with the second. It's about half an hour.

I searched for the address on the internet, but I couldn't find any pictures of the house. So, I have no idea what it looks like. But I'm hoping it's just an apartment in an apartment complex because that would be a little less expensive than an actual house.

As I leave the subway, I take out my phone and type the address in Google Maps. It says I have to walk for seven minutes.

I arrive and check three times whether I'm at the wrong address because it's not what I was hoping for at all. It's a house, all right—an actual house—a fucking contemporary house with a garage and everything.

I'm sorry, but who does he think will be living with us? Our ten children and grandchildren? Augustine and his choices are bad for my bank account. Very bad.

As I'm standing in front of the house with my mouth wide open, I hear someone call for me. "Hi, Ms. Armanious? I'm Jeremy, the realtor," he says while holding out his hand to me.

I shake his hand. "Hi there, Jeremy. Just call me Kristina."

I let go of his hand and turn to the house again, this time leaning back to take *all* of it in because it's not only big in width but also in length.

He looks at it as well. "Is it to your liking?"

"I mean, yes. It's very pretty, which means it has to be very expensive."

He laughs. "Naturally."

"So, enlighten me, Jeremy. How much are we talking about here?"

He hesitates. "One."

I blink a few times. "Hundred?"

"Million," he blurts out.

"What?!" I shout and immediately slap my hand against my mouth.

If it's one million, it means I'll have to pay half a million in about fifteen years' time, which means I'll have to pay around three thousand per month, which is one hundred twenty percent of my salary. So, I'll be living somewhere—which I can't even afford—but I'll die not long after because I won't be able to buy myself the necessities. And I didn't even take into consideration the interest rates.

I call for him. "Jeremy ..."

He doesn't make eye contact. "Yes?"

"Say ... can I pay my installments in installments?"

"I wish you could, but I'm afraid you can't."

I face the ground. Well, that settles it. I'm definitely not agreeing to this.

"Ha, Mr. Elias!" Jeremy says a little too happily, probably to get out of the awkward situation I've just created.

But wait, what? No. I look up and see Augustine approaching us.

"Mr. Elias? How are you even here right now?" I snarl.

"Surely, you understand that if someone is interested, the owner gets a call."

My eyes widen. "Owner?!"

"It's already mine," he says. "And this is yours." He hands me a set of keys with a diamond strawberry keychain attached to them.

I look at it. My set of keys. My *own* set of keys. I've never had them. Ever since

I was young, I wondered why I didn't have the keys to our house. My mom would tell me it wasn't necessary for me to have them because she would always be home to open the door for me. She also said I could lose them and that it'd be better for me not to have them to prevent that from happening. And I believed her. I always believed her.

So, when I got out of school early, rang the doorbell, and knocked several times, and she wasn't home to open the door for me, I would have to wait. In the winter, I would walk around in circles in the cold. I often walked around without cash on me, and that was the only way for me to have money since I didn't have a debit card either—I could lose that, too, of course. And if I ever needed something, I would just have to ask her to buy it for me. So, I couldn't go into a coffee shop to drink hot chocolate and warm myself up. Not that I wanted to drink. I just knew that ordering something was the only way to sit somewhere inside. To feel warmth while I couldn't feel my limbs anymore.

I would sit on a bench outside, waiting for her while freezing to death.

And for what possible reason? That there was a possibility I could bring guys over if I were home alone because she heard stories about that happening? She didn't trust me, never giving me the opportunity to prove her otherwise. Because she never gives me opportunities to prove myself.

So, having these keys in my hand right now brings up a lot of sad memories. But it also symbolizes that Augustine is the key to everything. To opening the door I have been stuck behind all these years.

I let the keys jingle by letting them jump in the palm of my hand. "I already told you, I don't want to be some parasite living off you. If it's meant to be my house as well, I want to pay for half of it."

He chuckles softly. "By paying your installments in installments?"

Of course he heard that. This man has timing, after all.

I shoot him an icy stare. "Are you mocking me right now?"

He puts up his hands, defending himself. "No. I would never mock someone about things they have no control over," he says. "Besides, I have another task for you."

"Oh yeah? And what is that?" I ask with lowered eyebrows.

He points at the keychain, which is dangling from my hand. "You will be on strawberry duty."

"What? What does that even mean?"

"Anything that is strawberry," he says, making intense eye contact, "buy it."

What is up with this man? I'm not being taken seriously, and if there is one thing I hate, it's precisely that—not being taken seriously by someone. He does things behind my back, doesn't ask my permission, and does as he pleases. As if my opinions don't matter and I have to accept things as they come. It's exactly the thing I'm running from, not toward.

I huff. "You know what, Mr. Elias? I realize now that I don't know anything about you."

"There is no need to know anything about me. It's for the best—to ensure our distance."

Seriously, now, he wants to distance us from each other because it's convenient for him? Or maybe he's finally realized that he wasn't acting distant-like when we had dinner together. "Oh? You were doing a very poor job at it at the restaurant."

His jaw tightens. "I've realized, so I'm adjusting."

Well, at least he realized it eventually. Good for him. But not knowing anything about him scares me. Because now, I don't know what he might be capable of. I don't want to know anything about him, but at the same time, I need to know *everything* there is to know to put my mind at ease. Cognitive dissonance—it's uncomfortable.

Furrows start taking over my forehead. "How can I trust you?"

"You can trust me."

"That is exactly what someone I can't trust would say."

He turns his head about thirty degrees, points his chin at his collarbone, and squints his eyes. "You can't trust me."

The furrows on my forehead become even deeper. "That's not what someone I can trust would say."

He scratches his temple and then holds out that hand to me. "Is there even a right answer here?"

Jeremy clears his throat, which makes us both turn to him. I forgot he was still here. "I'm sorry. Just to be clear, Kristina, you aren't actually interested in the house? And, Mr. Elias, you only agreed that someone could view the house because you knew it would be her?"

"No ..." I say hesitantly.

"Yes," Augustine confesses plainly.

"Yeah ... okay, I'm going to leave you both, so please, continue your lovers' quarrel," Jeremy says.

"We're not lovers!" I yell.

"We really aren't," Augustine adds.

"But you guys are going to live together?" Jeremy asks and then murmurs, "Yeah, good luck with that."

What is that supposed to mean?

"There's no need for that, Jeremy, because I'm leaving. Thanks for everything, and sorry for lying to you."

I don't say anything to Augustine. I don't even look at him before walking away from them.

As I enter my room, I notice a new item added to my collection that I like to call Things I've Unfortunately Received from Augustine. It's an envelope.

I open it and see a card with text on the front that says: *Dear Miss Armanious, your rule has an exception. No matter who asked whom, no woman should pay on the first date. Ever.*

I open the card and see four hundred dollars in cash. How does he even know that it was exactly four hundred? Don't tell me he went back to the restaurant to make sure how much I had paid? That would be ridiculous. He is ridiculous.

Augustine must have given it to Delano, and he probably thought it was a sappy love letter, so he put it next to the rings.

I've never thought about it, but the letter makes me realize it. Delano must also be why Augustine knew about me when I made an appointment to meet him in his office. Since Augustine already knew the surname Armanious, he probably asked Delano if he had a sister or something, and then Augustine somehow asked him if he knew any of his clients, and Delano obviously knows João. It has to be. That's why he already had João's file out. Augustine knew I was coming regarding João, he knew I was Egyptian, and he knew I was lying about João not knowing any Egyptian men.

So, that's what he meant when he said, "Your surname somewhat betrayed you."

I'm so stupid. How could I have forgotten there might be a chance he knew Delano when I tried to use the possibility of him knowing Alex to my advantage?

And how embarrassing.

I read the text on the card one more time.

With all the offense the world has to offer, I did not consider that a date.

But I have to admit, this would have been cute if it hadn't been from him.

CHAPTER NINE

Adam: Eve, I have been wondering about something for quite some time now, and I want to know your take on it. What do you consider to be home?

Eve: Adam. Home can be a place, person, feeling, or any object really. Home can be anything as long as it feels like one.

Adam: What makes a home feel like one?

Eve: Home has to be a safe haven. It has to bring you peace and comfort, the thing you turn to when life gives you the opposite.

Adam: And how can we let something become a safe haven?

Eve: By letting it be something according to your standards.

The last couple of weeks have been a dream come true. I've been meeting with Augustine regularly. Well, not actually, since that would have been a nightmare. But everyone *thinks* I have been meeting with him on a regular basis. I pretend to be with him all the time when, in reality, he is living his life, and I am living mine. To the fullest. And if this is life while being only engaged, imagine living with him. It will cause my leash to be severed *completely*.

I find myself in the library, devouring books. I'm also doing research on psychology-related subjects, which I'll be sure to use. And I have been very busy finishing up my application for the position of a crisis counselor. I've freaking loved every second of the last couple of weeks.

But I, unfortunately, have decided to turn it into a nightmare after all because, today, we will meet. More specifically, I will be meeting with him; he won't be meeting with me.

The truth is that I don't trust Augustine.

All I know about him is that his name is Augustine Elias and that he's old. I know he's an accountant, but I'm fairly certain that's not the only thing he is. He likes strawberries, which is hard to miss since he likes to remind me of it. He owns an expensive car, and he already owns an expensive house. How does one already have that at thirty-three?

Not only that, but he's also vague about everything. He wants to get married and seems to have no trouble purchasing an expensive ring and financing a wedding when it's all fake.

The last couple of weeks, we have been planning the wedding through text. I told him I really don't care about it and to keep it small. From that moment on, he would send me two options, and all I had to do was text him back with 1 or 2. Me being me, I would try to pick the less expensive option, but him being, well, him, he kept sending me the two most expensive options as the only options. But I admit, he does have taste. Sometimes, I'd have to think hard about which number to send him back.

When I went dress shopping with our mothers, Marina, and Alex, he gave his mother money to pay for the dress. She even encouraged me to choose the most beautiful and expensive one—which was a big, puffy princess gown. Eventually, I picked a trumpet dress because it's minimalistic—exactly my style—and less expensive. And also to show off the curves I don't have. And, of course, I don't want it to be a fairy-tale wedding, more like a tale I want to end.

And the most important thing I know is that Augustine Elias is a liar. He lied about not stalking me that Friday, and I'm sure he has lied about much more.

If all of that doesn't scream that he's a sick pervert who works in the underworld and is a rich Mafia boss who will kidnap me and sell me on the black market, I don't know what would.

It might be cute in books, but not in real life. Definitely not in real life.

I asked Marina what he usually does on Thursdays, and she told me he's supposed to be free but that he still goes to his office to grab files and run errands after. She probably thought I wanted to surprise him—I am, in a way.

And that's where I'll start my day, somewhere behind a bush near his office, in hiding. Hence me meeting with him, him not meeting with me.

So, I'm going to stalk the man after all. Sue me. But I don't trust him. I have this uncomfortable feeling I can't seem to shake, so I'm going to try to find out if the feeling is justified. I simply don't have time to get re-kidnapped; I was already kidnapped by my mother the minute the egg that was me was fertilized.

I have a life to live.

To be a detective, not only do you have to play the part, but you also have to wear the part. So, here I am, wearing black leather knee-high boots and black leather pants, making it look like they're attached to each other. I topped the outfit off with a black top and my nude trench coat. I'm also wearing black leather gloves and a black leather beret. In one hand, I'm carrying opera binoculars, and in the other, I'm holding a newspaper I just bought.

Now, I won't deny that I considered buying a pipe—not to smoke from, just to put in my mouth—but my frontal lobe decided against it since it would have been a *tad* extreme. Because what I'm wearing now is not extreme—no, not at all.

The outfit is supposed to be hiding my identity, yet at the same time, it screams that it is, in fact, me. Is it the trench coat? Probably. But would I ever leave the house without it? Never.

I have taken my position around the corner of the coffee shop next to his office. I check my pocket watch. As I've already stated, looking the part is vital to play it, so investing in a pocket watch was necessary. My frontal lobe somehow did not decide against that.

It's now two p.m., and there has been no sign of him yet—over. Over to God? Not that he would approve of what I'm doing, but I don't see him exactly jumping at the opportunity to stop me right now, so I doubt he disapproves of it *that* much.

About ten minutes have passed, and there he is, coming out of the building. I slowly walk behind him, but not long after, I realize he's walking toward his car, which causes me to panic because I'll be damned if I lose my suspect just because I forgot about transportation to follow the man.

I hold out my hand, stop a cab, and enter the back seat of the car.

"Good afternoon, miss. Where to?" the cab driver asks while pressing some buttons.

I point at Augustine's car, which is about to leave. "Good afternoon, sir. To wherever that car is headed."

He then turns to look at me, noticing what I'm wearing and holding. "Miss, are you stalking someone?"

I try to hide the binoculars behind the newspaper. "No ... that would mean that the someone in question would dislike being followed, and we don't know if that's the case."

"With you wearing that, I doubt anyone would want to be followed by you."

I gasp. "I'm sorry? But if I didn't know any better, I would say you think I'm a nutjob?"

He places his hands on the steering wheel and looks at me through the rearview mirror. "I'm just saying that actions speak louder than words."

I nod at him in defeat. "Touché, cab driver. Touché."

The cab driver follows Augustine, and after about five minutes, Augustine parks his car. The cab driver parks behind him. I wait inside the car until I see him enter the gym.

"Thank you, cab driver." I hand him twenty bucks. "Keep the rest."

"Yeah, happy stalking, miss."

"Yeah ... happy driving, sir."

We've all got a job to do. It's good to wish each other well at doing that job.

I get out of the car, look around, and see a bench across from the gym. It's perfect because there's a whole road separating me from him, which will ensure our distance—the distance we want, both physically and emotionally. And I came prepared. I can use the binoculars to have a better look at him. Not that I want to have a better look at him, but I can't stalk someone if I can't see them.

I cross the road and take a seat on the bench. Suddenly, Augustine leaves the gym. He was already wearing a white hoodie and gray sweatpants when he went in—so he does own sweats, after all—but he was also holding a black duffel bag, and now, he isn't.

Through the binoculars, I let my eyes follow him. He walks a little until he halts and crouches down. He's talking to someone. I see him hand the person something, and after a while, he stands up and enters the gym again.

Once he's inside, I cross the road and walk to where he was standing seconds ago. As I arrive, I see a woman sitting on the ground.

I hunker down next to her. "Excuse me, ma'am. May I ask what that man said to you just now?"

"Hello, darling. He just gave me money." She holds out three hundred dollars. "And his card, telling me I should contact him if I ever need something." She holds out the card to me as well. On it, it says his name, phone number, email address, and the address of his office.

"That man is too good to be true. It's suspicious," I say while looking toward the gym.

She smiles at me. "He was a very sweet man too. I told him it was too much, but he insisted."

I give her a soft smile. I look at the gym again. He'll probably be there for another twenty minutes, right? Which gives me time to run some errands.

I stand up again and say, "If you'll excuse me for a moment, I'll be back."

She nods at me, and I go to the nearest drugstore.

I grab a shopping basket and gather feminine hygiene products, such as tampons and pads. Then, I walk to the medicine aisle to grab painkillers, multivitamin pills, and bandages. I also put in toothpaste, a toothbrush, a few packages of wet wipes, tissues, and a nail clipper. Afterward, I collect a scarf, socks, gloves, and a blanket and put food and bottles of water in the shopping basket. Lastly, I grab a big box to put everything inside of it.

I walk toward the cashier. "Hi there. I would like to buy all of this, please."

The cashier starts to scan everything. As she's scanning, I grab what she has scanned and put it inside the box.

"That will be one hundred seventy-six dollars and forty cents, please," she says.

I hand her two one-hundred-dollar bills—ones Augustine put in the envelope. I also used that money to pay for the cab ride.

I walk out of the store while holding the box in my arms.

I crouch down to the woman. "Here you go, ma'am. Also, if you ever do need something, please don't hesitate to contact that man."

She puts her hand on her mouth. "Oh, darling! This is too much. I can't take this!"

"No, please do. It's the least I could do." Then, I tell her firmly, "We women need to look out for each other."

"Thank you so much, darling. This means the world to me!" she says as she places her hand on her chest.

"No worries, ma'am. You're too sweet!"

I keep chatting with her for a while and then return to my original post—the bench across from the gym.

About half an hour passes. I'm bored out of my mind and hungry into my stomach.

What is this man doing anyway? Training for the Olympics?

I groan as hard as I can and sit with my legs spread while looking at the sky. Being a detective is harder than I thought.

I try texting Adam.

Eve: Adam. I am in need of guidance. How does one cure boredom?

I wait a while, but he doesn't respond. Adam's probably not bored at all. I would even say he's busy doing something right now.

My stomach rumbles, and I decide to act on it by ordering sushi, a large Coke, and sweet popcorn. The combination might not make sense, but I crave it, so I might as well just listen to it. Besides, why else would they serve all of it at the same place?

Not long after, a woman holding her bike and wearing a delivery uniform approaches me. "Order for Kristina?" she huffs.

I squeal, "Yes! Thank you."

She holds up her hand to me, indicating that she has to get something off her chest. "Miss, if you're going to order something, could you please do so while you're at an actual place?"

I look around while sitting on the bench. "But I tried to describe where I am as thoroughly as possible. Did you have trouble finding it?"

"Miss, you described it as the bench across the gym with three bushes behind it, a lantern pole on the left, and a trash can on the right."

"Yes ..."

"You do realize that the gym has four sides, each one having benches, bushes, lantern poles, and trash cans?"

I was so focused on describing my own surroundings that I forgot about the possibility of all the sides being the same. And I was too hungry to even think about it, let alone check. I'm an asshole, I have to admit. I feel my cheeks heating.

"I'm so sorry. I did not think about that at all," I say, embarrassed. Very embarrassed.

"It's fine. I found you anyway." She hands me the food and the large Coke.

"How much is it again?" I ask.

"Forty dollars and twenty cents."

I hand her a fifty-dollar bill. "Here. You can keep the rest. Sorry for causing you trouble."

"Thanks. Have a nice day."

"You too!"

I use the binoculars to try to find Augustine, but the building is not entirely made of glass. I'm looking through them for a while, all the while satiating my hunger and thirst until my vision becomes pitch-black.

Someone is blocking my view. I remove the binoculars and see an officer standing in front of me with his hands resting on his hips.

"Ma'am, may I ask what you're doing right now?"

I can't tell an officer I'm stalking someone since it is a criminal offense. Nevertheless, I have to tell him the truth since I don't want to get in trouble for obstructing official business either. However, I can't use those exact words since anything I say can and will be used against me. It seems I'm facing a dilemma—fortunately, not the prisoner's dilemma.

But the frontal lobe that has been helping me a lot today—some would argue it's been doing the complete opposite of helping—especially my prefrontal cortex, plans the perfect comeback. I will frame them—both the officer and Augustine. Frame the officer by telling the truth while choosing my words *very* carefully. Frame Augustine by making him seem guilty when he probably really isn't.

I remind myself of the theater side I've somehow acquired since meeting Augustine and answer the officer while rubbing my eyes. "Officer, I'm finding out whether my fiancé is cheating on me!"

He gasps. "Oh no, that's terrible! Please, let me help you!" He sits next to me on the bench.

A sense of justice needing to be served, even if it isn't a criminal offense. That's very officer-like.

"Where is he now?" the officer asks.

"In the gym. He has been for more than an hour now." I hold out the plastic box with the last sushi piece to him. "Do you like sushi?"

"Are you kidding? I love sushi!" he says as he takes the last piece.

I realize he must be hungry, and I'm not full either, so I order another box of sushi.

As I stare through the binoculars again, I finally see Augustine leaving the gym. But he's not alone, and when the person he's with finally turns his face in my direction, I realize all too well who it is.

"Officer."

"Yes?"

"It seems he's cheating on me with my brother."

"No way?! Let me see!" He grabs the binoculars from me and puts them up to his eyes. "Which one is your fiancé, and which one is your brother?"

"The one with wavy black hair and a white hoodie is supposed to be my fiancé, and the one with curly brown hair is my brother."

"Oh ... but your brother does look handsome ..."

I point at myself. "Handsomer than me?"

The officer lowers the binoculars and checks me out. "No, definitely not."

I see the delivery woman from not too long ago approaching us. "Another order for bench girl."

"More sushi!" the officer exclaims.

"I bought more for us both. Have at it, please," I tell him.

The delivery woman gives him the box, and he starts eating from it.

I salute her. "Thank you for your service. You're a true veteran for finding me."

I hand her forty dollars, which leaves her another ten dollars as a tip. I owe her that much because I know I've been annoying her today.

"Miss, I have to ask, what are you even doing here?" she asks.

The officer speaks with a full mouth. "Her fiancé is cheating on her with her brother!"

Her nose wrinkles. "That's awful! You don't deserve that at all."

"Right? Behind my back at that," I say while nodding. Augustine keeps doing things behind my back.

"Yeah, well, cheating always happens behind people's backs," the officer says.

"I mean, it's supposed to happen behind one's back, but now, it's in front of my very binoculars at that ..." Wait, what? I mean, it's not supposed to happen at all.

He nods at me. "Yeah, that's awful."

"Would you like some sushi too? Have a break. You've been delivering enough," I say while holding up the box to the delivery woman.

She checks her watch. "You're right. I need a break, and I have time to have one."

She puts her bike to lean on the lantern pole and sits next to me, making me sit between them. I put sushi in the empty box from the first order and give it to her. I also grab the popcorn and put it on my lap, eating from it.

I gaze through the binoculars some more and see Augustine and Delano seated on a terrace close to the gym, having drinks. Then, I see Delano pulling out a notebook from his bag—*my* notebook.

"I can't believe this. My brother is giving him my notebook. It might be empty since I haven't written anything in it, but it's still mine. Why is he giving it to him?" I glower.

The delivery woman gestures for me to hand her the binoculars, and she looks through them. "Maybe he's trying to persuade him not to go through with it by showing something of yours."

The officer now gestures for her to give him the binoculars, and he looks through them as well. "Or maybe they took it to burn it with the memory of you along with it."

The delivery woman leans forward, and we both frown at the officer.

"Man, your job makes you say dark things," she says.

He shrugs. "It happens." He looks through the binoculars again. "Oh, miss! Duck! They're facing this way!"

I quickly grab the newspaper from under the popcorn box and hold it up to shield myself.

The delivery woman laughs and grabs some popcorn from the box. "You sure came prepared."

I turn to her. "I would be lying if I said I didn't plan this whole day out in a notebook, one that *wasn't* stolen."

"We're in the clear!" the officer announces.

"Say, Officer? Don't you have a bug thingy tool on you?" I ask him.

He shakes his head. "No, unfortunately, I don't."

All three of us keep eating the sushi and popcorn while passing the binoculars to look at Delano and Augustine.

Until we're interrupted. "Krissie?"

I direct my face to where the voice came from. "João! It has been ages. How've you been?"

"Good, *miga*. But what are you doing with two people who are clearly on the clock?" he questions.

The delivery woman looks at João. "Her fiancé is cheating on her."

"With her brother!" the officer adds.

"Fiancé?!" João grabs the binoculars from my hand and gasps. "Augustine, my accountant?! I thought you hated him."

The officer and the delivery woman turn their heads to me, raising their eyebrows at me. I avoid them and suck in my cheeks. This just got messy.

Believe me, I still do. João knows about the first encounter I had with Augustine since he's the reason I met him in the first place. He also knows about the second one because I texted him to guess who I had the displeasure of meeting again, which was Augustine, obviously. So, he doesn't know about anything after that, which means I can sell him the story I sold Alex. Well, not necessarily since, suddenly, she wasn't interested in buying it anymore.

"João, it was love at *third* sight. I just had to take a better look," I say, pointing at the binoculars in his hand.

Believe it or not, I hate lying. But sometimes, it feels like the world isn't leaving me a choice. It doesn't excuse my actions; I know that. Far too well. But at this point in my life, I've been caught up in the biggest lie, and I'm so stuck in it that I don't even know where to start untangling myself from it.

"Well, you know what they say. Third time's a charm," the officer says.

"Exactly!" I cheer.

João sits next to the officer on the bench. "Wow, I can't believe it. That makes me a matchmaker."

More like makes it possible for me to move out since no one is as crazy as Augustine to want to get married to someone they don't love. But also an *actual* matchmaker since all Augustine and I do is get into fights.

Thanks, João. I do owe you one.

"Thanks, João. I owe you one," I say, smiling.

The delivery woman interrupts us. "I wouldn't exactly thank him just yet. He picked someone who's cheating on you with your brother."

"Even if I have reasons to dislike Augustine, I know he's a fair man. So, knowing him, he's not cheating on her with her brother. Don't worry," João assures her.

The officer points at João. "You'd better be right; otherwise, you'll be arrested for being a bad friend."

All four of us laugh at that.

We sit there, talking and eating what is left of the deliveries I ordered, and eventually, we leave when Augustine and Delano do.

Today feels like a lucid dream. It's been like an adventure, and I haven't gotten to experience this much fun in *years*. Meeting new people, laughing with them, getting to know them. But also being able to help someone in need. That might have been the highlight of my day. Maybe true altruism does exist after all?

I've practically spent the four hundred dollars that was in the envelope Augustine gave me. I guess I could thank him for financing this day.

The verdict of today? Not guilty. Augustine has committed no crimes and can be trusted enough for me to live with him. And with that being confirmed, I start packing my entire room and preparing for the wedding and the move, which is in exactly sixteen days. T-minus sixteen until D-Day.

And then I will be free.

Having a nemesis with benefits *is* life-changing *change*.

CHAPTER TEN

Eve: Adam. New beginnings are a part of life from the very moment we are born. Even so, I wonder whether new beginnings are to be feared or welcomed with open arms.

Adam: Eve, you should know by now that the world we live in is too complex to be perceived in just the shades black and white—the absence of visible light or the presence of all visible light. We have colors. And in turn, those can differ in hue, saturation, and brightness. It's a spectrum containing both beautiful colors as well as less beautiful ones.

Eve: What does it mean?

Adam: It means that life can be beautiful, but it will always contain not-so-bright sides. In turn, life can be awful. Even so, it will have some bright sides to it as well. They overlap each other, just like a spectrum of colors. And yet, the same spectrum granted to us all can be experienced differently. How do you experience it, Eve?

Eve: Exactly as you described it. It feels like I'm experiencing the whole spectrum at once.

Today is D-Day, T-minus zero. The day I've been waiting for whole-souled, and the day I've been dreading wholeheartedly.

Just like the poet Edwin Brock wrote in his poem "D-Day Minus," which he addressed to his unborn son, who would still be alive for two more months until he would be born and begin to die. While for me, it's the complete opposite. The day I was born, it felt as if I was already dead. Until now. Now, it feels as though my nine months of life will start on D-Day and continue for as long as my heart pumps blood filled with oxygen through my veins.

He starts the poem by saying that his son won't see the world at first, that he will touch flesh, and that he will cry. Years later, he will cry because he has seen too much and touched too little.

As I see it, babies cry at birth to let oxygen fill their lungs for the first time. As we grow older, we cry again, wondering whether things would be easier if we no longer had oxygen filling our lungs.

I have seen a lot of things, things I wish I hadn't had to see, touched things I didn't always want to touch, and have been touched when I'd have rather not been touched. Now, I am content because I will see things I want to see, touch what I want to touch, and be touched by who I want to be touched by. Everything on my terms.

He then tells his son that he will be hungry for love and that love will feed him. But that it will also be the condition he will come to fear.

And with this, I can do nothing but agree. I was *starved* for love, and it has fed me for a while. Until it poisoned me. Because it was rotten. And, yes, love is something you will come to fear because no one eats rotten goods twice.

While he also tells his son to have children, to let them live for nine months, I can do nothing but disagree. Because I don't want to be responsible for putting a human being on this earth without having asked for it, creating a victim, only to be resented for the rest of my life.

He ends the poem by urging his son to die in good company since dying is a lonely occupation. And I will, since my own company is good enough, and I won't be lonely since I know we all die. That thought is all the company I need from others.

Every poem offers a deeper underlying message. I should know since I like to analyze poems in my free time.

This poem tells us that everything we once came to love and were comforted by, we will come to hate and be afraid of. Whether that be a place, a person, a feeling, or an object.

So, here I am—as a result of hating something I used to love, I assume—sitting with my back to a mirror while a makeup artist and a hairstylist are working their magic on me. Making me ready for D-Day. My wedding day.

As I sit on a chair in my living room, Alex, Marina, and our mothers are all dolled up on the couch. They're all wearing dark green. Our mothers are wearing similar dresses, both modest and reaching the ground. Marina's long dress has a split on her right leg. Alex—her dress isn't a dress. Alex is wearing a suit.

Since they're bridesmaids and Alex doesn't like wearing dresses, I picked out a suit and dress made from the same fabric and color. They both loved it, so we went with it. This way, Marina and Alex are still matching. And I like this even more than having them both wear dresses just because that happens to be the standard. Besides, Alex looks so damn good in that suit.

Now, I won't deny that I would love to see Delano in a dark green dress, but I doubt he would ever give me that pleasure. He's probably wearing a black suit since he's one of Augustine's groomsmen, along with George and Tony. All four of them are getting ready at Augustine's house.

"Done!" the makeup artist and hairstylist cheer.

They turn my chair around for me to face the mirror.

Alex shoots up from the couch and gasps. "Man, if I knew you were this beautiful, I would've married you myself!"

Marina laughs at Alex. "You look amazing, Kristina."

"*Ya amar!*" Marina's mother says.

My mother walks toward me, stands behind me, and puts her hand on my shoulder. "You are truly a woman now, *habibti*."

I give them all a soft smile and hold my mother's hand that's resting on my shoulder while looking at her through the mirror. Then I lower my gaze to look at myself.

I take a moment to take it all in. I have never seen myself like this. Sure, I've put on some makeup in the past and straightened my hair before, but right now, I don't even recognize myself.

It's a full face of makeup, but not in the sense that it has transformed my face into another; it just accentuates the features I already have. The contour and highlighter enhance my face shape, making my cheekbones and jawline appear more chiseled. My eyes have a smoky look while the inner lids are covered in a shimmery gold. The outer lids are almost black, topped off with a simple eyeliner wing. The creases of my eyes are black, and above them appears to be a lighter shade of brown. At the outer ends of my lashes are a few applied false lashes, making my eyes appear more oval-shaped. And the look is finished off with natural-looking nude lips.

My hair is up in a very big, fluffy bun, some strands falling out of it. All of it looks so elegant. So unlike me.

"Now, hurry up. Wear your dress, so I can put on your veil!" the hairstylist commands as she claps her hands twice.

I get up from the chair and go to my room, where I hung up the dress on the hanger on my door. I zip open the garment bag and put it on. It's a trumpet dress made of tulle, which hugs my whole body tightly, with a long tail flowing behind my heels. The dress is long-sleeved with a lot of details on them, and the back is V-shaped. I put on my white pumps and grab the veil that is so long that it makes me drag a second tail.

I take the engagement ring from my desk and put it on. These past couple of weeks, I would put the ring on before leaving the house. After hearing the front door close behind me, I would put it back in the box and in my coat. Before I entered my home again, I would put the ring on, and when my mother saw me arrive with it, I would take it off again since it's only natural not to wear a ring at home. So, I've never really worn the ring. Since I've been doing this for a while now, I've gotten used to it, and I've never forgotten when I have to put the ring on and when I can take it off again.

I take a last look at my room, which is almost empty, except for the furniture. All my boxes have already been taken to the new place I'll be living from today. I haven't been inside it yet, so I'm very curious.

I enter the living room and hand the veil to the hairstylist.

She puts it on me and holds up the mirror. "Well?"

"I love it. Thank you so much." I shift to the makeup artist. "And thank you. You both are so talented at what you do."

The makeup artist smiles at me. "No thanks needed. We love doing this; that's why it's our job."

Alex grabs her phone, texts someone, and then she turns to me. "We've got to bounce. Augustine and the others have already arrived at the church, and Delano is almost here to pick us up."

I thank them again, and they leave. Soon after, we leave as well and get into Delano's car. Since we're with six people and the car only offers five seats, I suggest that Alex can sit on my lap, but then I get yelled at by five people that I'm wearing a wedding dress. So, now, she's sitting on Marina's lap instead. Honestly, I don't get what the fuss was about; it's just a dress.

I'm looking out the window, and each passing mile causes me to be more anxious than the one before. I know I want this, but at the same, I don't want this at all. I look at my mother through the rearview mirror.

I know what I'm doing is wrong and that marriage is sacred. Seeing her being so happy right now makes me feel guilty. So much so that I'm about to stop this whole charade.

But I can't, and I won't. Because another thought just popped up, the one reminding me that what I'm doing now is very common within our culture. People getting married without even having had a proper conversation with each other because it was arranged by their parents. Is what I'm doing any different? It isn't, in fact; it's the same. Only this time, it has been arranged by the children.

We arrive at the church, and all of them, except Delano and me, get out of the car to go inside. Delano and I wait until everyone is ready, so I can also begin to make my way inside.

"You ready, corpse bride, who's very much alive?" he asks.

I can't believe he remembered. "You always have been funny in your own way."

His hand holds mine. "I wish I weren't the one to walk you down the aisle. It's an honor, but still. I wish Dad were here instead. I wish he were here, holding your hand right now, telling you how dull home will be without you and that you're a ray of sunshine, lighting up our lives."

My eyes well up with tears. "He is here, Lano." I put my other hand on my collarbone, where his name is written with permanent ink. "He always has been, and he always will be."

"I know," he says with wet eyes.

I'm glad that Delano looks so much like my father because, this way, it feels as if *Baba* were with me in the flesh after all. To walk me down the aisle.

Delano's phone chimes and he faces me. "It's time."

I exhale. "Okay."

Delano helps me get out of the car, and we enter the building. We are now standing with our arms linked together in front of the big door that leads to the church. Deacons are standing in front of us since they will be the first to enter. Once this door opens, there is no turning back. I will be walking down the aisle and standing next to Augustine, who's already there, waiting for me. That realization makes a knot grow in my stomach.

Suddenly, the door opens, causing me to flinch. Everyone stands up and turns around to face Delano and me.

O-okay. I wouldn't say I have stage fright per se, but I wouldn't exactly say I don't have it all. Because I'm about to do another play, and this time, it's getting married. But this stage is way bigger than the one I have behind the coffee table at home, and this audience is way, *way* bigger than the one I normally have seated on the couch. Can one consider this to be their debut as an actor?

As we walk down the aisle, as one who's about to get married does, I take in my audience. I see some familiar faces, like Mariam and Sarah—the girls from the time I embarrassed myself. I turn to the men's side and see João. It's the first time I've ever seen him in a suit. It makes me smile.

I look in front of me and see Alex being a bridesmaid, which causes my heart to flutter. And when I turn to the women's side again, I see Senait and Farah next to each other, which causes my heart to flutter even more. I'm so glad they came.

As I shift my gaze to the front again, I notice Tony and George, and then I finally direct my gaze to the man of the hour. And I, the woman of the hour, am walking toward him, enclosing the distance between us.

He's holding a bouquet of red roses, and he is wearing a beige three-piece suit with a white shirt, buttoned all the way up—there goes his signature style—and a black tie and pocket square. He's also wearing black loafers, but not the ones he usually wears. The ones he's wearing now are suede. But the thing that's completely new is that all his hair is slicked back. Not one strand is covering his forehead today.

While I let my eyes lock with his, Augustine is already staring at me. And as I pay more attention to it, it only gets more intense with each passing step. As if he wants to pierce this image into his hippocampus—that's how he's looking at me right now.

We arrive at the altar. Delano unlinks our arms and kisses my cheek. He then brings my arm to Augustine's. We link our arms together. With his free hand, he hands me the bouquet, and I receive it with mine. We stand in front of the priest while facing the men's side of the church, and everyone takes their seats again. And we unlink our arms from each other.

The priest starts the ceremony by praying, singing hymns, and reading from the Bible.

After a short while, we get dressed with the first pieces of royal adornments—golden capes with golden-red Coptic crosses embroidered on them. The cape being put on me is very short, reaching my ribs. The cape being put on Augustine is long, like an actual cape. This symbolizes that we will become the rulers of our new household.

Next, it's time to exchange the rings. The priest hands Augustine the wedding ring; it's white gold with small diamonds on the band. Augustine puts the wedding ring on my left ring finger. Then, he takes the engagement ring from my right ring finger and puts it on my left as well.

I take Augustine's wedding ring and replace it from his right ring finger to his left. God, his hand is big.

After that, the priest anoints us with holy oil on our foreheads. Which symbolizes that we are protected.

Then, it's time for the blessing of the crowns. The priest first puts a crown on Augustine's head, then on mine, while praying. And I know all too well what these crowns symbolize. The crowns symbolize the honor God grants the bride and groom during one of the Seven Sacraments the church has. They also symbolize that the groom and bride give their lives to each other and become one with each other through God.

Forgive me, God ... please.

I try to suppress my tears with all my might, but one gets out and rolls over my cheek. Augustine notices and places his hand on mine, his four fingers holding the back side of my hand, and his thumb caresses my palm. And for the first time, I let him.

The ceremony ends in *Zaghareet*—women celebrating the union with high-pitched sounds.

Augustine and I stand at the door to greet everyone with hugs and kisses.

A woman appears, and with her hands, she grabs Augustine's upper arm and brings it to her chest. "Oh, Augustinus, you looked so elegant up there." She turns to me. "Hiya, I'm Sofia. I'm his best friend. *Mabrook*! You're a little too lucky with him," she says and laughs.

I raise my eyebrows at her. "Uh, thanks? I guess?" *What does one even say to that?*

I'm sorry. I genuinely could not care less, but what if I did though? It's about principles. This is just plain rude. I mean, she can even have him tonight and let him make love to her, but still.

He sees me looking at her and releases himself from her. "Thank you for being here, Sofia."

She leaves, and then he opens his mouth to say the first thing he has said to me in weeks since the last time I saw him, which was with Jeremy. "She really isn't, I can assure you. Our mothers happen to know each other."

I scoff and laugh at the same time. "Oh, no. This is not something we're going to make a thing of. I really couldn't care less."

Then, our mothers approach us.

"It's time for the photo shoot," his mother says.

Oh. No. A photo shoot means photos and photos, meaning us embracing each other. PDA. Would asking for a rain check somehow be acceptable?

We arrive at a garden near the church, and I can already see the photographer standing with his equipment. Thank God it's only our mothers. I would have died of embarrassment if Alex, Delano, and Marina were here right now. But they're with everyone else, heading to the reception.

We take our positions in front of tall bushes full of all kinds of flowers. We stand next to each other, like two awkward toddlers who just got introduced by their parents. Our mothers are standing behind the photographer, facing us as well.

"Augustinus, put your arm around her," my mother tells him.

He obeys and puts his arm around me, letting the palm of his hand rest on my shoulder.

His mother shakes her head. "Around her waist, *ya* Augustinus."

He obeys her as well by slowly letting the palm of his hand slide from my shoulder to my elbow. Then, he slides his hand between my elbow and ribs, letting his hand rest on my ribs for a second before sliding down to my waist, holding it. It makes me tense up, and I'm sure he can feel it by the sudden movement I make.

Then, my mother has more requests. "Augustinus, kiss her hand for the picture."

He grabs my hand, the one on the side he is holding my waist from, and we turn with our sides to the photographer and our mothers. He lets the tips of my fingers rest on his index and middle finger and presses my fingertips with his thumb. He then brings our hands to his lips, gently kissing my middle knuckles.

And then, of course, his mother has more requests as well. "Now, embrace each other for the last picture."

His touching my waist already caused me to shiver, and his kissing my fingers made me want to jump out of my skin. But embracing each other is overstepping boundaries. Boundaries that are bound by a contract.

But Augustine somehow ignores that because before I can process what is happening, he's already standing behind me with both his hands on my stomach and his chin against my temple. But he isn't pressing me into him. I turn my head to where his chin is touching me, and out of reflex, I rest my hands on his.

I let out a small, frustrated groan.

He leans in and turns to let our eyes meet. "Just bear it. I'm not having the time of my life either."

"Don't tell me what to do," I hiss.

He's not wrong though. It's hard for us to keep our distance from each other when our mothers are so involved.

Eventually, the photo shoot comes to an end, and we make our way to the reception. It's a short car ride. Augustine is driving, and I'm sitting next to him.

We enter the hall, and everyone is already there. We greet them again, and then it is time to celebrate. If there's one thing Egyptians are good at, it's celebrating weddings.

I eye Delano, Farah, Alex, and Senait sitting at a table, so I make my way to them.

Both Senait and Farah look absolutely perfect. Senait is wearing a white *habesha kemis* dress filled with blue embroidery, and Farah is wearing a traditional red kaftan dress filled with gold details.

They stand up from the table, and I hug them together. "You both look absolutely beautiful. I'm so glad you could make it!"

"Thank you so much and for inviting me!" Senait says.

"Yes, *shokran*. I'm so happy to be here!" Farah says.

Alex and Delano give each other *the* look, the one you give your best friend when you have an inside joke. If anything, they're the ones who are the happiest that they're here.

Marina calls for me. "Kristina, your table with Augustine is ready now. You can sit there."

I want to sit at the table with Alex and the others, but I can't abandon my husband just yet. I have to hold on a little longer. If I accept everything today, it will be over before I know it.

I sit at the table next to Augustine, facing everyone in the hall.

Many Egyptian foods are served, but my favorite among them is macarona bechamel, which is basically lasagna, but the Egyptian version.

We dine, and then it's time for the actual celebration, where everyone leaves their tables and goes to the front of the hall to dance.

But before everyone gets to dance, Augustine and I have the *dis*honor of going first to slow dance.

We walk to the front, and "Allah Yebarekly Feek" by Tamer Hosny starts playing, which means *God bless you*. And if there's one song to let you know you're attending an Egyptian wedding, it's that one.

He grabs my hand, twirls me around to face him, and swiftly pulls me into him, letting his hands rest on my lower back. I wrap my arms around his neck, making my hands dangle behind him. The perfect way to strangle him.

In this position, we find ourselves only inches away from each other, allowing our personal spaces to intertwine, only leaving room for the oxygen our bodies need to fuel it. My temple caresses his jaw as we slowly move, swaying left and right.

I can feel his jaw move against my skin. "Are you enjoying yourself?"

"You are, by some miracle, not the worst dance partner."

"So are you. Consider me impressed."

People start to dance as well, and Tony approaches us. "*Mabrook*, you two, but, Kristina, I have to ask, why did you say you didn't know Augustine when we first met?"

I stammer, "I ... I, uh, I—"

Augustine cuts in on my stammering "I" speech. "That was just a lovers' quarrel."

Oh, I see. He's using what Jeremy called our bickering. Very clever.

"Oh, that's why you said it seems like you don't know her. Well, that's cute, I guess," Tony says.

He leaves, and I catch my breath. I almost dug my own grave there, and I'm far from ready to lie in it yet.

Then João approaches us. He puts his arm around my shoulders while Augustine and I are still holding each other. "Congrats, Krissie. You look stunning," João says.

I give him a soft smile.

He then turns his face to Augustine, who's raising one eyebrow at him, his jaw twitching. "Congratulations, Augustine."

Augustine nods at him once. I don't understand what has caused him to have such an attitude. I know they've had some disagreements in the past, but that's no way to treat him.

"I'll catch you later, João," I tell him.

He nods at me and leaves.

Farah and Delano, and Senait and Alex slow dance as well. It makes me very happy. Then, I chat with them and everyone else, and while Augustine and I are mostly with each other, we barely speak to each other. We mainly talk to others.

After a few hours, the reception ends, and everyone leaves. It's time for us to leave and go to our new home. The one I haven't gotten the chance to see yet.

He opens the door for me, and I get in his car. We don't talk the entire car ride, which is a good thing, I would say. We're alone, so we don't have to pretend.

We arrive, and he parks his car in the garage. He walks in front of me to the front door, sticks his key in the lock, and opens it. Then, he turns to stand with his side to me, holding the door for me to enter first.

I enter, and it's pitch-black. He closes the door behind me, which startles me.

He then turns on the lights, making my brain process all the new stimuli it's receiving.

It's filled with neutral colors. The floor is a gray laminate with a big gray shaggy rug underneath an acrylic coffee table. In front of the coffee table is a long black velvet couch, and two velvet armchairs are on either side of it. On the wall behind the coffee table, the TV has been hung up with a dark golden frame around it, as if it were a painting. The kitchen is on the right side of the room, which is entirely black, with some wooden surfaces. And across from it is a bar table with barstools of the same materials. The rest of the living room is filled with big green plants, art on the wall—specifically line art—and candles.

His low yet soft voice reaches me from behind. "Is it to your taste?"

I turn around and nod. Not only is it to my taste, but it's almost as if I decorated the place myself.

It's home.

He gestures to the black staircase. "Follow me?"

I follow him, and once upstairs, we're in a corridor with a lot of doors.

He starts pointing at them. "Storage room, bathroom, laundry room, and two small empty rooms, which can be used as closet spaces." Then he points at two doors across from each other. "My room, your room." He holds the knob of the door that's supposed to lead to his room. "If anyone ever comes by and wonders why we have two bedrooms, we'll just say one of them is supposedly the guest room but that we're using the extra space."

I nod at him, open the door to the room that's supposed to be mine, and see all my boxes, filled to the brim with my stuff. On the left, there's a made bed with white silk sheets and two small nightstands beside it. On the right, is a big, empty white bookshelf, and next to it is a white desk with an acrylic chair behind it. There are also some empty frames on the wall for me to fill and an empty clothing rack. It's so me, it looks as if Augustine had read my mind when picking out the furniture.

He stands in the doorway, leaning with one shoulder on the doorframe, with his arms crossed, not entering the room. "If you wish to change anything, let me know."

"That won't be necessary. I somehow like what you did with the place. Thanks."

I see the pocket watch I bought to stalk him dangling from one of the boxes. I grab it and look at the time. It says four thirty.

Okay. I'm out of sight, out of mind, so the sunrise I will find! If I hurry, I might still make it.

I take off my veil and throw it on the bed. I rummage through the boxes, but I can't exactly find my clothes.

I decide not to change out of the dress, toss my heels from my feet, and sit on the bed to wear the first flat shoes I can find—white high-top Converse sneakers.

Augustine is still standing there. "Where are you going?"

"Separate lives, Mr. Elias. Don't ask me questions about my whereabouts."

Now, he holds the knob of my door tightly. "It's the middle of the night?"

"Yes, that's exactly why I'm leaving."

As I make my way to the door to leave the room, he blocks the way by extending his arm, letting his hand rest on the other side of the doorframe, causing me to halt.

The corners of my mouth draw together, and my eyebrows lower. "What do you think you're doing?"

"It's late."

"Listen, if I wanted to have a curfew, I wouldn't have married you. So, move out of my way. Now."

"Let me come with you. Please."

I check the time again and realize I don't have time for this little "lovers" quarrel. "Fine, but don't slow me down."

I leave the house, and he follows me. The beach is not far from here; it's only a ten-minute walk. As I'm practically hopping, he walks right behind me.

We arrive at the beach, and I sit with extended legs on the sand, facing the sea and the horizon, where, sooner rather than later, my beloved sun will make its entrance.

It's a bit windy, which causes me to shiver. I feel something being put on my shoulders; it's Augustine's suit jacket. The jacket rests on my shoulders.

He crouches down and sits to my right, one leg extended and the other bent. "The beach?"

"The beach."

"Why is that?"

"Because, Mr. Elias, I've always wanted to see the sunrise, but I couldn't since I had a curfew and whatever the opposite of a curfew is called, so I could never be outside at this time."

He nods. "Wouldn't you agree it's time to lose the formalities? You aren't Miss Armanious anymore now that you're married."

I turn my head to him, only to find him already looking at me. "I agree. Let's replace them."

Let's see ... how can I insult him on a daily basis, more than I already do?

Augustinus, Augustine. August! Au-gust. Gus ... Goose? Geese have tall necks, and he has one too—to me, that is. Some of them even have green necks, and his eyes are also green—kind of hard to miss, especially now, when it's the only prominent stimulus I'm receiving.

It's not the insult I was hoping for, but it will have to do.

"Krista," he says.

I wince at him for saying that name. "No," I shout. "No ... anything but that, please." I try changing the subject by telling him his new nickname. "Goose."

"You're calling me Goose? After the bird?"

Be glad it's not Dog, that's what I called you the first time I met you. Actually? Why is it that Egyptians always use animals to curse at people? *hayawan* literally means animal, *kelb* means dog, *homar* means donkey, *baqara* means cow, *haloof* means pig, and *gamoosa* means buffalo. I guess Goose is good after all. "With good reason. They have tall necks, and you're tall too."

"Fine, *Teen*."

I close my eyes to try to register what he just called me, and then I lean toward him and open them widely. *Teen* means dirt in Arabic. Now, I know my name is Kris*tin*a, but that's way too insulting, even for me.

"With offense, Goose." I try out the name. "But your name also consists of the word *teen*. Your name even ends with it. So, maybe I should call you Dirt instead."

He shakes his head. "That wouldn't be right since my name is already Goose."

"But I'm not dirty! And you being tall is an observation."

He throws some sand on my dress. "You being dirty is an observation too."

"Asshole," I say under my breath while wiping the sand off my dress.

The sky starts to light up, and when I avert my gaze to the horizon, I finally see the thing I have been waiting for rising. It's revealing more of itself with each passing second. Its light caresses my cheeks, and I close my eyes to feel every sensation with just my skin, giving my tactile sensations all the room my brain has to offer to process it. I open my eyes again, and there it is—the sun, right behind the horizon. I'm truly mesmerized by it. It's everything I have ever dreamed of. In turn, the salty sea breeze blows, causing my messy bun to become even messier. And with the sun now fully risen on the horizon, it kisses every inch of my bare skin.

I keep gazing at the sun with squinted eyes. "The sunrise is beautiful, isn't it?"

"It is *too* beautiful."

And when I look in his direction, he is already looking in mine again. I let our eyes lock for a split second, and then I turn to the sun again. But from the corner of my eye, I can see him still turned toward me.

What I'm feeling now is what I felt at home physically, but now I feel it emotionally. The feeling of when you have been wearing heels all day with your toes being pushed against the small front of the heel. Leaving no room for them, causing them to be compressed. Uncomfortable. And then you finally get home at night to take them off, drop down on your couch, and rest your feet on any surface you can find. Suffering from blisters, but finally *free* of them.

With the sun rising, a new day has arrived, which marks for all kinds of new beginnings.

CHAPTER ELEVEN

Adam: Eve, the last couple of days, I've found myself burdened. This leads me to ask: is it always wrong if one fails to honor an agreement?

Eve: Adam. I would say it depends. If you change your mind about something that involves you alone, I would say only if you made a very important promise to yourself to stay out of harm's way. If it's something that involves another, then it could be wrong. Especially if there is an agreement.

Adam: If it involves another person, could I propose a new agreement?

Eve: You could. Or couldn't. You can try? Or not. Nothing is impossible, but maybe that is. It depends.

For the last couple of days, I have been very busy settling in, both mentally and physically. I unpacked all my boxes, filled my room with all my stuff, and bought the things I was still missing. But I was also struggling with sleeping since it was the first time I slept somewhere outside of my home without my mother or Delano. It even caused me to be homesick.

But today, I get to cure that homesickness. I've made the living room and my room Lady ready, and I am going to pick her up. I've missed having her next to me all the time.

I don't see Augustine all that much, which is a good thing. It makes me firmly believe that we can honor *our* little agreement, like Adam called it. Since he works long hours, he leaves before I wake up and comes home when I'm already cooped up in my room. And when we are both at home, we're both cooped up in our own rooms. He didn't have to unpack anything because he had already unpacked his stuff days before the wedding.

I leave the house and close the door behind me. The strawberry keychain dangles as I put the key in the lock. Since I'm on strawberry duty, I'll make him regret saying that. I will buy pillows, blankets, mugs, clothing, anything I can find related to strawberries that isn't actually edible. Because I know he meant edible things. If there's even the slightest chance of annoying him, I won't hesitate to take it.

I use public transportation to get to my house—well, old house. I arrive and ring the doorbell, and my mother opens the door for me.

This is the first time I haven't seen her in more than twenty-four hours. This is new for us. Very new.

She pulls me into her and hugs me. "Kristina, I missed you, *habibti*," she says while rubbing my back.

"Missed you too, Mama."

"Where is your husband?"

Oh, I totally forgot I have one now. Which is only natural. Everyone forgets they have a husband from time to time, right? But the reason I forgot is not that I actually forgot about him. I just prefer referring to Augustine as my roommate, nothing more, nothing less.

"He's working today," I say.

We go to the couch and sit next to each other.

She puts her hands together, as if asking for something like a toddler would. "*Mashi*, so tell me!"

I give her a questioning look. "Tell you what?"

"How was your wedding night?"

Well, Mother, my wedding night was not what you're thinking at all. You probably think I'm no longer a virgin and that I made love until the sun came up. And then some.

I mean, I did do something until the sun came up, impatiently waiting for it. And it was perfect. So, my wedding night was perfect. "It was perfect!"

"Did you save the bedsheets?" she asks.

"The what now?"

"The sheets you bled on." She cocks her head at me. "You did bleed, didn't you?"

Saved by the fucking bell because her phone rings. She gestures for me to wait a second and takes the call.

But, no, I didn't. Because I didn't exactly sleep with the man, even if I had, I wouldn't have necessarily bled. But that is something women in Egypt, and I'm sure women in many other countries, are taught.

The misconception of the hymen. The hymen can be found just at the entrance of the vagina. The majority has one, but some are born without. Every hymen is different since they come in different shapes, but there's one thing they all have in common, with the exception of an imperforate hymen: they allow things to both enter and exit the vagina. They can move out of the way, stretch, or tear through numerous things, which means there's no way to trace whether someone is a virgin by the presence or absence of one.

If the hymen were just like this thick brick wall—because, believe me, there are people out there who still think that—then that would make menstrual bleeding impossible. Which we women do every month. Unless you're me and you decide not to have the off week while being on birth control. I haven't bled in months, simply because I can't bear the pain. Yet those people turn a blind eye to this fact since it would invalidate their belief on the matter. Who would want to pay attention to something they can't explain? No one.

They're sowing fear too. A tampon is considered to be able to take away your virginity, for it is only meant to be used after marriage. Women in my culture have been brought up with this ideology; it has been pierced into them. So, even when aware of it being complete bullshit, you can't help but be scared of using it, not daring to, and feeling like you're doing something entirely wrong since it's all you've been told. Even when you know the truth, you still believe everything you've been raised with. Undoing brainwashing is a lot harder than meets the eye.

Menstruating is even considered not to be a topic of conversation. When you're on your period and have to change your pad, just taking it out of your bag is considered *3eeb*, shameful, and unacceptable. Instead, you have to hide it or take your whole bag with you. You absolutely do not let it be known that you're on your period around men. A fucking natural phenomenon.

It's traditional obsession. They get it taught and teach it to the next generation that the hymen is this thick brick wall that a man will destroy with his pickax on your wedding night, causing you to bleed on the sheets. Thus, its purpose is to indicate whether you're still this beautiful flower, only for the man to crumple by deflowering you. A cherry that needs to be popped, where red liquid flowing out, is of the essence. Which is supposed to be evidence proving your innocence of not having had intercourse before.

God, they really decided to run with anything *but* the actual purpose of it. Letting girls grow up with this fucked-up idea that sex is not *for* women but done *to* women. All women are taught is to fear sex instead of being pleased by it, that it's something they can't experience pleasure from. A wall that gets torn down? Being a disgrace—disowned even—if you let just anyone break the wall? Sex being something for the man to enjoy, and you're just the object used to do so? And they wonder why women are scared on their wedding nights. They feel obliged to let the man do what needs to be done. Taught that it has to happen then, even if they don't want to. The psychological impact is *beyond*.

I mean, I wouldn't know. Frankly, I'm scared of it, too, for those exact reasons ... and other reasons. But there are women out there who love sex and own it. If I'm going to draw a conclusion, I should use all the data at my disposal.

Virginity, which is rather a social construct than an anatomic one, is generally only ascribed to women. Men don't have a hymen, thus, there isn't something called virginity that can be taken away from them, and thus it doesn't apply to them. Let them do what they want, and let's turn a blind eye. Having sex before marriage is the "biggest" sin, but if a man does it, oh well. The premises were wrong, yet they used deduction to reach the conclusion. An invalid one. Talk about double standards.

Speaking of anatomy, I swear, the Y chromosome is called Y for a reason—*why* men?

However, in this day and age, there finally is a generation that has a mind of their own or, rather, who has decided to finally use the damn thing.

And all those damn sheets prove is that the man was too selfish and didn't take the time to make his partner wet and aroused enough for their hymen not to tear.

Admitting to her that I didn't bleed, simply because I didn't do anything, is obviously not the right card to play. Trying to explain to her about female anatomy won't land well either since she'll assume I'm cooking up the story because I didn't bleed, because I wasn't a virgin. If I can spare myself a headache, I definitely will.

She hangs up, and I answer her, "Oh, definitely. It was like a bloodbath. Blood clots everywhere. Blood on the cloth, I would say, so I washed it." I laugh away the lies.

She looks at me with a serious and stern expression. "You weren't supposed to do that, Kristina."

"Well, sorry? But you didn't exactly ever want to talk about sex with me until now."

This is all very new. I've always tried to have the talk with her, but she would never budge, telling me I should behave myself and to stop asking questions that didn't concern me. And suddenly, she's the one to make the matter a subject of our conversation. What exactly is the difference between a couple of days ago and today? Absolutely. Fucking. Nothing. It's infuriating.

But there is more to it. All my life, my opinions have always ended up down the drain.

Everything my mother thinks or feels is allowed to be said, and she never hesitates to do so. Whether it's criticizing me, telling me what I do wrong or how my actions affect her negatively. Everything is laid out there for me. Making it the absolute truth since it's the only side of the story that gets told.

Everything I feel, think, or say is, by default, not valid. I never get asked, *How do you feel about this matter?* or *What was something I did that you didn't like?* No.

I have to swallow everything she says, or rather, gulp it down because, sometimes, it's too much to bear. I have to digest it and make it my own. Absorb it into all my cells. Let it take over my body, feed on it, fuel from it. And the waste products, they leave my body through my very eyes. All my thoughts and feelings leave my body by my sobbing them out and getting rid of the waste that's me. Getting flushed down.

That's why her saying this infuriates me. I mean, I know all about the sheets. I know it's culture, hence bullshit. But it was her job to make me aware of it as a mother. Now, I'm supposed to be a woman who knows it all without having received the rulebook or the talk? Now, she decides to treat me like an equal? A woman?

It doesn't work like that, Mama.

Delano enters the living room and sits next to me on the couch. My mother leaves and goes to the kitchen to make tea. This is her way of showing me she's mad at me.

"Corpse bride being a corpse wife now?" he asks.

"Still very much alive, Lano, thank you."

He rubs his chin with his index finger while grinning. "Really? Even after all that sleeping together?"

I raise *my* index finger to stop him. "If there's one thing I'm not doing, it's discussing my sex life with you. Ever."

Not that I have a sex life. I suddenly have become the goddess of sex in this household. It's quite funny, my own little inside joke.

"Believe me, I don't want to hear it either," he says. "Do you like the way your new home looks?"

"I do! It's amazing."

He points with his thumb at himself. "I helped."

I frown at him. "How?"

"Augustine made a list with questions. A lot of them. It was such a pain. About things you like, decoration-wise and a lot of other things, so I basically stole your scrapbook with what you want your future home to look like, copied it into another notebook of yours, and gave it to him."

Oh. Oh? Oh! So, that's why I saw him hand one of my empty notebooks to Augustine that day. I was still so confused about it, but I let it go. I thought Delano maybe just needed a notebook, and I had plenty of them.

It's also why I suspected Augustine to be able to read my mind. It's because he practically did. That's why I love the house so much. He made sure I would feel at home in a new environment with a stranger. It's a little *too* thoughtful, if you ask me.

"I didn't know ... That was sweet of him," I tell him.

He nods. "Yeah, it was. He's a good man."

Why does everyone like to remind me of that fact? João calling him fair, Delano calling him good, the woman he helped calling him sweet, and Alex calling him thoughtful for asking for her pronouns. It's annoying me.

And all his thoughtful actions are annoying too. They interfere negatively with my vendetta against him, which I need to keep to avoid complicating our situation.

I sit there for a while, drink tea with them, and then leave with Lady on my back. More specifically, her in my backpack—my cat backpack. I'm sure the subway rides and the walk are a journey for her since the backpack is transparent and she can see everything.

As we arrive at the front door of our new home, I take off the backpack and hold it from the grab handle, letting Lady see what I see.

I open the door and walk inside. As soon as I do, my heart drops to my stomach. Because, suddenly, I see Augustine sitting on the couch with his legs spread, one shaking constantly. And his hands are in each other with his elbows leaning on his legs. As if he's nervous and impatiently waiting for something.

I put the backpack down, which causes him to turn to me and stand up, walking toward me.

I place my hand on my now-empty chest. "You startled me. I didn't know you would be here already."

He keeps walking until he stops inches from me, making me tilt my head back to face him since he's a tall, *silly* goose. O-okay, but this is a little *too* close.

He clenches his jaw and looks down at me. "May I hug you?"

I look up at him, disoriented. "Uh ... what? Why?"

He doesn't answer me. Instead, he repeats his question by nodding, asking for my consent again without using words.

I lower my chin, not even sure if it's a nod myself.

But he takes it as one and removes the remaining inches between us by putting one hand on the lowest point of my back and the other on my neck, holding it. Then he slowly presses me into him. My hands are not on him; they dangle at my sides like keychains.

But it doesn't take long, not even seconds, for him to pull himself off me, give me a troubled look, and then abruptly make his way upstairs.

I'm left here standing, speechless.

Maybe ... he had an off day at work and needed some comfort? I would say what a very quick way to be comforted, but I'm going to let it slide. It probably didn't mean anything, and I'm not bothered enough to find out.

I open my backpack, allowing Lady the opportunity to explore the new environment when she's ready to do so.

It has been three days since Lady arrived here, and she's finally gotten used to the place. But there's one thing, in particular, she's gotten used to, the shaggy rug underneath the coffee table. And frankly, I don't blame her; it's way too soft not to love. It's also somehow cured my sleeping struggles. I don't know what it is, but something about that rug knocks me out within seconds. Now, I know I'm dealing with a confounder here—Lady being it—causing me to sleep, but let's assume we're dealing with an interaction effect instead, where Lady is the moderator of me sleeping like a baby on the rug. I've taken my methodology exam thrice, so I'm pretty much an expert on the subject now.

We've been falling asleep there every day. And by some miracle, Lady and I find ourselves waking up in my bed in the morning. I know who's behind it, but I don't know how it exactly happens.

So, now, I'm fake sleeping. I can feel Lady's fur against my bare arm, so she's probably really sleeping, not bothered enough to find out what happens to us.

I hear footsteps approaching, and so it begins. I won't see what he does, but I will hear and feel it, which will let me fill in the rest. As I lie there, I can feel him standing next to me, on the other side of where Lady is sleeping, causing me to be between them.

I can feel him crouching down and hear the floor creak under his shoes. I feel his hand sliding on my hamstrings, and the back sides of both my legs are now resting on his arm. His hand is on my waist, holding it. Then, I feel a second hand sliding on my body, this one ending up on my shoulder. He lifts me up and brings my body to his, supporting mine with his. He moves the hand on my shoulder to my head and slowly brings it to rest on his chest. He then puts his chin on my head to hold it there. And we move. I can feel him walking, walking up the stairs and opening the door. I can hear my sheets rustle, and I feel myself getting put down, feeling my sheets against my back. He then puts my blanket over me and tucks me in. I hear him leaving the room and going down the stairs.

I quickly open my eyes because my tactile and auditory senses were overstimulated. *Especially* my tactile ones.

But I quickly close them again because I hear him walk up the stairs, bringing Lady to me.

I hear him enter the room and feel the sheets moving again, and then I feel fur against my arm. I assume he's also tucking her in because the sheets keep moving.

So, we're both tucked in, yet he hasn't left. I know because I can hear him, his slight movements and breathing.

He's walking, but not toward the door. He stops right beside me and does nothing. It's making me anxious, more than I already am.

My mattress dips, making me feel like I just floated an inch. Now, I sense him sitting on my bed, right next to my waist. And then I feel his hands on the mattress, closing me in. The mattress moves some more because he's moving, leaning into me.

I don't understand what's happening. My tactile and auditory senses are not receiving anything anymore. He freezes, but I still sense him hovering above me.

The next thing I know, I feel a cushion-like sensation on my forehead—lips. His lips are pressing against the skin of my forehead. He keeps pressing them for the longest three seconds—because I'm counting—and then releases, but he is still leaning above me.

Eventually, he leaves because I hear my door close.

I immediately open my eyes and sit up straight, taking in everything I couldn't. To look at Lady, my sheets, my mattress. Re-creating what just happened by filling it in with visual images in my working memory.

Maybe he didn't do this just today, maybe yesterday, and the day before that too.

What in the Snow White?

Did Augustine just princess-carry me and kiss me?

As I'm still very disoriented, disarranged, dis—anything, really—I've tried to avoid Augustine as much as possible today. Because a couple of days ago, he asked my permission to hug me. It was definitely weird, but I gave him the benefit of the doubt. And yesterday—and probably the two days before yesterday—he kissed me. I won't be giving him the benefit of the doubt twice. Now, I'm simply going to give him the downside of the doubt and assume the worst.

I'm going to avoid him some more and distract myself by doing something that's on two bucket lists of mine. The first bucket list is Activities At A.M., and the second is Men, Man, Male. I've already crossed off the first item on the first list, which is *watch the sunrise*. The second item on that list is *go to a bar at night*. One of the items on my second list is *make out with a stranger*. When combined, we get *go to a bar at night and make out with a stranger*.

Now, I know I'm the biggest virgin around. I haven't been touched, nor have I touched myself in eight years. But I want to change that. And I want to change that on my terms by picking out the stranger and taking the lead. Let him do to me what I want done to me.

It's almost midnight, and I'm almost done getting ready while going against my fairy godmother. My hair is still straight from the wedding, so I put it up in a high ponytail, my hair dangling down my back. I'm wearing leggings and an oversize T-shirt on top of it.

I grab my coat and kiss Lady's paw, who's lying on my bed.

I make my way to the front door, and as I grab the doorknob to open it, it's opened for me from outside. Augustine opens it, sees me, and walks inside, forcing me to take a couple of steps back. Then, he closes the door behind him and is now holding on to the doorknob, wearing no expression on his face. All his facial muscles are relaxed. It's intimidating.

"Where are you off to now?" he asks.

"Out. Bye." As I practically begin to charge to leave the house, he extends his arms, putting each hand on the walls of the thin corridor, blocking my way just like he blocked my way when I wanted to leave to see the sunrise.

This man is supposed to be the reason I can cross things off my bucket lists, not hinder me from doing so.

He pushes his tongue against the inside of his cheek. "It's late. You really shouldn't."

"Excuse me? You know it isn't your place to tell me that."

"Still—"

I stop him. "No. We're only living together, nothing more and nothing less. We agreed on that. You'd better start acting like it." I'm referring to the whole *kissing me* incident, but I doubt he understands that I am since he thought I wasn't conscious.

"Now, if you would, just excuse yourself and get out of my way," I demand.

He's still blocking the way, but now, his hands aren't resting on the walls anymore; they're in fists. He looks mad and restrained. Like he could grab me and lock me up at any second.

He keeps standing there, jaw twitching, until he turns with his side to me and removes the blockage.

I glance at him as I walk past him and leave the house.

That man is getting crazier with each passing day. I knew this would happen. Men first show you the colors you want to see, and then they show you their true ones. I should've listened to my gut. He can't be trusted.

I arrive at the pub I usually go to and see Ji-hye, the bartender from last time.

"The girl who's a psych major and was about to get married out of convenience, straight out of a romance novel," she says.

I sit on a barstool. "It's me, and I did."

She gasps. "No way. Actually?"

"Yes, but I might start to regret it now."

She holds up a bottle of wine—she remembers—and I nod.

She then pours me a glass. "How come?"

"He's acting all husband-like; it's creeping me out."

"Maybe he likes you?"

I look up at her in disgust. "No way. We hate each other."

Saying that makes me realize a lot of things all at once. What if blocking my way was his way of annoying me? What if he asked to hug me because my reaction would somehow be amusing? What if he kissed me because he knew I was awake after all? To mess with me? What if ... What if?

It has to be. This has to be his way of messing with me.

She shrugs her shoulders. "Maybe you hate him. That doesn't mean he hates you too."

"No, believe me, he does. And I think I'm starting to understand what his game plan is."

A man sits on the barstool beside me. A stranger. A possible target.

"I saw you sitting alone, and I had to make sure I was going to be the one sitting next to you," he confesses.

I smirk at him. "Oh, did you now?"

"I definitely did."

How convenient, Mr. Stranger, because I happen to like you sitting next to me.

"Could I offer you something to drink?" he asks.

I tap my nail on my glass of wine. "I'm all set. Thank you."

We both drink for a while, and then I make the first move—a very bold move at that.

I stand up from the stool. "If you'll excuse me, I'm going to make use of the restroom. Care to join me?"

He looks at me, as if surprised that it was that easy. "I wouldn't hesitate twice."

He follows me into the stall, and I push him against the wall. And without hesitation, I bring my lips to his and pull away.

I haven't done this in a very long time, so I might be very clumsy.

He puts his hand on my neck, tilts his head, and brings my lips to his again. I slightly part my lips to suck on his bottom lip, and then I softly bite it. That makes him shove his tongue inside my mouth and move it in circles around mine. Roughly—not the good kind.

As we're kissing, he puts his hands on my waist, bringing me closer to him, and letting me feel his hard-on. This is supposed to arouse me, but it's not. I don't feel anything. It's as if the sensory fibers of my genitals are damaged, making it impossible to transmit any signal to my spinal cord and brain. Only there to serve as an organ where I can menstruate and pee from. I don't like what's happening right now.

And I find my mind wandering to another person, which confuses me and makes me not like what's happening right now even more.

I push him off me. He looks at me, concerned.

I hold both my temples with one hand and exhale. "I'm sorry. I can't do this."

He backs away even more. "That's okay. I understand. Do you just want to drink something and talk instead?"

"No ... I-I have to get home. Thank you for offering," I say while swallowing away saliva.

I turn around, open the stall door, and leave him there.

I give my card to Ji-hye. She uses it and gives it back to me. I say goodbye to her and leave in a hurry.

I finally arrive home, carefully open the front door, and enter. As I walk into the living room, I see a blanket hanging from the couch. I walk to the dangling blanket, and then I see them.

Augustine is sleeping on the couch, and Lady is sleeping next to him, her body snuggled up against his shoulder and her little head against his cheek. The blanket is barely covering them.

Was he waiting for me to get home?

I can't help but smile at the image before me. I put the blanket on them properly so it covers them since I can't exactly carry them to bed.

I tiptoe my way upstairs and lie down on my bed with my arms and legs completely spread out, and I groan as hard as I can.

I thought I wanted this. I thought I wanted to do everything I wasn't allowed to do. I had rules confining me, so I wanted to be free by opposing them.

When we're not allowed something, we want it even more than before. And sometimes, we find ourselves wanting things we didn't even want in the first place just because someone told us we couldn't have them. We want to spite the people who told us something isn't allowed, show them who's boss. Show them we can't be controlled.

That's just human nature. We feel smarter and more capable and find ourselves in a very good mood when we break rules. So much so that it almost becomes addictive.

And that's not even the worst part.

As I was standing against that stranger, I was thinking about another—the one I know through and through, through words alone.

Then, it hits me. I realize what I want.

I want *Adam*.

CHAPTER TWELVE

Eve: Adam. Here's a question for you: can love be blind?

Adam: Eve, I think love should always be blind.

Eve: What do you mean?

Adam: It should be something not dictated by appearances but instead by everything beyond that.

Eve: And what would one consider to be beyond appearances?

As I try to grow closer to Adam, it feels as if he's distancing himself from me. But him saying that love should always be blind, doesn't that mean he's talking about us? Since we quite literally can't see each other. Or maybe I'm reading too much into it, as I always do. It's confusing, and I hate it. I thought I wasn't capable of feeling this way about another, and then all of a sudden, it just happens with someone I don't even know in real life.

I need comfort, and since Adam isn't responding anymore—and he's the reason for my discomfort—I try to find my second source of comfort. But I can't find her. She isn't in my room, the living room, or any room of the house. There's only one room I haven't checked yet, and it's the only one I've never entered before—Augustine's room.

I hesitantly knock twice.

"Mm-hmm?" I hear from behind the door.

I inhale deeply and open the door. He's sitting up straight, leaning with his back against the headboard of his bed, while holding a book that's resting on his knees. He's wearing Wayfarer-shaped glasses. And he doesn't have wax in his hair. All his strands are covering his forehead today, like wilted flowers in a flowerpot.

I also notice that he's wearing his wedding ring at home. I'm assuming he forgot about it.

And then I see her sitting on his lap as if she's reading the book with him.

He looks at his lap and then at me. "She followed me, and when I closed the door behind me, she kept meowing and scratching the door, so I opened it again, which resulted in her being here."

I hear him, but I'm much busier inspecting his room since it's the first time I've been in it. And the thing that immediately catches my attention is his desk, filled with art supplies, journals, sketchbooks, and canvases. In one corner of his room is a bookshelf full of books with their spines facing inward, not showing their titles, like in his office. And in the other corner of his room are at least a dozen paintings stacked against the wall with their backs facing outside, not showing what is painted on them.

He wears reading glasses. He *actually* reads, writes, draws, and paints. Five new things I didn't know about Augustine.

I avert my attention back to him and nod. I walk toward them and put my hands on Lady, trying to lift her up from him, but she digs her claws in his legs and starts hissing at me.

I let go, take a step back, and look very offended.

He puts his book down next to him. Of course, the spine is facing his bed. He tries to lift Lady off himself, but she digs her claws into his legs again and starts meowing.

He lets go of her and looks up at me. I can tell he's feeling very sorry for me.

She likes him more than me.

She would rather spend her time with him than with me.

My worst nightmare has officially come true.

"I ... I have to go to work," I say.

"Good luck, Teen."

"Thanks ... Goose."

I leave his room and enter mine. I could cry about what just happened, but I don't have time right now, so I will put it on my schedule for later this evening.

It's Thursday, which means Augustine isn't working today, which is why I made sure *I* am. This way, I can avoid him more.

Before the wedding, I had already applied for the crisis counselor position. I was accepted, and then I had my training. Now that my training is complete, I'm officially a crisis counselor, and today is my first day of working without supervision.

My training wheels have been removed, and now, I get to pedal with just two big ones, indicating that I'm ready to ride the journey alone.

And yet I'm very anxious about it. But I hope whoever calls today and has me on the other end can benefit from our conversation. Even if the benefit is so very small, I will be more than glad.

I leave the house and take the subway to get there.

When I arrive, I have a last conversation with my supervisor, and then I'm brought to a small room with a desk, a computer, and headphones.

There are two ways people can contact me, either via the online chat or by calling.

I see an incoming call pop up on my screen. It makes me jolt, and goose bumps take over my skin.

I put on the headphones, take a deep breath, and answer it. "Good afternoon. You have reached the suicide prevention hotline, Kristina speaking. How may I help you today?"

"Kristina is it? Well, I'm in crisis," says a manly voice on the other end.

"I'm here for you, and I would like to help you," I say in a calm voice.

"I've been in crisis for years now, and I thought I could never escape it. I still think, even while dialing the number and even now, as I'm telling you this, that I should just accept what's being done to me and suck it up like the man I'm supposed to be. And that ... *makes me want to die*."

"So, you have been in this situation for a long time and always had the feeling that you can't do anything about it?"

"Are you just going to repeat what I say?!" he asks angrily.

I keep the calmness in my voice. "No. I'm actively listening to what you're saying, and I'm doing that by repeating it to make sure I'm understanding you."

His voice breaks. "Don't, please. I just want a heartfelt conversation. Please, drop the protocol."

"Consider it dropped," I say while shoving away the binder on my desk, making it drop to the floor.

He exhales. "That's the beauty of being anonymous—you have only my voice; you can't picture me. I can say what I want without you judging me with my face in mind. You will never know me."

"I would never judge you even if I knew what you looked like, even if I knew you. I would never judge you, not then and not now."

He pauses before speaking again. "Then ... have you ever been physically abused?"

I don't respond at first but decide to after all. "Yes, I have."

"Did you want to end it all because of that?"

I hesitate but answer him again. "Yes."

"Why?"

"Because it felt as if my body didn't belong to me anymore."

He sniffles once. "How did you cope?"

"I tried to make it my own again. By tattoos, piercings, food I liked, clothes I loved. Things I wanted to be on my body and in my body. Things I chose to be there."

I can't help but tear up. I might not be professional right now, but I'm only human.

"What about the scars?" he asks.

"They are there. I didn't cover them."

"Why?"

"I use them as reminders, not of the abuse, but of the battles I won. That I overcame them. And that makes me feel so, so strong."

"Thank you," he rushes out.

"For what?"

"For showing me I'm not alone in this maze we call life. And seeing that you want to help others because of your experiences makes me believe it can get better, if you decide to see it through."

One tear rolls down my cheek. I was supposed to comfort and help him, yet it seems as if the roles were reversed.

"Thank you," I say, voice shaking.

"For what?" he asks in a way that I know he's smiling.

"For letting me believe I can actually help people."

"You did, and I won't forget it. Have a good day, Kristina."

"You too." *Beautiful stranger.*

He hangs up, and I roll my chair backward, looking at the screen.

I always give more love to strangers than to people I know, being more generous in giving it. Maybe because I don't know their flaws and only see their innocence, that's the beauty of having a lack of information. You see things differently when you don't have the whole story. And perhaps better because some things don't have to be known in order to see someone for who they truly are.

Strangers, the most beautiful souls you might encounter.

Before I know it, my first workday ends, and I find myself home again. Beat. And it seems I'm not the only one. Lady is lying on the rug, and I decide to lie next to her.

Not soon after, I feel hands on my body, which causes me to flinch and open my eyes.

I see Augustine kneeling beside me.

"Oh, I'm sorry. I thought you had fallen asleep again," he says while removing his hands from me.

"No ... I'm awake." I stand up, grab Lady, and rush to my room.

I change into pajamas, get into bed, and feel myself slowly losing consciousness. The beta and alpha activity in my brain slowly turning into theta activity ...

"Cut deeper, Krista. That's how much it hurt me when you crossed me again," he says.

The door is closed. The room is dark. The room is cold. And we're alone. Alone in his basement, where the floor and walls are covered in wet spots and bloodstains.

While I'm sitting on the floor, trembling, he's sitting on a chair across from me with crossed legs, a cigarette in one hand and a glass of whiskey in the other. He's drunk.

The stench of cigarettes and alcohol take over the room. It's sickening.

"When you're done reopening your old cuts, I want you to make new ones, so you can keep track of the new mistakes you made, which you really shouldn't have." He uncrosses his legs and spreads them out. "And you know the drill—when you repeat those new mistakes, you have to recut them. Each time you repeat the same mistake, it will hurt you even more than before."

I obey and bring the pocketknife even deeper into the skin of my inner thigh, tearing open the scar. I bite my bottom lip as hard as I can so as not to make any sounds. And it hurts. All of it hurts so damn much. It feels as if I'm inches away from death.

The knife and my hand are covered in blood; I can no longer tell whether it's my blood or the red color of the knife. And more blood flows out of my thigh.

He always carries this red pocketknife with him, which is only used on me. This pocketknife is his gift to me, and he gifts it to me at least three times a week.

Making mistakes should be punished. Repeating mistakes should be punished even more. I would rather cut myself than have him do it instead—aggressively. I have felt it before.

"Now, move to your other thigh." He points at it. "You see that spot right next to your outer lip? It doesn't have a scar yet. Let's fix that."

I'm sitting with the bottom of my right foot against the front of my left thigh and my left leg pointing outward, half-naked, only wearing a black T-shirt that barely covers my belly button.

I'm practically naked. And it's so very cold that I have shivers constantly.

I bring the knife to my other inner thigh and start a new cut and then another on top of it, forming the letter *X*.

I crossed him because I made two new mistakes today. First, I didn't tell him I had a free period, which made me get out of school earlier than I normally would. Second, I was alone with another guy in the library to finish our science project.

A hard thud reaches me. He put down his glass. He stands up, walks up to me, and grabs me by my hair, pulling it, which makes me stand up a little. Then, he throws me to the ground again while still holding my hair. "Deeper, Krista, much deeper. Or do you want me to do it instead?!" he yells through gritted teeth.

I sniffle. "No! I'll cut deeper, I promise!"

"Good. Discipline yourself," he says. "And when you're done, scrub your blood, sweat, and tears from the floor. It's disgusting."

So, I do exactly that and cut deeper while suppressing my whining to the best of my abilities. But I'm not suppressing it well enough because it burns. The sharp pain is unbearable, and it keeps intensifying. And I don't want it to. I just want it to stop. I just want everything to stop.

Please. Anyone. Let all of it just stop.

My tears reach the puddle of blood, my body fluids mixing on the floor next to me, forming another stain.

Will you let me bleed out? To end my suffering once and for all? I beg of you.

"Stop fucking whining, or I'll really give you a reason to whine about."

But his saying that makes me whine even more.

He tugs on my hair again, making me stand up completely, and pushes me against the wall. He puts one hand on my mouth and the other inside of me, shoving two fingers in at once—too deep.

He points his chin at me. "Go on. Whine as hard as you can for me. Show me that you enjoy everything I do to you."

As I try gasping for air against his hand, he pushes harder, hitting my head against the wall.

It hurts.

I'm in so much pain.

I don't want to feel anything anymore.

"I love seeing you in pain, and I love it even more when I'm the one behind it," he confesses. "I won't fuck you just yet; otherwise, you'll become boring. I will fuck you when I marry you. You'll be my own personal sex slave whose only role is to satisfy me, got that?"

No. I won't be around by then. Don't you dare long for me when I'm gone.

I nod at him fast because I'm scared of what he might do if I don't.

"Good." He lets go of me, unzips his pants, and pulls out his cock. "Kneel," he demands.

I kneel and bring it into my mouth. He then grabs my head and pushes it deeper inside, causing me to almost choke on it.

He pulls me by my hair again to make me stand.

"Best head." He brings his cigarette to my thigh and puts it out by pressing it on the freshly made cuts, thanking me.

I scream at the top of my lungs and start crying hysterically.

I'm sitting up straight, and I feel someone sitting behind me. I feel arms wrapped around me, one around my collarbones and the other right under my breasts, holding me.

"Shh, hey? Hey, I'm here, right behind you. I'm with you." I hear Augustine's soothing voice against my ear.

I open my eyes and immediately bring my hands to my thighs, squeezing them. My whole face is wet, covered in tears and snot.

I turn my head to look behind me. I see one of his legs dangling from the bed, supporting himself, and the other bent with his knee on the bed, supporting me. My shoulders are resting against his chest.

I lean further back, rest my head on his shoulder, and close my eyes again.

I was in REM. It was a dream. A nightmare. But it was so vivid and so real that it felt as if I were there again, in that enclosed space with him, experiencing that day. It feels as if I've just time-traveled to the future and that I found myself in this room when I opened my eyes.

The past has been making its way to the present lately, but it has never been this direct.

Eight years ago, when I was seventeen, I was looking for love. At that time, I felt my father's absence the most, and I wanted to fill that void with the presence of another man.

And then I met him. My first and only boyfriend. He was very sweet at first. He used to tell me I was special, that he wanted to take care of me, and that he loved me. It was everything that seventeen-year-old me wanted to be said to her. To me. To us. Someone caring for us and giving us attention. Showing us beautiful colors.

And then he changed. He started to show his true colors. I was special because I was the only one who got to experience the pain he inflicted, that he wanted to take care of me by slowly killing me, and that he loved me being in pain. Caring became controlling, and attention became obsession.

He was controlling, so much so that it felt as if I were a puppet and the strings were glued to his hands, unable to ever escape his command. He wanted to know everything there was to know—where I was, with who, and why—and he would get pissed if I didn't answer my phone immediately. And he would get even more pissed when things didn't go his way.

That was where the punishment came in. He would always tell me that crossing him meant hurting me. And that it did, in a very horrendous way at that. He loved punishing me. And he loved it even more when I did it myself; he called it *disciplining oneself*. When I hurt myself, he would watch me do so and enjoy it.

Every cut, he enjoyed.

Even after he changed, I still loved and obeyed him, regardless. Because I thought that the sweet man I'd first met was still inside of him somewhere. And that all the punishment was for my benefit. That he cared for me so deeply that he made sure I learned things the hard way. I was so fucking young. I didn't know any better.

That one experience traumatized me in more ways than one, making me the person I am today.

He was the only experience I had with men, and so he became the prototype of what a man was like. The average man. *Every* man.

I was disgusted by all men and did not trust them because I knew what they were capable of. It made me repulsed by love because I knew it wasn't sincere; I knew that every man would be sweet at first and then change. It made me fear marriage because that meant you'd be with a man behind closed doors, all alone, where he could do everything and anything to you, and no one would ever find out.

It's why I thought I would never fall in love again because I didn't want to go through *that* ever again. But somehow, Adam has become an exception on every front.

My experiences regarding sex aren't good. It's one of the reasons why I don't like to be touched. I have never felt pleasure because the line between pain and pleasure is nonexistent to me. I don't know any better; it's all I know. It's made me not engage in anything related to sex for the last eight years, knowing nothing about my own body.

It's why I wasn't surprised when I tried to make out with that stranger, and it did not affect me. Why I felt numb when he was aroused. I fear that not only my soul is shattered but my entire female anatomy along with it, because all of me is broken beyond repair.

I have scars. A lot of them. Scars from many different sharp objects and cigarette burns, covering both my entire inner thighs. In all kinds of patterns. Each one reminds me of a mistake I made, and some were just for his fun. They're the reason I don't like wearing dresses. When I wear a dress, I feel exposed, as if I could reveal my scars to everyone if I make one wrong move. A mistake. And the friction of my thighs when rubbing together hurts, so I always wear shorts underneath when I have to wear a dress, even on my wedding day.

It's why I never change clothes in front of others. It's also why I haven't gone swimming in almost eight years and always pass on vacation. Why I love the beach so much because you don't have to wear swimwear in order to dip your toes in the water.

It's why I needed the piercings and tattoos even if I wasn't allowed to get them. I *needed* to feel that my body belonged to me, even after everything it had to endure against my will.

It's why I barely befriend people, unable to form new connections. Who would want to connect with me? For the longest time, even I didn't feel connected to myself.

I wanted to escape my body so badly, especially when I was eighteen, and wanted to end it all myself—even attempted to do so when I thought the suffering would never end.

People with suicidal thoughts don't like pain; it's almost always the very thing they try to escape. Taking one's life is painful, but it's the price they decide to pay.

What's a second of pain compared to a lifetime?

But they aren't the only ones to experience pain. With them ending their sentence, they hurt the people they love most. Some decide to stay in pain, to exist for their loved ones, and not let their loved ones experience what they experience day in and day out.

It's why I decided to major in psychology. To understand him, to help people like him. But above all, to help people who are victims of people like him, to help people like *me*.

It's why I want to specifically help people who have suicidal thoughts because I've been where they are; I've experienced it firsthand. And I know that the feeling of wanting to escape it all can change, and I want to share that with them.

It did for me—eventually. With time. With professional help. And when it did, I realized I wanted to change things. Because when I stopped living my life for him, I was living it for my culture.

It's why I became this fucked-up human being who is *obsessed* with wanting to live her life for herself for once and not be controlled by anything or anyone. Not my culture, my mother, or my ex. I even married someone to do so. And by doing that, I have several prices to pay. And I'm having a hard time paying them. They are Augustine, Augustine, and *Augustine*.

When I first met him, he wanted to close his office door behind us. I protested against it because I didn't want to be alone with a strange man in a closed room.

The second time I met him, I cried because he told me that holding his tie and him holding my hand were the consequences of my actions, reminding me of the consequences I'd had to face when crossing my ex.

When Augustine kept touching my hand or wrist, I hated it because I didn't want to be touched by a man—and one I barely knew at that.

Now that I'm living with him, I'm scared all the time. Because we're alone all the time, behind closed doors. He could do anything to me, both consciously and unconsciously. And he does. He carries me, kisses me, and intimidates me when he plays alpha man.

It's why I'm also scared right now, him being alone with me in my room as I'm resting my head on his shoulder. We're touching each other. I'm getting comforted. And feeling myself losing consciousness.

Even when my ex is no longer in my life and hasn't been for a long time, he has dictated my whole life and continues to do so. The one thing I can never completely escape, is him.

I open my eyes. I'm lying in my bed. I look next to me and see Lady sleeping—*only* Lady. And I feel that my face has been cleaned.

I make my way downstairs and see Augustine in the kitchen. I take a seat at the bar. He's standing behind it, making breakfast.

Since we have been living together, we both cook our own meals and never eat together. I always eat my meals in my room, and I assume he does too. It might be lonely at times, but it just so happens to be that way. It's something I have to accept since I wanted to move out.

"Good morning, Teen," he says without facing me.

"Good morning, Goose ..."

"I knew it would cause you worry if I stayed with you, so I left as soon as I made sure you had fallen asleep again."

What worries me more is whether or not you kissed me again.

"Yeah ... thank you."

He stops what he's doing and faces me. "If you want to talk about it, I'm here."

"I don't, but thanks for offering."

As I try to stand up to make myself breakfast, he slides a plate in front of me—scrambled eggs with red bell peppers and mushrooms. And the other plate is exactly the same. I look up at him, surprised.

He grabs forks from the kitchen drawer with his back to me. "That's how you like your eggs, don't you?"

"How do you know?"

I mean, I know how he knows. He has a whole notebook of mine, full of all kinds of facts about me.

He turns to me and hands me a fork. "I just happen to know."

I take it from him and notice that he's still wearing his wedding ring when he doesn't have to because he's home and we're alone. Why?

He grabs his plate, places it next to mine, and sits next to me. "Roommates can share meals, you know."

I nod at him hesitantly. "You like bell peppers and mushrooms with your eggs too?"

He puts his fork in the eggs. "I'm about to find out, and I will tell you whether I do."

And thus we have our first meal together in our new home.

And it is delicious.

And he thinks so too.

CHAPTER THIRTEEN

Eve: Adam. Is there something you like to do when you find yourself with free time on your hands?

    Adam: Eve, I would say that I like to cook. I find it therapeutic somehow.

    Eve: Are there more things you find therapeutic?

    Eve: What is your favorite food?

I have been trying to change the conversations that Adam and I have by making them more personal. I want to get to know him, *about* him. Anything I can get out of him, I want it. But it feels as if it's getting harder and harder with each passing day because he doesn't respond right away, like he used to, and sometimes, he doesn't respond at all. And if he responds, it's terse. He's changed, and I don't know if it's because of me or something in his personal life. And I hate it.

It's Sunday morning, so Augustine is probably getting ready for church now. Good for him. I'm going to make myself breakfast.

I walk downstairs to the kitchen. I open the fridge, grab the cold brew coffee and milk, and make myself iced coffee. As I bring the straw to my lips, I'm interrupted from having the heavenly first sip of coffee in the morning.

"Don't," Augustine says while standing in front of the bar, holding the edge with both hands.

I face him, still holding the straw, letting it touch my lips. "Don't?"

His grip tightens. "Don't drink. Get ready. We have to leave."

When we go to church, we have to be fasting. Which means you don't eat or drink anything before the service because you take communion during it.

I chuckle and point at him with my index finger briefly. "You mean, you have to leave."

"No, we have to leave. You have to go on Sundays now."

I put my mason jar down on the counter with a lot of strength, making it bang against it. "Why?"

He puts on his watch as he says, "We're married now. Going to church together is kind of what married people do."

I shake my index finger. "No, see, I got married to do things my way, not to do things the way they're supposed to be."

"Which I understand, but sometimes, you have to sacrifice something to gain something better or what you desire." He tilts his head. "Wouldn't you agree?"

That ... that was more Adam than Adam himself in our last conversation. I don't like comparing them, but sometimes, Augustine says things that remind me of Adam or things Adam would say if he were the one standing in front of me right now.

"Maybe, but I don't want to sacrifice this. Have fun at church. Pray for me, will you?" I grab my mason jar and bring the straw to my lips again.

"Don't ... Don't!" He rushes around the counter to stop me.

I immediately remove the straw from my lips and hold out my hand to stop him. "If you come any closer, I will actually drink from it."

He takes a step back and sighs. "Look, if your mother asks me why you aren't with me, it will raise unnecessary suspicion."

He's not wrong. If I don't go today, my mother probably will find it suspicious and annoy me with questions that I have answers to, but I can't exactly give without outing myself.

But I'm not convinced enough. He notices and tries to convince me. "We will leave right after the service. There's no need for us to stay."

My chin points at my breast, and my eyes narrow at him, like I don't trust him. "Really?"

"Really. You decide when we leave. Do you accept?"

I shrug my shoulders. "I think I can accept."

"Good. Now, get ready. I'll be waiting in the car."

And I do. I get ready; we drive to church, and now, we're attending the service. I see almost every Egyptian person I know in one place. I see Delano and my mother. I see Marina and her mother. I see Alex—I love Alex. And Tony, Sarah, George, and Mariam from what I like to call the Egyptian ensemble, are present too.

The service ends, and I already see Alex running toward me.

She grabs my arm. "Tell me everything now! How was it?"

I decide to break our traditional greeting by hugging her. The last time I saw her was at the wedding, and we've barely spoken since then. I've missed her so much, and now, I realize that more while she's in my arms.

I let go of her. "How was what?"

"Uh, being deflowered?"

Oh? Oh. Oh! I forgot yet again that everyone now thinks I'm the new goddess of sex. It's exhausting, taking on all these new roles when I'm not actually fulfilling them. Leaving me no choice but to lie or try to use an excuse. "Alex! I can't talk about that in church."

"Of course you can. It's written about in the Bible, so it's perfectly natural. And since I'm not planning on letting a dick ever enter this"—she gestures circles with her hands around her reproductive organs—"beautiful creation by God, I need to know everything there is to know, so spill!"

I give her a tense laugh. "It was ... awesome."

"Awesome?" She looks in Augustine's direction and then at me again. "Was he big? He looks big." She checks him out again. "He's definitely big."

Oh my God. I don't know, Alex. How about you ask him?

But now that she mentions it, he does look ... big. I've always known his hands to be big with the backs covered in a few hard-to-miss veins, and his fingers are thick and long. And if they say that the size of a man's hand says something about his other measurements ... I wonder what else is big—wait. Why do I even care? I don't. Alex is getting in my head.

I see her deep in thought.

I sigh, unamused. "What are you thinking about now?"

"I'm picturing you having sex with him."

No. Please, stop. That's an image I refuse to ever see. But then my thoughts wander in very wrong directions, and I need to stop us both from picturing things.

I snap my fingers. "Alex, snap out of it and stop!"

"Stop what?" Augustine asks from behind me.

Jesus, all this man has is timing.

Stop picturing us having sex, but we're not going to tell you that.

Alex is going to come up with something completely unrelated to what we were just talking about. She's the best at coming up with things right on the spot, a natural even.

"Picturing you and her having sex," Alex tells him.

A disaster. I'm so glad I'm not facing him right now. I want the ground to swallow me whole, and I don't care if the destination is hell. I would be satisfied with anything to leave this very moment.

"And?" he asks her.

Alex answers him with a question. "I'm having a hard time picturing it. Who was on top?"

What the actual fuck is happening right now? I mean, God, are you hearing this? Help! Please? Let Judgment Day be now.

"We both were. We kept switching until the sun came up for a week straight."

No, we didn't? I mean, sure, we kept switching turns to talk until the sun came up at the beach, but that was it. After that, we kept avoiding each other for a week straight. This man sure can lie.

Alex scratches her temple. "Man, that must have been hot."

"Very," he says.

Delano and Marina walk up to us.

"What are you guys talking about?" Delano questions.

"I was picturing Kristina and Augustine having s—" Alex is about to finish that sentence, but I stand behind her and put a hand on her mouth and an arm around her chest.

I whisper, "Don't even think about finishing that noun. I will literally strangle you right in front of all these people, no hesitation. I will even ask the priest to pray over your dead body right away. Do we have an understanding?"

Alex turns her head to me and nods slowly.

"Good," I say, releasing her.

She then whispers in my ear, "I don't believe you guys switched. You were definitely on top and had him tied up."

Augustine looks at me and blinks several times, probably having heard what I said since he's standing close to us and is surprised I have this side to me.

"She was picturing us having sushi because she loves it and I don't," Augustine tells Delano.

I guess he *doesn't* want to be strangled by me. And how does he know I love sushi? Of course, the notebook.

Well, nice save, Augustine, far better than what Alex did, actually telling you what we were talking about.

And how does one not love sushi?

Delano faces Augustine. "You don't? Maybe we should all go out and eat it, convince you it's good since your wife is sushi-obsessed."

Well, I am, definitely, but please don't call me his wife. I can't get used to it, and I don't want to.

I see Sarah, Tony, George, and Mariam approaching us.

"Do you guys want to join?" Delano asks them.

"Join what?" George says.

"To eat out. Sushi."

"Yeah, sure. When?" Tony asks.

Delano pulls out his phone to check his calendar. "Tomorrow?"

All four of them check their calendars as well and confirm that they're available.

"Oeh, I could bring Senait!" Alex says enthusiastically.

"Yeah! And I'm going to try and let Farah come too." Delano turns to Marina. "Marina, you should bring your fiancé along as well."

"Yeah, I'll ask him."

"If everyone is available tomorrow, we can have a"—Delano counts how many people are standing in a circle right now—"a sextuple date."

They all confirm and chatter away with each other.

I can't believe we were just talking about sex, trying to hide it from Delano, only for him to end up saying *sextuple*. That's hilarious. But I'm sorry? I'm available, yes, but I don't want to be part of a sextuple date. Count me out. Make it a quintuple date, and while you're at it, adopt Augustine as your eleventh wheel.

"I can't. I'm sorry," I say.

Augustine glances at me.

"Why?" Alex asks.

The real reason is, I'm not trying to have an Egyptian ensemble 2.0, that's why. But the fake reason is going to be, I have work. I do actually have work, so I'm not lying. It's a *truth by omission* kind of situation again. "I have work."

"You can come after. I have work too. There will be enough time to get ready," Delano tells me.

Lano, for once in your life, could you, I don't know, shut the fuck up? "Right ..."

"Great. I will make a group chat and send everyone the details. See you guys tomorrow," Delano says and walks away.

The others walk away as well, and I'm left standing with Alex, Marina, and Augustine.

Marina stands between Alex and me and whispers, "You were picturing them having sex, weren't you?"

"No, she wasn't." I try to convince her by waving my hand.

"Yes, I was. Kristina, you absolutely cannot lie in church. You have to be honest."

Damn you, Alex. I should have strangled you after all.

Marina laughs and leaves.

"So much fun. See you tomorrow, babes." Alex kisses my cheek and leaves too.

Augustine and I are now alone, facing each other.

"Not only did we not leave right after, but now, I also have to hang out with them tomorrow. Good job, Goose! I didn't think it was possible, but I hate you even more now."

He puts his hand on his chest. "May I defend myself?"

I glare at him. "I would like to see you try."

"Walk with me?" He takes my hand, links our arms, and brings me to walk with him to the candles where no one is standing.

He then releases and faces me. "First of all, we didn't leave because you were talking with Alex. Then, your Egyptian ensemble arrived, and Delano was the one to introduce eating out with everyone. While they were planning everything, I didn't vocalize a single word. I didn't even confirm that I would be there."

"But you were the one who said sushi, thus putting food out there."

He snickers. "Would you rather I told them that she was picturing us having sex?"

I look at him, shocked, shocked that he just repeated it as if it were nothing, as if it were normal.

"I—you—" I breathe out. "Why did you tell Alex all of that?"

"Because it had to be believable, and you were probably doing a poor job at making it so."

"No, I didn't," I protest.

He runs his fingers through his hair. "Oh? Then what did you tell her?"

I pause, realizing what he meant. "I said it was ... awesome."

"That's doing a poor job at making it believable that we had sex."

I look at him again, angrier than before. Angry because I don't like the words *we* and *sex* in one sentence, and it feels as though he keeps repeating them.

He smiles softly. "I know what you want to do. You can strangle me when we get home."

"Don't tempt me."

The time has come to meet with the Egyptian ensemble 2.0. Unless ... unless I try to run away. But there's a good chance that Augustine the goose will chase after me, and I don't want him to even though it'd be a wild goose chase, because if I don't want to be found, I make sure that I'm unfindable.

But I've been stalling for quite some time already, and Delano, Farah, and Augustine are waiting for me downstairs. I can't do this to Farah, so I decide to woman up after all and leave my room. Because we're late and I'm the reason why.

I make my way downstairs and see Farah sitting on the couch. She sees me and stands up. We greet each other, and Delano and Augustine enter the living room.

"Delano, where exactly are we going?" I ask him.

"Didn't you read the group chat?"

No. Because I woke up to a thousand-plus messages, and I sure as hell was not about to read all of that just to find out where we're going to eat.

I shake my head.

"It's like a karaoke bar, minus the singing, so we get a separate room, and we can play our own music while we eat."

Oh, that does sound like fun. And since Alex, Senait, Farah, and Marina will also be present, I can enjoy it. I just have to make sure that I sit next to them, not Augustine, and then I'll get through it.

"Everyone ready?" Delano asks.

We confirm that we are and drive to the place. Farah and Delano are carpooling with us.

We arrive and ask the hostess which room is reserved under the name Delano. She takes us to it, and I open the door. All of them are sitting around a big rectangular dining table. I walk toward the seat next to Alex and sit down.

"There you guys are, but there's a small problem," Tony says.

"Which is?" Augustine asks.

Sarah stands up to face Augustine. "We're missing a chair, and we already asked if they have one extra, but they don't because the whole restaurant is booked. And since you guys are late, you'd better fight it out."

Farah turns to Delano. "But didn't you make a reservation for twelve people?"

"No, eleven. Marina's fiancé wasn't coming anymore because of work, but I guess he got out of work earlier than expected."

Delano and Farah look at me while I'm sitting. Waiting for something. *Why are they looking at me?*

"Kristina, share the chair with Augustine," Delano urges me.

I look at him, moon-eyed—the full-moon kind.

I'm sorry, but why don't *you* share a chair with Augustine?

"Wh-why don't you share a chair with Farah?" I ask.

"We can't exactly do that ..." she says.

God, I know you guys can't, but please, I don't want to share a chair with Augustine. It wouldn't even be sharing. He's way too big to share anything.

I can't believe I did this to myself. If we hadn't been late, I could've just sat on a chair alone. But I can't exactly protest against it since it'll be suspicious for me to do so. He's supposed to be my husband, and we're supposed to want to be all over each other since we're supposed to still be in our honeymoon phase.

I stand up—reluctantly—and step away from the chair, wanting to step out of the room altogether.

Augustine sits on the chair and taps his fingers on his upper leg. I roll my eyes at him and sit. On his lap. With my behind on his groin and his other leg between my legs.

We order food and start eating. I also order red wine and drink the whole glass in a matter of seconds. I need something to get me through the situation I've been put in.

As I'm sitting, I'm trying very hard not to end up on his crotch, but I keep sliding down to that area. And I also feel something warm poking me. I squirm on his lap to try to find a comfortable angle.

"What are you doing? Stop moving," he murmurs against my ear.

I don't listen and keep moving. "What is that? Oh, can you take your phone out of your pocket? I'm sitting on it."

"No, that's all me, love, so stop before it gets worse."

Love? Why is he calling me that? No one can hear us anyway.

"What do you mean all—" Oh? Oh. Oh no. It hits me, and I freeze. I stop breathing. I become a statue. He is ... hard? Now? No, I'm leaving.

I try to stand up, but he pulls me back to him with his hands on my waist. And when I land on him again, he groans softly.

Against my ear, he whispers, "You can't. I'm wearing slacks; it'll be noticeable."

I mock him. "What? Insecure about your measurements?"

"Very, so keep covering them, please."

Which means he isn't. Not at all. If there's one thing a man who isn't insecure would say, it's that he is.

And I can feel that he shouldn't be.

But then something happens that turns my whole world upside down at this very moment. Because I feel my heart racing, my body turning hot, and a tingling sensation. Down there. I start to get aroused myself.

No. It can't be. It must be the suspension bridge effect. I'm not aroused because of him, but because of the glass of wine. It has to be. Who am I kidding right now? I normally don't get aroused when I finish a glass of wine in seconds. Not like this. *Never* like this.

And I don't understand the why or how of it. Why now? Why him? How is this possible? Because I've never felt this before. I don't even know if I'm aroused right now because I don't know what that feels like. All I know is that I'm confused and that I need to leave—now.

I try standing up again, but he holds me down by my waist.

His grip on me tightens. "Don't. I know you don't like me, but please."

"It's not just my head thinking it; my body doesn't like you either," I sneer.

Alex turns to us. "Are you okay? Why are you so red?"

I feel even more heat climbing up my face. "No, I need to—"

Augustine places two of his fingers on my lips. "She had seaweed on her lips. All taken care of."

Alex nods and turns back to Senait.

I bite one of his fingers, and he removes them. "Just bear with me, please? If you stop talking and moving, it'll be gone before you know it. Just act like you aren't here."

So, I do exactly that. I don't talk, and stop moving except to bring food to my mouth.

Eventually, I stop feeling something hot poking me, and we all leave. During the drive and when we arrive home, we don't talk either. I rush to my room, close the door behind me, slide down with my back against the door, and sit. Panting. Processing.

Knocking hits my body, and it startles me.

"I'm sorry if I made you feel uncomfortable," Augustine says.

I don't respond.

"Lady's in my room. Do you want me to bring her to you?"

"No!" I swallow some of my spit, almost choking on it. "K-keep her."

The door of his room closes.

I bring my fingers into my underwear. And I can feel the undeniable truth. I'm ... wet.

It's that time of the month again, or rather, that time of the year for me. I've been taking birth control pills nonstop for the last six months, which means I'm now forced to have the off week. And it's unbearable. I'm lying on the couch, and I'm a mess. I'm experiencing the most awful cramps, my head is throbbing, and I'm sweating like crazy. And my hair is an even bigger mess, but putting it in a bun would feel like a whole exercise. Also, I wanted to be close to the kitchen because I have the weirdest cravings when I'm on my period, and I can't keep walking up and down the stairs every time I get hungry, which is all the time. And since my heating pad—Lady—likes the rug in front of the couch, I didn't have a choice, to begin with.

"Lady." I tap the area where my uterus is. "Here, please."

She tilts her head at me and lies on her back to roll around on the rug.

So much for physical support. She's doing a poor job at it because every time I grab her and put her on my stomach, she runs away.

I hear the front door open and close. It's Augustine.

He walks toward me and stops right in front of me, looking at me.

My eyelids are lowered, and I give him a numb look. "What are you looking at?"

"Are you okay?" he asks.

"Do I look okay to you?"

"No. To me, you look like you're on the verge of dying."

"That's exactly how I feel, so leave me alone."

"Let's change that." He sits down next to me with his legs spread and taps the space of the couch between them.

I gaze at his crotch and then at him in disgust, replaying the events of a few days ago in my mind.

He notices and realizes what I'm thinking about. "Don't worry; I won't let it touch you again."

"Liar."

He beams. "If you want me to tell you lies, I can tell you lies."

I sit between his legs but not against him. He braids my hair, all of it in one big braid.

"Where did you learn how to braid?" I ask because he's doing such a good job at it.

"I lived with two women most of my life. They taught me a thing or two, braiding hair among them."

Delano lived with two women most of his life, but I don't exactly see him jumping at the opportunity to braid hair. Hell, I even doubt whether he can put hair in a hair tie without messing it up.

He stands up and takes me with him from my shoulders, and we're touching each other for a *hot* second. Then, he leaves from behind me to go to the kitchen. I lie on the couch again.

"Are you hungry?" he asks.

"I'm starving. I could eat paper and be satisfied."

"I'll make you something. Here." He puts a heating pad on my stomach and wipes away the sweat on my forehead with a wet cloth. He then walks back to the kitchen and starts cooking.

When he does things like this, I catch myself thinking, *Maybe he isn't* that *bad after all*. What if he actually doesn't mean any harm? Or am I being too naive? He has done things to make me doubt him. I don't know, but what I do know is that I can't keep living on high alert all the time because it's exhausting.

I feel fingers stroking my neck. I open my eyes and see him carrying two plates in one hand, placing them on the coffee table. One is filled with sushi, and the other with strawberries covered in chocolate.

I sit up straight. "You ... you made sushi? I thought you didn't like it at the restaurant."

"It's not that I don't like it. I just don't love it."

"But you searched for the recipe. Why?"

He glances at me. "Because you love it." Then, he immediately adds, "And I happen to like cooking."

Adam likes cooking too—no. *Stop comparing them, Kristina. Why do I keep doing that?*

I take a piece, dip it in soy sauce, and eat it. It's good—*so good*—even better than the sushi we had at the restaurant.

"Well, it seems that sushi is dealing with unrequited love because it loves you; it obeyed your cooking." I eat another piece. "It's delicious."

He looks at me, enthusiastic. "Here, have some strawberries. I know you like those too," he says while bringing one to my mouth.

I hesitate before parting my lips.

He sits next to me and takes one too.

"I thought I was on strawberry duty," I tell him.

"You deserve a free pass now."

As we're eating, it's quiet for a while until he starts talking again. "I want to be your friend, if you'll let me."

I shrug my shoulders. "I guess I could consider us frenemies. After all, you did grant me freedom, and I can't ignore that."

He smiles so very softly. "Good. I would love that."

Maybe I should give him the benefit of the doubt after all. All I keep thinking about are my negative experiences with him. And I know, as a psychology major does, that humans remember negative things better than positive things. It's the *negativity bias*. And once I'm aware of a bias, I should *un*bias.

Besides, the mere exposure effect is not something I can deny. When seeing someone day in and day out, you grow to like—tolerate them, even if you don't want to admit it. Which I'm doing now—I'm not admitting it.

It's just science.

CHAPTER FOURTEEN

Eve: Adam. Would you say that you're happy right now?

Adam: Eve, I'm content with what I have, yet there is one thing I find myself chasing after, and I can't seem to stop.

Eve: And what is that?

Eve: Adam?

What could it be he's chasing after? I mean, one thing is for sure: it isn't me. Sadly. But it's unlike him to read my message and then ignore it completely.

What is going on in his personal life? I want to know. I *need* to know.

Love truly is a silly notion. When we fall in love, it's such a strong feeling. We get utterly and unreservedly consumed by another, so much that we sometimes can't even recognize ourselves anymore.

Every little thing that person does or says is interesting. It's meaningful to us, which is why everything becomes important. We wonder what the person did the day we didn't get to spend with them. What made them laugh and how we weren't there to witness that delightful laughter of theirs. What upset them and we hate not having been there to comfort them. Hating not being able to be with them for all the hours their day consists of. To be a part of *everything*.

We want to become this shield to them, to make sure they stay protected from this sometimes-cruel world and take all the bullets instead. Sacrifice ourselves if that means that their happiness is ensured. Be the only one for them, like they are the only one for us.

Sometimes even getting jealous when we realize that others realize how amazing our person is. Getting greedy because of it. Getting scared of losing them to those other people because we know they deserve the world, and we doubt whether we can give it to them.

All of it is so intense, making it almost undeniable that love, in fact, does exist. And we know we experience it when we read something related to it, and the image of the person arises in our mind. Yes, like *that*.

It's almost too beautiful to be true that we humans can get so infatuated with someone that it dictates our happiness daily. It's alluring.

It's frightening because love is solely based on memories.

There is no such thing called love. There is something called having fond memories of someone, and in one way or another, it just clicks in your brain and is labeled as love.

What is love? we wonder. *That is love.*

Love is nothing more than a feeling we use to describe a sequence of experiences with another that means more to us.

And I never claim things without presenting evidence along with them. That's not something a psych major does. We like to use evidence-based practice, and I like to evidence-base my claims. When a person has retrograde amnesia, they might not remember anything prior to the event that caused them to have the amnesia. And what if they were married for years? They don't recognize their partner anymore. To them, their partner is nothing more than a stranger, and they greet the person with, *Hey, do I know you?*

Thus proving that love lies within our memories, in our head. It's not a feeling we feel within our heart, like we think we do; it's a recollection. With the memories gone, so is the love.

It's why when we have a broken heart—more like a broken head—we keep reliving memories of experiences with that person in our head. To smile at them briefly, only to wish we could erase them. Erase the love. Ease our pain.

Because love is pain, and we can feel it physically when we're experiencing heartbreak. Our brains don't distinguish between emotional or physical pain; it all gets processed in the same regions.

There is another thing we label as love—the type of love we experience with someone who hurts us. Who abuses us. Who doesn't love us. And we let them because the simple truth is, we don't love them either; we are addicted to them. We label our addiction as love. Like alcohol or drugs, even though we know it's bad for us, we can't seem to stop wanting it.

We find ourselves more infatuated with them than we initially thought we would. We try to leave them, only to end up in their presence again. We spend all our time on them, be it trying to leave them or failing and actually being with them. We crave them constantly. We are unable to manage our personal life because of them. We still are with them, even when it gets in the way of our relationships and friendships. We neglect our recreational activities because of them. We are with them, even though we know how bad they are for our mental and physical health. We find ourselves staying, even though we know we are putting ourselves in danger.

Nine of the eleven DSM-5 criteria for substance use disorders can be used to describe being addicted to a person. If you experience six or more of these symptoms, it indicates that the severity of the addiction is severe.

Isn't that alarming?

And somehow, every relationship ultimately ends up being addictive, or rather, the person it's with. It feels as if the person becomes a drug, and we become addicted to all the substances that make up the person: their touch, voice, and presence. We find the old conversations, pictures, and voice memos aren't enough to satisfy us anymore. We need more to feel what we felt when those conversations were held, those pictures were made, and those voice memos were played for the first time. We need new memories to feel what we felt back then.

We have built tolerance.

And when, suddenly, we can't have more because they're out of reach, because the relationship has ended, and we came to depend on them, our appetite changes, we experience difficulties with sleeping; we experience mood swings; we get irritated easily, we're restless.

We go into withdrawal.

Eleven of the eleven DSM-5 criteria for substance use disorders can be used to describe being addicted to a person. It fits like a puzzle.

It's alarming.

Even if I view love from all these different perspectives—and there are many more I'm not considering right now—there is one thing everyone can agree on: love is just as painful as it is beautiful. But we accept the pain that comes with it because we think the journey is worth it. We walk through fire, hoping we don't get burned. We know it's going to end up killing us, but we get resurrected again and find ourselves walking a different path that will ultimately end up the same way. We keep walking different paths over and over until we reach a destination, a person. A person we like to call our stop. And then, at last, we stop traveling altogether.

This is how I have perceived love for as long as I can remember, convincing myself that what the world perceives as love doesn't exist to me. Something I won't be taking part in. Because it's more frightening than it is beautiful.

But it's something you can't control; it's something that just happens to you. And I understand that now far too well.

Because even if I approach this whole thing from a rational perspective that argues against all love, I can't help but feel my heart flutter when I think about him. Adam. About his words, since that is all he has given me, but it is enough. Enough to make me say that he is the only man who has never made me feel uncomfortable. That if I were to see him, I would be able to pick him out of a crowd of thousands.

I just got back from work, and when I make my way to the living room, I see a very large picture printed on plexiglass hanging on the wall. It's a picture of Augustine and me on our wedding day. He's standing behind me with his hands on my lower stomach and mine on his. And our heads are slightly turned to each other, letting my temple touch his chin.

I try to remove the picture from the wall, but then a hand from behind me stops mine—the large hand that belongs to Augustine.

"I know you want to, but you can't," he says.

I lower my hand and turn to him, making him take a step back. "And why is that?"

"It's a gift from my mother, and she and Marina are coming over today. It would be rude if we didn't put it on display, wouldn't you agree?"

I mean, yes, it would be rude, but I don't like seeing such a *big* picture of us every day, as if we were happily married. It's giving me the ick. Just glancing at it makes me uncomfortable.

"Fine, but can we remove it after they leave?" I ask.

"No," he says almost immediately.

"No? What do you mean, no?"

He clears his throat. "What if they visit us unexpectedly? We can't keep putting it up and removing it; it would be a hassle. Let's just leave it, and if it bothers you, don't look at it."

"Yeah, well, Goose, it might not be a big deal to you, but the picture is almost bigger than me. It's kind of hard to miss."

As I say this, I realize I saw his wedding ring around his finger when his hand was on mine, even though he's at home. And this isn't the first time. I thought he kept forgetting about it, but how does one forget something every time? They don't. He's wearing it on purpose even though he doesn't have to, and I decide to confront him about it. "Why do you keep wearing—"

The doorbell rings and Augustine leaves to open the door before I can finish my sentence. The man is quite literally saved by the bell.

Tant Samia and Marina enter the living room, and I greet them.

His mother looks at the picture while smiling brightly. "It looks so beautiful in your living room!"

I'm the worst. I was just arguing against the whole thing, and now I'm going to act like I completely love it. Despicable. "Yes! *Shokran tant*, it's very thoughtful of you." I hug her.

I make tea, and now, we're all sitting in a semicircle—Augustine and me on the couch next to each other and Marina and their mother on the armchairs.

Augustine takes a sip from his tea. "How are you, Mom?"

"I'm fine, *habibi*, just tired," she answers.

He gives Marina and her a troubled look, but she proceeds to smile at them.

I know it's common to ask someone how they are, but it somehow felt as if there was more behind his question. As if something had happened to her in the past, and he wanted to make sure that she was okay now. The question felt loaded. Or I could be completely wrong, and he just wanted to know how his mother was doing. I don't know Augustine well enough to assess what he means by saying or doing certain things.

I haven't even asked him about his father, whether he's in the picture, which I highly doubt because it's common in our culture for the father not to be involved in the lives of his wife and children. I shall present the gender roles of our culture. Almost all marriages of the generations before mine were arranged. Which means they weren't based on love but rather on everything *but* that.

The woman's family asks around about the man's family, who came to ask for their daughter's hand in marriage. Some of the criteria are whether the man has a well-paying job, whether his reputation and the one of his family are good, whether he drinks, and if he's a womanizer. And when he passes—because he's just that good at concealing things—he gets accepted to take her as his. He chooses her because he heard she's a modest woman who can take good care of his house and children. Plus, she doesn't look half bad. She accepts him because her family advised her to.

Then, they live their "separate" lives, she as the caretaker and he as the breadwinner. Which typically ends up with the woman being the only one having an actual relationship with the children since the man is busy winning bread all day. Among other things. He is probably committing infidelity while he's at it since he can, and it won't feel like cheating if he doesn't love her in the first place.

They think that this is the way to balance their household when, in reality, it has the opposite effect. It's *disbalancing* love. A child doesn't know better than to assume that their dad doesn't love them enough to want to spend time with them. And then, they grow up with the same assumption because nothing has changed for them to assume otherwise.

Which typically ends up with the man not having a proper relationship with his children. A person the children call their father but isn't exactly their dad.

It was doomed from the start. Unless ... unless you are somehow lucky and being together brings you close enough to realize each other's worth. To respect one another. Then, the love might come after. And then that love can be shared with the children. Straying away from the gender roles. Breaking stereotypes. Becoming a *lovely* household.

In my culture, marriage is something you work toward to start living your life. When a man reaches a certain age and has a job and a house, there is only one next step he can take. And since a woman is often viewed as a body to carry children, there also seems to be only one next step for her to take. And sometimes, they take that step at a very young age. Both of them take the step when there's a good chance they don't even want to in the first place. However, the cultural norms they have found themselves living with put it as though you're deviant if you never reach that part. That you will die as pathetic, worthless even, because you couldn't find someone to spend the rest of your life with. Because to them, not wanting to get married is inhumane, impossible even. What is life worth living for if you don't live it with a partner? If you don't get to reenact that part of life?

It reminds me of the speech of Jaques in *As You Like It*, written by Shakespeare:

All the world's a stage,
And all the men and women merely players;
They have their exits and their entrances;
And one man in his time plays many parts.

We are all born to be actors, entering the world from stage right, with the curtains already drawn open because the performance has been performed for a very long time now.

We take our places on center stage and start acting out our assigned roles. The role of a crying infant, the role of a young lover. Each consisting of many scenes that we play daily. We all get assigned the same roles, yet our scenes differ.

In the audience, our loved ones are seated, watching us. Applauding when we reach our milestones. Laughing when we mess up our lines tremendously. Weeping when we suffer. Supporting our play, our life. *Us.*

And then we die, exiting the world from stage left, with the curtains not closing behind us because the performance doesn't end with us. Other actors will soon follow in our footsteps, and our part will be forgotten over time, no matter how well it was performed. This will continue to happen until it doesn't anymore.

God, I love analyzing poetry.

While daydreaming about Shakespeare, I hear a very hard thud outside and rush to the window. "Oh my God, a tree has fallen on two parked cars, damaging them completely."

Marina rushes to the window as well. "That's horrible! What if someone is still sitting inside?!"

I turn on the news, and it says that the wind force is at least ten, if not higher, and that it's advised not to go outside if not necessary.

"But we have to go home," his mother says.

I face her. "No! Of course not. It's too dangerous. You can sleep here."

"Mom, I'm not letting you leave. End of discussion," Augustine tells her.

"*Tab*, where will Marina and I sleep?" she asks us.

Oh. That is a very good question. They can't exactly sleep on the couch since we have an extra bed. And they probably think we sleep together and that the extra bed serves for situations like this—which it really doesn't. I think, yet again, I've been put in a situation where I have to get a little *too* close to Augustine. But I won't, not if I have something to say about it.

Augustine looks at me briefly and then turns to his mother. "We have a guest room. It's just filled with her stuff, but you can sleep there."

"Yeah, his—" Wait. What? My room is the guest room? We didn't even discuss this. Why isn't his room the guest room?

I shuffle back to sit next to Augustine and whisper in his ear, "Why is my room the guest room?"

While looking me in the eyes, he whispers, "My bed is bigger. Do you want more room, or do you want to sleep on top of each other?"

I don't want to sleep with each other at all. And we're not going to. I have it all planned out. I'm going to sleep on the couch. So, I'm good. It was a false alarm, after all.

My eyebrows lower at what he says. I keep my voice low. "What are you talking about? We have the same bed."

"We don't actually. Mine's bigger."

"What? Since when?" I hiss.

"Since you're smaller and since I didn't think you would need all that space."

"That's unfair."

"It really isn't if we compare our sizes to one another."

He holds up his hand and gestures with his head for me to put my hand on it. Without thinking, I bring my hand to his, comparing them, and my fingertips barely reach his top knuckles. As I try to retract my hand, he slides all his fingers in the spaces between mine and wraps them around the back of my hand, holding my hand. My fingers are still pointing upward.

He then pulls me in one swift motion to him and whispers in my ear, "I will sleep on the floor if you want me to."

I lean back a little and shake my head, still too startled to retrieve my hand from his. "No ... I can sleep on the couch. It's what I was going for anyway."

He lets go of my hand himself. "You can't. They can enter the living room. We have to share my room."

"Can we sleep now then? I have to leave early for work," Marina says.

I stand up. "Of course! Follow me. I'll grab you and *Tant* some clothes."

She follows me. "Thank you, Kristina. I'm so sorry for the intrusion."

"What? Not at all! You're always welcome here."

I grab some clothes for them and hand them the necessities. They get ready for bed and are now in my room, probably sleeping.

Augustine is already in his room, ready for bed, and I'm still in the bathroom. I'm also ready for bed, but I'm not ready for *his* bed. I'm contemplating what I should do. He's not wrong about me not being able to sleep in the living room because there's no way I'll be awake before Marina is. So, she would see me in the living room, and I have no idea how I could possibly explain why I was sleeping there. Maybe I could say that we had a fight? Married people fight, right? And then they don't sleep together. Why would you want to sleep next to someone you just fought with? That doesn't make any sense. Or do married people sleep with their backs to each other when they fight? Do they? What do they do? I'm this close to searching it on Google.

But I don't want to worry his mother with us fighting, so I can't exactly do that. Maybe *I* should just sleep on the floor. Yes. I'm going to sleep on the floor. Problem solved—again.

I leave the bathroom, knock on his door, and enter his room. He's sitting up straight on his bed with one leg extended and the other bent.

"I will sleep on the floor," I say.

He gets up and walks to stand in front of me. "I'm not going to let you do that," he says. "I already told you, if you want me to sleep on the floor, I will. I don't have a problem with that. I will make myself comfortable."

I mean, I'm supposed to say yes. This is what I want, but I somehow can't bring myself to say it because I would feel guilty if I let him sleep on the cold floor.

I glance at his bed. It is significantly bigger than mine, which means we can share it if I put a lot of pillows between us. We won't be touching each other; we won't be seeing each other either. I think I can compromise that way.

It's time to quit being such a scaredy-cat, Kristina. You're not Lady.

"We can share the bed. I'll just put all the pillows I can find between us. You stay on your side; I stay on mine. Deal?" I propose to him.

He grins. "Deal."

Thus begins my journey to find pillows. I find some in the living room, on the couch and chairs, and in the attic. I enter his room again and start putting them in a straight line on the bed. Then, I rearrange some.

Augustine stands behind me with crossed arms, observing me. "Do you want some measuring tape with that?"

"Why?"

"Because you're trying to put the pillows so that we both have the same amount of bed space."

I rearrange some more pillows on the bed. "Yeah, because it needs to be fair."

"You call giving us the same amount of space fair?"

I stop replacing them and face him. "Isn't it?"

He squints his eyes at me teasingly. "No, love. Equity is fair; equality isn't."

He called me that before, first, in front of my mother, which I understood. Then at the restaurant, when we were with others, even though I was fairly certain no one could hear us. I thought I was maybe wrong, so I kind of understood. This is the third time. We are entirely alone, which makes me not understand at all. But I decide to ignore it and act like I didn't hear it. Because even though he's the one who said it, I'm the one who somehow ends up feeling embarrassed.

"Oh? You're going to teach me about equity now?" I ask.

"If you want me to, I can lecture you."

"There's no need," I say as I put the pillows in a way that leaves him almost the entire bed.

He laughs and puts them back in their original state—the equal one.

We get into his bed on our respective sides. I'm hugging a large pillow with my back to him. I can't see in which position he's lying, even when I turn my head to his side because of the many pillows separating us.

It's quiet, and I can't help but wonder about his father again. I decide to ask him about it after all. "Say ... Goose?"

"Mm-hmm?"

"I've never asked, but I was wondering, is your father ... uh—" Fuck, I should've thought this through. Isn't it rude to just ask someone if their father is dead? I know I don't like getting asked the question, and now, I'm doing exactly that. How hypocritical of me.

"Alive?" he asks.

That sure is a nicer way of putting it.

"Yeah ..."

He sighs. "He's alive, just not in *our* lives."

I understand. I already had a feeling too. And I feel for him. Because even though I don't know what it's like to have a father, I don't wish it upon anyone to have one who's alive and doesn't want to spend time with you. As if he were already dead. That's worse than having a father who's actually dead because then you assume that he would have loved spending all his time with you. Augustine's situation is so much worse.

"I understand," I say. "If you want to talk ... I'm here."

I can hear him smile by the exhale from his nose. "I appreciate it, Teen."

After a while of quietness, I assume that we both fell asleep. I know I did ...

I'm still hugging my pillow, is what I think. As soon as I open my eyes, I see reality as it is. Almost all the pillows are scattered over the floor, even the pillow I was hugging at night. I look at what I'm hugging—more like *who* I'm hugging. Augustine fucking Elias.

My head is resting on the left side of his chest, and my hand is on the right. I have also managed to put one of my legs, bent, on his. And his left arm is wrapped around my waist, holding it.

How the fuck did this happen? No.

I jump away, and it wakes him up.

He rubs his face with his hands and looks at me with his eyes barely open, confused. "Good morning?" he says in a very deep, sleepy voice.

"Not good. Bad morning!"

He sits up straight. "And why is that?"

"Do you see the pillows? Do you see where you woke up? I woke up there too. We broke our deal."

He nods at me, indicating that he heard me. "We didn't exactly break our deal. No one got on the other person's side. We ended up where the pillows were. Therefore, deal unbroken. All good."

"Not good enough!" I get out of his bed and leave his room.

I enter the bathroom and sit on the toilet with the toilet seat down. I'm so glad he didn't see us wrapped around each other. That would have been way too awkward. It sure as hell startled me.

But I wonder about the pillows. There is no way we made all of them fall on the floor with our movements alone, even though I know I move a lot. It just seems impossible.

How did they *all* end up there?

CHAPTER FIFTEEN

Eve: Adam. Are you okay?

Adam: Eve, yes. Why do you ask?

Eve: You've just seemed distant lately. I wanted to check up on you.

Adam: I'm sorry. I have a lot on my mind.

Eve: Do you want to talk about it?

And I do too. You. I have all of you on my mind, and with each passing day, I find it harder and harder to ignore. I want to see you. I want to hear your voice. I want to have the conversations we used to have but in real life. You are comfort to me. I don't want to lose that, but it feels like I can't do anything to prevent it from happening. Like I have no control over it.

I want what they have.

I'm sitting on a terrace with Alex and Senait. Even though I haven't known Senait that long, I feel like we clicked the minute we met, and I'm so grateful that I get to consider her a friend too.

They're sitting next to each other, and I'm sitting across from them. I can't help but smile at them; they're adorable together.

"Say, Senait, why don't you come to our church?" I ask.

Alex turns to her, a little too excited. "Please do! There are lots of Eritreans and Ethiopians who go to our church. Even though they don't understand the service completely, they can feel it in their hearts. And I can feel you in mine."

She gently pushes Alex away and laughs. "You just want to see me more than you already do."

"Yes, and I'm not ashamed of it."

"I mean, I can come by, but not permanently, since I have duties at my own church," Senait says. "By the way, Kristina, how has marriage been treating you?"

"It's everything I hoped it would be." And by that, I mean freedom, freedom, and more freedom. I love it.

Now that I think about it, I've felt so much inner peace since I got married,. I have the safe haven I longed for. I've found a routine that works for me. I can leave the house without anyone interrogating me about it—except when it's at night because, somehow, Augustine interrogates me then. But he never refuses me. He either accompanies me or lets me go after I practically demand he get out of my way.

I have dates with myself, silly things like eating out or going to the cinema to watch a movie I know no one wants to watch. But I don't let that stop me from going because why would I? I love kids movies, and I'm not ashamed to show it to the world.

I have gone to a spa by myself, which I highly recommend everyone does. And once I have the time, I'm going to take myself on vacation. Alone. That's my biggest dream that has yet to be achieved, but I can do it, and that's what matters. Although I wish I could take a specific someone with me—Adam. I would love to spend time with him on vacation. This is my newest dream.

"Have you ever gone on vacation together?" I ask them.

"No, but since we're both girls and our parents think we're best friends, we can actually go," Alex says.

Senait nods. "Yeah, but it still sucks because I want it to be known that she's my girlfriend, but telling my parents might cause them to drop dead from shock. I don't exactly want that happening."

"So, you both are allowed to go on vacation with people other than your family or husband?" I ask.

"We both are. I don't know what it is, Kris, but your mother is a different type of Egyptian. It's as if she brought not only the language with her but also the traditional culture that even Egyptians living in Egypt don't follow anymore. I'm glad you found love and moved out," Alex tells me.

I bite the inside of my cheek. "And I'm glad you guys can go, but ... have you ever thought about the future?"

Senait gives Alex a look and then turns to me. "This might sound crazy, but we actually discussed it once and said that we should both marry some random dudes, maybe even a gay couple who has the same issues, and then we can all leave our houses and just live with each other. We know it sounds crazy, don't judge us. But it's the only solution we have come up with for our situation."

I laugh nervously. Almost *too* nervously. It's not crazy at all. Why? Because that's exactly what I did. And them saying this makes me question whether they mean it or if they are telling me that they know about my crimes and that it's time for me to fess up about them. It's too accurate to be a coincidence. Too suspicious. But I won't trap myself by admitting the truth. Besides, what if everyone is as insane as me, and we all want to escape our houses? It is a possibility. Who doesn't want to live their life for themselves? "That's crazy! But a crazy good plan as well!"

"Right? It certainly is an option." She caresses Alex's cheek with her temple. "I would do anything for her."

Alex looks around her like crazy. "We are in the clear!" She gives a peck on Senait's lips and rests her head on her shoulder.

I envy them. They don't give up on what they want, even though there are many reasons to. They know that their families will never accept them as they are, yet instead of letting go, like people expect them to because it's the "easy" thing to do, they keep fighting for each other even if their battles are only going to keep getting harder.

It's like wanting to live according to your parents' wishes but also want to stay true to yourself. You can decide not to choose, even when you feel like you're being forced to make a choice.

Because a lot of people who experience their situation leave the religion and culture altogether and cut ties with their parents. Some are even bullied away because they're told by others that they can't be queer and believe in God.

Yeah, well, I say, what a bunch of fucking hypocrites. You can't lie, gossip, judge, curse, cheat, use violence, get drunk, have sex before marriage, watch porn, and believe in God. Yet here they are, doing exactly that on a daily basis. People always make sure that they're in the clear, *no matter what.*

Nevertheless, they try to stay true to themselves, even with all the shit they have to deal with that wants to get in the way of that. They decide not to let go of the things that reject them because those still feel part of them. And they never do to those what those do to them. They don't judge the people who judge them; they ignore it. And to even forgive those people for not knowing any better than to blindly follow rules without respecting others.

To me, that's character. Traits not every person has the honor of possessing. But they do, and all I can do is envy them for it.

After a while, Senait and Alex leave together, and I do too. I buy some groceries and am now finding myself in a shop where they sell fruit-themed items. And since I'm the one who's on strawberry duty, I will not leave this store before I have found something strawberry-related that is one hundred percent unnecessary to have. Maybe even two things. Why not annoy Augustine twice?

More like annoy him five times. I've gathered a jewelry set, lamp, kitchen timer, travel bottle, and shower curtain, all filled with strawberry patterns. It's perfect. I'm buying them.

On my way home, I can't help but think about confessing one's love to another. It somehow always goes like this: one person finds themselves madly in love with another. They tell their friend about it; they're basically confessing their love to their friend, and they do it so easily. It's almost as if they're giving this beautifully prepared speech about the one they love; they explain when they fell in love and why; they explain why they love the person even more for those reasons, and then they explain how much they want that person to become theirs and how they can't imagine their life without the person in it. And then their friend smiles because it's so genuine, so beautifully so, and asks them whether they told the person it's meant for. And almost always, the answer to that question is *no*.

The most beautiful confessions rarely reach the people they're meant for.

Why? If the person you love heard that same confession—if they didn't love you already—they would probably fall in love with you on the spot.

But they don't confess because they're afraid. Afraid that the love is unrequited. Afraid of being rejected. So, they decide it's better not to know, to linger in this thing called ignorance. Shielding themselves with it.

But aren't you limiting yourself that way? What if the love is requited? Then you get to share your life with that person.

Not knowing might be protection, but I would rather know, be rejected, and try to move on or maybe even have the off chance at being happy. Maybe not knowing isn't always better than knowing. Maybe ignorance isn't bliss after all.

I arrive home and see Augustine sitting on the couch.

"I come bearing gifts," I say as I take out all the strawberry-themed items from the plastic bags and put them on the bar.

He giggles. "You know this isn't what I meant when I said strawberry duty, right?"

I give him a surprised look. "You didn't?"

He walks to the kitchen counter, grabs a vase with flowers, and holds out his hands for me to take it. "Here, for you."

This isn't the first time he's given me flowers in a vase like this. He has been doing this ever since we got married. Every few days, he buys a new bouquet of flowers and puts it in a vase, only for him to hand me the vase and for me to put it down again. And he always gives me a different type of flowers. I've seen white acacia flowers, bellflowers, gardenias, orange blossoms, and skeleton flowers.

I don't know much about flowers, but apparently, he does. I know their names because of the tags he leaves on them.

Now, he's giving me a bouquet of ... clovenlip toadflax flowers.

I take the vase from him and put it on the bar. "If they're for the house, why do you always give them to me first?"

"I never said they're for the house."

"What?"

His phone rings, and he leaves to take the call.

If they aren't for the house, then what are they for?

He comes back and goes to the kitchen to put on an apron.

"What would you like to eat today?" he asks, rolling up his sleeves.

"What can you make?"

"I can make anything you desire. You name it, I make it."

It's incredible living with someone who can cook. I can cook, but I wouldn't say that Gordon Ramsay would tell me I did a good job. He would probably make me cry because I did a very poor job at a probably very simple dish. Let's just say I can cook to survive, not to work in a private restaurant and serve dishes to royalty. I would probably end up giving food poisoning to the whole monarchy. Okay, who am I kidding right now? I can't cook to save my life.

"Hmm ... then, can you make phyllo meat pie?" I ask.

"You mean, goulash? Consider it done."

Oh my God. How can he even make that? Goulash is an Egyptian dish, a savory pie filled with beef that lies between layers and layers of crispy phyllo pastry dough. I consider it to be macarona bechamel's long-lost twin because they look alike and always end up being served together.

"I'll help you." I walk around the bar to put on an apron as well. "Let me cut everything that needs to be cut."

He points at the box with onions. I grab a few and start cutting them.

He stops gathering the ingredients and looks at my hand holding the knife. I stop cutting. He faces me and immediately turns away to grab a pan.

I break the awkward silence that has taken over the room. "How did you learn to cook Egyptian dishes?"

"I used to watch my mom when she was cooking, and I wrote all the recipes down in a journal. Then, I ended up being the one to cook almost every day, so I got better at it. She still helped, of course."

My eyes are burning and barely open. All I see is a blurry Augustine. "That's so sweet," I say, sniffling.

"I didn't pick you to be the sentimental type, Teen." He washes his hands and dries them off by rubbing them on his apron. He then walks over to me and wipes my tears with his thumbs from my eyes and cheeks.

"You not-picked right, Goose. How are you not crying right now?"

"Tolerance, love."

Fourth strike. I should say something about it. But I can't seem to do so because it's embarrassing. I'm going to keep ignoring it; maybe it'll eventually go away if I do.

After a while, we finish preparing. Or more like he finishes preparing, since I was standing there like a child, learning how to make the dish. We've put it in the oven, and now we wait.

I fill the new strawberry bottle with water and take it with me to sit on the couch. As I'm drinking, I see Augustine gazing at me—more specifically, at my hands. He always looks at them, and I don't understand why. What's so special about my hands anyway?

I frown at him. "What are you looking at?"

"You," he says, walking toward me.

His saying that startles me. The lid of the bottle falls on the floor.

"Why?" I ask as I bow down to grab it.

But he beats me to it and grabs it by kneeling on one leg between my legs, like he's going to propose.

Suddenly, the atmosphere completely changes because now we find ourselves staring at each other, not saying a word.

He extends his arm hesitantly and grabs a lock of my hair. He slowly lets it slide between his fingers until it falls back against my chest. I don't move an inch.

He then extends the leg he's resting on, bringing our faces to the same level.

And finally, he leans his body into mine, bringing his face closer to mine as his eyes hold mine hostage.

He brings his thumb to my lips and wipes off the gloss, wiping it all off in one hasty motion.

His face is only inches away from mine now, and he averts his gaze from my eyes to my lips. And he leans into me even more, enough for me to hear the sound of his shallow breathing.

He's nervous.

Even though my heart is beats away from breaking out of my chest, I don't dare move. To even tremble. I'm just observing what he's doing because I'm too stunned to say or do anything back. I don't even understand what's happening right now.

All I manage to do is close my eyes, and I squeeze them as hard as possible to *stay* closed.

I can feel his breath against my lips—that's how close he is right now. His lips aren't touching mine, but it feels as if they are. As if they'd already been put on mine. I don't even know if I hallucinate it, but I feel something grazing my lips for a split second. *His.*

Only the warm sensations of his exhale touch me, and the coldness of him abruptly pulling himself away from me follows. Then, the fast-paced taps of his footsteps reach me.

I open my eyes. He's leaving the house because the thud of the front door getting shut reaches me next. Gone is the man with the lid of the bottle I'm holding.

Did he just ... try to kiss me? But for what possible reason? I thought we had agreed to be friends-ish because it was only logical to do so. Because ignoring each other was harder than we'd thought, and being friendly with each other would still mean we get to live our separate lives. But him doing this? It just complicates things even further. And it makes me doubt his intentions with me again. But it also makes me doubt my own body again because why did it feel ... *not bad*?

God, since when do so-called friends try to kiss you?

CHAPTER SIXTEEN

Eve: Adam. I have been thinking a lot ... about you. And I can't keep it to myself anymore. I want to share it with you. We have been talking to each other for a long time, and I have always appreciated every moment I spent talking with you since the very beginning. I would even say that I considered you to be my friend for the longest time. But that changed. I wonder what you look like, what your voice sounds like, and who you are as a person. And that is because I have developed feelings for you ...

Adam: Eve, I have always thought of you as a wonderful person, and I cherish our conversations deeply. Except I don't feel the same way about you. I have feelings for someone else. I apologize, Eve ...

Eve: There's no need to apologize. I understand. Thank you for your honesty. And I hope it works out between you and her.

Adam: Thank you. I appreciate it.

Eve: Can we keep talking to each other and stay friends though?

Adam: Yes, absolutely. I would like that.

I have been rejected. Getting rejected is hard, but not having him in my life would have been even harder. So, I'm glad I asked to stay friends even though I was embarrassed to do so.

Ostracism means ignoring and excluding individuals from a group, often without an explicit declaration as to why. Rejection is an explicit declaration that an individual is not wanted. For example, Adam's reason for not wanting me is he wants someone else.

When we experience either ostracism or rejection, we find ourselves in a temporary state of abject misery. Our blood pressure increases, and our dorsal anterior cingulate cortex—a region in our brain—becomes more active. This region is also active when we experience physical pain.

With good reason. Being excluded or ignored signals as a threat, which causes a reaction in the form of pain or distress to survive. Because to belong is a fundamental need for safety, procreation, and mental health. And being excluded threatens that need directly. If we didn't feel the pain that came along with being excluded, we would ultimately end up dead. Exactly like how we have reflexes when we touch something hot, without them and without pain, humans would not survive.

That's why evolutionary mechanisms like immediate pain are necessary. Being excluded also leads to sadness. And it also directly influences our self-worth.

People are social animals because of evolution. We survive in groups. So, sometimes, the feeling of wanting to belong gets so intense that people can't distinguish between good and bad anymore, resulting in them finding any group to be a part of, whether it be a cult or even a terrorist organization.

After the reflexive phase, the reflective phase follows, determining how you will react to being rejected. It all boils down to four ways of reacting: tend-and-befriend, fight, freeze, or flight.

Some try again because they don't want to give up on the group or person. They try to act in a way to get accepted anyway. Some might display antisocial or even aggressive behavior; they get hostile. Some are too stunned to react and display catatonic behavior. And then we have the people who try to escape the situation altogether. Escape, get distracted.

And that's exactly how I react to being rejected. I distract myself. Usually, I do so with alcohol, numbing the pain with it. But I'm sick of alcohol. So, I will go to the second-best thing. The man next door.

He made me feel something when I sat on his lap and maybe even when he tried to kiss me. I don't know what it was, but I need to find out and test my hypotheses to do so.

When I was sitting on his lap, I thought I got aroused because of the alcohol and not him—the suspension bridge effect. I was dealing with a confounder. But since I'm sober as a judge, which means I'm controlling for confounding, it's time to judge whether there's a correlation between my being aroused and Augustine Elias. Or rather, even further than correlation, I'm looking for causation.

The null hypothesis being that Augustine Elias's body does not cause Kristina Armanious to get aroused.

The alternative hypothesis being that Augustine Elias's body does, in fact, cause Kristina Armanious to get aroused.

Now, it's time to do my research by doing an experiment. It's time for me to gather some data.

It will probably be very awkward. We haven't really talked since the whole almost-kissing incident because he has been avoiding me for a change. But I will use that incident to my advantage to persuade him.

I look at myself in the mirror. My hair is in a messy bun, and I'm only wearing an oversized T-shirt, covering up my scars. I inhale and exhale deeply and leave my room to knock on his door.

"Mm-hmm?" he says.

I open the door and see him sitting at his desk, wearing his glasses and looking kind of blue, guilty even. As if he has the need to comfort more than I have the need to be comforted. He rolls away from his desk and turns to face me. Scanning me. He forms fists while his arms are dangling beside him because the chair he's sitting on has no armrests.

How does one start? I don't even know what I want. I only know that I want something and that he can give it to me. "I need something from you."

He puts his hands in each other on his lap. "What do you need?"

I take cautious steps toward him. "I need you to go back on your word." And I now stand in front of his legs.

"My word?" he asks with a throaty voice.

"Yes, the one where you stated you have no desire to touch me. I need you to go back on that one."

His eyes ... he looks awestruck, as if he isn't sure whether I said that or if he's hallucinating that I did.

"Wh-what are you saying right now?" he asks.

I slowly put my hand on his shoulder. "Can you create desire?"

He looks away, facing the ground. "You don't know what you're saying. You're drunk—"

"I have never been soberer," I say while holding his shoulder now.

"Stop. Please."

"You don't want to? Is that why you kissed me?" I ask.

He looks up again, alarmed. "I didn't. I left."

"But you did—when you carried me when I was asleep."

He doesn't say anything. He looks at me as if he feels embarrassed, ashamed even, that I caught him and know what he did.

"You have done something you wanted; it's time to return the favor," I plead.

"No. You don't want this. You will come to regret it and come to hate me."

"I do. And I already hate you, remember?"

"Then I don't want you to hate me even more. So, please, just stop. *Please*," he begs me, trying to remove my hand from his shoulder.

I exhale. "Listen, even if you're not up for it at all, can you at least try to—"

Before I can finish saying that, he grabs the wrist of my hand that's holding his shoulder and pulls me into him, which makes me land on him. He then adjusts me with his hand on my lower back, pushing me to his front until I'm sitting on his crotch, straddling him.

He has both his hands on my waist now, holding me there. "Do you feel that?" he says in a thick voice.

He's stopped resisting me. Since I'm only wearing underwear underneath the T-shirt, I feel it all too well, as if I were not wearing anything. He is so hard; it somehow excites me that I'm the reason.

I put my hands around his neck. "I do."

"I wanted you the second you walked through that door. Don't assume shit when you know nothing," he grits out.

"Show me what you want."

He takes off his glasses and shifts his eyes to my lips. "If we do this, I won't be able to stop. Do you understand what that means?"

"Good. I don't want you to."

He holds the back of my head, already bringing us closer to each other. "Even if you beg me to."

I answer him by softly pressing my lips against his. I lean back an inch to look him in his eyes, and then I go in for another taste of his lips, tilting my head and parting mine to do so while holding his cheek. His lips are delicate against mine, and warm. *And sweet.*

As we're kissing, he removes my hair tie from my hair, making all my hair fall against my back. He then brings it to his wrist, wearing it.

He's still holding the back of my head with one hand, and he puts the hand that was on my waist on my cheek, holding me tightly, as if I might disappear if he doesn't.

He slowly brings his tongue against mine and touches it. Our lips are gliding against each other as we keep going back to tilt our heads and forth to lean back into each other.

So deep into kissing one another.

Then, he places his hands on my behind, stands up, and lifts me along with him. Still kissing me, laying me down on his bed.

He pulls himself off of me and holds the hem of my T-shirt with two fingers, rubbing his thumb against it. "I want this anywhere but on your body."

No. The scars. I'm not wearing anything underneath. If I take this off, everything will be shown. *All* of me will be visible.

"There is no need for that since it'll be quick," I tell him.

"Quick? It won't be a quick fuck. That won't be enough to satisfy me, love," he says. "I need to feel all of your skin against mine." He's still rubbing the hem of my T-shirt.

I nod slowly, and he begins removing my T-shirt. I'm sitting on his bed in only a black lace thong. Both my chest and scars are now visible to him. He looks at my chest for a brief moment, but as soon as he sees my scars, he stops looking at the upper half of me and directs all his attention to them. I feel uncomfortable and uneasy, so I immediately put my hands on them, covering my inner thighs.

He brings both his hands to mine. "Don't hide from me, please. It saddens me you feel the need to."

I look at his hands on mine, and he continues, "The only way they define you is how strong you were when the weight was only getting heavier. You are wholly and thoroughly perfect."

He slowly removes my hands and proceeds to give my scars small kisses. Taking his time in doing so, giving every scar his undivided attention. Making even that part of me feel loved by someone.

If only you knew they weren't made by my own volition … but thank you for paying attention to all of me. Even them.

After a short while, he makes his way up, kissing my groin, my abdomen, and then he stops to look at the image on my right ribs.

After my other tattoo—the one he will see any second now—I wanted to put something on my body that wasn't in the spirit of the pain but rather one of healing.

I wanted to be confident because with confidence comes assertiveness—the trait I most desired. But I also wanted something to represent everything that was me, everything I wanted to become and be. I combined everything and turned it into one simple black-inked scenery.

It shows a summer day at the beach with only more freedom beyond the horizon. The sun god Ra of ancient Egypt is sailing on the horizon, only to descend over it at sunset since he's also perceived as the physical sun itself. Which is the center, the self, and the planets orbit around it, representing things like growth and courage. It's a force to be reckoned with, that goes its way. An assured force. It also represents happiness, peace, optimism, and always looking on the bright side.

Since I wasn't shining enough, I made it shine by adding wavelengths around the sun. Not any wavelength, but the long wavelength of five hundred eighty nanometers, which we call yellow. I wouldn't say I ever disliked physics since it and psychology happened to be good friends. The wavelength of yellow stimulates the brain; some might consider that to be a positive thing, while others find the mere sight of it obnoxious. It's not one way or the other; it's complex. As am I.

But I didn't want to be alone on that beach. I didn't exactly want to be with someone either. So, I chose the next best thing—animals. Animals that fit in the little scene I created—a lionfish, a bluebird, and a butterfly.

The lionfish is on the coast, representing letting go of negativities and freeing myself of pain. To be able to swim in the depths of the sea. The bluebird represents the blue of my father's eyes, who's with me in spirit. Reminding me to take control, not let anyone steal away my happiness, and embrace change. Which introduces the butterfly, symbolizing rebirth and the transformation from a colorless larva to a colorful butterfly. Both the bluebird and butterfly have their wings spread across the vast ocean with no destination in mind, solely to keep flying.

Since it was there to stay, it had to be more than meaningful. But I probably went a little overboard with the symbolism. I don't regret it though, not one bit, because, for the past years, it reminded me every day of who I am and want to be. Every time I shower or change my clothes, it is there. To remind me.

He brings his index finger to my left nipple, touches it, and licks his lips. I have a piercing there.

I'm very insecure about my breasts since it seems they forgot to grow along with me as I got older. But he doesn't seem to mind their size.

Then he brings his lips to it and starts kissing my nipple and licking it. I let out a soft sound.

He leans back, rests on his knees, and takes off his T-shirt by grabbing the back and pulling it over his head. And then I see it. I already knew he was muscular; I knew because of the tight button-up shirts he always wears, showing off his arms. But seeing it catches me off guard. His chest and stomach muscles are well-defined, and his V-line is even more defined.

And not only that, but he also has tattoos. I already knew he had them, I just didn't know what they were. A warning would have been nice. On his left chest, his mother's name—*Samia Elias*—is written in Arabic. On his left upper arm is a big cross. On the right side of his stomach is a phoenix with its wings spread and covered in fire. It's so detailed; that must have taken hours to tattoo. It makes him ten times more attractive, and it somehow makes me a hundred times hornier.

But I also see something else on his lower abdomen. A scar shaped like a crown.

I bring my fingers to it and trace over it. "Who did this to you?"

"A stranger."

"How did it happen?"

"There was a man hitting on a woman who clearly wasn't interested, uncomfortable even. He thought I wanted to steal her away from him when I was actually helping her get rid of him. Then, he smashed the bottle he had been drinking from and stabbed me with it."

I give him a troubled look. "Drunkards are the worst."

He brings his hand to my face. "Don't give me that look," he says. "It's my crown. I'm a king."

I laugh; he's funny.

He smiles and starts to draw a crown on my abdomen with his fingertips. "Will you be my queen?"

"Just for tonight," I say.

"I'll take it." He slides his hand into my underwear and starts stroking me with his finger, carefully and gradually increasing the tempo.

And it feels ... *so good*. I can feel it all the way in my brain. Dopamine is being released. It's the first time I'm experiencing this, and I love it. Is this what true pleasure feels like? I feel like levitating to God knows where.

Heaven.

He then holds the elastic of my underwear with his other hand, rubbing it with his thumb, like he did with my T-shirt. "May I take this off? Please?" he says in a hoarse voice.

I pant a little. "You may."

He brings both his hands to the elastic and takes off my thong for me. He looks at it for a moment, clenches it in his hand, and throws it on the ground.

Then he grabs both my legs and places them on his shoulders. He looks at my center—or rather, at the spaces between my outer lips and thighs.

"*Love hurts*?" he asks.

That's my other tattoo, the one no one has ever seen besides the tattoo artist. And now Augustine. I have the word *love* in cursive on the right side of my opening and the word *hurts* in bold with the letter *t* shaped like a red pocketknife and blood dripping off of it on the left side.

Love has hurt me both emotionally and physically. Since the line between pain and pleasure was always absent to me, I thought the act of making love must hurt too. And even more so. When a man makes love to a woman, he pins her down with all his weight; he suffocates her in a way. He then pushes something inside of her and takes it out again. Over and over and over again, as if being stabbed repeatedly, and when done roughly, the woman bleeds.

Love, first love, falling in love, being in love, unrequited love, making love—it all hurts *tremendously*.

He leans in, grabs my waist, pulling me toward him while my legs are resting on his shoulders, and brings his face to my center, wetting it, *teasing me*.

And ... oh. It feels so hot. The blood that is supposed to circulate through my entire body is only circulating down there. My toes curl, and I grab his hair for support.

He leans back to look at me and grasps my wrists with one hand, bringing them above my head. "Keep them there, love. I'm going to make you feel so good."

I obey because I want to feel good. I want to reach the stars while lying here, getting eaten out by him.

He dips his tongue inside of me, making me whimper. Not one whimper, an elongated whimper, because my body is getting washed in pleasure. Every inch of it is soaked in it.

He looks up at me. "Keep telling me how good I make you feel."

My moans get louder, and I arch my back because he's doing things I can't even describe at this point—only my face can. I want more. I want more of him. I *need* him to give me even more.

He groans. "You're so wet; it's driving me fucking insane."

He removes my legs from his shoulders and places me on my side. Then, he gets up from the bed, and from behind me, I can hear him taking off his pants and … fondling himself. My back is turned to him, so I can't see him, but I can hear it, hear him too. Moaning. And the sound of it turns me on even more. I didn't know that the sound of someone experiencing pleasure could have this kind of effect on me. It's ridiculous how much it makes me want him.

I feel his touch again. He's lying behind me, spooning me, until he places one of my legs over his. He wraps his arm around my waist, putting his middle finger inside of me, and while moving it, he lets the end of his palm stimulate my clitoris, sliding back and forth against it. His other arm wraps around me, his hand cupping my breast, rubbing it. With his hands on and in my body, he keeps pulling me into him, making my entire behind touch his front. His chest is against my bare back, and his cock—which feels even harder now—is nestled between my cheeks. He's kissing and sucking on my neck, slowly making his way to my earlobe, nibbling on it.

And I feel all of it so intensely; I don't even know what to focus on anymore.

My whole body is being stimulated, and I feel so fucking complete. Like I needed this, like I *longed* for this. He has me body and soul; at this very moment, I'm his for the taking.

"You once said that your body doesn't like me. How does your body like me now?" he asks, pushing a second finger inside me.

All I can do is gasp because with each passing second, I'm experiencing things I never knew were possible. To feel on fire and to savor every burn.

His voice turns husky. "Answer me in words."

"It feels—" I moan the words. "So fucking good."

"It will feel even better." He searches for my lips and kisses me while holding me in the same position.

He's pleasuring all kinds of my body parts. My heart can't keep up.

He then brings me to lie on my back again and rests on his knees between my legs. It's the first time I see him completely naked. And all I can do is be shocked to my core. I even start sweating because I had assumed he was big, and just now, it felt big, but what I'm seeing now is way too much. That will never fucking work.

I panic. "I-I'm still a virgin!"

"I thought you wanted freedom?" he says, holding *it*.

"I thought so too, tried it even, but I couldn't exactly feel anything ..."

With his other hand, he holds my chin up with his index finger and thumb for me to face him. "What about now? Do you feel anything now?"

I stutter, "I-I do. A lot."

He chuckles. "It's because you're attracted to me, like polar opposite sides of a magnet."

I raise my eyebrow at him. "I'm not though? If you mean we're opposites, then, yes, you're correct. It just so happens to be true in physics, but opposites don't attract in psychology, and that's my field."

He ignores it. "You are." And he gives a peck on my temple. "But I won't force you to admit it now."

He leans into me, causing me to lean back and lie down, and he hovers above me.

"Let me be inside of you and fuck you. I beg you," he begs.

I want him to because all I have felt up until now is pleasure and even things beyond. And he has got to be experienced because he seems to know exactly what he's doing. But somehow, the size of his cock is making my hen chicken out.

"That"—I point at it, almost as if I were disappointed—"will never fucking fit."

"That"—he points at mine—"will welcome me like I was custom built to be inside of it," he says. "It will fit perfectly."

He leans into me again, with one hand holding my head and the other still holding himself. "I will be gentle, love."

He rests his forehead against mine and slowly slides his cock inside of me, but not all of it. The second he does, we both gasp against each other's mouths while maintaining eye contact. He pulls out a little and slides half of it inside me again. He repeats that a couple of times with the hand that was holding himself now resting on my hip to support his movements.

And I ... don't feel pain. Instead, I want to shove all of him inside of me myself. It feels *celestial*, and I want to feel even more. I want to feel divine. I can feel my heart pulsating in my center—hard. As if it's trying to keep up with pumping all my blood to it.

I fucking knew it. I'm too aroused to think about hypotheses right now. I only know that both I and the null hypothesis have been rejected. But that all of me and the alternative hypothesis are now being accepted—by him. Being researched even further. And I'm fairly certain that I'm not making a type I error. I can feel it in my ... insides. Oh God.

"Can I keep going?" he asks me.

And I want to scream yes—until I sense it grow inside of me, even bigger than it already is.

"M-make that stop. I can't handle that!"

He grins. "I can't, love. This is my way of showing you how I've longed for this. Only you have this effect on me. May I show you more?" he asks, putting his hand on my lower stomach, feeling me, feeling himself inside of me.

I exhale—hard. I want to see it all.

"Yes." I bite back a whimper. "Please."

He thrusts more of him inside in one go, making me moan uncontrollably. Not because of pain but because I feel so whole, *full*. I don't want him to pull out. Ever. But he does and immediately fills the void again by gliding inside of me, harder than before, even better. The thrusts become harder, and I become hotter.

"You're so fucking tight," he whispers with a raspy voice.

Still inside of me, he leans back to sit and pulls me with him, making me sit on him and support myself with my lower legs. I'm straddling him again, only this time, without any clothes between us. This time, without even oxygen between us.

He lies down as I'm sitting on him. "I want you to ride me."

All the heat travels to my face because now, he gets to see me from up close, all my insecurities along with it. I automatically put my hand on my chest to cover it, but he grabs it and the other and places them on his chest, holding them there. Watching me.

I begin shifting my hips back and forth, finding a rhythm that makes us feel good. Because as I'm riding him, he groans, closes his eyes, and holds on to my hands tightly.

And I understand why. I close my eyes and almost immediately feel everything more intensely. With every motion I make, I feel myself reaching climax.

He suddenly sits up and lets his forehead touch mine again, his eyes piercing into mine. Then he holds my hips and pushes himself even deeper, making his eyebrows furrow and his eyes almost roll back. And mine too.

He then places one hand on my cheek, cupping it, as if he needs all of my attention—and I give him exactly that. "Kristina."

That immediately sends shivers rushing down my spine because it's the first time he has ever called me by my first name. The first time I've heard it in that familiar, gruff voice.

His throat bobs, and he almost gulps down his words. "Call me by my name."

"Goose," I breathe out.

"No. Not my nickname. My real name. I won't let it go," he says, putting force into cupping my cheek.

I have said his name before, multiple times even. But I never did it to address him or in front of him when talking to others. It makes me feel awkward to say it now. "Aug-Augustine."

He breathes out, moves his hand to hold my chin, and closes his eyes. "Once more."

"Augustinus," I repeat quietly.

A beam takes over his face, as if he's thankful. "I have found you—at last," he says, cupping my cheek again.

He brings his lips to mine and starts kissing me, but not as gently as before. Rougher—much rougher—and I adore it. He tenderly bites my lower lip and continues to make love to my lips with his.

He then places his lips on my neck and starts kissing it, sucking on it again, and it makes me feel like I'm about to finish because, as he's doing that, he's also moving me with his hands on my hips. Guiding me. Making me ride him. Making him lose control. Going faster.

He has become a beast that finally lost its leash. I don't recognize him anymore. The gentleman I thought I knew is gone. *Forever.*

"Fuck," he huffs. "I need to pull out. I didn't use a condom. I should've fucking grabbed one."

Wait, why does he even have condoms at home in the first place? I mean, I don't care. I'm in no state to think right now. Because as he's even deeper inside of me, I feel myself reaching something. I feel like my soul is overflowing with God knows what and that I'm even wetter than I already was. And—

Oh. Fuck.

I came.

I had a fucking orgasm.

My eyes widen.

"I can feel it. You came on me. I fucking love that," he says, biting his lower lip. Then he grunts. "I want to come inside of you, and it's taking everything in me to resist."

I wrap my shaking arms around his neck. "Then don't. I want you to come inside of me."

He shakes his head fast, as if shaking off my words, and closes his eyes. "Fuck, don't say things like that. It turns me on, more than I already am."

Now, I wrap my still-shaking legs around him and hold them there. Unable for him to pull out of me.

He gives me a very unsettled look.

"I'm on birth control, so you can lose your control." I put on a smirk. "Come, Augustine."

And before I know it, he moans in my ear and comes, flooding all my insides with it. Dripping out of me.

Sex really is ... fucking *awesome*. Even more, it's extraordinary, addictive, and awe-inspiring. I can't believe I've wasted years of not having sex, of missing this gratification. Such a fucking shame.

I try to get off him, but he holds me in place with trembling hands, still inside me.

"Where do you think you're off to?" he asks.

I yawn and stretch my arms. "To sleep."

He chuckles. "One round would never satisfy me, love. I need at least three more rounds, and that is me going easy on you."

My jaw almost hits the floor. Three rounds? Who does this man think he is, the Hulk?

But not soon after, I feel his cock growing inside me again, becoming harder.

He sees that I'm feeling it. "See? Not completely satisfied yet."

And I somehow don't mind. "Fine. Then, let me satisfy *you* completely."

I get off him and kneel on the edge of the bed. He gets off it and stands in front of me.

He looks down at me. "Touch it."

I bring my hand to his twitching cock and start stroking it. I keep pulling it down to the base and up again, making him whimper.

Then, I bring the tip to my mouth, giving it soft kisses. Giving it small licks as I hold it, teasing him. I do so while looking up at him. Wanting him to beg for more.

He puts his hand on my head. "I want to be sucked dry by you."

Tis but the work of a moment, Augustine.

I lick the shaft from the base to the tip, and then I put it and more of his cock inside my mouth. Sucking on it and tasting all of it. I keep putting it inside my mouth and take only about half of it out. Over and over. And it makes him groan, mutter things under his breath, and tighten his grip on my head. God, that's hot. I keep his tip between my lips and wet the underside with my tongue. It's so thick.

He comes on my face, and I lick away what remains on my lips.

He smirks and wipes it off. "The only way I want liquid flowing down your face is when it's covered in my cum. This is the only way I want to see your face ruined."

Then he holds my face, brings me to him, and tries to kiss me.

I jolt back. "I just sucked you off?"

"And I loved every fucking second of it? Let me show you how grateful I am." He leans in and kisses me so passionately.

When I used to give head, gratitude was expressed with cigarette burns, but now, everything is different. Everything I thought I knew about sex has been debunked by this man right here. The man who's laying me down again and is now on top of me, still feeling me up and lustfully kissing me. As if he can't get enough and doesn't want to.

As if he's set on savoring every inch of my skin.

I open my eyes. And I know far too well where I am. In Augustine's bed. Waking up next to him. Even though he has cleaned our fluids from my body, I have no choice but to let what happened yesterday dawn on me. And it makes me feel uneasy because now that I'm awake and not high on pain or arousal, my rationale is starting to take over my thought process. And it disagrees *completely* with what I did yesterday.

I tiptoe around his room, trying to find any of my clothes and having no luck. So I decide to make a run for it. As I try to open his door without making any noise, a deep morning voice reaches my ears, startling me.

"Leaving so soon, love?" he asks.

I turn my head to him and see him lying on his side, supporting his head with his fist against his cheek. And holding out my T-shirt to me.

I practically jump to him, grab the T-shirt, and put it on.

"Where is my underwear?" I ask.

Without even looking around for it, he shrugs his shoulders.

I don't want to leave it here, but I don't want to stay any longer either. I will look for it later—when he *isn't* here.

I nod, turn around, and leave his room. I enter mine and close the door behind me.

He knocks on my door. "We have to talk about it."

"Oh, we will, definitely!" I shout as I find myself new underwear and wear a tracksuit.

I open my window and start climbing out of it—more like falling out of it, scraping my elbows. *Fuck, that stings.* And I flee the scene.

So I jumped out of a window to avoid confrontation. Sue me. But I don't know how to go about this.

Everything is ruined. I ruined everything because I let my curiosity get the better of me. Everything had been perfect the way it was. I had my freedom. I was living my life. And now, I have complicated everything.

It was a mistake.

Even so, if I ignore how bad the situation is, I do get to cross off having a one-night stand off my bucket list. Since I had one with my "husband," which has a very weird ring to it. I also get to cross off walking the walk of shame. I walked—ran—mine out of my own house, which sounds even weirder.

After a few hours of eating and drinking—while hating myself and my poor life decisions—I return home. I'll just make my way to my room without him noticing that I'm home—and hopefully, he isn't.

I go to my room and carefully close the door behind me.

Mission accomplished, is what I think.

But the second after I close my door, it flies wide open, Augustine entering and closing it behind him. Locking it with the key and putting the key in his pocket.

My soul almost left my body there, probably because he caught me red-handed.

I place my hand on my chest. "God, you startled me. Wait, why did you lock the door and take the key—"

"To prevent you from running away again. We are going to have our conversation—now," he demands, putting his hands inside of his pockets.

I start taking small, hopefully unnoticeable, steps back. "I-I mean, are we really?"

He takes one step forward and holds up his finger to me, warning me. "Don't you dare jump out of the window again."

I freeze. "I'm just no good with words," I say, blowing out air.

"Aren't you an aspiring therapist?" he asks.

"So? All of a sudden, I'm supposed to be the dictionary, having all the words?"

He frowns. "What?"

I frown back. "What, what?"

He changes the subject. "I am too. Well, was, until last night."

"You were too what?"

"A virgin."

What? I don't believe that. That simply cannot be true. That was a virgin fucking? No fucking way.

"Yeah, right, and I'm the queen of Egypt."

"I had done other things. I just never penetrated someone. You were the first one."

I sit on the edge of my bed, trying to process the words he said just now, still not entirely believing them.

"I wanted to share that moment with someone special to me," he says.

"What does that even mean? Wait, don't answer that. This was a one-time thing, a mistake on my part. I'm in love with someone else," I tell him, as if throwing this bomb at him and giving him no time to even try to figure out how to dismantle it.

Even if I was rejected, I can't just press a button to let all my feelings for Adam disappear. I wish it were that easy. If it were, I probably wouldn't be here, having this conversation with Augustine.

His jaw clenches. "You said you don't fall in love."

"And you said you have no desire to touch me. I guess we're both still liars."

That was really low of me, but I'm so desperate to defend myself right now.

He comes to stand in front of my legs and holds his forehead. "Fuck, Kristina, you can't do something and then just brush over it by calling it a mistake when others are involved."

Guess we're on a first-name basis now. It's new and somehow ... unnatural.

I swallow some of my spit and stutter, "I-I'm sorry. Can we please just go back to normal?"

He nods and accepts, yet also disapproves. "Your wish has always been my command."

He grabs the key from his pocket, opens my door, and leaves my room.

He has every right to be mad—I know he does. I just hope we can actually go back to normal and that we can act like nothing happened.

Just hit the reset button on yesterday. Is that too much to ask?

Augustine

Eve: Adam. I have been thinking a lot ... about you. And I can't keep it to myself anymore. I want to share it with you. We have been talking to each other for a long time, and I have always appreciated every moment I spent talking with you since the very beginning. I would even say that I considered you to be my friend for the longest time. But that changed. I wonder what you look like, what your voice sounds like, and who you are as a person. And that is because I have developed feelings for you ...

Adam: Eve, I have always thought of you as a wonderful person, and I cherish our conversations deeply. Except I don't feel the same way about you. I have feelings for someone else. I apologize, Eve ...

Eve: There's no need to apologize. I understand. Thank you for your honesty. And I hope it works out between you and her.

Adam: Thank you. I appreciate it.

Eve: Can we keep talking to each other and stay friends though?

Adam: Yes, absolutely. I would like that.

I'm sorry, Eve. I wish I didn't have to put you through what I go through day and night. I don't wish that upon anyone, not even my worst enemy.

Kristina, the first time I saw you, I was mesmerized by your beauty and elegance.

As you were checking yourself out in my office door, I was checking you out. Enjoying every second of it. Taking you all in.

Unfortunately, I knew why you came to be in my office. I couldn't care less about the money that peasant owed me, but I had to prioritize not letting someone make a fool out of me. It had happened before. Therefore, I stopped looking at you. I stopped thinking about you. And I opened the door and was as rude as I could be.

I convinced myself that you were superficial. But you have been contradicting all my assumptions about you since our very first encounter. And you continue to contradict them by living with me, by letting me watch you. You surprise me. You show me I don't have it all figured out, that I can't assess someone. It intrigued me. You have intrigued me ever since.

I found myself slipping when I proposed to you. And I tried to distance myself from you again after that, suppressing those thoughts about you and feelings for you. Ignoring them. Apparently, not enough. I was on a slippery slope, waiting for the inevitable to happen.

I wanted to see you in a wedding dress, walking toward me. And when I did, you had me captivated. Then, I fell completely as I watched you watch the sunrise. You were so beautiful. Too beautiful. And I told you this. But I knew I was already on the floor with broken bones, unable to get back up again, when I experienced the days at work as long. When I would impatiently wait to get home, pass on dinner with my coworkers. Because I wanted to see you, all the time.

And when I realized this, I rushed back home, but you weren't there, so I impatiently waited for you to get home. And when you did, and I asked permission to hug you, I knew I was far gone. I knew I was doomed. Because I just needed to touch you for only a second, and I could immediately feel my body reacting to yours against mine. Confirming what I had already known. It took everything in me to pull myself off of you and leave when all I wanted to do at that moment was take you and make you mine. And I have been resisting doing just that ever since. Or rather, trying to.

I'm falling even more, to the core of this earth.

When you had to use me as a seat, I knew you would be uncomfortable. Even so, I was overjoyed. Overjoyed because I wanted to feel you against me. I loved having you there—all of me did. My body even shared this little secret of mine. And when you wanted to leave, I told you that you couldn't because it would be visible—the effect you have on me. But that was rather an excuse. I could have easily covered myself with anything else. I didn't want it to end—the opportunity that had presented itself to me.

I put my own wants above your needs. I'm scum, Kristina. I know that all too well.

Because I didn't just do that, I did more. When we slept next to each other, I waited for you to fall asleep. And the minute you did, I threw all the pillows separating us away. I even removed the one you had been hugging so tightly. I was jealous of a fucking pillow, wanting it to be me. Making you hold on to me. I got to feel your body against mine for a whole night. I adored it. It fed my starved soul.

I just couldn't contain myself. Not anymore. I used all of those moments as an excuse to bring us closer to one another. Denying what reality is.

That I'm inexpressibly and excessively in love with the woman who is my wife.

I can't describe my affection for you, but I want to be with you all the time. When I'm not with you, I wonder what you're doing, what you're thinking, and what you see, hear, smell, taste, and feel. All that you sense. What you're wearing and whether you have your hair in a messy bun or not. I want to know the small things. I want to know what made you laugh, what made you happy or angry. Because I already know your favorite color and favorite food. I did my research.

But what I'm truly interested in are your deepest desires, the things you never say out loud. I want to know the side of you that you only express when you're alone. When you're anonymous. I want to know the side of you that you show no one. The side that you even try to shun yourself.

Kristina, you are my sanctuary. The one I find myself always drawn to. You *are my first love. My only love. I have never wanted anyone before, and I know I will never want anyone else. I have never felt this way. You make me feel things I didn't know could be felt. I want you emotionally and physically, body and soul. Everything.*

And I wish for you to perceive yourself through my eyes. You only see yourself in the mirror. I see you when you laugh uncontrollably. I see your happiness when you cross something off in your notebook. I see you cuddling with Lady and telling her, "Bless you," when she sneezes. You would understand me if you could see what I see all the time.

I hear knocking on my door, and it can only be one person, which excites me and surprises me at once. She rarely enters my room.

"Mm-hmm?" I say for her to come in.

She opens the door, and I turn to face her while sitting. I immediately notice that she isn't wearing pants, only a long T-shirt. Her legs are showing, and I see them for the first time. Making room for opportunities.

I form fists, trying to suppress whatever it is my mind started wandering to at the mere sight of her bare legs.

"I need something from you," she says.

And that does it. Her wanting something from me, *needing* something from me. The way she said it, her graceful voice, hesitant.

Don't be. Anything you desire is yours, my love. I'm yours. My body is ready to prove it to you.

I put my hands in each other and cover the thing I failed to suppress. "What do you need?"

She is walking toward me now. "I need you to go back on your word."

She is so close. I can't think straight. What word?

"My word?" I ask her, hesitant myself now.

"Yes, the one where you stated you have no desire to touch me. I need you to go back on that one."

I must be imagining things since I only live off my imagination when it comes to her. Her being so close must have caused me to have a wire loose.

"Wh-what are you saying right now?" I ask.

Unsure, she puts her hand on my shoulder. "Can you create desire?"

She is touching me.

Create? This is my desire. You are my desire. I tried restraining myself to the best of my abilities, but seeing you all vulnerable and asleep, I couldn't help but steal a kiss or two. Planting them on your head, cheeks, and hands. Even when my guilty conscience was so against it.

My desires—the ones you are responsible for, the ones you create—if I were to act on them, on all the perverted things I thought of doing just by laying my eyes on you, I would be put behind bars immediately, serving a life sentence. And I would serve it gladly if that meant I get to have you. Even if it was just once for a mere minute, I would serve the sentence. Gladly. While reliving that minute for the rest of my life. That's how much I want you. I would take anything you offered me. Even crumbs.

And yet even I know there are boundaries that should be respected.

I look away from her. "You don't know what you're saying. You're drunk—"

"I have never been soberer." Her grip on my shoulder is getting tighter now.

Lower, Kristina. Touch me lower. I'm hard for you. Feel it.

Feel me.

"Stop. Please." *No. Don't throw yourself at me. I won't be able to resist you. Please. You should fear me.*

"You don't want to? Is that why you kissed me?" she asks.

I face her, fearing she can read my mind because I did that when she was unconscious. "I didn't. I left."

"But you did—when you carried me when I was asleep."

And my fears become reality. *How does she know? When? Fuck.* This is even worse than if I had actually kissed her that day. She will never trust me now. And I give her every right not to. She shouldn't because even I can't trust myself around her.

"You have done something you wanted; it's time to return the favor," she says.

What if I can't resist her?

"No. You don't want this. You will come to regret it and come to hate me."

"I do. And I already hate you, remember?"

"Then I don't want you to hate me even more. So, please, just stop. *Please.*"
I grab her hand to remove it from myself.

I can't endure this any longer. *You need to leave. Now. Before it's too late and I start doing things I can't take back.*

Every night, I hear you turn on the shower and the water running. Knowing you are unclothed, water dripping down your nude body. Being so close to me. It drives me fucking insane. Only my restraint standing between us. I'm aching to have you in those moments. *Aching.* And it takes everything in me not to act on my thoughts. I would imagine things. Unorthodox things. Things I would do to you. Things you would do to me.

Oh, the things I imagine you'd do to me. If only you knew about them, you would move out of here immediately, break out of here without looking back at me twice.

I keep thinking to myself: *How long can I hold back? What if I lose control completely?* The temptation is too big to bear with you being in the next room all the time, unguarded. Alone with me in one house. For me to take. For me to make mine. Showing you how in every room, corner, and against every surface this house has.

You trust me too much, Kristina. Way too much for your own good.

She exhales. "Listen, even if you're not up for it at all, can you at least try to—"

You are irresistible, Kristina. I won't win this battle, no matter how hard I try. At this very moment, I'm dreaming with my eyes wide open. From envisioning it to reality.

I grab her wrist instead and pull her to fall on me. Arranging her to sit on the thing I tried covering the moment she walked through that door.

I hold her down by her waist for her to keep using me as a seat. "Do you feel that?"

She wraps her arms around my neck. "I do."

"I wanted you the second you walked through that door. Don't assume shit when you know nothing," I grit out.

"Show me what you want," she demands of me.

I knew she was assertive; it's one of the reasons I fell in love with her. Now, it turns me on.

I take off my glasses and focus on her lips. "If we do this, I won't be able to stop. Do you understand what that means?"

"Good. I don't want you to."

I spread my hand out on the back of her head, slowly bringing it to my face. "Even if you beg me to."

She gives me a peck on the lips. Then she gives me more than a peck and holds my face. She tastes so damn good, even better than I thought she would.

There is an entire fireworks show happening inside my head right now. Celebrating a hopefully happy, new beginning.

I remove her hair tie while we're kissing. I love it when she has her hair down, and I need to stay true to how I imagined this moment would be. I wear the tie around my wrist. I'm taking it, and I won't be taking it off. Letting something of her be on me forever.

While still holding her head, I put my other hand on her cheek, or rather, I grab it, making sure that this is happening and that I'm not hallucinating. Making sure that it can keep happening by not letting go of her.

I kiss her more fiercely, and she answers it by kissing me back the same way.

I want more. *Now.*

I don't stop. I put my hands on her bottom to stand up and take her with me. Laying her down on my bed.

I lean back and graze the hem of her T-shirt. "I want this anywhere but on your body."

She doesn't answer right away. "There is no need for that since it'll be quick."

Knowing her, this will probably be the first and last time. I don't want this moment to end. I will make it last until I'm on the verge of passing out.

"Quick? It won't be a quick fuck. That won't be enough to satisfy me, love," I say. "I need to feel all of your skin against mine." The hem of her T-shirt is still between my fingers.

She consents, and I take off her T-shirt, only underwear covering her body now. I've wanted to study everything that her T-shirt concealed all this time—until my attention shifts to her thighs, which makes her cover them, distressed.

This isn't the first time, and it pains me.

When she had a nightmare not too long ago, she appeared to be so frightened. I wanted to keep holding her that night, hold her until she woke up again. So I could make sure that she went through it without distress, guarding her from the terrors of the night.

It pains me to see her in pain. I never want to see her cry again. If I can prevent it, I will. I will deal with anyone who hurts her. Kill those who hurt her to the extent of her hurting herself.

I've said it before. *I want to know every side of you, even the side you try to shun yourself.*

I place my hands on hers. "Don't hide from me, please. It saddens me you feel the need to."

She doesn't say anything. She only looks at our hands.

"The only way they define you is how strong you were when the weight was only getting heavier. You are wholly and thoroughly perfect," I tell her.

Don't carry that weight alone anymore, please, my love.

Every inch of you is loved deeply by me.

I gently remove her hands from her thighs and brush my lips against all her scars.

Then, I work my way up, brushing my lips against other parts of her skin. Until I come across a tattoo, one I didn't know she had. I already knew she had her father's name on her collarbone, the symbol of psi on her arm, and a cross on her right wrist—since it's common for Coptic Orthodox to have one there.

It appears to be the beach with some animals and, of course, the sun.

My love, you are the center, and my world revolves around you. Like the sun you adore so deeply, you blind me with your beauty, burn me with your body, and blaze my entire being.

I continue working my way up with my eyes, bringing my finger to her nipple while wetting my lips.

She has a nipple piercing, and, fuck, that turns me on even more. Her breasts are beautiful and round and would fit perfectly in my hands.

I'm mesmerized.

Is this what your clothes have concealed all this time? I want to rip them to shreds, so you can never wear them again. So you can never conceal yourself from me again.

I kiss her nipple and wet it with my tongue. She makes a sound, a sound I have imagined her making.

I get off of her and take off my T-shirt. I'm too impatient.

I want to hold her.

I want to touch her.

I want her to touch me.

She is staring at me.

She puts her fingers on my scar, caressing it. "Who did this to you?"

"A stranger."

"How did it happen?"

"There was a man hitting on a woman who clearly wasn't interested, uncomfortable even. He thought I wanted to steal her away from him when I was actually helping her get rid of him. Then, he smashed the bottle he had been drinking from and stabbed me with it."

She looks at me, unsettled. "Drunkards are the worst."

"Don't give me that look," I say, holding her face. "It's my crown. I'm a king."

She laughs. I love the sound of her laughter. It fills me with such joy, especially if I'm the one causing her to laugh.

With my fingers, I start drawing a crown on her lower stomach. "Will you be my queen?"

"Just for tonight," she says.

"I'll take it." I slip my hand into her underwear, feeling her clitoris against my finger and touching it in hopefully a pleasurable rhythm.

But I want more.

I want to lick every square inch of her skin. Taste all of her.

I bring my other hand to the band of her underwear, grazing it. "May I take this off? Please?" I ask hungrily.

You wearing jeans. Them hugging your behind. Your front ... tightly. Letting my imagination run wild.

"You may," she huffs.

I bring her underwear down.

This, you will never find again. I'm keeping it as a souvenir. I need something to remember this by and to use to pleasure myself.

I clench it in my hand and toss it on the floor.

I put her legs on my shoulders, giving me a view of what her underwear concealed. Another tattoo for me to discover. Her body is like a scavenger hunt.

"*Love hurts?*" I ask, but she doesn't answer me, not in words, at least.

I will take her silence as an answer.

I hold her waist and bring her closer to me, so I can go down on her.

And she tastes so damn good.

She tugs on my hair.

I lean back to face her and grab her wrists with my hand, placing them above her head. "Keep them there, love. I'm going to make you feel so good."

I insert my tongue, and she expresses how I make her feel with sounds.

The sound of you in pleasure? I want to record it. Replay it repeatedly. I love your soft whimpers. I need to hear more. I can already picture you touching yourself, making these sounds. I need to see that.

I look up at her. "Keep telling me how good I make you feel."

I could orgasm just by watching you make these expressions and hearing you moan.

Fuck, she's wet. Do I make her feel this good? "You're so wet; it's driving me fucking insane."

I want to feel her against me. I remove her legs from my shoulders and let her lie on her side. I get up, stand behind her, and take off my pants. And, fuck, this view—her legs, her behind, the two dimples on her lower back. *Her back.* The way her spine shapes it. The way her entire body is shaped like an hourglass. I'm aching. All my sand is in the lower glass bulb now.

I receive pleasure by giving it, but seeing you like this, I can't contain myself anymore.

I start touching myself.

And I want you dripping, Kristina.

I lie behind her, wrap my arm around her hip, and insert my middle finger inside of her with my palm resting on her clitoris. Stimulating it as I move inside of her. I wrap my other arm around her breasts and pull her to me. My entire body is touching hers now. And my mouth is pleasuring her erogenous zones.

Foreplay has never felt this good.

"You once said that your body doesn't like me. How does your body like me now?" I ask as I insert my ring finger as well.

She gasps.

"Answer me in words," I demand of her.

"It feels—" She moans. "So fucking good."

"It will feel even better," I tell her while finding her lips to put on mine, still holding her against me.

I want to be in her.

I make her lie on her back, and rest on my knees in front of her, making her look at me.

"I-I'm still a virgin!" she yells.

You ... are?

The day you wanted to leave the house at night, I knew what you were after. And I tried my very best to keep you with me, even if I had no right to. It enraged me.

I didn't want you to have it. Not with someone who wasn't me.

"I thought you wanted freedom?" I ask, holding myself.

"I thought so too, tried it even, but I couldn't exactly feel anything ..."

Yes. Good. I'm so glad, relieved even. Happy beyond words. I want to be the first one. I want to be the only one. The only one to enter you. You are mine, my woman. Only I get to pleasure you. I don't want anyone to touch you besides me.

I hold her chin up with my index finger and thumb. "What about now? Do you feel anything now?"

"I-I do. A lot," she stammers.

I chuckle. "It's because you're attracted to me, like polar opposite sides of a magnet."

She raises her eyebrow at me. "I'm not though? If you mean we're opposites, then, yes, you're correct. It just so happens to be true in physics, but opposites don't attract in psychology, and that's my field."

I disregard her denial. "You are." And I kiss her temple. "But I won't force you to admit it now."

I *need* to be inside of her.

I lean forward, hanging above her as she lies down. "Let me be inside of you and fuck you. I beg you."

"That"—she points at my crotch, dissatisfied—"will never fucking fit."

"That"—I point at hers—"will welcome me like I was custom built to be inside of it," I say. "It will fit perfectly."

I will make it fit.

I lean further into her and hold both her head and my cock. "I will be gentle, love."

I then put my forehead against hers and gently insert myself inside of her, the tip and a little more.

That makes us gasp against each other, and we're not ashamed to look away. We're being vulnerable with each other for the first time.

I pull out, but not entirely, and gently insert about half in. I keep thrusting with only that while holding her waist with one hand and her head with the other.

Through sheer willpower, do I not push more of myself inside of her. All of myself.

You feel so good, love, and it excites me even more.

"Can I keep going?" I ask because I feel myself getting harder.

"M-make that stop. I can't handle that!" she almost urges me.

Adorable.

It makes me grin. "I can't, love. This is my way of showing you how I've longed for this. Only you have this effect on me."

I need to hear you consent to me. I need you to invite me in. I will enter slowly, but all of me will enter surely.

"May I show you more?" I ask, placing my hand on her lower stomach, trying to find myself.

"Yes," she breathes out. "Please."

Good.

I press a lot more inside of her, and she seems to love its effect. Which, in turn, I love. I love that I can make her feel this good. I was born to love her and make love to her.

I keep thrusting into her, with more strength with each thrust. More pleasure washing over me. "You're so fucking tight," I whisper.

And my mind starts wandering to the image of her on top of me.

I need to make that reality.

I hold on to her and lean back to sit. Letting her straddle me.

Then, I lie down. "I want you to ride me."

She covers her breasts with one hand.

Don't hide from me, love. I love your breasts too much. I want to spend every waking moment looking at them.

I take her hands and bring them to my chest, keeping them there while looking at her.

She starts moving her hips. Riding me.

I want to capture this moment. You being on top of me, me being inside of you. Paint it, frame it. Build an altar for it and honor it ceaselessly. And I will. To me, you are a goddess sent from heaven itself. And I would grovel and worship at your feet if only you would let me.

I close my eyes.

We have started a dangerous game. I have craved you all this time. Once I get a taste, there is no turning back. I won't be able to stop. Ever. I'm addicted to how you make me feel right now, to the feeling of having you around me. To your insides, gripping my cock, hugging me tightly.

To you.

But there is one more thing I found myself dreaming of. Longing for.

I sit up, put my forehead against hers, and look at her. I then place my hands on her waist and push myself deeper inside. That almost does it. I almost come. But I won't. Not until I'm about to pass out.

I hold her cheek. "Kristina."

She flinches.

"Call me by my name," I say, almost choking on my words.

"Goose," she exhales.

"No. Not my nickname. My real name. I won't let it go." I hold her cheek tighter now.

Please.

"Aug-Augustine."

How I have longed for those lips to vocalize that name, to hear it in her voice. Ringing through my ears.

I breathe out, place my hand to hold her chin, and shut my eyes. "Once more."

"Augustinus," she repeats.

Heaven.

Suddenly, I remember what Tony told me the day he got engaged. *"You will find her, August. Your soul mate, your other half, the one who is meant to be yours."*

Finally.

I smile. "I have found you—at last." And I hold her cheek again.

I lean forward and kiss her. Aggressively because my restraint has officially expired. I can't use it anymore, and I don't want to.

Kissing her neck and throat. Sucking on her skin while holding her waist and moving her back and forth. Fast.

"Fuck," I puff. "I need to pull out. I didn't use a condom. I should've fucking grabbed one."

I hope she doesn't pay too much attention to why I have them in the first place. It was out of a little hope, hope that there would be a time we would feel drawn enough to each other and express it.

Strawberry flavored—our favorite.

I feel something.

She came on me.

Fuck me. I could get used to that.

Her eyes widen.

"I can feel it. You came on me. I fucking love that," I tell her, biting my lip.

Seriously, I want to come inside her so badly, fill her up to the brim. Filling her with me, leaving traces of myself in her. Marking my territory.

Mine.

I grunt. "I want to come inside of you, and it's taking everything in me to resist."

She puts her trembling arms around my neck. "Then don't. I want you to come inside of me."

I can't form coherent thoughts anymore. I want to. I *need* to. But I shouldn't.

I shake my head and shut my eyes. Looking at her will instantly make me come. "Fuck, don't say things like that. It turns me on, more than I already am."

Then she wraps her trembling legs around me. She's so provocative. I love her all the more for it.

Even so, I can't help but hesitate.

"I'm on birth control, so you can lose your control." She smirks. "Come, Augustine."

The words of a goddess who is addressing you by your given name. How could anyone disobey?

My orgasm courses through me and I moan in her ear, then I relax entirely. I've marked her, and the ink comes dripping right back.

She starts getting off of me, and I hold her in place with now-trembling hands. "Where do you think you're off to?"

She yawns and stretches her arms. "To sleep."

I won't let you. Not yet.

I laugh softly. "One round would never satisfy me, love. I need at least three more rounds, and that is me going easy on you."

I want to lock you up in my room and stay here forever. Screw the daily activities we have to participate in without each other. I don't want this moment to end.

She looks shocked. I start getting hard again, and she feels it.

"See? Not completely satisfied yet," I say.

"Fine. Then, let me satisfy *you* completely," she says while getting off of me.

She kneels on the bed, and I stand in front of her.

I look down at her. "Touch it."

She strokes me, and all I can do is make sounds, showing her that she's stimulating me.

Then, she puts it in her mouth, teases me, looks up at me. That fucking look. She's seducing me; Satan sent straight from hell.

I place my hand on her head. "I want to be sucked dry by you."

And she does just that. Things I can't even begin to put into words.

I have masturbated to the thought of you more times than I can count. It's disgraceful.

Those hands. I always stare at them, washing things, holding things. Drinking. I would watch your fingers with long almond-shaped black nails tightly wrapped around a bottle, bringing it to your lips.

Lips around it. Sucking on it. Swallowing.

I imagined you having the same grip around my hard cock, stroking it up and down, bringing it to your mouth. Lust would take me over completely. The thought of it alone made me so hard. I could hardly resist the urge to touch myself. Imagining that it's you touching me. How I longed for your fingers to be wrapped around me instead of mine. Wish granted at last.

But it also pisses me off that it feels so good.

Who did you do this to? I want to kill him. All of them, if there's more than one. Erase the memories they have with you by getting rid of them.

I-I'm coming undone, entirely.

I come on her face, and she licks her lips.

I smirk and wipe her clean. "The only way I want liquid flowing down your face is when it's covered in my cum. This is the only way I want to see your face ruined."

Then I grab her face and try to kiss her.

She jumps away. "I just sucked you off?"

"And I loved every fucking second of it? Let me show you how grateful I am." I bend down and kiss her with all my might.

I keep kissing her as I lay her down and get on top of her.

Recurrence always gets associated with weariness. *But you could never be dull to me. Instead, I worry more that I can't get enough of you. How will I ever get things done if I can't even pull myself off you?*

So, after this, my love, I hope that you'll let me take you on dates. So you can wear the clothes I know you have, but don't seem to have an occasion for.

This was more than sex. It's a new beginning. We got to know each other's bodies. Every freckle, mole, scar, and piece of art. All those things have stories of their own. And I want to know them all.

You are my favorite map, the one I would love to navigate through daily.

I didn't sleep all night. I cleaned you. Then, I watched you. Taking you all in again. In my bed, by my side. Where you belong. I regret from time to time how I treated you the first time we met and after. And yet I also don't. If I hadn't, everything might have turned out differently. And I wouldn't have wanted that. It means there would have been a chance that you wouldn't be by my side right now. Not in my arms, but in someone else's—God, I hate that idea.

And what I hate right now is you trying to escape from my room. Why do you always run away from me?

"Leaving so soon, love?" I ask.

She flinches and faces me. I'm lying on my side and holding out her T-shirt to her since she's looking for it. She grabs it and wears it.

"Where is my underwear?" she asks.

In my second drawer on the left, hidden behind my boxers.

I shrug my shoulders.

She nods, leaves my room, and enters her own. I put on underwear and follow her.

I knock on her door. "We have to talk about it."

"Oh, we will, definitely!" she yells.

And then I hear a hard thud. I immediately open her door, only to find her gone and her window open.

You are always good at doing the unexpected.

But why do you feel the need to run away from me? I should put you on a leash or chain you to me. And yet I find myself not minding chasing you to the ends of this earth.

I don't know, Kristina. Perhaps you're right to want to distance yourself from me. Taking away the opportunity of me ever hurting you. The thing I fear most in this world.

But I might misbehave along the way since love doesn't play by the rules. And neither do I when it comes to you.

I have been waiting for her for hours until I hear her trying to sneak into her room.

I'm sorry, love, but I'm going to have to confront you.

I open her door, enter her room, and close the door behind me. I lock it from the inside and put the key in my pocket.

She places her hand on her chest. "God, you startled me. Wait, why did you lock the door and take the key—"

"To prevent you from running away again. We are going to have our conversation—now." I put my hands in my pockets.

She takes hard-to-miss steps back. "I-I mean, are we really?"

I take a step forward and warn her with my finger. "Don't you dare jump out of the window again."

She stops moving altogether. "I'm just no good with words." And she exhales.

"Aren't you an aspiring therapist?" I ask.

"So? All of a sudden, I'm supposed to be the dictionary, having all the words?"

I frown at her. "What?"

She frowns back at me. "What, what?"

I'm going to confess to her. "I am too. Well, was, until last night."

"You were too what?"

"A virgin."

"Yeah, right, and I'm the queen of Egypt," she says.

No, but you're my queen though.

"I had done other things. I just never penetrated someone. You were the first one."

She takes a seat on the edge of her bed.

"I wanted to share that moment with someone special to me," I tell her.

"What does that even mean? Wait, don't answer that. This was a one-time thing, a mistake on my part. I'm in love with someone else."

I break.

She doesn't even give me the opportunity to confess anything. To finally be honest about my intentions with her. Rather than fireworks, they were bombs. Destroying rather than celebrating. Me along with it.

I fucking knew it. I knew I had every right to be jealous of João.

When we were at our wedding, dancing, holding each other, he came hugging you. I hated seeing him touch you. I hated how he got to call you by a nickname—Krissie—and I couldn't even call you by your first name. I got so jealous that I jumped at the opportunity to say we should address each other differently. And when I wanted to nickname you something I hadn't heard anyone call you before, something only I would get to say, you refused it. I want to fucking kill him. Remove him from the picture if that's what it takes for you to see me in it. The only good thing he did was let us meet, and I'm grateful. Simply put, his absence in our lives is long overdue.

I clench my jaw. "You said you don't fall in love."

"And you said you have no desire to touch me. I guess we're both still liars."

Why are you doing this to me?

I stand in front of her and hold my forehead. "Fuck, Kristina, you can't do something and then just brush over it by calling it a mistake when others are involved."

She starts stammering, "I-I'm sorry. Can we please just go back to normal?"

Jesus, I don't fucking want that. I am in love with you, my wife. It's only natural. I can't believe I'm not allowed to, that you won't let me. That fucking contract—I regret it. If only I had known back then, I would have never signed the damn thing.

I nod, not accepting it, but tell her I am for her sake. "Your wish has always been my command."

Your wish has always been my command indeed. I promise you, I will never touch you against your will. Only if you ask me to—and I hope you do. Please do, my love.

I grab the key from my pocket, unlock the door, and leave her room.

But now that I know what I've been missing all this time, what you feel like, I will chase you until you're mine. Willingly.

No going back now. That is too much to ask of me.

CHAPTER SEVENTEEN

Adam: Eve, I need a new perspective on a particular matter, one that you undoubtedly have experience with. Once you got a taste of the forbidden fruit, were you able to restrain yourself from devouring it completely?

Eve: Adam. I see we are leaving our modern days behind again and are going back to where it all began, our time in the Garden of Eden. I would say I wasn't. In fact, I would be lying if I said that I didn't want to devour all the forbidden fruits the garden had to offer. And I still want to devour them.

Adam: Even if eating from it will grant you new knowledge that will only cause you to want even more and to have to live with the hardships of restraint, which is hanging by a thread as thin as your control?

Eve: Even then.

Adam: What's a little pain in light of so much pleasure?

Eve: Worth every sensation.

My whole world has been turned upside down, and it's exactly by the man I married in the first place to make that happen. Although, apparently, I had another world that wasn't rotating elliptical around the sun, let alone on its own axis. Now, that particular world is not only spinning on its own axis and revolving around the sun but it has been completely shot out of its orbit. It has spun, rotated, whirled, moved in every possible way, and now, I've officially lost it somewhere in the vast universe filled with galaxies, stars, and black holes. Unfindable—the control I thought I never needed but do if things aren't standing still anymore and are moving mercurial.

I have been doing things. Things I did not know I wanted to do or needed to be done. Touching myself, imagining the events of a couple of days ago, while closing my eyes. Trying to re-create the things he had made me feel. And I have been failing miserably. Even bought a vibrator, and I still couldn't feel what I had felt then. I hate it and him for turning me into this uncontrollable beast that's constantly craving pleasure.

I used to be scared of being touched, but somehow, by him, I *want* to be touched. The thought of it alone makes me want to grab a hammer and turn my brain into goo just to not think thoughts at all. I know I don't love him—I've already established that. I mean, how could I? It took me a long time just to be able to tolerate the man.

And I love Adam. *I love him.* I'm emotionally attracted, attached even, to him since he is not a physical entity—at least, not to me. Which means I'm physically attracted to Augustine. It has to be. But that's not love. Love is emotional, right? Right.

I'm glad Adam still wants to be friends and that our conversations have somehow returned to how they used to be. And since he's talking about having had a taste of something, I'm fairly certain that he's making progress with his *actual* Eve. I'm rooting for him and the woman he loves. I truly am, from the bottom of my heart, from my very ventricles. I want him to be with the person who makes him happy. But being happy for someone doesn't make it hurt any less that that person couldn't find such happiness with you.

I haven't seen Augustine since ... well, since the moment we removed all the distance two people could possibly have. He has been on a business trip for three days and two nights, but he returns today. Which means I've had the entire house to myself and Lady. Which also means I didn't feel embarrassed enough to do things to myself. Which I absolutely won't be doing when he's home again. Which is a good thing. This way, I can cleanse my body and soul from anything related to sex and pleasure. Since I was bathing myself in it and I'm not entirely proud of that. Probably because it didn't feel as good and that was frustrating, to say the least.

I tried to escape the thoughts by escaping the place and am now waiting for Delano on the not-so-unfamiliar couch of my family home to get ready, so we can leave and catch up.

Delano walks out of his room and puts on his coat. "I'm ready. Let's go."

"Where to?" I stand up and walk to the door.

"Rather than a place, to a feeling."

I close the front door behind me. "We're going to a feeling?"

"You'll see. You'll probably even find a way to drag psychology into it, since you always do that."

We get into his car and drive for about fifteen minutes. He then parks the car, and we walk toward a food stall. Or rather, a drink stall—a juice bar.

"What does this remind you of?" he asks.

I can't help but laugh. "The nights in Egypt."

Because in front of me is a stall where they serve freshly squeezed sugarcane juice, mango juice, and guava juice. Nets filled with mangoes and guavas dangle from the ceiling at the entrance, and sugarcanes are stacked behind the counter. And even here, you have the option to get your drink in a small plastic bag, tied with a straw inside of it to drink on the way, since finishing the glass it gets served in is simply a mission for some. It's a very generous amount.

This place is definitely run by an Egyptian because even the way it's equipped looks exactly like the juice bars you would find on the streets in Egypt.

I stand there with an open mouth, observing the place. "How did you even find this place?"

"Farah. She brought me here because we can't exactly go to Egypt together, so she wanted to bring Egypt to us. Or rather, a fragment of Egypt that's only minutes away instead of hours. Those were her exact words."

"This is amazing," I say.

We enter, and Delano orders. "*Salam 3amo*, could we have an *3asir manga* for her and an *3asir asab* for me?"

"*Salam*. Of course, coming right up. You can take a seat. I will bring it to you."

"*Shokran 3amo,* we'll just order something from the back and then sit."

He nods, and Delano gestures for me to follow him to the back.

"Order something from the back?" I question while walking behind him.

"Yes, because it gets even better."

We reach a door, and it leads us outside.

And he's completely right. Because outside is a man seated behind a wooden table with sweet corn stacked on its husks on the left and a small grill on the right. He's holding a hand fan made out of feathers above the grill while corn is being grilled.

Roasted corn, which we call dora mashwey in Egypt, is being served outside.

Have I just been teleported to Cairo? Because this is beyond insane.

Delano grins. "I told you it gets better."

"*Ezayak ya 3amo,* could I please have two dora mashwey?" Delano asks.

"*Salam 3alikom, t'mor ya habibi.* I will bring it to your table."

"*Shokran.*"

We walk back and take a seat. After a short while, our drinks and corn get served.

"Now, I want you to take a sip of your drink and then take a bite of the corn. I can't describe it, but it's pure nostalgia," Delano urges.

I do exactly as he said. I take a sip from my glass. And, oh my God, the last time I drank this was years ago. I remember exactly when. It was our last day in Egypt, and we ended our vacation in the most traditional way possible, with all my uncles, aunts, cousins, and their children, drinking at the juice bar until late at night. Taking pictures, telling jokes, making fun of each other, and laughing because of it. Crying because we didn't know when we'd see each other again. And even if we had promised to call each other every day, our busy daily lives would make us forget to follow through with that promise. Sometimes, when people are distanced from each other physically, it also causes them to distance themselves emotionally. Unwillingly.

I close my eyes to take in the smell of the freshly grilled corn, tingling at the back of my nose. It makes me smile. I then take a bite of it. As the hot sensation touches my tongue and I *hashafashasha* my way through it until I can start chewing, another memory arises.

Those days in Cairo, with the city sleeping during the day and awake at night and corn grilling almost everywhere. During Ramadan, people break their fast when the sun sets, and we all celebrate iftar. It doesn't matter if one is Christian or Muslim; everyone is outside, eating, drinking, and having fun. People in Egypt usually don't distinguish themselves regarding religion. There, everyone is just Egyptian. They grow up together, live in the same small street their whole lives, and play outside with each other almost every day.

Egypt, the land that is considered to be the mother of the world. *Masr om el dunya.*

"So, how is this related to psychology?" Delano asks as he *hashafashashas* his way through the corn.

"The Proust effect. It means to unexpectedly relive past emotions or memories caused by present experiences of our senses related to them."

"I just knew it," Delano says as he continues to eat.

Rather than the past making its way to the present, I find myself going to the past. The taste of the drink and the smell of the corn, causing me to relive memories as if I had time-traveled again, only this time, to a place of comfort rather than a place of pain.

The French author Marcel Proust wrote the novel *In Search of Lost Time*. In his work, he explains how he raised a spoonful of tea from his cup with a small piece of madeleine cake soaked in it, and the second it reached his mouth, and his senses were exposed to the strong scent and taste, he felt extraordinary changes throughout his entire body. Unexpectedly reliving memories of his childhood.

Which isn't strange at all, especially for the sense of smell. Because scents are processed differently than all the other sensory systems, those make their way to the thalamus, and odors bypass that region. Which causes smell—anatomic-wise—to be closely related to our emotions and memories since scents enter our limbic system and that same region is responsible for linking emotions to memories. This is why when we smell something related to a specific memory, we go back to it almost instantly.

This phenomenon isn't limited to smell; other senses can cause the same effect. For instance, if there's a playlist you used to blast on repeat during a specific period of your life and you play it now, unconsciously, you will even know which song follows, and that activates the reward system of your brain. It will cause you to have this indescribable fuzzy feeling because you know what you will experience next.

Since we can remember sounds, we can also remember how someone's voice sounded when they told us something. We can remember it so vividly, as if the person were repeating it, the only difference being that they aren't standing in front of us to do so. Which is especially special when that person is no longer in our lives or alive ...

Reliving memories is such a strong yet vague concept.

I look up at Delano to share something I somehow got reminded of from sitting here with him. "Lano, remember when we used to take the bus to church when we were little? Mama was too scared to drive because of *Baba's* accident, so we would sit behind the driver and pretend that we were the ones driving the bus until we reached our stop."

He leans back in his chair to look at the ceiling and grins. "Oh yeah! We would even make a schedule for whose turn it was to drive. It's hilarious how serious we took the whole thing."

I nod. "And then we would tell the driver that it was his turn to make sure people reach their destination safely before we got off, that we were entrusting him with the task since arriving somewhere safely meant more to us than others."

"The good old days. We didn't know better," he says.

The good old days. Every moment becomes the past, and every moment becomes part of this thing we call the good old days. Even sitting here with Delano, I'll catch myself thinking about this moment in the future, wishing I could go back to it because what I'll be facing then will be so much harder. Because we somehow always end up praising the past, never completely satisfied with the present. Only to end up praising every moment before we get off the bus, having reached our last stop.

Which is in line with the expression of a glass being half-empty rather than being half-full—for Proust's sake, a cup. We always look at the half-empty part of our cup not the half-full part. But our cup, it was empty at first. And if you were to ask yourself how you would feel if your cup were filled with mere droplets, you would probably answer with being delighted beyond words. And yet we aren't when that moment arrives when we have achieved something we've wanted for as long as we can remember. Since we're already busy searching for the next thing to pour into our cup of achievements—to win a cup we can put on display. But we should dwell upon our achievement before we immediately go looking for another.

To live more in the present instead of pining for the past or planning for the future.

After you've achieved something, you consider it to just be there. Disregarding it even when there was a time you craved it. You will only realize this when the cup spills. When what it contained is gone. When it's empty again. When it's too late. People take things for granted, which is why showing gratitude daily will completely change that.

And that will cause you to interpret all the cups of life differently. Then, looking at things with the cup half-full mindset translates into being someone who always looks on the bright side of things. An optimist. Something terrible could happen to that person, yet that same person would tell you that it could have been so much worse and that they are grateful for what happened, that their cup still contains something and can only be filled from this point. Whereas a pessimist, who only pays attention to the half-empty part, considers the cup to constantly be knocked over after the hurdles of life.

Framing ourselves, telling ourselves the same thing with other words, can really change how we perceive things.

We all have many cups in life, each representing something different. Some are empty, some consist of droplets, and some are filled to the brim. Sometimes, people invite us to drink with them from their cups. Some invite us to drink from their cups with abundance. And sometimes, some people want to share their less fortunate cups with us, the ones that are shattered and barely cups anymore.

I think it's important to always pay attention to our own set and not comment on others'. We also shouldn't be jealous since we only see the cups they put on display and the ones we get to drink from. Not their whole set. *Never* their whole set.

This is why when someone tells us to be happy that we don't have something they have, it's plain wrong, even if we all find ourselves guilty of doing it. For instance, when women complain about having children and tell other women that they should be glad they don't have them, not knowing that those other women are infertile and have been trying to have children for years.

Even if the intention wasn't to hurt someone, it doesn't mean that the accident didn't cause another to be wounded.

I get out of my head. "Lano, why is it that you love Farah?"

He smiles. "I'm unable to ever put that into words, but if I really had to try, I would say ... Farah brings me *farah*—happiness. Adding to my own. Because there's no one like Farah. It feels as if she had been made just for me, even when I literally can't have her. The irony, my misery."

"Have you ever thought about your future together? Would you both ever decide that ... it might be best to let each other go and get married to someone with the same religion?"

That makes him shake his head. "I can't do that, not to Farah, another woman, or myself. Marrying someone without actually loving them? No one deserves that. So my plan is to just keep living like this, loving her from the shadows and being there for her if she ever needs something. It isn't nearly enough, but I'm satisfied with anything she can give me."

That's ... beautiful. And heart-wrenching. *It's love.*

"You're the modern retelling of *Romeo and Juliet*," I say.

"That's cruel, Kristina. They died way too young. I want to love her for a lifetime. Did you even hear me just now?"

We both laugh.

Delano has told me before that he could never see himself love someone else. That, even if he ever would, it could never compare to his love for her because Farah is unique. Everyone is. Everyone is one of the seven billion, each with their own set of cups, special simply because they were born. There's only one version of you on the planet with seven billion. You're irreplaceable. *Don't let anyone ever tell you or make you feel otherwise.*

We sit there for a while and reminisce some more about the past. I, of course, don't finish my drink, so I ask for it to be put in a plastic bag with a straw inside to drink on the way. Delano drives me home. Now, I open the front door, and it's likely that once I open this door, I will face Augustine for the first time after—well, after ... *that.*

I enter the house and see his suitcase next to the door, which means he's here. I walk to the living room while nibbling on the straw and see him sitting on the couch with Lady on his lap, giving her chin scratches.

He looks up at me. "Kristina."

This whole *being on a first-name basis* thing is not going to work for me. I can't believe him saying my name alone lets my mind wander to sleeping with him. This is ridiculous. How am I going to go back to normal if his addressing me by my name is abnormal? Fucking name calling?

"Augustine."

He clenches one hand in a fist and points at my drink with the other. "Did you get back from a trip yourself?"

I hold up the plastic bag. "No, I wasn't in Egypt. There just happens to be a juice bar exactly like the ones there."

He puts Lady on the couch, stands up, removes the distance between us, and holds the straw from just above the knot in the plastic bag. "Let me taste it."

"What? No! I drank from—" On second thought, he has tasted other quite *extreme* body fluids of mine, so my saliva is child's play to him. Is this how I'll think thoughts from now on? If so, I regret sleeping with him more than I already did. I also never thought I would regret sleeping with someone. This sure is new, not being the holy Virgin Mary anymore.

He tilts his head for me to finish my sentence like Lady does when she stares at me. But he's also smiling smugly at me. As if he knows exactly what I was about to say.

I push the bag farther into his hand. "Have at it."

He barely has swallowed and already has something to say. "It tastes good. I want to go."

I nod. "Okay, you should. I'll send you the address."

"No, that won't be necessary, since you already know."

"What?"

"You are going with me."

I don't know, but he's ... changed? He's way too direct. Since when is drinking something together something we do? It isn't. So, I'll just say no how every Arabic-speaking person does when they want to kindly decline something. By saying if God wills, with God unwilling. "*Inshallah.*"

I go to my room, change into pajamas, and then I go to the bathroom to brush my teeth. As I'm doing that, I see Augustine in the mirror, leaning with his shoulder against the doorframe. He has his hand under his T-shirt, exposing one of his V-lines and inches from the phoenix I know is drawn there. Just standing there, observing me.

It makes me anxious, among other things ...

I take the toothbrush out of my mouth and look at him through the mirror. "What are you doing?"

"Waiting."

"For?"

"You to finish brushing your teeth."

"Can't you just stop looking at me and brush your teeth as well?"

"Do you want me to spit on your neck?"

I frown. "No?"

"Then, I can't."

What is up with this man anyway? He's acting unusual.

I finish brushing my teeth and step away from the sink for him to brush his. As he does that, I brush my hair next to him, both looking in the mirror to brush.

He finishes brushing his teeth and just stands next to me, observing me again, while I search for a hair tie until I see one around his wrist.

I point at it. "Give that to me."

He puts his hand behind him, hiding it. "No, this one is mine."

"What do you mean, yours? It's my hair tie. You took it when—" Don't. Finish. That. Sentence.

He gloats. "When?"

"When," I say as if I said more than just that word. As if it were the closing sentence of a life-changing speech.

If I want things to go back to normal, I have to act normal. And what does one normally do when someone returns from a trip? They ask how it was. "How was your trip?"

"Very ... insightful."

What does that even mean?

I avert my attention away from him by opening the drawers underneath the sink, and I finally find a hair tie. I brush my hair again and start putting it up to tie it. I still see him through the mirror, and he's looking at me through his eyes alone, turned ninety degrees to do so.

"Is that for me?" he asks, smirking.

I roll my eyes. "I already told you, it was a one-time thing."

His smirk disappears almost immediately. "Don't roll your eyes at me."

I turn to look at him through only my eyes and lift one eyebrow. "Or else?"

"Or else I'll fuck you so hard that they'll be stuck at the back of your head, unable for you to ever roll them again."

My mouth falls open, and it feels as if my eyes are about to fall out of my eye sockets.

He smirks again, as if he has achieved exactly what he was going for. "Good night, love. Dream of us, will you?"

Then, he walks away and leaves me standing there, still speechless, with one pounding heart in my chest and the other between my legs.

Because not only am I astonished by the fact that he just said that, but I'm also astonished by the fact that all I wanted to say to him was show me to never see again. I can't pretend it didn't happen when all he says or does reminds me of it. Fuck, I need to avoid him.

But what truly astonishes me is that it's as if his personality has completely changed after that night, as if he's someone else entirely. Or maybe this is who he has been all along, and he decided to start showing it.

Which is both spine-chilling and spine-tingling ...

God, I hate myself and this new type of cognitive dissonance I have to deal with.

CHAPTER EIGHTEEN

Eve: Adam. I find my thoughts wandering to a not-so-unfamiliar topic for us. Choices. Up until now, we've always discussed the choices we make. Now, I wonder about the choices we don't make or, rather, the options we don't choose and what could have been. What is your take on this matter?

Adam: Eve, I choose not to occupy myself with it since I know far too well that if I had made the choices I didn't make, it would have hindered me from having certain things I cannot imagine myself living without.

Eve: Would you say you don't regret any of your choices because of those certain things?

Adam: Beyond any doubt.

"The Road Not Taken" a poem by Robert Frost. The poet finds himself walking through the woods, only to find the road diverging into two. A junction has been reached. To move forward, a choice on which road to take has to be made. Which one will he choose? He's standing there, studying each road, as far as humanly possible. One a beaten path, traveled by many. The other, wearing nature as its attire, off the beaten path. He chooses this one and wants to leave the other road for another day, even though he knows he won't have the opportunity to travel it. He's also aware of the fact that he will look back on this choice, sighing that he took the less traveled one and that it made all the difference.

My interpretation? A road that has been used frequently is well regulated with road signs and traffic lights, granting time to even think while traveling the road. There's room for anticipation. Accidents don't occur as often; mistakes get avoided. Avoiding risks, wanting to play it safe, and conforming to the norm. The beaten path traveled by all.

A road that isn't used as frequently isn't as well regulated. Which makes anything possible on that road, it's accident-prone. And there must be a reason why it isn't used as frequently. Is it nothing but a dead end? Resisting taking that risk. Resisting being the only one to find out.

Roundabouts, where you're convinced that you are moving when, in fact, you aren't at all, you're just wasting energy. Standing still, not traveling. Postponing the inevitable—exiting.

Choices, which are being made every second of every day. From the moment you wake up and decide to put on black socks instead of white ones to the moment you decide to get married or not.

Choices, which often have many options we choose to disregard. Since we can't choose them all, unable to live multiple versions of our lives as one could if parallel universes were to exist. Neither can we alter our decisions once they have been made. The options, dictating both our miseries and blessings. The other options were only there to define everything that didn't happen, that *could* have happened.

Making the right choice being essential, but how can one? Our future depends on it. Giving thought to it is of the essence. Even if a choice seems unimportant at first glance, it will make all the difference in the future—yes, even if it's about the noncolors of our socks. Nonetheless, just like Robert stated, you can see only so much with the unaided eye when analyzing a road. Beyond is a mystery, as are *all* the consequences of our choices.

After taking any road, doubt and regret start pouring down, wondering if it was the right one. This is life, unable to travel all the roads to see which destination is most desired and valuable to us, no matter how hard we wish for it.

Many roads, sacrificing most of them. When traveling one, you cannot travel the others. One-way roads where U-turns and wrong-way driving aren't allowed. Here's to all the lives we could have lived. Better? Worse? Hit-and-runs?

Adam, what you're describing, to not have certain things if you chose otherwise—although, I'm sure you're talking about a certain someone—is called the butterfly effect. And I wish I could tell you all about poetry and psychology, the things I use to make sense of this world. But I don't want to annoy you with my rambling about my interests, which certainly wouldn't interest you. So, I'll just ramble to parts of my brain, letting neurons fire while I do so.

The butterfly effect, also known as the chaos theory, coined by meteorologist Edward Lorenz, is the sensitive dependence on initial conditions in which a small change in one state of a deterministic nonlinear system can result in large differences in a later state. The most minimal air movement due to a butterfly flapping its wings can cause a tornado on the other side of the world. Indicating that climate change is sensitive to many conditions, thus, nearly impossible to predict.

In human behavior, it suggests that the smallest change can have a drastic impact.

So, what's the difference between catching the bus at ten thirty or ten thirty-five? Nothing. Wrong. When riding the first bus, you might accidentally bump into your soul mate, taking your breath away. When riding the second bus, you might be in an accident yourself, taking your last breath. And we will never be able to predict the cascading effects of every choice. Which cascading effects are favorable, and which ones should be avoided. Isn't that something to be feared? What if we have been escaping the clutches of death all our lives by choosing right in every gamble?

You are always—and I mean, *always*—one decision away from living a completely different life.

Adam, I don't think people realize how special forming connections with other humans is. There are people you didn't get to meet because of your choices or because of theirs. There are people you didn't get to meet because they are no longer alive or weren't even alive in your epoch, to begin with, unable for you to ever meet. All being born at random in different epochs.

Meeting you, the chances were nil, but all our butterfly effects led us to each other. And, sure, if most of our choices were kind of coincidental or at random, led us to one another, wouldn't you call that fate? Out of all the roads, ours intersected.

At this very moment, I'm also finding myself on a road—or rather, at the end of it, since we're about to park. We're going to go grocery shopping since Augustine decided that us going grocery shopping is the new method we'll be using from now on. The old method? That was my putting a notepad on the kitchen counter for us to write down what's missing—or almost missing—and how much we want of it. The one who found themself going to the grocery store had to buy the whole list. The method was perfectly fine and effective, I might add. Our fridge was always full, and we never wasted food. If there's one thing I hate, it's wasting food, and apparently, he does too. So, why does he want to change things?

Augustine is holding the cart, and we're walking through the different aisles. I'm walking next to him, holding the notepad and a pen to cross off what we put in the cart.

I see eggs. "We need eggs," I say while skimming through the notepad.

He grabs a box. "We also need some avocados, so I can make you sushi again."

Yes. That I love. Almost loving him along with it. Because I can't deny it; the sushi he makes is something else entirely. "Thank you."

We walk past the aisle with nuts.

"Oh, Delano mentioned that you like pistachios and cashew nuts, but you dislike almonds, right? Since they're sources rich in protein and that is needed for muscle gain, try peanuts. I looked it up, and they're the ones with the most protein." I grab some bags of the nuts he likes and peanuts and put them in the cart.

Nuts. How ironic. I'm going nuts right now. Why can't I let sleeping together go? I know it's a big deal, but still, I can't even have a proper conversation without my words or mind running to it.

He stops walking and bows down to lean with his elbow on the cart handle, supporting his temple with his fist. He's smiling. A little *too* satisfied.

I exhale, frustrated. "What is it now?"

"You remembering all the little things, even when you supposedly don't care about me, makes you all the more attractive."

Before I can process what he just said, he adds to the things we need, "And we need strawberries."

He straightens himself and walks again.

"Yeah … we also need mushrooms and red bell peppers," I say.

It's how I like my eggs that I can't live without. And he happens to like it too.

We arrive at the vegetable aisle. I grab the mushrooms and red bell peppers and put them in the cart.

"But we also need strawberries," he says.

"Yes, I understand. But now, we're at the vegetables. First things first."

I grab some more vegetables.

He tugs at the hem of my top, like a toddler would when they want to be given attention. "Strawberries, love."

I'm going to kill him. He always decides to run with the only thing we have in common to bond over.

I get it, but enough, Augustine. You're annoying me.

I wrap my hands around the cart handle and push it toward the fruit aisle.

He's also holding on to the cart handle, following my lead.

I grab five boxes of strawberries and throw them in the cart with a little too much force. "Strawberries. Happy now?"

He stacks them on top of each other, treating them as delicate items while I treated them as everything but. "Very. We also need eggplants."

Eggplants? We just needed eggs though. Wait. Don't tell me this is his way of teasing me about us sleeping together?

I try giving him a look, an ignorant one, as if I were slow. "For what?"

"To make mesa'a'ah, eggplant being the basic ingredient."

Oh. Mesa'a'ah is an Egyptian dish filled with fried eggplant, tomato sauce, and a bunch of other cooked vegetables. Anything you can think of, it's in there. It's very healthy and very vegan. Okay, so I was reading too much into it.

Fine. My bad, Augustine. Forget that I thought anything.

Apparently, I'm the only one who thinks of food as genitalia.

"And pomegranates," he adds.

My bad, my ass. He's doing this on purpose, acting all innocent-like, clearly knowing that I understand what he means. He's enjoying this way too much.

"Pomegranates?" I ask defensively.

"They taste exquisite," he says, bringing his fingers together, slowly guiding them to his lips, and barely giving them a peck. Gesturing chef's kiss with closed eyes. "Wouldn't you agree?" he asks.

His eyes slowly open, piercing into mine. It was as if, by closing his eyes, he could re-taste its taste—*my* taste.

Two can play this game, Augustine.

"I don't know. I've never tasted them before." I grab one and put it in the cart. "Here, for you, the *only* available pomegranate." I walk away from the cart, but he's still standing in front of the pomegranates.

He points at the tag. "But it says buy one, get one free."

Wait. I wanted to make a point, but I'll set my pride aside for any discount. I mean, it's a discount. Not only that, but it's also getting something for free. And I do love pomegranates, damn it.

I don't turn around. I slowly take steps back and halt next to him. "Wait, really?"

"No, I was just pulling your leg," he says and chuckles.

You always know what to say. Not only that, but you always have a saying ready for it too. Maybe you should stop using sayings to say what you want to say and just say it. Oh well. I'm going to startle you. Maybe that will teach you. Because you've been annoying me since the moment we entered here.

I grab both his arms tightly for him to face me. "Want me to pull your third?"

He flinches and looks bewildered. "Wh-what?"

I simper. "Nothing. We need bananas," I say, walking away since he's too stunned to move.

Who's left standing speechless now? Idiot.

After a good ten seconds, he follows me, and I put the bananas in the cart. We arrive at the vegetable aisle again.

He points at an eggplant, the biggest one. "Grab it."

Okay, that is it. I'm sorry, but am I the only one noticing what he's trying to do right now? I know I did it, too, but he started it. Fine, I started it, but who cares?

"You grab it. You have a hand, don't you? Use it because you won't be getting mine."

"But you just offered, Kristina."

"Sayings aren't meant to be taken literally, Augustine. You ought to know."

We walk toward the register and pay. After putting everything in bags, we leave the grocery store, only to bump into not-so-unfamiliar people—although, the little one is.

"Augustine, how are you, man?" George asks.

They hug each other, and I greet Mariam and, apparently, their daughter. I didn't know they had a daughter. But my baby fever is kicking in.

"This is Maria, our baby girl. She just turned one," she says to me.

I caress the back of her little hand with my index finger. "Hi, beautiful."

"Could you guys look after her for a little while? We just need to quickly return something to a store nearby," George says.

What? No. What if I drop her? What if she breaks? My intrusive thoughts aren't helping, but I am thinking them. Get out of my head!

Augustine looks at me and somehow reads my mind because he extends his arms to take her from Mariam. "Yes. We'll be sitting on that bench, waiting for you to return."

"Thank you, Augustine," Mariam says as she and George walk away.

Augustine gestures for me to follow him with the cart full of our bags to the bench. I do so, and we sit down next to each other. He's holding Maria in an upright position with one hand on her head, caressing it, while she rests it on his shoulder, facing me. And now, he's leaning his head against hers. They're adorable—I mean, she is. She's adorable.

I caress the back of her hand that's resting on his shoulder with my finger again. "You're good with children," I tell him.

He tilts his head to face me. "Is that a fact?"

"Yes. Maybe you should have some of your own someday."

"Will you make them with me?"

"Are you asking me to sleep with you?"

He shakes his head. "No, I'm asking whether you want to have children with me. Don't confuse the two, love." And he asks, "Will you be their mother?"

"No?"

"Then, I don't want them."

I look in front of me, only to see an actual goose, which isn't weird since there's a pond nearby. But the irony.

I point at it. "The resemblance is uncanny, Goose. Tall, grumpy-looking."

"You find me grumpy-looking?"

Maria giggles. Which makes me giggle as well.

"Apparently, I'm not the only one who agrees." I carefully lift her hand and high-five it.

He breathes out. "I could get used to this."

I cock my head. "To what?"

"We're back! Thank you," Mariam says as she takes Maria from Augustine.

"She's adorable," I tell her.

"Thank you so much, Kristina. We'll be going now, but we'll see you guys again."

"Thanks for everything, *salam*," George says.

We say goodbye to them, and they leave. Then we walk to the car, put all the groceries in, and drive home. We don't talk. His eyes are on the road, and mine are on a blur of faces, buildings, and nature.

Now, we're putting the groceries away in the fridge. I used to do this with my mother since I always did the food shopping with her. Now, I'm doing it with Augustine.

So, I wonder about the butterfly effect again, only this time, about mine. Especially now that things have changed since I decided to travel a bumpy road while being scared to drive—literally and figuratively. Requiring a leap of faith. What would be of me now?

In these past few months, I have done things I couldn't have done in ten years' time. For instance, making plans and following through with them. When I was still living at home and made plans, my mother was obviously aware of them since I had to ask a year in advance, but often, I could not follow through with them. My mother would somehow decide on the day of the plans that she wanted to go somewhere and that I was tagging along. As if I had no plans or life of my own. If she suddenly made plans, I had to drop everything. Being dragged to places like a suitcase. As if it were nothing, as if it weren't embarrassing to tell people, "Sorry, my mother decided that we're going to do this today instead. Rain check?" A rain check was never granted. People just didn't invite me anymore, which I completely understood. But it didn't make it less hard. It didn't feel less lonely.

Although there was one type of plan I always disapproved of myself. Swimming. Not because of the scars. This was before, when I was younger.

When swimming, skin is exposed. Now, as an Egyptian woman, I have body hair—a lot of body hair. Everywhere. You name it, I have it. The better question would be where I don't have hair, and the answer is on my palms and the soles of my feet. Of course, my lips and nipples are hair-free, but around them, hair is welcome again with open arms—obviously, not by my hairy arms.

When I used to ask whether I could remove it, I would get lectured as to why no was no and would stay no until it wasn't no, which was when I got married.

See, most women in my culture are taught that the day before your wedding night, you'll shed your fur. This means, we shed for the man, right? Our body belongs to him, not to us anymore. Doing things for him, not for us. The removal of women's body hair is being sexualized by women who don't consider it as something natural and something people can choose to remove for various other reasons or even keep if they want. Since, again, it's something natural, there for several anatomical reasons.

I wanted to remove it because I was just so insecure. Bullied because of it. Blame it on society since the beauty standard is to be as naked as a newborn, which is disgusting if you start thinking about it.

I made my eyebrows as thin as possible. I removed my sideburns and upper lip hair, epilating all of it. *It hurt so damn much.* But I would rather experience physical pain than the emotional one when I used to be called a man because I had a beard and a mustache. Or more hair on my body than the average boy in my class. Being the only one of the girls who had that. Feeling disgusting in my own skin, unable to escape it.

How is a man's opinion of *my* body more valuable than my own? How is following some stupid cultural norm about my *own* body more important than my say, than my own mental health?

Of course, I removed all of it and was yelled at for doing so. Getting bullied for something isn't always a good enough reason for people. It was for me.

Unbelievable, I have always had a reason not to go swimming.

And now, I have this man right here to thank. I don't like comparing Adam and Augustine, but I can't deny that the comparison has to be made.

Because, Augustine, all our butterfly effects have somehow led us to each other as well. Especially the one where we chose to drink our sorrows away that day. Our roads happened to intersect. And yet, seeing as you already knew everyone I knew, it would have only been a matter of time before we met each other one way or another. The intersection would have happened. If it wasn't then, then it would have been at another junction. Many exist.

And if an encounter goes from coincidental to inevitable and that is called fate, then it truly is a silly thing, Augustine.

It appears that Augustine is on his period today. Well, not actually, but it sure looks like it. Now, he's the one lying on the couch, covered with a blanket, and my guilty conscience can't ignore it since he helped me when I was going through it. But not only that. He's actively making sure that I can't ignore it by groaning every thirty seconds. I've counted. Four times. Exactly every thirty seconds. I swear he must be timing it.

I grab Lady from the ground and put her on him. She walks to lie in the space between his shoulder and head with her head against his. He leans into her.

"Emotional support cat who's warm. Check," I say. "I'll make a wet cloth for your head and soup. I will also bring you chocolate. That'll ease the cramps."

He nods, approving of the plan.

I place my hand on his forehead. He really is burning up.

As I try to retract my hand, he holds it there. "Do you feel that? I'm burning hot."

"Yes, apparently so," I say while trying to pull my hand from his evil clutches because, "Do you feel that?" is exactly what he said when we ended up sleeping together.

I finally retract my hand after a lot of force. Man, that man is strong.

I put the cloth on his head and bring him some chocolate. Then, I put some soup in a bowl and place it on the coffee table.

He sits up straight, removes the cloth, and puts the blanket over his head. "Feed me."

"May I advise you starve to death?"

"Feed me," he repeats.

As I'm standing, I look down at him and shrug my shoulders. "Beg me."

He kneels on the floor and grabs my fingers and kisses them. "Please?"

I take back my hand immediately. "Don't actually beg, you idiot!"

He sits on the couch again, and I sit next to him. Turning to him, I bring the spoon to his mouth. It's burning hot. Like he is—I mean, like *he said* he is.

"Blow," I urge.

"Me?"

"Never again."

"Then nurse me back to health and blow on my soup."

If annoying could take on a human form, its name would be Augustine.

I blow on his soup and feed it to him like the toddler he is. Once the bowl is finished, I bring it to the kitchen.

"Anything else I can assist you with?" I say sarcastically.

"Yes. Feed me chocolate."

"Of course."

I remove the wrapper from the chocolate bar and break a piece, bringing it to his mouth. I then break another piece and eat it myself. It's melting in my hands, probably because of the warmth of the soup.

"Do you want more?" I ask.

"Yes, one more."

Of course you want more.

I bring another to his mouth, but he doesn't eat it. Instead, he keeps staring at me and brings his thumb to the corner of my mouth, rubbing it before sucking the top of his thumb. "That was the one I wanted," he says.

God, I ... I can't do this anymore.

I stand up abruptly, and he looks up at me.

"I'm going to shower," I say.

Before he can say anything—and he is about to—I shut him up. "No, you can't join me. Yes, you did want to say that. No, I won't believe the thing you just came up with to prove to me otherwise."

He smiles and lifts his eyebrows. "You have me all figured out, love."

"Unfortunately."

I walk up the stairs and shower. He's getting crazier with each passing day. First, he made small remarks, implicit ones. Now, he's just too direct with both his words and actions. I don't know what to think or do anymore.

Once I put on some clothes, I go downstairs again, only to find the couch empty and the blanket on the floor.

"Augustine?" I yell.

I look in all the rooms, but he isn't here. Where could he have gone? He's sick, for God's sake.

I try calling and texting, but he doesn't answer either. Which kind of worries me because he never just takes off. I never ask about his whereabouts, but he always likes to inform me about them. Every time.

I decide to call Marina. "Marina? I'm sorry to bother you, but do you know where Augustine is?"

"He didn't tell you?"

"Tell me what?"

"Our mother ... she isn't doing all that well anymore. He's probably already at the hospital, and I'm almost there."

"What?! I'm—I'm on my way. What happened? What department is it?"

"Oncology ..." She hangs up the phone.

Beep. Beep. Beep.

My heart drops, and I stop moving. Stop breathing even. Because I didn't know. And I'm assuming Marina doesn't know that I didn't know. I didn't know that their mother has had cancer all this time. I ... I don't know what to think. All I know is that losing people scares me.

Please don't let that be the case.

Please.

CHAPTER NINETEEN

Augustine

Where to even begin? At the beginning, I suppose. My mother and the man who is supposed to be my father, who I refer to as Mario, met in Egypt. They used to go to the same church there, and their marriage was arranged by their families. He told her that he chose to marry her because he loved her from the second he laid his eyes on her. And it was the truth—until it wasn't anymore. My mother, a pure soul, ended up being married to vermin.

He wanted to move to the United States after a year of marriage. Even when she didn't want to move, being taken away from her family, she agreed to it. Thinking that she could give her unborn children a better life if she sacrificed her own. She thought he wanted to move for the same reasons as her, but his reasons were to remove themselves from the people that could keep an eye on them. Her family. His own. The people they knew. Because the selfish bastard wanted to have a better life for himself. Surrounded by women, sex, and substances.

When her family called, they would tell her she was lucky. Living the American dream with the love of her life. She had to lie her way through it, denying what reality was, confirming their assumptions as the truth. That he was the sweetest, that he treated her so good. That he filled the void that was her family. Lies. Not exactly. It was the truth without the adverb not.

He abused her in all the ways one could get abused: financially, emotionally, physically. Sexually. Which is possible when married. Being married is not equal to having the right to do what you want when you want it. Marriage isn't equal to consent forevermore. Consent has to be granted every fucking time.

He completely changed after they moved. From a man from a well-respected family, swooning all over her, to a man who was anything but.

My mother would find receipts for lingerie which she never received. He never bought her anything after that first year of marriage, not for their anniversary, or her birthday. He didn't even know when either was. The only thing he would gift her was a very small amount of money, which was to be spent on only the necessities—barely the necessities. Mass-market clothes and toys not being one of them. But my mother, the woman who never wanted to refuse her children anything, who wanted to give her children the stars if only humanly possible, wanted to give us the life everyone around us had. She wanted to buy us the clothes our friends wore and buy us the hottest new toys.

So, she picked up several jobs behind his back to do so, being a housekeeper, a cleaner at schools, and working in waste management. They were all jobs in which speaking the English language wasn't required to earn money. So she could make ends meet. While raising not one but two children. Alone. While trying to figure out how this new society she had been put in works. Trying to learn the new language she had to use eventually. She was focusing on how to change things instead of crying about it.

I envy her.

All this time, she didn't have a phone. He didn't want her to have one. He didn't want her to communicate with others without him being present. He told her it wasn't necessary, that she wasn't worth caring for. Once she got one—having bought it herself, the first expensive purchase she had ever made for herself, a flip phone—he obviously had to punish her. Women started calling her. Asking her what her opinion was on the fact that her husband was now lying next to them. She could always hear him laughing in the background. Sometimes, they would even knock on our door, calling her names and throwing stuff at her. At her own home.

He laughed at her when he found out about the jobs. Telling her she was just like the dirt she picked up daily, that it suited her after all. He would steal what she had earned. Telling her that *her* son had stolen it. Not his, only hers. And he broke her phone after he had his fun with it.

I would wake up to my mother and him fighting and yelling almost every day. Mostly him yelling at her. I would sit on the highest step of our staircase to watch them. I tried shielding Marina from it all to the best of my abilities. When she would wake up and come to me, I would take her back to her room. Then I would play with her dolls with her and put on *Sailor Moon* for her to watch. Put on music using a cassette player. To cancel out his loud voice, his harsh words. I wanted to do anything to stop him. And I almost did.

Once, I was watching TV, and I saw someone place a pillow on another. They screamed and struggled for a while, but after, they stopped resisting. They stopped moving. They stopped *breathing*. It was quiet. Finally.

He was sleeping alone. They never slept next to each other. My mother always slept next to Marina or me. I grabbed a pillow and almost put it on his head. But I couldn't go through with it.

All I wanted was for him to stop moving, to not lay his hands on my mother again. To not almost choke the life out of her with his bare hands, to not throw anything he could find in our living room at her head, to not pull her hair when she wanted to walk away from him when she was having a full-blown panic attack in front of him.

He once threw an ashtray at her head, causing a severe head injury. He told her it was her fault for annoying him. He would deny everything he did to her. And then blame her for his behavior. Denying and admitting at the same time. The man wasn't right in the head. She tried to tend to her own wound, unable to see it, only being able to feel it, the pain. For her to see the blood on her hands and cry because of it.

There isn't a day I can remember when my mother didn't cry. Because if she wasn't crying about her pain, then it was about ours. That started out as emotional but became physical as well.

When he got violent, especially when he had been using any substance really, he would express it by hitting anyone. Anyone who happened to be standing closest to him. Every time he wanted to hit Marina or my mother, I would jump in front of them. Shielding them, taking his punches as mine. Making bruises cover my arms and back. But I didn't mind. I just wanted them to be safe. At those very moments, as I was holding them, I would wish I could teleport us to any place but home. Freeing ourselves from his clutches. Because the emotional pain used to hurt more than the physical pain inflicted on me. I wished for peace. I was *sobbing* for peace, like the child I was.

We are all bad people. What makes you good is being able to control or resist the bad urges. To not act on the bad thoughts since we all have them. But Mario could never *resist* any of his urges, a word and its meaning both unfamiliar to him.

He only came home to sleep, to sleep with her, and to sleep shit off. When she refused, he would say it was her duty as a wife. She was raped every damn time. She was nothing but an object to him, the last one on his list. The one to end his day with.

I remember all of it so vividly. The bedroom door would be ajar, my mother barely covered in clothes, and him holding her mouth. He would be half-naked himself while suppressing her screams, standing behind her with his other hand holding her hands on her back. Forcing his way into her. Committing sodomy. He used to see me with my eyes filled with tears because all I understood was that she was in pain. He would smile at me with lowered eyes, bringing his index finger to his mouth. Gesturing for me to keep quiet, to keep what was happening in front of my eyes a secret. Now, I understand far too well what was happening in my presence all those times. I was seven.

He used to threaten her. If she were to tell anyone—the church, her family—about what happened between them, he would cut her off financially. He said this before she started working herself. He would put us on the streets without hesitating twice. She didn't care about herself. She only cared about Marina and me having a roof above our heads. She endured him for our sake even when a way out was presented to her when she was pregnant with Marina.

In our religion and culture, divorce isn't allowed. There is even a taboo on the subject. It simply isn't an option one considers. It almost doesn't exist. Even if you don't love each other anymore, that isn't a good enough reason. You ought to try loving each other again and work for your marriage. But that's what enables abuse. There are only two reasons in which the church considers allowing divorce. Either someone abuses the other or one commits infidelity. He checked both boxes. The man was so cruel that even the church realized divorce was the only option.

But the poor woman still had hope. She thought being pregnant with her second child would bring them closer together. As close as they used to be when they were still living in Egypt. When he still loved her. Before he changed.

She didn't want her children to grow up without a father since there were many children who did. She wanted us to have one. She decided to stay for us. Only for him to keep breaking her heart and not actually be present. Only for him to keep leaving behind the small amount of money for us to live off. All of it was brutal, to say the least.

Her intentions were from the heart, but I believe we could have spared ourselves a lot of suffering if she had divorced him back then.

Because all that time, we were surviving rather than living, and it was hard and lonely.

Eventually, he left us when I was twelve. Forcing me to grow up a lot sooner than one would. There was no time for me to have a childhood. It had been taken away from me the minute Mario changed. All this time, but even more so after he left, I was Marina's father figure, treating her like a daughter instead of a sister. And my mother treated me like Marina's father. I was the man of the house, with two women to care for.

Both Marina and I didn't want to get married. For different reasons—hers being that she was scared she would have to endure what she had seen our mother endure. But she found love after all, even if it was me who was playing hard to get—hard to get my approval. I made sure that the man who is her fiancé loves her genuinely, treats her with the utmost respect, and is a good man. Otherwise, I wouldn't have allowed it. Never will what happened in our household repeat itself.

A few years ago, my mother was diagnosed with breast cancer. In her left breast.

She has been undergoing treatment ever since and has been wearing a wig. Not telling a single soul about what she has been dealing with, acting as if she were the happiest woman to walk this earth. It's why I tattooed her name on the left side of my chest. Because of her illness and because she will always stay in my heart, no matter what happens to her.

Because I knew it was only a matter of time. And I knew her wish was for me to get married and to have a wife and children. To see me as the excellent father she knew I would be. Anything she wishes for, I want to grant it to her, wanting to give *her* the stars, if only humanly possible.

Which is why I proposed to marry you, Kristina. Out of convenience, never having told you the actual reason. It was for my mother, Kristina, to fulfill her dying wish, for me to start a family of my own after taking care of this one, fulfilling Mario's role.

The idea of it being arranged means it's a contract. Which means it isn't real, that it only means to live together. Which was perfect. This way, I couldn't hurt a woman if I kept my distance from her. Not be close to her. No strings attached, just convenient for the both of us.

Because I never wanted to get married in the first place. I look exactly like the man, especially now. I'm the spitting image of my father. People always used to tell me how much I looked like him. To me, it means I must be like him as much as I look like him. My father's son, capable of cruel things.

It's why, when I caused you to cry, Kristina, the second time we met, I was hell-bent on apologizing. I didn't want to leave things unresolved. I needed you to have closure, and then I would never approach you again. Not for you to end up experiencing what my mother had, not being apologized to when all my father had done was make her cry. I didn't want any of my actions to resemble his. It *scared* me.

To hurt a woman in a similar manner as my mother has been. Being afraid of what I'm capable of. Accordingly, I swore off women. So I could always be there for my mother and sister, whom I love dearly. That was good enough for me. I promised myself that I would dedicate my life to working for them. To never struggle again, as we used to when I was still too young to do anything about it. And I did. I worked my way to the top, owning a successful accounting firm. Having other small businesses on the side. Providing for the only women in my life. We have had it good ever since.

And ever since, people I had never talked to approached me. Wanting to befriend me. While some of those very people did not look at me twice when all I did was draw my attention to my studies. I wasn't oblivious. I knew their motives. Yet it didn't hinder me from accepting their requests. Since I dedicated my whole life to my family, I had few friends besides George and Tony. I grew up with them.

But people with money aren't really loved. Those people honored me with their lips but not with their hearts. Manipulating me into giving them what they wanted from me.

I never really had genuine connections either. I thought I could never form them as long as people knew who I was and what I did. But I was lonely and longing for someone to talk to, which made me set up an account on an app called Pen Pals Penning. Every user is anonymous, so no one knows who anyone is. I felt as if it was the only way to genuinely connect with someone. No identity, no status, just two people talking and listening to each other.

I named myself Adam after the first man who had been put on this earth. Being the first must have been a big responsibility, and my entire life, it felt as if I had to be responsible. Then, an Eve approached me, who for the longest time was the only person I considered to be a friend, at one point even more. Until Kristina, of course. The second person I have ever felt a genuine connection with.

Because even if you stated that I was nothing but a pawn in your getting your freedom, you were honest about your intentions from the very beginning. You were honest about what it was you wanted from me.

When you didn't want me to pay for the bottle of wine you were drinking from. When you paid for our coffees, telling me that the one who asked should pay. When you wanted to compensate me for buying you a ring. All these things might mean nothing, but to someone who is only used to being used, it meant *everything*.

Not only that, but when we started living together, even if you said that you hated me, you would end up taking care of me. You would wash my clothes if you happened to see them lingering in the laundry room, even fold them. You would buy the things only I ate while you did grocery shopping. And every morning, I would find my coffee mug on the counter, with coffee already having been made by you.

You doing those things, it might have been you honoring us being roommates. But I have always been the caretaker. To end up being taken care of, I can't describe how grateful I felt each time you did those things. It made me fall in love with you even more, more than I already had been. I really tried to distance myself from you, to not be able to ever hurt you. To protect you from what I must be capable of. But I simply couldn't, not when you have had my heart in your angelic clutches ever since.

There is so much more that has happened, more that I cannot remember and my mother did not want to share. Because she already feels guilty that I know these snippets of what her life used to be all those many years ago.

I rush to the hospital, knowing exactly where she is because we have been here before. Many times. For surgery, radiation therapy, and chemotherapy. Every possible treatment has been implemented, but the tumor has metastasized to different organs, which means that the treatments she has now are only meant to slow it down and to ease her pain.

Even if you know how it's going to end and you can anticipate it, it doesn't hurt any less. If not more, because the pain was there all the time. While waiting for the inevitable. The thing that is bound to happen sooner rather than later.

I open the door to the hospital room and see her lying down, turning only her head to me.

"Augustinus," she says, her voice barely coming out of her mouth. "Do you know why I decided to name you that?"

I close the door behind me and walk to the chair next to the hospital bed. "It means to increase, for me to grow and be a tall, muscular man."

The corners of her mouth move slightly away from each other. "Yes, that is what I used to tell you when you were still a young boy. But did I tell you the actual reason?"

I hold her hand and shake my head.

She holds my hand back. "Being venerable. It means to be respected because of character and wisdom," she says. "St. Monica, the mother of St. Augustine, persistently prayed for him for seventeen years, for him to convert to Christianity and to leave his immoral life behind. I used to pray for you before you were even born, up until now. Not because you are living an immoral one, but for you to live a *mortal* one. To live a life full of happiness, to die a happy man."

Behind every man is a great woman. Behind me is the one who raised me. And the one I hope to raise with.

I want you to be the mother of my children, Kristina. I want them to look like you, but more than that, I want them to *be* like you. For them to take after you, share your traits and your character. To merge and unite us through and in another. It symbolizes unity.

I want us to be one like that. I *yearn* for us to be one like that.

I smile at her and nod, bringing her hand to my cheek. Not saying anything for her to share everything she still wants to share. To not leave anything unsaid. To tell me the things only she can tell me ... before it's too late. I want to hear her speak and hear her voice, because I know it will be the last time. I know because her eyes are telling me that it is.

"Like his mother, Monica, who had to endure abuse, my suffering and sacrifices, the ones I know you are aware of, weren't for nothing, Augustine.

Even if your father never returned to us, all my tears weren't for nothing. Look at you, my sweet boy." Her brows draw to each other. "You are everything a man should be. A child of tears like hers shall never perish."

Mine start rolling down my face and onto her hand.

"Her purpose was fulfilled when he finally converted. My purpose is fulfilled now that you are married and Marina is about to."

"Please. I know it's selfish of me to ask, but please, just hold on a little longer, for her. *For me*," I beg of her.

She smiles and shakes her head at me. "As she told her son on her deathbed, I'm telling you this on mine, Augustine. I have seen everything I had to see of this earth, all of its delights. My purposes have been fulfilled. I have no reason to stay anymore. But the greatest delight is your marriage."

For me, the time was ticking too, Kristina. And now, it stopped. I made it in time.

She looks at the ceiling. "What else? I need you to always keep an eye on Marina, no matter what. Don't let the past ever repeat itself."

"Never. I will always do so. You have my word."

"What else … ? There is so much to say, but I don't know where to start," she says, then laughs, in complete pain.

"Anywhere, Mom. Tell me anything you wish to tell me."

"I need you to make sure that Marina doesn't call off her wedding when I'm gone. I need you to celebrate it for me."

I nod and shift her hand from my cheek to my mouth, kissing it.

"I will see you again, but I hope not for a very long time. I wish you could have lived all your years full of love. I'm so sorry, *habibi*, but I hope that your future will make up for past and the pain your father and I caused you."

Nothing could have prepared me for this, not these past years, nothing. The hardest goodbyes are the permanent ones.

"I was loved, Mom. You were perfect."

She tears up, as if she needed me to redeem her, and now that I have, she exhales, as if she's relieved.

Then she sobs and shakes her head again. "I'm not afraid of dying. I'm just afraid of leaving you behind in this sometimes-cruel world."

All she knows is pain. The pain my father caused her. The pain the cancer has caused her. And the pain of the future she won't be here to witness, what the unknown is causing her.

I kiss her hand again.

"But I know everything will turn out all right because you are strong, Augustinus. Stronger than you can possibly imagine. I want you to use this moment to remind yourself of it when you find yourself wanting to give in to weakness," she says. "To remind yourself that you are loved, so deeply."

I wish it were the truth, Mom, but I'm not loved. At least not by the person I want to be loved most by in the world. And it hurts, especially because you think it's genuine, but mainly because I wish it were.

We hear knocking, and we both turn to the door. It flies open, and Kristina enters the room, panting.

Her hair is damp, and she's wearing her pajamas, which means she came here immediately.

My love, you are going to catch a cold like this. I don't want you to get sick. Ever. Please.

My mother wipes away her tears, looks at her, and then sits up straight a little to whisper something in my ear. "She's the one."

I look at Kristina, and she looks at us, tilting her head. Questioning, but not with words.

"Can you give us a moment alone, Augustine? I want to talk to her," my mother says.

I stand up. We glance at each other as I walk past her, leave the room, close the door behind me, and sit in the waiting room. Waiting. Thinking about my mother's words.

Mom, you told me my name means wisdom. But this wise man has no idea what his next step will be when you are about to take your last.

CHAPTER TWENTY

The door closes behind Augustine, leaving me alone with his mother in the hospital room.

I don't want to lie to her. I've never wanted to lie to her, especially not when she's in this state. She deserves nothing but the truth, I know that. But what I don't know is how to even begin explaining that I didn't know my mother-in-law was terminally ill. That I never asked about her health. Never having done anything for her. Guilt is starting to take me over *completely*.

"Kristina, you don't have to pretend anymore. Not in front of me," she says.

I flinch. "What ... what do you mean?"

She gestures for me to sit on the chair next to her bed. I walk toward it and take a seat.

"What was your reason to marry out of convenience?" she asks.

I don't respond. Instead, I just look at her with my brows raised, my eyes wide open, and my jaw falling to the floor.

Then, the realization dawns on me. She knows.

She knows about ... *everything.*

"It's okay, *habibti*. You can tell me anything," she assures me.

My chest feels hot, and I feel myself getting dizzy. "I ... I wanted freedom. I wanted to live my life for myself and not for other people anymore, and since I couldn't do that while I was still living at home and the only way to move out was marriage, I married your son."

She nods and smiles. "I understand. Do you know why he wanted to marry you?"

I used to wonder at first, but then I let it go. I was too self-absorbed. I couldn't care less about his reasons. But now that she mentions it, to this day, I still have no clue what Augustine gained by marrying me.

I shake my head at her in answer.

"He did it for me. I know my son all too well. He wanted to grant all my wishes, seeing him married, being one of them. His whole life, he has put others' needs above his own, never going after what he wants. As have you." She places her hand on her breast. "When the cancer spread, it was only a matter of time. He was aware of it, and that was why he married you."

"I didn't—I didn't know his reason. I only knew that he wanted to. I'm sorry for everything. I know it's wrong to marry if you don't love each other."

"Maybe at first, but things have changed," she says.

I give her a questioning look.

"I can see the way he looks at you. That is a man *in love*. I only hope that you can somehow feel the same along the way."

"No, you've got it all wrong—"

She interrupts me. "He has prioritized my happiness his whole life, and he knew marriage would make me the happiest. I approved of it because I just hoped you two would fall in love eventually. I even tried to make it happen at one point when I realized that it wasn't going the way I'd hoped it would."

"Tried? What do you mean?"

A weak chuckle leaves her lips. "I knew you didn't have a guest room and that the extra bedroom was yours. So, if someone were to ever sleep over, it would mean that you had to share a room. Which was why I made sure I visited you the day there was a storm. I should thank the news for telling me about it a week in advance," she says. "But the pillows in the living room were gone in the morning. I'm assuming you took them to separate you, so unfortunately, my plan didn't work out the way I'd hoped it would."

I gasp because I can't believe my ears. "You planned that?!"

"I will always be a romantic, even on my deathbed, as you can see," she says, gesturing at it.

I smile at her with tears in my eyes. And then my smile fades as fast as it appeared. "I'm sorry. I'm so sorry for never checking up on you. I would have. It's just that ..."

"Oh, *habibti,* you can't do something if you don't know something. I knew you didn't know about my illness because I knew Augustine wouldn't share that with you." She removes her wig from her head. "Besides, I didn't want anyone to know. I didn't want people to just know me as the woman who was terminally ill."

My tears roll down my cheeks, and I shake my head. "No, you are so much more. You're such a sweet woman. Even before I knew Augustine, you were always so good to me. Remember? You would find me sitting alone, eating breakfast, after church every Friday, and invite me to sit with you. Making me laugh. Talking about the things I wish I could talk about with my mother. You are so much more."

She tries to put her wig back on, but I stop her. "You are beautiful, just as you are."

Her expression lights up, and she holds my hand. "My sweet girl, don't cry." She wipes away my tears with her other hand. "I know it isn't real, but please, take care of him. Even if you don't love him, please be there for him. I don't want him to be lonely or alone."

I sniffle. "I will take care of him, I promise. You can count on me."

"I know."

"And please, don't tell him I know he did it for me," she adds.

I confirm that I won't. Because I was never planning on it. Everything she has told me, I will take with me to my grave.

"And, Kristina, one more thing. He does love you. I know because his father used to give me that same look before everything went downhill."

"Downhill?"

"You will understand once I'm gone. But I need you to remember something the moment you understand. He might be the spitting image of his father, but he will *never* be him. I can assure you of that because *I* raised him."

She breathes out. "Now, I have done everything I wanted to do, I have no unfinished business anymore. I will leave things in your hands now."

"Don't say that, please."

She presses her lips into a thin line. "I'm just very tired."

I nod at her and stand up to embrace her. "I know. You should rest now. I will be here, next to you, as you do."

"I'm glad that you are. I wouldn't want it any other way. This is *perfect*."

I hold her, hug her. And I feel her muscles relax in my embrace. She must be asleep.

It's quiet. Only the sound of the heart monitor echoes through the room, its pace decreasing.

Until there isn't a pace anymore. Until simultaneous beeps become one long one, taking over the entire room.

I immediately shift my head to the monitor, only to see a flat line on the screen.

I hold on to her as tight as I can.

No.

I feel a lump in my throat.

I feel my whole body heating up. I feel cold, goose bumps rising on my skin.

My heart rate increases. It scares me.

I can't breathe.

And I give in to crying hysterically.

"No, please?" I shake her body, still not pulling myself off her. Not able to bring myself to see her face. Because I find myself now in denial. Once I pull away, I can't turn back. "You still have to forgive me! We haven't finished our conversation yet!"

I scream at the top of my lungs, "YOU CAN'T DO THIS! YOU'RE THE ONLY ONE LEFT! MAMA?! PLEASE!

"AUGUSTINE!"

The door blows open. I see spots through my tears that are supposed to resemble Augustine, Marina, and doctors, standing in the doorway.

Marina starts crying immediately and rushes over to me; she also holds on to her mother.

"I-I'm so sorry! She was supposed to just sleep!" I yell, the words barely reaching them because I can't stop bawling my eyes out.

Because Marina didn't get to say goodbye, and it's all my fault.

Marina hugs me while we both hug her mother. Her body slowly turning colder.

A doctor walks to the monitor and turns it off.

"I'm sorry. I know how hard this is, but we have to move her," the doctor says.

I turn my head slightly, seeing him from the corners of my eyes behind me, and like the guard dog I am, I tell him, "Don't you dare take her away."

The other doctors start whispering for Augustine to intervene. He first grabs Marina, who resists but then kisses her mother on the head and leaves the room.

I'm still refusing to let go of her.

He then walks to me, hugs me from behind, and whispers in my ear, "I know this is hard, but you have to let her go now."

"I can't—I can't look at her."

"You don't have to. You just have to close your eyes, turn around, and hold on to me instead."

I close my eyes and slowly bow down to let her rest on the bed. I turn around, and Augustine immediately grabs me and buries me in his chest. Tightly holding my head with one hand and my waist with the other. I'm unable to move.

I can hear the other doctors start walking, and the hospital bed wheels squeak on the floor. It's loud. Harsh. And definite.

She is being taken away.

We stay in that position for a moment, for me to sob to my heart's content against his.

Eventually, Augustine leaves to fill out forms, and Marina and I end up comforting each other in the waiting room. Then, her fiancé comes to pick her up, to be with her. I keep waiting for Augustine, and eventually, we leave too.

We are now driving home. I look out the window and see my reflection. My eyes are puffy, and I look numb. I haven't cried like I did today in *years*. But losing her is affecting me way more than I would have ever expected. And I feel guilty that her last moments were with me and not them, guilty that I didn't know.

"Why didn't you tell me?" I ask, still looking out the window.

"You wanted distance. Telling you would have hindered that."

"It was unfair, Augustine."

"I know. I know it wasn't fair," he says. "What did she tell you?"

I can't tell you because I promised not to. But I also want you to believe that you made her happy in her last months since it was your goal. I don't want to shatter that. So, I will do the thing I did the very first time we met—tell you the truth by omission.

"We were just reminiscing about our breakfast dates that we had when I used to go to church on Fridays."

We arrive home, and I clean the bowl he had soup from. I completely forgot that he's sick, acting like he isn't. Acting like he's okay on all the fronts he shouldn't be okay on.

He's showering now.

I find myself looking at the big picture of our wedding day, the one she gifted us. I'm standing so close to it that I have to look up to see it. And since the lights are out and it's the middle of the night, I can't see it all too well.

I feel Augustine approaching me. He places his hands on the picture from behind me and closes me in. I turn around, and he almost immediately bows down to rest his head on my shoulder, making me stand against the picture.

He breathes out. "I know I've been unfair already, but I'm going to be unfair again."

"What?"

"The distance; can I remove it once more?"

"What do you mean—"

"Sleep with me."

"Augustine, I don't think—"

"No, not that. Let me just hold on to you tonight." And he whispers, "Please? Just this once."

I don't respond at first, not because I'm hesitating, but because I'm not. Because, somehow, I'm okay with it.

But my silence makes him ask again. "May I?"

"You may."

He lifts his head and looks at me. He then removes his hands from the picture and takes my hand, guiding me to his bedroom.

Once we enter, he closes the door behind him. I don't look at him and get into his bed, facing the door. Then, he gets in, too, and I feel his hands on my body, pulling me into his embrace with one arm wrapped around my collarbones and the other around my lower stomach.

We don't talk. And I can't sleep. Not because of discomfort but because of today dawning on me. That someone died in my arms. Someone I had a personal relationship with. And it hurts. It hurts because if I had known, I could have spent more time with her. Gotten to know her better, beyond the conversations we had on Fridays. That it's just too late for that. And I hate it. I hate that I didn't know.

And I hate that Augustine is trying to hold himself together. I know our bond is odd, and I know I'm mostly responsible for it, but I want to be there for him, to be his friend.

He sniffles against my ear. I turn my head around, only to find him sleeping. And crying. A tear is rolling down his face.

As he holds on to me, I turn my whole body around to face him. I wipe away the tear with my finger and hold him back.

Somehow along the way, I've started to feel safe in his presence, even behind closed doors.

When the funeral had to be planned, Marina told Augustine something I didn't quite understand. She told him he had done enough. That he had carried their family on his back since he was little. That it was time to stop giving and to start receiving. He resisted at first but eventually gave in, trying to distract himself with work. Because even when I thought he was acting like he was okay, he wasn't. He just needed time to realize what reality was. He has been grieving for his mother ever since in his own way. And Marina is resilient. She was grieving for her mother too, but she turned all her grief into making her mother's funeral the most memorable one. She asked me to help her instead, and I did. It was an honor.

First, there was a prayer at church, and then everyone gathered at the cemetery for the burial. Everyone was offered the chance to take the shovel and be a part of burying her. Taking a moment to do so. To say goodbye. And after that, everyone gathered at church again to talk about her and to share memories and stories. To laugh, to cry. Everything about it was beautiful and memorable, exactly what Marina had wished for. But during it all, I realized some things that troubled my mind.

Many leave this world with no warning. Whether it's because of a car accident, an illness one wasn't aware of, or on purpose—though often, there are signs prior to it that others decide to ignore—things get left unsaid.

Their mother was sick. Somehow, even when she thought people didn't know, a lot of them did.

And all those people who shared good memories probably hadn't spoken to her in a long time. Because some mentioned that there was so much they still wanted to say. Which made me not understand why they didn't. Why they didn't when it wasn't too late yet.

We celebrate birth, and we gather at death. And we won't know when it's our turn. We won't know when people will gather for us. And we won't be there to witness it. We won't know what kinds of things are going to be shared, what kinds of things people remember us by. How people truly feel about us. We won't know because those confessions don't reach us. Like most confessions don't.

I wish we would let our loved ones know what it is we would say at their funerals. Let the living be a part of what happens when they aren't.

We should tell our loved ones we love them a little more often.

Not long after the funeral, Marina's wedding date approached. She wanted to call the whole thing off, and her fiancé told her, anything she wished to do was going to be done. But Augustine intervened and practically forced her to go through with it because their mother had already known this would happen and explicitly told him not to let her call off the wedding. That was enough to persuade Marina.

It was beautiful, the whole wedding. But also heart-wrenching.

Because Augustine was the only one of her family there for her, walking her down the aisle. I can't imagine how she must have felt then. Marrying someone you truly love, only to not have the person you loved truly first celebrate it with you. Afterward, Marina told me she wanted to get married before her mother died. And that she regretted not having her wedding sooner. She regretted she was too late. And that hurt me deeply.

So, a lot has happened in the span of a long ten days, and I need a drink.

I enter the not-so-unfamiliar pub, where I somehow always end up when things get rough.

I sit on a stool and see the not-so-unfamiliar bartender turning to me.

"Is it just me, or are you always here when I'm going through it?" I ask.

She laughs. "Maybe I'm your guardian angel?"

"It wouldn't surprise me if you were."

"What brings you here today?" she asks while drying off a glass.

"The better question would be, what doesn't bring me here?"

She pours me a glass of wine. "That bad?"

I drink from it. "That bad. My faux husband's mother died. Apparently, his reason for marrying me was because it was her dying wish. She ended up knowing that everything was fake, telling me that his love for me isn't. And he doesn't know that she knew."

"I already told you, I don't think he hates you."

"But it just doesn't make sense for him to love me. He's also never said he does."

"Don't you love him? Even after just living together?"

I shake my head. "I'm in love with someone else. Someone I don't even know since it's someone I talk to on the internet." Then, I sigh. "I mean, the whole *hating each other* thing, I've let that go. He even offered for us to be friends, and I accepted that since roommates can be friends, that it's normal to be friends."

"But?" she asks.

"But then we kind of slept together, and that made our whole dynamic change. All we do is tease each other about it. To see who's better at doing so."

She laughs again. "That's cute."

"It's annoying," I say, somewhat glaring.

"Do you think that if the person from the internet wasn't in the picture, you would love him?"

I lean back, thinking about the question. Because I don't know. Would I? I wouldn't exactly say I would. "I don't think so. All this time, I've just considered him to be the key to my freedom. I've never wanted to take a better look at him to not complicate that."

"But you have. I mean, you slept together. That's very intimate. Even if people say sleeping with someone doesn't have to mean anything, it's still two people choosing to be vulnerable with each other."

"I mean, I guess you're right, but still. I'm in this weird state where everything is just standing still. I can't move because I can't move on from the internet person and I can't move back from sleeping with him. I'm just there, standing."

"Maybe you will move again, if you decide to be open for someone else," she says.

"I don't think I can ever do that."

"Never say never. Who would have thought that the day you sat here all those months ago would be the answer to all your problems? I'm guessing not me and especially not you."

A customer calls for her, and she leaves to help them. As I'm finishing the glass of wine, I find myself thinking.

Even when I know that it's expected for me to love Augustine and not Adam, I somehow can't bring myself to. Because I simply don't feel anything toward him. And I can't force myself to love someone. Anyone would agree; love is something that has to be felt, not something that has to be made.

I leave the pub and arrive home. Not soon after, Augustine does too. I can hear the front door from my room.

Making my way downstairs, I see a vase with flowers on the kitchen counter. It's that time again, the time when he buys a bouquet of flowers, puts it in a vase, and gives it to me, only for me to put it back on the counter.

I walk toward him and extend my arms. He smiles, grabs the vase, and gives it to me. I put it back on the counter and look at the tag. This time, they're called bleeding flowers. They're pink, and their branches bend out of the vase.

The kettle whistles, and I turn off the stove.

I go to the cabinet and hold the handles. Before pulling on them, I turn around. "Do you want some tea?"

He nods at me.

I open the cabinet. The cups are normally on the highest shelf, so I must climb on the counter. But this time, they're on the middle shelf, so hopefully, I don't have to climb to get them. It would be embarrassing to do that in front of him.

I stand on my toes and try to grab the cups with both hands. But of course, I'm failing miserably because I'm too short by a freaking inch.

He catches on. Without saying anything, he puts one hand on my shoulder and the other on my hand, which is up in the air, in the cabinet. Stroking it. He then brings the hand on my shoulder to my waist, making me put that arm down.

It reminds me of the time he was at my house when he proposed in front of our families. We were grabbing cups. The only difference is, he isn't being coy. Instead of not touching me, his whole front is touching my entire back. He's even pushing himself into me, closing me in, causing my hip bones to press against the edge of the counter.

He slowly lifts me up with the hand on my waist, allowing me to reach the two cups. I immediately slide two fingers into their handles and hold them, bringing our hands down. I place the cups on the counter. Then he puts me down again but doesn't let go of me. He's still standing behind me with his hand resting on mine, his other on my waist, and his lips near my ear.

His body heat radiates into mine. But my body heat somehow ends up in one place—my center.

I breathe out shakingly.

In order for me to release myself from him, I have to push myself into him even more. I take a step back, pushing him with my behind to free myself from his arms. He takes a step back too.

I turn around and tell him, "How about you grab the tea bags from the other cabinet?"

He opens the cabinet next to the one we just grabbed the cups from and takes out the box of tea bags. "Strawberry?"

"Do you really still have to ask?"

He takes two and puts the box back into the cabinet.

Then, he opens the first one by ripping the package with his teeth, spitting out the part that's between his teeth, and putting the bag in one of the cups.

And he repeats it with the second one. Only this time, when he's ripping it and spitting it out, he locks eyes with me. I'm unable to look away because he's staring so intensely at me.

And it looks as if he's ripping open a condom wrapper. And heat takes over my center even more.

He pours water into the cups, spilling a little on his hand. "It's burning hot.

Be careful, love."

I'm trying, Augustine, but I can't seem to let go of things causing me to feel hot and bothered.

I put sugar in the cups, and we take them to sit on the couch. The second Augustine sits down, Lady jumps on his lap and keeps tossing and turning until she finds a comfortable angle.

I pout. "She used to do that with me alone."

He pets my head while petting hers. "Don't be jealous, love."

"Yes, well, I kind of can't help it. She's supposed to be my loyal familiar."

He scoffs. "You're a witch now?"

"I could be?"

"Beyond any doubt. After all, you have me under your spell."

"I—" All this man does is leave me speechless with his witty remarks. "How did you even get so close to her?"

He's thinking. Thinking of the perfect response—I can see that he is. "I'm just very lovable," he says, shrugging his shoulders.

I knew it. "I would say you're very funny."

He slightly tilts his head, looking at me with puppy eyes. Or, for Lady's sake, pussy eyes. No, I mean, cat eyes. Not—oh, never mind.

"Do you think I'm very funny?" he asks.

"I think you very are."

"Good. I want to make you laugh."

I laugh. Because he really is funny and his remarks are always funny too. Even if I don't like to admit it.

You do make me laugh, Augustine. Thank you.

CHAPTER TWENTY-ONE

Eve: Adam. When giving someone a gift on the day they were born ... what can you possibly give them that they don't already have?

Adam: Eve, funny you should mention the day a person was born.

Eve: Funny why?

Adam: For no particular reason. However, I would say that anyone would appreciate any gift as long as it is from the person they want it from. Then it wouldn't matter what it is. Even their shoelace would do.

Eve: But what if you want to gift something thoughtful?

Adam: Then you can always just try to question them about it. Perhaps they will tell you exactly what it is they want from you. I know I would.

Today is Augustine's birthday. A couple of months ago, I couldn't have cared less about the day he happened to be born, but now that we're friends, I do care. And I have no idea what to give him. Then, I have an epiphany. The reason I have no idea is because I don't really know anything about him. I only know snippets because of things I happened to see lingering in his room, but I don't actually know what he likes or loves. And I never asked about him. And I think I'm feeling guilty because he happens to know exactly all those things about me. Because he *did* ask about me.

I considered buying him art supplies, but I don't know what he would need since I'm no expert on the subject. I almost wanted to buy him a set of one hundred brushes, but I didn't go through with it. It seemed a little ... too much. And too little. Then I wanted to buy him books because I know he reads, but then again, I don't know *what* he reads since all the shelves he owns consist of books with their spines facing inward. I considered jewelry, but I haven't a clue what he likes. Although he probably likes his wedding ring since he never takes it off.

Eventually, I gave up. Or rather, I gave up on finding something on my own. I'm just going to ask the man once and for all what he wants. Since Adam advised it, and I trust his judgment *blindly*.

I knock on his door. But he doesn't answer, which means he isn't in his room.

I go downstairs, only to find him sitting on the couch with Lady on his lap, looking at his screen. He's texting. Probably responding to all the birthday wishes.

And he's wearing a suit. Black.

I stand in front of him. "Augustine, happy thirty-fourth. Is there something you would like to have?"

He quite literally throws his phone next to him while staring at me. I, on the other hand, follow it with my eyes and turn back to him. He lifts Lady from his lap. Fortunately, he doesn't throw her as well.

"Are you offering?"

"Well, yes?" I say as he stands up, making me look up at him now.

He slightly tilts up his chin while looking down at me. "You."

I sigh. "I can't give you myself."

"Fine. Then I want you to kiss me. Kiss me for a good thirty-four seconds. That's what I want you to give me."

My neurons aren't communicating anymore. They have been fried. On fire rather than firing. I can't believe what he just said right now. He must be joking. What? "You? What—"

He cups my cheek. "It's not too expensive, is it, love? I'm very humble when it comes to you."

They're supposed to be thirty-four candles for you to blow air on, not thirty-four seconds for you to be gasping for air against my mouth.

And I didn't expect him to be so blunt either. But I suppose I could give him what he wants since I already refused—

Wait a fucking second. Did he just manipulate me by using a method *I* learned about myself?

The door-in-the-face technique is a compliance technique—but I consider it to be a technique to manipulate someone—where one first makes an extravagant request, only to end up requesting the thing they truly want. Knowing that the first request would have been refused. And since people don't want to refuse twice, they somehow end up agreeing to the second request. Whereas if the second request had been made from the get-go, they would have been likely to refuse it since they normally wouldn't agree to it in the first place. This way, the *manipulatee* tries to meet the manipulator halfway. Not actually, just making it seem so. Since hello? Manipulated to see so?

The nerve.

The man is evil.

I was meant to use that on people, not it winding up being used on me. I'm ashamed, deeply. I'm a disgrace for a psychology major. A poor excuse even.

I scowl at him. "Clever. The door-in-the-face technique? It makes me want to slam the door in your face and deny your request just out of spite. And it makes me want to literally slam one in your face."

"I don't know what that means. Teach me?"

"Apparently, you don't need the lesson since you've just created a perfect example of it, one that can go straight into social psychology textbooks."

"But I'm the birthday boy, love."

"But you're the birthday boy indeed."

"You can't deny me. That would be cruel." His other hand cups my cheek. "Even for you."

I guess you deserve it. Almost making me fall for it. I can't help but respect that. Gifting me awareness that I shouldn't forget about techniques. Fine, Augustine, I will gift you what you want from me. It's just an exchange, not of saliva, but of gifts.

"Request granted."

He lets go of me to grab his phone and starts tapping on the screen. "I'm a righteous man. The timer will go off in exactly thirty-four seconds once I press Start. Seconds won't turn into hours."

"Believe me, I would notice."

"Would you? Time flies when one finds themself immersed in pleasure." He holds my cheek with one hand now. "Where were we?"

"Nowhere still."

"Let us change that." He puts his lips on mine, and not after three whole seconds does he press Start, making the timer tick.

I wrap one arm around his neck. And kiss him back.

This familiar taste, the one I think about, even when I don't want to. But he still tastes as sweet. It still feels as good.

Then it gets a little rougher.

Much rougher. Like he was hungry for this. Like this is the only way to satiate his hunger, and he decides to do just that. To even go beyond satiation.

I'm unable to even breathe. But I don't mind because this, seems like a good way to go.

The timer goes off. Very loudly. It's impossible to miss.

Instead of letting me go like the righteous man he is, he throws his phone on the floor and puts that hand to rest on my behind. Squeezing it while pressing me against him. He presses me against him even more because the hand that was on my cheek is now on the back of my head with force.

It keeps going off, and he doesn't give any mind to it. Instead, he's focused on the way his tongue moves against mine.

Another thirty-four seconds pass.

Augustine, you didn't turn sixty-eight. But I suppose you could. One day, you will, right? Consider this an early birthday present.

Suddenly, the doorbell rings. Making my auditory cortex in my temporal lobe temporarily go berserk. Because now, a timer is going off, a bell is ringing, and the sound of smooches is taking over the room.

But because of the cocktail party effect—being able to steer my auditory attention to just one stimulus among others, making the others appear in the background—I find only the sound of kissing being processed. The ticking and ringing are just extras, while our lips are the main characters. And they have a lot to say. A whole story to tell.

He pushes his lips even deeper for a last second and then abruptly pulls himself away from me.

We keep staring at each other. Panting. Hard. With both our chests rising and falling, synchronized with each other.

He walks away from me as he wipes his mouth with the back of his hand; I'm guessing that he's wiping off the saliva that we exchanged since he's going to open the door to God knows who.

But God knows who saved us by ringing the door. Because if they hadn't, I don't know what would have happened. All I know is that he wouldn't have stopped, that *we* wouldn't have stopped.

Saved by the bell, literally. I turn the timer off.

I see Alex, Sarah, and Tony walk into the living room with Augustine behind them.

I didn't know she was coming. She didn't even tell me she was. "Alex?"

"Kristina? I didn't know you lived here too!"

I narrow my eyes at her. "Alex."

She narrows her eyes back at me. "Kristina."

"Sarah ..." Sarah says.

Alex and I laugh. I greet them both and wave at Tony since he's talking with Augustine.

"We just came to congratulate your husband on being old," Alex says.

"Well, you aren't wrong. He *is* old," I tell her. Apparently, even older than sixty-eight by God knows how many years—I lost track of the seconds.

We all sit down. I'm sitting in the middle with Alex and Augustine beside me on the couch. Sarah and Tony are sitting on the armchairs across from each other.

Sarah stands up. "Augustine, happy birthday."

"Thank you, Sarah."

"Tony and I brought you this." She takes out a bottle of red wine from her bag and hands it to him.

I wish that were for me instead. It's a bottle of Gaja Barbaresco. That must taste good. I mean, I could steal a few sips without him noticing, right? Definitely.

He puts the bottle on the coffee table.

"My gift will be revealed later," Alex says, grinning.

I bet it's a sex toy. It has to be. It's written all over her face. Why doesn't that surprise me?

"Can I offer you all some tea?" I ask them.

I see nodding from several heads, meaning tea is a good idea. It always is.

I get up.

Alex gets up as well. "I'll help you!"

I let her since I betrayed her that time I let Augustine help me instead. I owe her one.

She walks with me to the kitchen.

"Okay, I'm glad, you're taller, so you can actually reach the cups. Because I was definitely not about to climb," I say.

"I already thought so, shorty."

She opens the cabinet and grabs five cups. "So, how is your sex life? Is it still awesome?"

I can't believe that I actually don't have to lie to her now. Now, *that's* awesome.

"It's very awesome and even more so," I say as I put the kettle on the stove. "I finally understand what you mean by second and third base feeling just as good."

She nods at me fast because her point has finally been proven to me after all this time. "Right? Right? Who needs dick?"

"Apparently, no one. Completely unnecessary."

"Hey, if you want to play for both teams, be the chameleon. I, as a coach, approve," she says and winks.

I shoot her a look, thinking about it. "I will definitely consider it."

The kettle whistles, and I turn off the stove. "Do you know which flavors Tony and Sarah like?"

"Yeah, green tea. You and Augustine drink strawberry, right?"

"Yes."

Alex grabs the tea bags from the tea box and puts them in the cups. I fill them with water.

"Kristina?" Tony yells.

"Yes?" I yell back.

"Come here for a sec."

"Go. I'll put them all on a plate and bring it to the living room," Alex says.

I mouth, *Thank you*, and go to the others.

"Yes?" I repeat to Tony.

"Do you guys have plans for tonight?"

I try looking at Augustine as discreetly as I possibly can. But, all he does is tell me with his eyes that I should say yes. Now. It's scary how I understand him with his bright green eyes almost blinding me.

I nod fast. "Yes!"

"Bummer. We wanted to eat out with you guys."

"I'm sorry. Maybe next time?"

Alex approaches us with a plate full of cups, walking around to give everyone theirs.

"Did you guys ever go on a honeymoon?" Sarah asks.

No. We didn't. And we won't. But fortunately, this is the only lie we have ever prepared since we got married. We're natural at telling this one. We even prepared this one so well that we take turns telling it.

"Too busy," I say.

"With work," he says.

"So, when are you going then?" Tony asks.

Our preparations have unfortunately come to an end. This we didn't prepare. We didn't think that far ahead. Wait, can't I use that thought as my answer? Of course I can. "We didn't think—"

Augustine interrupts me. "Soon."

Soon? What do you mean soon, Augustine? Or are you just lying through your teeth right now? Are you? You'd better be.

"You guys should. Mariam and George said that the whole experience was amazing," Sarah says.

Tony nods. "And Sarah and I find ourselves more hyped about our honeymoon than our wedding."

She smiles at him. "Yeah, we actually are."

They smile at each other now. I know my first impression of them wasn't good, but as time passes, I realize they're good people.

It has also made me realize I shouldn't judge people just because they happen to be a part of something. The whole doesn't have to define one. Because even though people are part of the mean, form it even, it doesn't define them individually.

We keep chatting, mostly about Egypt and our vacations there. How we see people carrying their groceries on their heads and how auto rickshaws, known as *toktoks* in Egypt, are the main means of transportation. How the cinemas still have intermissions. That everyone's experiences are universal—being there for a whole month with your family in the summer, sleeping during the day because the weather is too much to bear, and being awake at night when there's a nice breeze.

Then the weather inside of *me* starts to be too much to bear. My heart rate has increased, as if I just ran a marathon and actually made the effort to reach first place. And it feels as if my whole face is red. I feel flushed. Hot even.

I turn to Augustine. He looks uneasy as well and has his hands in fists on his lap, holding them with force. His knuckles turn white while his hands turn red.

What is happening?

Alex gestures for me to scoot over. I do, and she sits between Augustine and me, putting her arms around us. "The timer is set for fifteen minutes."

God, please don't remind me of timers being set.

"What?" I say.

"What you guys are feeling now will worsen in fifteen minutes. Although I would say will better, but everyone is entitled to their own opinion."

"Whatever do you mean?" Augustine asks.

"I laced both your teas with a substance like Viagra. Don't worry; I did extensive research. It's not harmful. I wouldn't have done it if it were. It will kick in, in fifteen minutes, which is why we're all leaving in one."

Oh my God.

No. I knew it tasted weird, but Augustine didn't say anything, so I thought my taste buds were playing tricks on me. Since my body loves doing that to me—confuse me.

Tea is *not* always a good idea, especially not when Alex is somehow involved.

She turns to Augustine and whispers, "Happy birthday sex, Augustine, this is my gift to you. Her horny, you aroused."

She jumps to her feet. "Can we leave? I just realized I have a ton of schoolwork."

Sarah and Tony get up as well.

"Enjoy your day!" Sarah says.

"Yes. Be sure to enjoy your night, too. And morning. Basically till the sun comes up. Since you guys like doing just that," Alex says, wearing her mischievous grin.

I wish it had been just a sex toy.

I will kill you for this one, Alex. Kill.

We say goodbye to them for a while since it's something Egyptians do.

They leave, even though I want to pull Alex back to strangle her. I'm resisting urges on a whole different level. And that will probably be the case now as well.

Because Augustine and I are in the living room. Three meters away from each other. Slowly panting this time—exactly where we left off.

The timer that wasn't actually set has gone off in my center. Fifteen minutes have passed. I can't hear it, but I sure as hell feel it. *Contractions.*

He loosens his tie, tightens his jaw, and looks as if it's taking everything in him to say, "I have to go to, go."

He has to go to, go?

The man can't even think straight anymore. And neither can I.

He slowly walks away. He can't seem to properly walk anymore either. And I don't want him to because there's only one thing I want right now.

For him to stop walking away from me and to take me instead. I want him to fucking take me. So hard that *I* can't properly walk anymore.

I walk—unfortunately properly—over to him and grab his wrist from behind him. "Where do you think you're off to?"

He doesn't turn to me and starts shaking his hand for me to let go. "Don't touch me, not right now, love. Please."

"This will be the last time," I say to convince him. To convince myself. That it's okay if we give in, if we promise that it won't happen again after this. So we don't make things even weirder than they already are.

He slightly turns his head, watching me from the corners of his eyes. "Is what you said last time."

"There won't be a third time. Ever. No holy trinities in sex. This is just to relieve ourselves."

And he finally turns to me completely. I'm still holding his wrist. "You know that one round won't satisfy me and that I won't be able to stop. Especially now. Can you handle that?"

Now, *my* mischievous grin takes over my face since I solemnly swear that I am up to no good. "Yes. In fact, I think I'm capable of doing more rounds than you. Positive even."

He wets his lips while looking down at me. "Good girl. Show me."

Augustine twists his hand, holding my wrist now instead. He pulls me into him by bringing the hand holding my wrist to his shoulder, and with his other hand, he lifts me from the ground. I wrap my legs around him.

He makes us sit on the couch. I'm hovering above him with my knees on the couch beside his legs, lifting myself.

He takes off his suit jacket and tie and starts unbuttoning his shirt, exposing his upper body, but doesn't take it off. "Let us actually finish what we started before they came, interrupting us."

He kisses me. And he wasn't lying. He's starting where we left off. Because he isn't kissing me gently as he always starts his kisses, he's kissing me as roughly as before. Still as hungry as before. Even hungrier than before.

He stops. "Kristina, lower yourself on me—now."

I do as he says, placing my center on his erection. Which almost immediately sends shivers down my spine. As he starts guiding my hips back and forth, we continue kissing.

I feel his hands on the collar of my T-shirt, and then I hear the sound of fabric ripping. I pull away from him to find my T-shirt has become an open cardigan without buttons. "Hey! That's my favorite T-shirt!"

He points at his unbuttoned shirt. "Now, we both have our shirts open. It's only fair. Equity, my love."

I squint my eyes at him, annoyed. Very annoyed because I want to laugh.

"It was in the way, love," he says, holding the outside of my thighs.

I pout.

He smiles at me. "I will buy you ten new ones in all the colors your favorite

T-shirt is available in."

"Well, in that case, it's available in three colors."

"Then I will buy you thirty. I'm a man of my word."

Not exactly. Not as righteous as you said you were. But I don't want you to be. I want you to be as gluttonous as you can possibly be right now.

He kisses me again while squeezing the outside of my thighs. Until we get interrupted again. By fur. A lot of it.

By Lady walking in on us and walking *on* us, wanting me to get the hell off the lap that's her resting place. She's sitting on his stomach while her face is resting on mine. Staring at me while wagging her tail at him.

We both freeze.

Only my mouth moves. "Well, this sure isn't awkward at all. Is it just me, or is this what people feel when their child walks in on them doing it?"

He chuckles. "Well, in essence, Lady here is your daughter. And I'm practically her dad by now."

I hold up my finger to him, warning him. "Stepdad."

I lift Lady. "Lady, as you can see, I'm busy with, well, being a lady. So, shoo and let me finish. In more ways than one?" That is rather meant for Augustine than Lady.

I gently throw her on the ground since cats always land on their feet. Although Lady's somehow an exception to this rule, she always survives.

"I can make that happen," he says.

"I'm counting on it."

He looks at Lady, who just jumped on the couch again. "Thank you, Lady. You gave me an even better idea."

He squeezes my thighs again to take me with him as he stands up. I wrap my arms and legs around him.

"Where to?" I ask against his throat.

"Our first destination is the bathroom. Then we will start making our way to all the other rooms. Did I ever even give you a proper tour? Shame on me. You are deserving of one. To test out all the surfaces."

"I can't help but agree."

He opens the door to his bedroom and goes to his nightstand.

"What are we doing here?" I ask.

"Condoms," he says, bowing down while rummaging through his drawer.

"What? No, I don't want to feel latex. I want to feel skin." I wrap my legs tighter around him.

That makes him straighten up again. He takes a moment before answering. Probably thinking about my answer or what I just did with my legs. "On second thought, I like your view on the matter better."

He closes the drawer again, and we leave his room. Once we enter the bathroom, he closes the door behind him, making me see my reflection in the mirror. Which is hilarious because I look like an annoying child that doesn't want to let go. And it's the truth. I don't want to.

He walks to the sink, puts me down, kneels, and gestures for me to put both my hands on his shoulders. I do, and he pulls down my leggings, taking them off for me. He plants four big kisses on the inner sides of my thighs, assuring me he didn't forget and that he won't. And then he plants small kisses on my underwear, which makes *me* form fists for a change.

Augustine then stands up again to take off my new *cardigan* and bra. He strips me of my clothes in mere seconds, too fast for me to process what's happening. He tosses everything on the floor until I'm only left standing in a white thong and socks.

He takes off his own new cardigan, starts tugging at his belt, and unzips his pants, all with one hand. He lets them rest on his waist. Then he takes out his cock and holds it. And even fondles himself for a moment.

Augustine looks at me through the mirror. "I want us to see each other enjoying what is being done to us. I need you to see the pleasure taking over our facial expressions."

He rests his chin on my shoulder. "I *need* you to see what I see."

I keep staring at him through the mirror. Not saying anything. Not thinking anything. Just taking in all his words. Wanting to take him in instead.

He retracts his chin and grabs my hands, putting them on the sink from behind me. "Don't let go. Keep holding on to the sink." A faint breath leaves his lips and caresses my ear. "Bend over, Kristina," he whispers.

I bend over, and he places his hand on my stomach and slowly slides inside my underwear. And the first thing he touches is the most sensitive part. It makes me arch my back, pushing my behind against his front.

He gives small kisses on my neck as he strokes me.

It feels good. It always feels good. And I can see it on my face. But I don't have time for foreplay. I'm already wet. I don't even think it's humanly possible for me to be any wetter than I already am.

"Just put it in," I whimper.

He puts his middle finger inside of me, gliding inside of me almost too easily. Like there is room for so much more.

And I want to be filled to the brim.

I exhale the words, "You. Now."

He stops kissing my neck and faces the mirror. "Are you sure?"

My eyebrows furrow. "Positive."

He brings the finger that was inside of me to his lips, kissing the top, slightly sucking it. Tasting me instead of a pomegranate. And his eyes flutter shut. "Consent to me."

"You may, please," I beg him rather than consent to him.

He pushes the fabric that's between my legs aside, holding it there, while his other hand rubs my clitoris.

Then, he jostles inside of me, not even entirely.

Once. Only. Fucking. Once.

Why the fuck did he stop?

He lets go of me and brings his other hand behind me, making me unable to see what he's doing right now. Until I hear fabric ripping again, and my thong falls on the floor.

I turn around and look at it between my feet. "Augustine! Stop tearing apart my clothes!"

He holds my shoulders, guiding me to turn around again. "It was also in the way. Literally. Step out of it," he urges.

I step out of my underwear, and he shoves it away with his foot. He then widens my stance by putting one of his legs between mine and slightly pushing my foot aside. Holding it there.

Then he places one hand on the lowest part of my abdomen and his other on mine that's holding on to the sink.

Without warning, he makes his way inside of me again. This time, with much more force.

We both gasp at the same time, looking at each other through the mirror. But I somehow feel embarrassed, so I duck a little to look at the sink.

I see the hand that's on mine moving to grab my chin, forcing me to look up. He doesn't let go of it. "Look at us. If you don't, I will pull out."

No. Don't, please. I'm going to look at us. At myself. At you.

He keeps thrusting inside of me and sucking on my neck. And I keep moaning because of it. My eyebrows are knitting together, my eyes are fluttering, and his expressions aren't any different from mine. Only his sounds are lower. His soft moans—there's something about them that I can't explain, but they ignite my body.

To feel on fire and to savor every burn.

I missed this *so much*. Can't we just start a marriage-with-benefits arrangement? God, that would be great.

He removes his lips from my neck, only for me to find a bruise. The man gave me a ... fucking hickey?

"Augustine, what did you do?"

"I marked what's mine."

"I'm not."

He groans. "I don't want to hear it."

He proceeds to give me another, still thrusting inside of me. Briskly. Like he has to reach climax before another timer goes off. Sucking even harder than he did before. I want to push him away, but it feels too good, so I'm willing to risk a mark or two.

But that is it. Not a third. This reminds me I have to hold my ground and that this is, in fact, the last time.

"This is the last time," I rush out of my system.

"You talk too much. Stop talking, love." He decides to talk some more though. "Let me enjoy you."

He pulls out, turns me around, and lifts me up to sit on the edge of the surface next to the sink. He then slides inside of me again to finish what he started.

He's kissing me. Shutting me up. Making me accept it.

And he's pushing it all in and pulling half of it out. Over. And over. And over again. Harder. *Deeper*. His testicles slapping against my skin.

It makes my toes curl because I feel something cooking up inside of me.

He places his mouth against my ear and whispers, "I want you to give yourself to me, body and soul."

I shake my head against his lips.

"Give yourself to me, Kristina. I promise I will be so good to you," he says.

Instead of words, sounds leave my lips—high-pitched ones.

"Keep making those heavenly sounds. I love them just as much."

As much? As much as what?

As much as I don't care because something else is happening. Something is *throbbing*.

I dig my nails into his back, tracing to the lowest end. Clasping because the satisfaction is taking control of my body.

He grunts and beams, enjoying the little pain I'm inflicting on him.

I'm soaking wet, and I feel a tingling explosion everywhere, reaching to my toes and fingertips.

And then he comes inside of me, cum sliding down my thighs.

We're resting our heads on each other's shoulders. Huffing and puffing.

He lifts his head, which makes me do the same. He's looking at me with lowered eyelids. "*Alors*, we shall now commence round *deux*, ready, *mon amour*?"

I'm guessing *something*, *two*, and *my love* in French. I didn't know he knew French. It's a new fact about Augustine to know.

My eyelids are lowered as well. I'm still not sober from the orgasm I just had. "Born ready."

He removes his pants and underwear, throws them on the floor, and shoves them next to mine.

We went at it like starved animals. Doing rounds all around. After the bathroom, he brought me to his room just to pin me against the wall and kiss me lustfully. Telling me that we knew this room well enough as it was. That it was just a pit stop.

Then he grabbed my wrist, bringing me to my room. Telling me that we never had the pleasure of getting acquainted with my bed. Not at the same time, at least. He confessed that he happened to—his words, which I wouldn't believe even if my very life depended on it—*just* lie in my bed when I wasn't home *sometimes*. We did another round there. I liked the round there. My sheets were soft against my back. He suggested we power nap for thirty-four whole seconds—*actually*, thirty-four whole seconds this time because we had reached a bed on our journey.

So, for only five seconds, we did because he lifted me up again to go to the laundry room. Telling me that our hands were busy in this particular room with rubbing stains off clothes, pulling them out of the washing machine, and pushing them into the dryer. So he rubbed me with his fingers and pushed them inside of me. And I pulled him with mine. He told me that handiwork wasn't as intense and that we had been given a pair of hands for a reason. That a recovery period wasn't necessary after it. He is so damn witty. So we continued to travel down our road.

He put his hands on my shoulders, guiding me to our next stop. The kitchen. Where he insisted on feeding me something. Himself. That the journey of walking down the stairs must have been hard after all and that it was time for me to eat. That I should blow him instead of his soup for a change. So, I did. And the chef was far too happy to serve his personal dish—it was meat. And then he waited for me to invite him to eat something, that he happened to be hungry as well since he had been traveling with me. He mentioned that he was greedy and would like two chicken breasts and a pomegranate. That only that would satiate his hunger once and for all. I served him the three-course dinner since evening started dawning on us. He loved my cooking. Especially both our sauces tasted exquisite.

Eventually, we found ourselves in the living room again. He assured me that Lady wouldn't be here to interrupt us again, to give the living room a fair chance, like we had the other rooms and that we should punish Lady for doing so in the first place. So, he pushed me onto the gray rug that she likes so much and laid on top of me. And then I was on top of him. And then we switched a couple of times. Exactly like he had told Alex that one time, we kept switching until the fucking sun came up.

If I had to sum up every orgasm, I have had in the last couple of hours in one word? *Oxytocin*.

Augustine's summary was a little longer. He said, and I quote, "Best birthday ever."

It is now very early in the morning, but since we didn't sleep, it's very late at night. Augustine filled the bathtub with water and poured us two glasses of the wine Sarah and Tony gifted him. The bottle is with us in the bathroom, so we can refill it.

We're in the bathtub now. Since we were both covered in sweat—among other liquids—he insisted on getting clean together, to even help one another because we caused each other to be dirty. And that I, Teen, was extra dirty. He also said that at the end of every tour, you had to find yourself exactly at the place you had started it.

I'm sitting in front of him, between his bent knees. Even when I feel his cock against me, I can't possibly get aroused anymore. Now, it's just there. And I'm guessing he feels the same way. We have expended all our energy and are actually *just* taking a bath.

He's rubbing my back with a sponge. I'm leaning forward a little for him to do so.

"Kristina?"

"Augustine?"

"Be my girlfriend."

I ... I don't understand him anymore. I thought that all the remarks he made and everything he did, that it was just him messing with me, teasing me. Or that it was just him being in the moment. That he was still high on sex when he told me he wanted his first time to be special. But more than one person said that it was sincere. I have to find out once and for all. Even if I don't want to.

"Augustine ... are you still pretending?"

"I'm not, I haven't been for a long time now. Thank you for finally noticing."

There isn't a single trace of him joking in the sound of his voice or in his tone. They were right, and I was just too blind to see it on purpose. Believing that I had everything figured out, like I think I always do. In the way it suits me. But this is complicated, and I don't like it being complicated.

"But the contract stated—"

"God, Kristina, fuck that piece of paper. That's when I didn't know."

I hesitate. "Didn't know what?"

He wraps his arms around me and pulls me into his familiar embrace. His lips are against the shell of my ear to whisper his confession. "How much you would mean to me. How infatuated I would be with you. How much we would—" He breathes in and out deeply before resuming. "How much you would consume my very being, Kristina. I—"

"No," I blurt out.

"No." he repeats until the realization hits him. "No? You can't reject a profession of love."

"You—you are not in love with me. It's an illusion."

He grabs my jaw and turns my head slightly to his. Kissing me briefly. To shut me up again because he doesn't like the words I'm uttering.

"I don't want to hear it. You not having feelings for me is an illusion," he says. "Give me a chance. I want to be your person, Kristina, your friend just as well, but I want to be so much more than that, if only you would let me."

I shake my head. "I can't. I'm in love with someone else."

"Don't love me. Let me love you. I will love for the both of us. I have plenty of love. I'm overflowing with it. Please, love?"

"No, Augustine. That isn't how love works."

He runs his fingers up my head and grabs a fistful of hair, tugging on it, so my head leans on his shoulder. "You might be mine unwillingly, but you are mine. And even if you don't want me, I am yours. You break my heart, and I will still let you do what you want. You get to decide what to do with what's yours."

"Augustine—"

He brushes his lips against my earlobe. "Shh, *shh*. My birthday is not over yet. Gift me not denying me," he whispers.

I scoff. "It's after midnight. You're too late, Cinderella."

"Don't shatter my glass slipper, love. That's cruel."

Silence takes over the bathroom as he traces something on my back with his fingers. He puffs out a breath and says, "I wish it were my birthday every day."

I'm denying him like a broken record, both his body and soul. I don't like doing it. I really don't. But accepting him without requiting his love would be just as cruel. Even more so. And I understand now, to break is far crueler than to get broken.

He finishes tracing his fingers on my back. And if what he traced got processed correctly, then it was one word—in Arabic, at least.

Hbini.

Which means, love me.

And with that, the real timer of today *officially* goes off.

Echoing through both our hearts.

CHAPTER TWENTY-TWO

Adam: Eve, now I'm in need of guidance. How does one even begin to cure emotional pain? To at least cope with it?

Eve: Adam. I find myself believing, actually convinced, that it isn't any different from physical pain. We even describe it as such. The lump in one's throat caused by keeping in the sadness, heaviness in one's chest from a broken heart. A wounded soul. Pain is caused by injuries. You have to treat it in order for it to heal.

Adam: What if you don't know what treatment will suffice? When you don't even know the diagnosis, the severity of it all. When all you know is that it is simply too much to bear.

Eve: Then, exactly as a doctor who doesn't know either, you give it time. Trust your immune system to deal with the invader, any invader. Put it in the hands of your white blood cells, your natural killer ones. To kill the unnatural emotional pain altogether.

Adam: Putting things concerning myself in other entities' hands, gets accompanied by a heap of uncertainty. I wish I could kill it with mine instead.

Eve: You could—the source causing you pain, at least.

Emotional pain, Adam? Rather, emotional discomfort for me, the one that is caused by Augustine. I'm feeling discomfort because of the comfort of sleeping with him. But especially the comfort of being held, of being loved. To be distracted and numb to the pain of the past, even when attention is being paid to it.

When people experience something, they tend to evaluate it. To think about it, reliving the experience to do so. Naturally, you don't remember the details of it all, which is an absolute shame when the experience was phenomenal. Even the things you loved, your mind filters those out of the memory. And yet, when you relive it, there is almost always one prominent detail that gives the experience the special notion it has. What stuck out? Which detail do you find yourself repeating when thinking about the experience as a whole?

The kitchen. That's where he placed me to lie on the counter of the island, to do things down there. But that's also where he was kissing the inner sides of my thighs and *holding* them. The kisses aren't new to me, but something else is. It's all about him holding my thighs. Touching them for a long period of time. Not being disgusted by them to do so. I never actually showed that side of me. All I did was share it in words with Alex.

You are the first and only one, Augustine. And how you handle it, it just means so damn much to me.

Thank you, truly.

Nevertheless, after having slept it all off since it felt like I'd been hit by a truck, it hit me. The realization that we have slept together again. And now, I have to face him. I hope I can postpone the inevitable since sleeping with him and facing him afterward makes me all giddy and awkward.

It's midnight right now, and I have a night shift. He's probably sleeping, which is a good thing.

I wind my way to the living room, only to find Augustine not sleeping, wide awake even.

Act normal, Kristina. Remember Newton's third law—the law of action and reaction. When two bodies interact, they apply forces to one another that are equal in magnitude and opposite in direction. If my action is the magnitude of normal, then his reaction will be too. I'm intentionally ignoring the opposite direction part of the law; otherwise, it wouldn't make sense.

The apple doesn't have to fall far from the tree. Actually, it couldn't have. After all, it had to fall on Newton's head for him to come up with the law of gravity in the first place.

"You're awake?" I ask him. I mean, it's normal all right, but also very dumb. I know dumb questions don't exist, but I can create anything out of nothingness. Even dumb questions.

Of course, the man is awake. His glittering green gaze is impossible to miss.

His eyes sparkle as he speaks. "Just came home. Long day."

"I'm about to have one—or rather, night."

"You have work?"

I nod. "I do."

"You need to eat first. Let me feed you. Pancakes?"

"Yes, please."

He knows because he takes feeding me so seriously that he has made an actual menu. Yes, I'm talking about the ones with a leather cover you find in restaurants. The name of his restaurant? Mine. No, seriously. My name, *Kristina*, is carved into the leather cover in big cursive letters, and underneath, very, *very* small, the word, *mine* in all caps, is carved into it. He thought I wouldn't notice, the idiot.

The menu is divided into breakfast, lunch, dinner, and dessert. Filled with global cuisine dishes. He wasn't lying when he said, "You name it, I make it." In each division, there's a section named Egyptian cuisine since he knows I like that best.

So, almost every day, he hands me the menu to pick what I want to eat the following day, so he can prepare it. Yesterday—or rather, today, very early—he asked me what I wanted to eat while we were in the bathtub. And I said pancakes.

"Full stomach, happy heart, love." That's his mantra.

I take a seat behind the bar counter, and he starts making breakfast—for me, that is. This is his midnight snack since he was working all day and I was sleeping.

I turn the stool around and see Lady playing on the ground with many new toys. All kinds of toys. It looks like an infant lives here too. She's now playing with a tower filled with balls stuck in their circuit. It resembles those round parking garages.

Balls, ironic—no, stop that.

I point at it. "Augustine, what is all of this?"

"Toys for our daughter," he says from behind me.

I roll my eyes because of the word *our*. "Why?"

"A peace offering, since I said to punish her for interrupting us when she was sleeping. I don't want to be scratched to death while I'm sleeping myself. She's especially frightening when she hisses at me for removing her from my lap."

Kristina, you can still act normal even if it's being brought up by the other body. Although now, the opposite direction part of the law doesn't have to be ignored. It turned out to be true. He's going in the direction I don't want to go in at all.

So I'm not going to. *You won't get to manipulate me into being confronted by you again, Augustine. I know better now.*

He places two plates with fluffy pancakes on the counter. He also puts a bowl full of strawberries, a sauce cup with Nutella, and a container with powdered sugar.

"*Bil hana w shifa,*" I tell him.

"*Shokran,* love, you too."

We devour the pancakes and all the toppings. And then there is only one strawberry left. And we are both aware that we don't have any strawberries at home anymore. *Right ...*

And let's just say that Augustine and I get competitive when it comes to strawberries.

We begin staring at each other, counting down, our eyes being the screens and our blinking the ticking.

And then I immediately grab it and put half of it in my mouth. But he doesn't exactly compete with me. He's slow on purpose. Oh well. Who cares?

While I chew on half of it, I squint my eyes at him. Out of spite.

He smirks at me. And then, in one swift motion, he leans into me and bites off the half that is still outside my mouth, brushing his lips against mine.

An error has occurred. The answer has been expressed in the wrong units. A common mistake when solving problems in physics. The physical events from before I went to sleep are happening after I went to sleep. Where the unit is supposed to be words again, not touch.

When dealing with angular velocity and acceleration, you need to set your calculator from degrees to radians.

Augustine, you are using degrees to calculate angular velocity and acceleration. Impossible. Wrong. No.

He leans back and starts chewing. "Sweet of you to share half of it with me, as I shared half of the extraction of my strawberry tea bag with you."

"Yeah. Unwillingly?"

He shrugs his shoulders. "Sharing is caring, they say."

I care. Not about you. About you being slow on purpose. You planned this. I know you're guilty as charged—120 Volts (V) and everything—but you would deny it, just like your resistance to touch me being 0 Ohms (Ω).

Why is physics taking over my brain today? I don't care that opposites attract with you. Get out of my head with the speed of light (c = 2.99792458 m/s).

My physics professor should see me right now though. I can't help but enjoy it since he always thought I was too incompetent for the subject. Well, look at me now, not being unsure of my knowledge anymore. Physicist Heisenberg who? Don't know him. He's too uncertain.

I wipe my mouth off. From the pancakes. From his. And stand up. "I'm going. Good night."

He stands up as well. "How are you going?"

Not this again. When I have a night shift, Augustine either drives me or forces me to take a cab if he can't drive me. Which only happened once. He's somehow always able to drive me. But cabs are a waste of money, and I like public transportation. "Public transportation …"

"No."

"But—"

"No. Take our car." He pulls out his keys from his pocket and holds them out to me with his index finger in the clasp, letting them dangle.

Our car? You mean, your car. And no, I don't drive … "I—I don't drive."

"You can't drive?"

"I mean, I have a license. I can drive. But I just don't drive. Because I can't …" My voice trails off.

He spins the keys around once and holds them when they return to his palm. "Time for a driving lesson, then."

"What? No. Absolutely not. I don't want to learn."

Augustine grabs me by my wrist and guides me to the front door. "*Yalla,* love."

He's still holding on to my wrist, making me wear my shoes, and only lets go to put on my coat for me. Then he continues to drag me to the garage. He's too strong, so even if I pull away with all my might, to him, I'm nothing but a bag he's just holding.

He opens the garage, then the car, gets in the driver's seat, and spreads out his legs. Tapping the fabric of the car seat between them twice for me to sit.

Reluctantly, I get into the car and sit between his legs. He refreshes my memory of where everything is—the brake pedal, the gas pedal, and how I should not use my left leg since this isn't a manual car. Why that's easier—his way of assuring me, I can do this. He shows me how to use the turn signals. And he lets me adjust all the mirrors since he's a tower—especially when sitting behind me.

He extracts himself from behind me and gets into the passenger seat. It's time for me to turn the car on. I press the ignition button, and the car purrs to life, but I'm still pressing on the brakes as desperately as I can.

"You can let go now," he says.

"I know," I say, still not letting go.

"What is it?"

"What if I wreck your car completely?"

"You're worried about the car and not yourself?"

"Of course I am. This thing must be worth a ton."

"Adorable." He leans over to kiss the top of my head. "And you are of innumerable worth."

I look at him through the rearview mirror, as uncertain as Heisenberg. Which is something I find myself doing more often lately—looking at him through mirrors.

"Focus on the road, love, not the car. The rest will come naturally."

I take a deep breath and slowly release pressure off the brake pedal.

And I start driving. Actually, fucking driving, even though it's only nine miles per hour. Leaving the garage and turning to get on the road.

"No need to act all coy. The gas pedal isn't scared of pressure either."

I laugh at him for saying that and slowly start pressing on it.

I'm driving. And it somehow feels ... *liberating*. The windows are open, so I can feel the breeze against my skin, and my hair dances because of it. As am I, with my feet.

"At the next traffic light, turn left," he says, exactly how the GPS tells it.

"What? What's left?" I hysterically shove away the sleeve of the hand that's holding the steering wheel, only to find my tattoo there, which means that's right. Wrong. I put on the turn signal and breathe out.

A small chuckle leaves his lips. "You always use your wrists to distinguish left from right?"

"I just get confused under pressure."

"Easy, love." He leans over to kiss my shoulder this time. "You're in control. Believe in yourself as I believe in you. I'm here if you need any assistance, but the real reason I'm here is for moral support only." He pauses. "And to tell you directions, of course."

He must know. He must know about my fear of driving. Delano must have told him. It has to be, which is why he's doing this. To tell me to overcome fears

I have had for years without using those words.

And he isn't wrong because I'm obviously still scared shitless, but it's a different fear. I'm scared but also very excited to do the thing I see badass women do in movies in high heels and suits or dresses. And then, they get out of their car with a cup of coffee in their hand. That's the kind of woman I aspire to be.

I just needed this. Comfort. Support. Encouraging words. I needed someone accepting my fears rather than invalidating them because they don't understand them, because they can't imagine having them. Him.

I needed *him*.

Not long after, I arrive at the parking lot of the building I work in.

Survived. Arrived. Safely. Thank God.

"Thank you for driving me. I'll see you at home," I tell him.

"You drove yourself. And you will again after your shift. I'm not leaving."

"But you have work in the morning. You need sleep. You barely even slept today ..."

He picks me up, places me on his lap, and pushes the car seat all the way back in a single action, making us recline.

"I'll manage, love. Your second driving lesson cannot be postponed if your driver's test is almost approaching."

He brings the seat back up again, and I start opening the door.

"This was a big accomplishment in itself, believe me."

"I believe you. Leave good reviews, will you? Also, payment is in kind."

I groan. "Good night, Augustine."

I get out of the car, but he stops me from closing the door by grabbing my wrist to say something. "Someone who reaches for the sun but is just as satisfied with a red dwarf. That is the kind of person you are, Kristina."

The sun ...

It's as if its warmth covers my cheeks. "You sure do know your physics, astronomy even."

"By heart, my love. By heart."

God, physics.

When I finished my shift, I saw that he did manage. He was sleeping so peacefully with the seat just a little leaned back, his arms crossed, and his jaw resting on his left shoulder, facing the window. Eventually, I had to wake him because he had to get ready to go to work, and it was time for me to sleep. I drove back, as he had said I would, and I felt more comfortable than going there. I hope with every drive, I gain more confidence. But I only want to do it if he's sitting next to me since I felt safe that way because of his ability to intervene if I were to screw up, but also just his presence.

I just woke up and am going to meet João since it has been a very long time since we last saw each other.

I can't believe when I used to live at home, I had to lie when I wanted to meet him just because he's a man.

I get ready and hear my phone ring. It's Alex.

I pick up. "Hi."

"Hi. What are you up to?"

"I just woke up and am now going to meet João at that juice bar I told you about since he wanted to taste Egyptian beverages."

"Oeh, fun. Never mind then."

"Why?"

"Senait and I are going to go shopping, and we wondered if you wanted to go with us. Have a girls' day, like they call it."

"Oh, rain check, please? I would love to."

"Yes, definitely, babes. I will let you know. Talk to you later."

"*Salam.*" I hang up the phone.

I take public transportation, and since it's raining like crazy, I'm completely soaked. I arrive at the juice bar, only to see João already sitting at a table.

"Krissie!"

"Hi, João. Have you been waiting long?" I ask while sitting down.

"No, just got here. The weather is awful, even though it's warm."

"Yeah, I completely forgot about bringing an umbrella, but I can dry up here."

He points at my neck. "Are those hickeys?"

Fuck. I was wearing a turtleneck at work, but it's too warm to wear that now, so I tried covering it up with concealer, but it obviously isn't full coverage, like it says on the damn package.

"No ..."

He laughs, and I try to cover them, embarrassed.

I call for the waiter, and he comes and takes our order from us. Our beverages are made almost immediately, and now, we're drinking them. João loves it.

We reminisce about the past until I see a few missed calls from Alex and some texts.

And while I'm looking at my screen, I completely miss the person who comes sitting next to me.

A high-pitched sound runs out of my mouth because I'm startled. "Augustine?!"

How did he even know I was here?

Alex.

I read the texts she sent me, and it states that Augustine called her to ask where I was because I wasn't home and that she told him I was meeting João here and that Augustine sounded annoyed when she told him.

"Hey, Augustine," João says.

But Augustine ignores him and keeps looking at me instead. He's mad. Annoyed. Jealous?

Acting childish, that's for sure.

Eventually, he turns to João, who's looking at me, or rather, at my hickeys. Probably because the one who planted them there is sitting next to me now.

Augustine follows his eyes, which are on my neck. I know they are because not a second before Augustine sat next to me, João was teasing me about them again. But Augustine follows his eyes to my top—my white top, which is soaked and see-through now. Making my bra visible. And I didn't bring a coat with me.

His jaw clenches, and so do his fists, and if dead stares were a thing, João would be lying in his grave right about now.

He stands up abruptly and tugs on my arm, making me stand up as well. "We're going," he says.

"No. You're going," I tell him.

He bows down, grabs me, and throws me over his shoulder. "No, *we* are going."

He doesn't say anything to João, walks over to the counter, pays for both drinks, and leaves a very generous tip. I see it when he turns around to leave the place altogether.

"Put me down! I said, no. Don't you have the word *no* in your vocabulary?!" I shout.

"No."

Clever. Very clever. I'm going to kill him once he puts me down. I. Swear. To. God.

"You don't own me!" I yell while slapping his back.

"Well, I should!"

He slides me down a little, wrapping his arm underneath my behind. Bringing our faces to the same level. While he holds me, he uses the hand that's underneath me to undo the Velcro strip of the umbrella he's holding and pushes open the umbrella above our heads.

He's looking furious now. "I don't accept anyone seeing you dripping wet, except for me. Understood?"

And he slides me down for my feet to finally touch the ground. Making me stand in front of him, just as close as when he was holding me. "You were supposed to take me there, not him," he tells me. "I don't like him. I don't like any man in your life who isn't me."

If only you knew about the one I talk to on the internet. Which I'm obviously never going to tell you. You would probably break all the devices in the world for us to never talk again.

"I'm going to kill all the men in your life," he says.

Or you would kill him.

He hands me the umbrella, takes off his coat, and puts it on my shoulders, closing the few first buttons to cover my upper body. He then takes the umbrella back and holds it above our heads again.

I see him looking at something behind me. And he frowns at it.

"Krista."

And at the exact moment, that name in that voice reaches my ears and gets processed, thunder strikes, and even more rain pours down.

My heart is not in my stomach, it's lower. It's in my feet; it's making my knees tremble. My entire body starts trembling. And there is only one person who causes me to tremble uncontrollably, unable for me to even move. To even breathe. Frozen. Cold. Shivers.

No. Please tell me this isn't happening. Please tell me that he isn't here. That he isn't standing behind me in the flesh.

I slowly turn around. My eyes reflect horror; Augustine notices and looks alarmed. I give him my back, only to see my worst nightmare playing out before my very eyes.

"You're married now? I thought you vowed to never be touched by a man again after being with me."

I used to wonder when my heart would heal. Because, sometimes, it felt like the wounds were only getting deeper.

But seeing you is like cutting the wounds open all over again.

Vomit climbs up my throat; I feel like I'm going to be sick. To think you've been trying to put the past behind you for years, only to be confronted by it in a matter of seconds. Healing, it's hard when the source of all your pain decides to make a comeback. My past, in the present. *Now.*

The power people have over you ... it truly is a cruel, unpredictable world.

Not only that, but Augustine also wanted to call me Krista, and I refused point-blank. Which means he now realizes why. But I don't want him to understand the why. I don't want him to know what my abuser has done to me.

And even when all I want to do now is run away to prevent that from happening, I can't. Stuck like I used to be. In his grasp. Like I want to give in.

"Look at you, all grown up. And your body did some growing too," my abuser says.

He starts talking to Augustine now. "Let me guess. You've already fucked her. Was she good? I'm the one who taught her all the foreplay. You're welcome, by the way. I basically prepared her for you," he says. "Is that what you did, Krista? Got over me by getting under him? Or were you on top? Riding him? Man, that must be a sight to behold." He bites his lower lip while looking down at me. Hungrily. Disgustingly.

My abuser tries to put his hand on my shoulder, but Augustine pulls me back to him and grits out, "Don't you dare touch my wife."

He scoffs. "Your wife? Because you marked her, no?" He points at my hickeys. "We all seem to want to do that. I marked her too," he says, pointing at my thighs. "She has always been mine. At least I fucking marked her in a unique way."

Terror is taking over my face. My eyes, even when wide open, still find a way to keep the well inside. They're resisting still. Then, my eyelids lower a little when the realization hits me that the truth has made its way to the surface. And finally, I close my eyes in acceptance; it was foolish of me to think I could escape the past, escape him. And as I close my eyes, tears leak out of them because resistance is *useless*.

Augustine must realize now that all my scars, the ones he thought I was responsible for myself, were caused by him.

I can't see Augustine's facial expressions. I can only hear the pain in his voice when he tries to utter his next words; it's breaking even. "You ... you did that to her?"

He shrugs his shoulders. "Sometimes. But I mostly let her do it to herself. That was way more fun. Don't you like to see her in pain as well? Hilarious."

"Here." My abuser takes out a pocketknife—*the* pocketknife. The one I felt against my skin many times. "You can use this too, like I did. I always carry it with me as a memento." He turns his attention to me now. "Remember this, Krista? You must have fond memories of it. I know I do. I've kept it all these years. It especially helps me at night, if you know what I mean."

He extends the knife and licks it.

The umbrella Augustine's holding falls to the ground.

And now, Augustine has realized that the tattoo between my legs, the one with that pocketknife, has meaning. I can't see his realizations, but I can hear them in how he inhales and exhales air.

I can't stop him. I can't physically move. I can't do anything. Powerless, like I used to be. Like I always have been. Like I am. Like I always will be.

Augustine says something under his breath; it sounds a lot like profanity.

"What? I can't hear you," my abuser says.

Augustine's face twitches; he brings me behind him and walks to my abuser. "I'm going to fucking tear you to shreds," he says through gritted teeth.

Augustine grabs him by his collar and pushes him against the wall, making his head thud against it. Then, Augustine pulls him from the wall and brings his foot behind my abuser's, letting him stumble, falling on the ground. Augustine kneels, hovers above him, and beats him to a pulp with his fists.

"Augustine!" is the first thing I manage to say because the sound of his hard punches somehow pulled me out of the trance I was in. The blood splattering, dripping from my abuser's face and from Augustine's hand on the floor, makes me able to move again.

I run toward them and start pulling Augustine from his shoulders, but without success. So I try using my words instead. "He's not worth it. Let go!" I shout.

But I can't seem to get through to him. Now, it looks as if he's the one in a trance.

People start running and yelling. Chaos is taking over the street we find ourselves on.

And more blood flows.

Like he wants every last drop to reach the floor. Like that is his goal and like he's going to reach it, no matter what.

A police officer rushes to them, removes me from Augustine's back, and immediately tries to grab Augustine's hands to arrest him. Augustine resists at first, but eventually, the officer has the upper hand and puts the handcuffs on him, and pulls Augustine to stand up.

Augustine looks down at my abuser. "Be glad someone intervened. I swear, I would have made you suffer in unimaginable, horrifying ways for what you did. I would have taken your life right from you, like it's nothing."

He's barely conscious but still finds the energy to grin. "You're a monster. That's what she's into, after all."

Augustine stomps on his face with his foot, knocking him out while handcuffed. The officer doesn't appreciate it, so he pushes Augustine to move.

Blood is dripping from his hands, and there is blood on his shirt. But it's not his blood. Augustine remained unharmed, even when my abuser tried to punch him back. To Augustine, it looked like child's play.

I rush behind them. "Wait!"

The officer stops and finally looks at me. "Stalker girl? I'm sorry, but I'm going to have to arrest your fiancé."

Augustine slightly turns his head to face the officer. "Husband. I'm her husband."

"Does it really matter right now?" the officer asks while shoving Augustine into the back seat.

Augustine faces me. "It does to me," he says before his face disappears and the car door closes.

After I bailed him out, we finally got home. I'm not one for violence, but

I'm glad Augustine hit him. My abuser deserved it. Augustine planted all the punches I have always wanted to plant. And that kick? Now, that was a closing sentence to remember since my abuser ended up in the hospital because of it. I don't know how he's doing, and I couldn't care less either. I only know that it was bad, which is good.

We haven't talked yet. When we got home, he immediately went to the bathroom. I'm guessing he's processing things since he has been "showering" for over an hour now. I can't blame him. I was processing things, too, while waiting at the police station.

I'm sitting on the couch when I hear footsteps descending.

He sits next to me and holds my hands, which makes us slightly turn to each other.

"Kristina, sometimes good people need to do bad things to let the bad people pay for their wrongdoings."

I nod at him.

"Are you ready to tell me about his?"

I nod at him again and start taking in all the air that's at my disposal to tell him *everything*.

As I tell him my story, he's suppressing his pain. His eyes are even red and wet.

He looks at me, worried. "Did I ever … remind you of him?"

"No!"

He shakes his head at me. "You used to hate me touching you; you'd sometimes even flinch. The first time we met, you told me not to close the door firmly. The second time we met, I told you to face the consequences of your own actions, like he used to tell you, causing you to cry."

"That was—"

He throws himself at me and stands up, taking me with him. To hug me even tighter. "I'm so sorry. I'm so sorry, my love.

"The first time I saw them, I thought you did it to yourself. I thought I had it all figured out without asking you. Without taking the time and effort to comfort you while you were being vulnerable with me. I can't apologize enough for everything I have ever done that made you relive the past again."

But you did! You so did. You were perfect at comforting me.

"It hurts. It hurts me so much." He pauses. "I wish I could hold you like this forever, protect you from any harm that should ever befall you. I wish I could have done it back then. I wish …"

Pain turns into anger again. "I want to kill him even more now," he growls.

I hold on to him. "He's in the hospital, Augustine, in critical condition. Barely alive. You can't kill one bird twice, right? That's not how the saying goes. And you adore sayings."

"I adore you."

Silence takes over the room, our embrace.

"What did the officer mean by stalker girl?" he asks.

"You caught that …"

I tell him everything about that one day I described as an adventure, which he happened to finance.

"You love me," he says, smiling.

Since he loves sayings and I want him to get off my back, but we're hugging, I decide to run with that. "Get off my front," I say as I try to remove myself from his arms.

I can't believe my stalking him came right back to bite me in the ass, even though I told him a long time ago that stalking him was the last thing I would do.

He lets go of me. "One last thing. I have something for you."

He pulls out the pocketknife from his pocket, hands it to me, and closes my hand around it. "Do with it what *you* want to do this time," he says while holding my jaw and caressing my cheek with his thumb.

He leaves me to be in the living room alone.

I look at it in *my* grasp.

I can't believe … he took it from *him*.

Dear Kristina,

Usually, our present selves write our future selves letters. This time, I will write you—my past self—a letter. To heal. Both you and I. We're broken, shattered. But shards bring luck, Kristina; they do.

I finally grasp the notion now. We should never regret having met certain people. The good bring you enjoyment in life, and the bad give you the experiences of what you don't want in life. The worst give you lessons you learn from forever, and the best grant you beautiful memories you get to cherish forever. The bottom line is that one can't come without the others.

Because the truth, Kristina, is that you are involved with a person who has psychopathy. Of course, you don't know this now, but I have studied it. I know all there is to know.

Psychopathy is a personality disorder part of the dark triad, together with Machiavellianism and narcissism. These traits get especially expressed in interactions with others.

People with this disorder can be problematic and dangerous to others. At first, the person appears sweet and charming, manipulating you to perceive them that way. But then they drop the act. They start showing their true colors. They become cruel and apathetic. They hurt you and blame you for it. Because the people who cross them always end up regretting it. I did. They want to control you. You're the puppet, and the strings are glued to their hands. They get pleasure from your suffering, sometimes sexual pleasure. They become easily bored, causing them to go looking for excitement, engaging in crime and abuse. They can be very insensitive to their problematic nature, but the people around them, they suffer greatly for it. I know you do.

And there is so much more that fits his profile. You will understand what I mean when you learn about it.

But you will also understand that not everyone with this disorder is as extreme because of homogeneity, that there are people who are diagnosed with it and live lives society considers to be normal. It's a disorder, something that happened to them. You might even pity him that his brain anatomy and activity are different from others. I understand. I can't blame you. I pity him too.

He wanted to control someone. He wanted to inflict pain on them. All out of boredom. I was merely the collateral damage of his boredom. While for me, his boredom damaged my entire being, my very soul.

It's fucked up, Kristina.

I want to apologize to you. I don't know how you do it, how you can stay in that basement and go back every time. Endure it over and over again. I'm so sorry you have to put up with it until time saves you. My heart aches for you, for us. For everyone who has gone through abuse and everyone who still does.

But somehow, everyone ends up accepting the roses while ignoring the thorns. When, in reality, it's been a cactus all along.

Your future shouldn't be found in the past, Kristina. It never could because it simply isn't there. Looking for it would be wasting your time. And I have wasted more than enough of it, believe me.

You wonder whether the bells will toll for you next. You fantasize about the moment you will finally get to rest. While people fantasize about a beautiful future, you are fantasizing about none.

You wonder in letters whether you will ever get through it, addressing them to your future self, addressing them to me. You are existing rather than living. Surviving even. And I remember exactly which words you always use to end the letters: Does it ever get better, Kristina?

At first—and especially today, when I saw him—I would say no. It doesn't. You should ask yourself about the horror that awaits you instead.

But now, after I have processed everything. After being comforted by the only other person who knows about our situation. By the one who even knows more than the first person now. The one who knows the whole story. I can stand proud and tell you this: It does, sweetheart. It so fucking does.

Because I always used to think that I could never escape him. I know you do too. But I learned something, Kristina, and it's just a matter of time until you do as well. I only hope that you figure out using said knowledge much sooner than I did.

The self-fulfilling prophecy means that an originally false expectation leads to its own confirmation.

I always thought I could never escape him, which is how I lived my life up until now. I did everything in his name. Ending up exactly like that, not being able to escape him.

My new expectation is that I can escape him. And I will.

After finishing this letter, I will take matters into my own hands. I will destroy both this letter and the pocketknife. Getting rid of it once and for all. Removing the thing that was always in the way of me truly healing. Physically and mentally.

Because even though I was scared today, and I thought it would consume me, I was more mad. I felt more than just fear toward him. I wanted to punch him myself, punish him for what he had done to me instead of the other way around for once.

The past will always hurt, but I'm not afraid to show what it did to me anymore. The scars are a part of me, not just as reminders of how strong I am but also as reminders of how loved I can be beyond them.

That's the only thing that counts—that someone sees more in you. More than you knew there was.

Augustine, it appears that my driver's test indeed came sooner rather than later. The test to drive him away from my mind. To drive him off of me, once and for all.

I passed, and you helped me in doing so. Isn't it time to celebrate?

Yours healed,

Kristina

CHAPTER TWENTY-THREE

Eve: Adam. I find myself in what one would call a happy state. And I only hope that you do too. Happiness comes from within, right?

Adam: Eve, I'm glad that you are. It does me good to hear that you are doing well. As am I, thank you for asking. It definitely does, and others can add to that, causing happiness to overflow. But you can never have enough happiness since we have been born with enough cells to absorb it. Similar to photosynthetic cells absorbing sunlight, it should always be welcomed with open arms to grow, to blossom, and to become even happier.

Eve: Oh, I hear you. I will be sure to wear a welcome sign from now on and walk around with my arms wide open.

Adam: I actually like that idea. Why not welcome more good things into our lives?

Eve: The more, the merrier!

I hope you're happy, Adam. Especially in the love department, but also just in general. I wish you all the love, happiness, health, and blessings. Everything you wish for, I hope it will be gifted to you sooner rather than later.

I never thanked you, and I probably never will, but you played a key role in my journey. The first man I got to know after everything that had happened to me, who didn't make me feel skeptical. It started with you, letting people in. When I had to deal with men, at work or just in general, I gave them a chance by thinking, What if they are just like Adam?

I met some amazing men, men I had the honor of helping with their mental health, like Thomas, but also the person who called me on my first day as a crisis counselor. Although I would say, he helped me more than I helped him.

I met Augustine's assistant, who was respectful. I met Augustine's realtor, who was genuine. I met the sweetest officer when stalking Augustine. I met Augustine's friends Tony and George, who are so good to the women they love. And I met a stranger who respected my boundaries when I didn't want to continue making out with him.

And many more good men.

Not all men, yes. But you have to experience some men firsthand in order to believe the statement.

And, of course, I met Augustine. I used to hate comparing you to him, but now, I'm glad. It means that you two are the same, which helped me trust him. And I have him to thank for introducing me to all these men. He also played a key role in my journey.

You both did.

Thank you, Adam. Even if I never meet you to tell you in the flesh, you mean the world to me. And so does your friendship.

I find myself at the juice bar with Farah and Delano. Or rather, the modern-day star-crossed lovers, as I like to call them.

And I find their situation difficult still. I always will. See, most of the time, we're born into a religion. Which means we could have easily been born into another one. We would probably practice it the same way we practice our current religion. It makes me wonder, *Is being able to be with someone based on sheer chance?*

In some religions, it isn't possible to marry someone from another religion. Some parents even take it up a notch and forbid you from marrying someone outside your culture or ethnicity even. And then they wonder why it's taking so long for their children to find love. They have the audacity to turn on all the filters to find zero search results, to end up being confused that's the case. Parents disapprove of real love because of rules. Urging you to find possible love. *No* love.

I understand the rules. But I also don't understand them. I disagree even. And that's the problem.

Because Delano and Farah are love. An insight to love. Exactly how I feel about Aug—Adam.

Wow? No. Now, hold on a second. That was simply a slip of the cerebellum. I meant to think Adam. I was thinking about Adam. Augustine infiltrated my mind by classical conditioning, a type of unconscious learning. Causing me to make an implicit connection between him and love since he calls me that. That must be it. Freaking Pavlov, who has a cat instead—who also happens to be my cat, for God's sake.

"Farah, you wanted to become a flight attendant, right?" I ask.

"Yeah … I actually already discussed it with my mother after finally gathering the courage to, but I'm not allowed to travel alone, so a job that's exactly that was an instant no. She told me to find another passion and that I can't travel without my family until I'm married. Which I can't exactly do …"

Delano puts his hand in front of his eyes. "Don't remind me, or I might actually cry … for the millionth time."

She pats his shoulder. "I'm sorry, Del."

"Call me *habibi* to make up for it."

She chuckles. "I'm sorry, *habibi*."

He tugs at the end of her sleeve and kisses it. Not her, just the fabric. They never kiss. They barely even hug.

"Be careful," I say. "Make sure no one you know sees you, since every Egyptian comes to this particular juice bar now."

Farah nods. "I know. Thank you, by the way, for coming with us. It's just easier if we aren't alone, even though we aren't doing anything wrong. You know how they twist rumors into worst-case scenarios. And then we can wave our reputations as respectable women goodbye."

We toast our massive glasses with juice to the reputation of a woman in our culture. "Oh, I hear you, sister."

With our lives depending on our reputations, we get suppressed in just living them out. It's as Farah said—you have a passion or dream job? If it isn't between the bounds of what is allowed, then you can't do it. Best to just forget about it. Ignore your wants and needs.

For instance, being artistic is a big no. You want to go into acting? Your mother would probably throw a slipper against your head for even thinking about it to set you straight. Because what would others think of you? A woman who is into acting? No man would want to marry her. That isn't being modest at all. Women in our culture simply don't do that. End of discussion.

What if I want to become a writer though? I like books, love poetry, and adore literature. But, of course, I would probably get burned alive. Especially if I were to write in the genres I love, like romance, among others—men written by women in general. I would write about Adam because he feels like a man who's written by a woman. Augustine too.

It's true what Farah just mentioned, how if someone were to see her alone with Delano—a man who isn't her husband—hell would break loose, and rumors would go around with the speed of light.

But it's also about our clothes and anything else really.

Actually, scratch that. It's *everything* a woman does. Nothing is good; everything is wrong.

Because women tend to always wrong our dear society. Being insecure is too attention-seeking in the "right" way and being confident is too attention-seeking in the "wrong" way. When will it ever be just right in no way?

And don't even get me started on the double standards. Actually, I won't. Just thinking about it makes my blood boil.

Just one thought then. A man rules his own life. After all, he gets to rule a whole family. So, no rules for them! Do whatever you want!

Besides, a man can't exactly be "not modest." How would that even work? They don't even wear dresses! *insert mocking laughter* They can, and most of the time, they aren't. Being modest isn't about your clothes but your intentions and actions. And definitely not about your gender.

Our lives depend on our reputations, the stakes being getting disowned by your whole community and your parents right behind them. We're suppressed by the fear of it all. It's exhausting, to say the least. To be on guard all the time. To think through every little thing you do. To not be able to just *live.*

Farah and I continue trash-talking the double standards in our culture while Delano just sits there, kind of being insulted. It's fun though.

Eventually, I leave them because they decide to go watch a movie, and I'm going home to meet Augustine because we decided to go to the cemetery today to visit our parents.

I arrive home, and while I wait for him to get ready, my phone rings.

I pick up and put my phone on speaker on the floor since I'm petting Lady. I need two hands to pet Lady. "Hi, Marina."

"Hi, Kristina. Could you do me a favor?"

"Yes, of course. Tell me."

"My husband's little cousin also studies psychology and is having trouble with her thesis. Could you maybe help her with her questions?"

"Yes, totally. When is it due?"

"In five days. I'm so sorry. I know it's short notice."

"No! Don't apologize. I'll manage. Just send me her contact information, and I'll contact her."

"Thank you. I owe you one."

"It's okay. See you. *Salam.*" I hang up.

Augustine clicks his tongue a few times, indicating disapproval.

I turn around and look up to face him. "What is it?"

"You know you're too busy to help someone with their thesis, and yet you try to squeeze in favors in your schedule. You bite off more than you can chew, love."

Oh? You really shouldn't have said that to me.

"It didn't look like that when I completely sucked you dry. I can handle more than you think."

He chuckles. "Of course, you have something to say against a saying. Rebutting it. You always do."

"What can I say? I'm unable to be left *sayless,*" I say and wink.

That is a complete lie. All this man does is leave me at a loss for words.

"If you want me to shut you up, I know a way or two. You just have to promise that you'll suppress your whimpers."

Kissing him and giving him head? Of course, he goes there too.

Well, here's a saying for you. "Bite me, Augustine."

He takes my hand, lifts me up to stand, and gently bites my neck.

I push him away. "*Ay,* not actually! I thought I was the only one who took sayings literally."

He rubs my neck. "You have infected me, and I don't mind being sick with you. I would accompany you anywhere, even if our destination were the infernal regions."

You could have just said hell. No need to get all dramatic, Auguspeare.

Lady is using his leg as a scratching post, meaning she wants to be held. He grabs her and pets her.

He then reaches with his other hand for me and pulls me into his embrace while we crush Lady. "A long-awaited family hug."

I release myself from his clutches. "No time. We have to go. I still want to go to the flower shop."

"Then, let's finish what we started when we get back—"

I interrupt him. "There will be no such thing as finishing what we started ever again."

He really thinks I'm an idiot. I know exactly what he means. We finished having started kissing in this very room too.

We leave the house and drive to a flower shop close to the cemetery. It's the one where I always buy bouquets of blue roses when visiting my father's grave.

I leave with two bouquets of nine blue roses, one for my father and one for his mother. Augustine is waiting for me outside the flower shop.

And then I see a woman all over him. Sofia, his so-called best friend, who told me I was a little too lucky with him.

Seriously, I'm not jealous. But what if I were? I'm going to pull the wife card now, for the sake of what-if.

I approach them. She has her arm linked in his, and he's trying to retract it.

"Hiya. How are you, Kristina?"

"Sofia, is it?"

"Yes."

"Could you not throw yourself at my husband like that?"

"Excuse me?"

"Yes, excuse you indeed. Get your hands off of him. Now."

She unlinks their arms. "You can't be serious?"

"I'm dead serious, love."

I can see that Augustine is enjoying this a little too much. Especially when I called her love, and he started pursing his lips.

I hand him one of the bouquets and link my free arm in his. "We're going."

"Your wish, my command," he says.

He waves at Sofia with the hand of the arm I'm holding, and we walk away from her.

I'm normally not like this, but she just annoys the crap out of me with her behavior.

"See? I didn't say that *you* are going. I obeyed. If only you had done the same when you were with that peasant," he says.

"His name is João, your client. And even if I didn't obey, you made me obey by dragging me out of the place. Besides, he didn't do anything. She was all over you."

He shrugs. "Debatable. Are you jealous, love?"

"Please, I'm not. The wife I'm supposed to be got jealous. I wasn't going to just stand there and let her think I'm that ignorant, fuck."

"I love hearing you use profanity," he says and grins.

"You love hearing me say fuck?"

"Once more, slower this time, and a little higher."

I unlink our arms and hit him with the bouquet I'm holding.

We arrive at the cemetery and are now at my father's grave.

I kneel down and put the bouquet on his tombstone. Someone has already removed the wilted ones—probably my mother or Delano.

"I always give him nine blue roses. Since blue represents him being mysterious to me and nine represents eternal love," I say, standing up again. "I bought one for your mother, too, but maybe you should come up with something that's more personal to you."

He turns to me. I can see it from the corner of my eye. "So, you do know your flowers?"

I face him. "What do you mean?"

"Nothing," he says as he averts his gaze back to the tombstone. "I wish I'd had the honor of meeting your father and asking him for your hand, Kristina."

Not having had the chance to meet someone because they are no longer alive … I have thought about this before.

"I wish that too …" I lean my head against his shoulder, and he follows by leaning his jaw on my head.

We stand there in that position for a while until we go to visit his mother's grave. Only for us to end up in that same position again.

I hear the doorbell ring and make my way to the front door to open it. Before me materializes a man with bright green eyes and pitch-black hair.

"Hello, sir. Can I help you?" I ask.

"Is Augustinus here?"

"May I ask who you are?"

"Mario."

"Mario .... ?"

"Elias. Is Augustinus here?" he repeats.

I look at him, surprised. Don't tell me ... it's his dad? I thought he wasn't in their lives anymore. What brings him to our doorstep?

"You're his ... dad?"

He shrugs. "I suppose."

You suppose? What kind of answer is that?

I can smell the alcohol on him. I don't know if I should let him—

I don't get to make that choice because he shoves me out of the way to enter the house himself.

This can't be good. I close the door and rush to follow him into the living room to warn Augustine.

Only to find Augustine and him already staring at each other. Augustine looks startled, but hints of fury and fright are also on his face. I can't see the face his father is making because I'm standing behind him.

"You're here for the money," Augustine says.

"So, you were expecting me? Good boy."

"I'm not giving you anything, Mario. That money was meant for her if something were to ever happen to me. Never for you. Now that she isn't here, everything will go to Marina."

"My boy, then you should have sorted your things out. I have been informed, so I'm here to collect."

His father is cold. Harsh.

I hate him.

I don't need to know anything to understand that he's awful. His whole aura screams at me that he is.

I walk toward a drawer in the living room to grab something, and then I stand between them at a distance, seeing both their faces.

I intervene. "I'm sorry. Mario, is it? I don't think you can demand something that wasn't yours in the first place."

Augustine looks at me, alarmed, as if talking back to him were a crime. As if I were about to serve a life sentence for it.

"Who even are you? His wife?" Mario shifts his attention to Augustine and laughs mockingly. "You got married after everything you saw me do to your mother?"

Mario faces me again. "Tell me, does he abuse you? It's the only thing he saw, the only thing he knew and used to breathe from. It's the only thing I ever taught him—how to treat a woman."

Then, it hits me. Her words. Her words about how I would understand once she was gone. She knew he would do this, that he would come knocking on our door for money, money that was meant to be hers.

And then I remember the other thing she said, her exact words being, "I need you to remember something the moment you understand. He might be the spitting image of his father, but he will *never* be him. I can assure you of that because *I* raised him."

Fill in the blanks, Kristina.

It means that his mother was ... *a survivor of abuse.*

A woman I knew I felt more toward because of something I couldn't quite understand. But now, I do, and this is her abuser. A man who looks exactly like Augustine. His father. *Her husband.* My fears for never wanting to get married, she lived them out firsthand.

And it enrages me beyond words.

"He doesn't. He treats me with love and respect. Just because he looks like you doesn't mean he takes after you," I tell Mario.

Augustine looks at me, almost grateful for my saying that, as if he's needed this confirmation his whole life and finally got it from someone other than himself.

"He won't be able to escape everything I made him see, young lady. Sooner or later, he's going to want to inflict all of it on you. And you'll let him since you're his wife and you appear to love him so much. You. Will. Let. Him."

His words only hurt because they're true—or they used to be. *But I've changed, Mario, and I won't let you get away with what you did to them—God, things I probably can't even imagine.*

Mario shrugs his shoulders. "He's my son, after all."

"He's his mother's son. You were only there to serve as sperm, nothing more," I say.

He laughs and points at me while looking at Augustine. Augustine isn't laughing. He looks like he doesn't know what face to make anymore.

"Women are nothing but ovens to carry children and objects to fuck. It's not the other way around," Mario says.

You fucking misogynistic bastard. You did not just say the thing I hate most—the so-called actual role of women in our culture.

I'm mad. I'm pissed. I'm fucking fuming. My chest is burning with rage. "It's exactly the other way around, and you're the walking epitome of it. A poor excuse for a human being, as useless as your role in their lives. You think abusing your wife and children is something to be proud of? You're nothing but scum, Mario, and the depths of hell are reserved for you. I can't wait for you to burn into fucking ashes."

"What the fuck did you just say to me?" his father grits out.

"Oh, you heard me loud and clear, but if you want more, I have more to give you. I hope you live a miserable, penniless life. Go grovel somewhere else for money because you won't be getting anything from Augustine. I'll make sure of that."

His entire face starts twitching, and he begins walking toward me, growling words under his breath.

Augustine gets out of his trance. The one I know all too well, the one where you can't move and you let everything just happen until your instincts take over.

He grabs his father's wrist, who is about to put his hand on me. "We might be having a disagreement, but don't ever lay a hand on my wife. That you were able to hurt your own doesn't mean that you can hurt mine."

Mario grins smugly. "Then I'll give them to you, my son, since you were always so good at taking the punches that were meant for the women in our house. See? History is already repeating itself."

Augustine closes his eyes, giving in to history.

But not on my watch, Augustine. Not now, not ever again. Not in the present and definitely not in the future. The ticking stops here. I will break the hands of this watch, just like I did with my clock. I will break his hands for you to stop him if I have to.

I grab the thing I just took from the drawer and spray it in his father's eyes.

He almost growls like an animal. "You fucking bitch! You will pay for this. *He* will pay for this!"

Mario wraps his hands around Augustine's throat, squeezing it. Augustine is resisting, but at the same time, it looks as if he isn't. As if it's hard to resist what you're so used to.

I run to the kitchen and grab the first thing I see—a frying pan.

"I can't fucking see shit," he growls as he lets out his frustrations on Augustine.

"Good! Now, sleep!" With all my might and *my* pent-up frustration, I aim for his temple and hit it with the frying pan, knocking him out and making him collapse on the floor. *Thud.*

Augustine's jaw almost hits the floor, and his eyes are about to fall on it. "Did … did you just—did you just pepper spray my father and hit him with a frying pan?"

I rather 'broke' his father's eyes and head than his hands.

"As I said before, drunkards are the worst," I say, panting. "He was about to hurt you. I-I panicked!"

"Why ... why do you even have pepper spray in the first place?"

My breathing finally calms down. "I ... I was about to live with a stranger. It was meant to be used on you ..." I have more hidden around the house. I didn't know when and where I would need to use it in advance.

He looks at me, stunned. "I think ... I think I have a new nickname for you."

I give him a questioning look, still holding the frying pan, as if I'm about to go for another round of hitting.

"You have long hair, you were stuck in your own tower—your family's home—and you hit people with frying pans. Rapunzel, the brunette one."

I gasp and lower the pan. "You watch Disney movies?!"

"All the time with Marina."

"It's not Disney, but do you know *Corpse Bride*?" I ask.

"Always the bridesmaid, never the bride?"

"Oh my God, Augustine, yes!"

"Do you love me now?"

"No?" I say, frowning.

"When will you? If I watch more Disney movies? If so, I will watch every one that has ever been made."

I shake my head at him. "You're crazy."

"Crazy about you."

Eventually, we called the police, and they took care of him. Augustine hadn't wanted to do it initially, but I had urged him to. There is no such thing called family in abuse. Abuse is abuse, no matter who's responsible for it. We shouldn't distinguish between the who as an excuse. He listened, and so his father was taken away.

Which made me realize that I should have done the same with my abuser and that I still should. Because it's never too late to seek justice, it's never too late to hinder people from doing something like they did ever again, to anyone.

I can't even begin to explain how I ended up injuring his father twice. I'm not one for violence, especially not for inflicting it. But my instincts just kicked in. When facing a threat, you go into survival mode.

I also owed him one. Augustine and I were like Bonnie and Clyde, not in crime, more like in getting at people who we have to thank our misery for. I always thought that Bonnie and Clyde were Adam and me—Adam and Eve—but I guess things change.

I decide to text Adam.

Eve: Adam. Maybe it's called a happy state for a reason—because it doesn't exactly last long. How do you cope with having had an awful day?

All I can think is, *How unbelievable.* How unbelievable it is for a spouse to go from vowing all these things to ending up doing the exact opposite of those things. It's frightening to know that feelings can change so drastically. If I had known about this before meeting Augustine, I would have used this as the perfect example of why I never wanted to get married. But I know better now. Now, I know that rotten apples live among fresh ones because, most of the time, they used to be fresh too. It's how every apple usually starts out before it gets plucked, ending up God knows where.

I knock on Augustine's bedroom door.

"Mm-hmm?" he mumbles for me to come in.

I open the door and see him lying with one hand on the back of his head and the other on his stomach.

"Do you ... want to cuddle?" I ask.

He sits up straight. "You don't have to do this for me. I know you don't like us being in one bed."

"No, I want to cuddle. Do you want to cuddle?" Believe me, I'm doing this for me. I want this. Need it even. The comfort.

He squints his eyes at me and nods slowly.

I sit next to him on the bed. "But I think we have to talk first ..."

"You want to know everything? I'll tell you everything."

And he does. He tells me *everything*—things I didn't know were possible, things I didn't know could happen, things that are simply inhumane. Making me tear up.

"Kristina ... are you sure I never reminded you of your ex?"

There's one thing that stuck out to me: he was convinced he was his father's son rather than his mother's son. I think he's still convinced of it, which is why he's asking me this. It's his fear. Now, I understand all his actions up until now. Now, I understand him as a person.

"Augustine, I need you to understand something about genes and environments," I say. "You might look like him, sure, because of genes. But a person is more than just their genes. Their environment plays just as big of a role. Some would argue even bigger. There are two types of environments, the first being your shared environment. Which is your household, the one you share with the people who gave you the genes in the first place. And the second is your non-shared environment, your unique environment. This is everything beyond your household, such as friends, school, and work. Anything really. Since it's the only thing identical twins differ in, it causes them to be two completely different people, personality-wise. It practically rules them.

"Your unique environment—you can control that. The environment you chose is the exact opposite of what your father offered. And don't forget that your mother was also a part of your genes and your shared environment. And she was love. It all adds up to the person you are today, sitting here next to me. He doesn't outweigh the other things. If anything, he's only such a small part of it. After all, book covers almost always only depict one element on them from the entire book." I exhale. "What I mean to say is, you're nothing like your father. Everything beyond appearances is too different to even compare. Even if your soil wasn't entirely healthy, you still got to bloom and blossom because you went looking for light and warmth when all you knew was darkness and frost."

I point at his stomach. "That's why you have a phoenix on your stomach, isn't it? From the ashes, you'll rise. And you did."

He smiles so brightly, blushes even at my words, and nods. I have never seen this look on his face, and yet I want him to continue showing it to me from now on because it's beautiful.

He's so very beautiful.

"I'm going to stop rambling now before I start explaining gene-environment correlation and gene-environment interaction and bore you out of your mind," I tell him.

"You could never bore me."

I laugh tensely.

He studies me. "This is what you get taught?"

"Do you find it interesting?"

"I find anything about you interesting, so if this is a part of you, then yes. Mad interesting, love."

We lie down and cuddle, and then cuddling turns into sleeping.

Just sleeping.

CHAPTER TWENTY-FOUR

"Eve." Eve, the name I never thought I would hear being said to me in that particular gruff voice—in Augustine's voice.

He probably doesn't mean anything by it, but I can't help but feel that he does. His tone. It's all in his tone, as if I'd been caught red-handed.

I turn around, blink several times, and try to laugh off the nerves. "What? Why would you—"

"I saw the notification of a message from Adam from that pen pal app."

"So? Why would you assume I'm called Eve? Also, why are you looking at my phone? And how do you even know that app?"

Yes, those are many questions indeed, and I need answers. Now. Because Augustine knowing about Adam's existence was never in the cards. It was never the plan. And if there's one thing I dislike, it's plans not being followed through.

"Unless ..." I say.

He nods and presses his lips against each other. "Unless ..."

No.

I hesitantly pull out my phone and open my conversation with Adam. The last thing he answered was that he had an awful day as well and that he decided to just sleep it off.

I type Adam, hit Send, and immediately look up at Augustine.

His phone chimes, the sound echoing through the room. The sound of the app. Of only that app. My temporal lobe can't believe its ears.

He takes out his phone from his pocket, reads it, and holds it out to me. "Eve," he repeats.

I look at his screen and see what I wrote on my screen displayed on his. My occipital lobe can't believe its eyes.

He retracts his arm, letting it fall beside him. "When you fell asleep, I responded. Then I heard your phone chime under your pillow. I wouldn't have looked at it if it hadn't made that specific sound. But it did. And I thought I was imagining things. Believe me, I thought something like that would be *too* good to be true. Until your screen showed me the irreversible truth. My message, sent to you."

I shake my head at him. Desperately.

Two completely different worlds are starting to share one orbit, and their clashing makes my brain split in two, separating my left hemisphere from my right hemisphere. Breaking my corpus callosum. Making me unable to think, to even function.

He's standing at the opening of his door, and all I can think of is leaving. I need to leave. Immediately.

I start moving to the door, but he isn't moving out of the way. I duck to leave his room from under his arm, but he ends up grabbing mine to stop me. "Don't. You don't have to run away anymore. Please? Don't you see that this can work? All this time, I thought you were in love with that peasant."

"What? João? No ... he's just a friend. I'm in love with—"

Wait. My brain doesn't even get the chance to make connections when it has lost its biggest one. If Adam is Augustine, then I'm in love with ... Augustine?

Surreal.

My eyes widen. And his soften.

He slides his grip from my arm to my hand, placing it on his chest. "Do you feel this? Beating, as if it can't keep up anymore. It has been doing this the entire night while I waited for you to finally wake up. Leaving me with only my thoughts. Causing me to enact a million different outcomes as to how this could go. I'm nervous. I'm excited. You are causing this. You are it, my heart."

I can feel his heartbeat through his clothes, reaching the nerve endings in the palm of my hand. The trembling of my hand synchronizes with the beating of his heart.

"Augustine ... I need you to let go of me. I don't want to be touched by you right now."

He looks alarmed, releases me almost immediately, and moves away for me to leave his room. I leave him behind in the room. I leave him behind in the entire house.

While he had the whole night to think, I didn't even get one second.

Think, Kristina.

I'm in love with Adam. Not with Augustine. How are they one person? It's impossible! I can't begin to fathom ...

Who is the real Adam? Who is the real Augustine? Are they both him? Are they not? Who even is "him" in the first place?

God, all the conversations ... were with Augustine? Fucking Augustine?

This isn't thinking. This is wondering. I can't think. I only have questions. For Adam? For Augustine? For both? No. For the universe. How is this even humanly possible?

I need to talk to anyone. I need someone to help me make sense of what reality is now.

Alex.

I ring her front door. I didn't tell her I was coming, but I know she's free today. So, yes, I am, in fact, about to just barge in. To come clean to her once and for all. To be guided by her wise words.

The door opens. "Kristina?"

Seeing her immediately calms me down somehow. "We need to talk. Now."

"Come in. Go to my room. I'll grab something for you to drink."

I do as she says and enter her room. Only to not find the floor, but all of her clothes scattered on it. Her closet is an even bigger mess.

She walks in with a glass of orange juice and hands it to me.

"For someone who has been in the closet for so long, I thought it would be cleaner," I say.

"Believe me, I wish I had cleaned the time I was in it too, when I had all the time in the world and no one was watching me. I hate cleaning out my closet, but I wanted to donate clothes I don't wear anymore, so I decided to love it, and then it completely blew up in my face."

I chuckle. "Alex, your closet was see-through to begin with, no offense."

"None taken. Was it the short nails? The short hair?"

"No. Really, it was just the rainbow pride flag printed on your T-shirt."

She puts on her mischievous grin, the one I love so much. "Well, you know me, proud to be queer, using it as my gear."

"I know, and I'm proud of you too."

We sit on the edge of her bed, and she taps my knee. "So, tell me? 'We need to talk. Now.' About what?"

"Brace yourself, because I'm about to dump almost half a year's worth of information in approximately four sentences." I chug the glass of orange juice to prepare myself.

She holds up her hands like a keeper does. "Hit me."

I inhale as deeply as I can and start dumping. "Augustine and I married out of convenience. Augustine fell in love with me. I fell in love with Adam. Augustine is Adam."

She lowers her arms. "Yeah, no, I completely let that one slide—0-1 for you. Hold the fuck up. Let me do the math. What?! I fucking knew it!"

"What?"

"That there was something about you guys. It didn't make sense to me why, all of a sudden, you wanted to get married when you had been so against it all these past years. But then it didn't matter because I was too happy for you that you had found love regardless of your past. I didn't want to ever bring that up again."

"I'm sorry I didn't tell you because I knew you would stop me."

"Of course I would have stopped you. This is insane. But wait, in love with Adam? I thought you said he was just a friend."

"I thought so—until I didn't anymore."

"The *Augustine being in love with you* part doesn't surprise me—that's just too obvious. That guy is obsessed."

Well, it surprised me it was real.

She looks up at the ceiling. Thinking. "But wait ... if they're the same person, isn't that actually a good thing?"

"What? No! Of course not. I can't even begin to wrap my mind around that part. It just doesn't make any fucking sense. He said the exact same thing you're saying, and it made me run away."

"Okay, but the fact is that they're the same person, which brings us to our following question. Why did you fall in love with one and not the other?"

I shrug my shoulders. "Because they can't be the same person. This must be some sick joke—"

She interrupts me. "Kristina, your past made you perceive every man as the same, right? So, even if you were aware of the 'not all men' statement, you would never risk tasting a cookie if there was a chance it was poisoned again, which is only natural. People then decide to only eat cookies when they know all the ingredients and how the cookies have been baked. But you decided not to taste anything ever again. You let your trauma become these handcuffs holding you back from living and loving.

"You have been living in fear all this time. It consumed you. Protecting yourself had become a leash you held on to dearly. Adam? He couldn't hurt you. You talked to him while you were comfortable, from your own room even. There was no fear, which made room for forming a connection. With all the men in your life, you were probably too busy being scared because of what you had been through. It's automatically different. You thought you weren't capable of falling in love anymore, but that was never the case. You are capable, if the need of feeling safe is met."

And then it hits me. Needs. Maslow's pyramid. "You are using Maslow's Pyramid."

"Who? I thought they were the Pyramids of Giza? Did Maslow steal our fucking pyramids? It's literally the only thing we have. Come on."

I can't help but laugh. The humor department? Alex is the fucking manager.

"No, you idiot. It's a hierarchy rather than a pyramid, actually. It all bottles down to this: basic needs have to be met before psychological ones. Safety before belongingness and love."

I kiss her cheek. "Thank you, Alex. I needed to hear this to actually start thinking in the only way I do."

"Psychology? Poetry? Academia in general?"

"Yes!"

"God, you're such a nerd. Anyway, if you need me to come up with other pyramids, you know where to find me. I'll be here, in my closet. Maybe stay in it to not be a disappointment for once."

I start laughing again. "I like you better outside of it. You *belong* outside of it."

Suddenly, Adam exists. Adam has a face. Adam is a person. I met Adam. I know Adam. I dine with Adam. I live with Adam. I slept with Adam. I *slept* with Adam. What a great example of anaphora.

Adam turned out to be comfort. And after a long time, so did Augustine.

Is it now time for the next step in the hierarchy? *Love?*

Because now that Adam isn't just an entity anymore but an actual person, it's the one I've been ignoring since the very beginning. I have been rejecting what I want most for the longest time.

But I can't decide to love him now just because he's Adam. That isn't fair.

The need for safety required to be met to form a bond. But isn't Eve my true self? And if Augustine doesn't like Eve, then he doesn't like the *real* me.

Humans tend to self-categorize themselves; it makes up our self-concept. And since we're part of several groups, it makes up our social identity. For instance, involuntarily, we have a specific ethnicity or an assigned gender. Voluntarily, we're part of a major or club. In each group, we behave in the way that's in line with the norm. But when one finds themselves being anonymous, there is no norm that binds you. This means you display your true self, the one that isn't bound by those unspoken rules.

To conclude, our situation has been doomed from the start, and we will never work because we don't love each other. Source? Trust me, I'm a psychology major. I know things. And if you don't, I researched it. My manuscript got peer-reviewed, and I even published the paper. Kristina et al. All being all my doubts.

My phone beeps with a normal text message.

Nemesis with Benefits: Don't forget the man you are destined to be with.

I ignore it. *But how could I? All the planets revolve around you now. You're the sun for a change.*

I suddenly remember my conversation with Ji-hye. She asked me if I would love Augustine if Adam wasn't in the picture. Since they're the only ones in the picture now, would I? Do ... I?

I decide that she's going to be the one to help me figure that out.

I make my way to the pub, and my prayers have been heard because I see my guardian angel pouring a glass for someone. The only things missing are her wings, really.

"Kristina? What brings you here again?"

"Ji-hye. I'm here to tell you that you were right, right about him being in love with me. But I'm also here to tell you a few other things."

I pour out everything, and all she can do is pour herself a glass of wine while pouring mine. We drink in silence. Her processing. Me *trying* to process.

She finally breaks the silence. "Okay, you know what I think? Something I didn't tell you back then but have been thinking ever since."

"Well?"

"You have loved him all this time too. You were just too busy denying it by loving Adam. Believe me, sleeping with someone twice is not just for the hell of it. Especially for someone like you."

I frown. "Someone like me?"

"You were about to hook up with that stranger that one time, but you left not two minutes later. Now, I know people are quick, but no one is *that* quick. Which means nothing happened, right?"

"Yes, because I couldn't feel anything ..."

"But you felt something with your husband, didn't you?"

"I mean, yes, when I sat on his lap this one time, which made the whole sleeping together happen, but it's just physical attraction."

She shakes her head at me. "You made it that way because being emotionally attracted to two people is something you didn't consider. Humans always disregard that, it being illicit. If it were just physical, wouldn't you have figured that out at the very beginning? Did you think he was handsome the first time you saw him?"

"Yes ..."

"Did you want to sleep with him then?"

I hold up my hand at her defensively. "No, absolutely not. I just wanted to scratch open his annoyingly pretty face. Ruin it."

She gestures for me to fill in the blanks with her hand.

"Only after I got to know him and formed some kind of bond with him ..."

She tilts her head a little. "An emotional one, emotional attraction. *Love.*"

She continues, "You love him. Adam, Augustine, whoever he is, it's one person, one soul. The way I see it? You fell for him twice. You will always choose him, no matter what shape he appears to you in. If that's not your soul mate, I don't know who is."

Even when my mind was supposed to be secured by Adam, Augustine kept infiltrating it.

I used to compare them and hate it. But now? It makes sense why I did. Comparing them. I was benchmarking Augustine with the standard Adam, a perfect match. Of course, it is. Of course I hated that. Because admitting to it would have meant admitting to my emotional attraction toward Augustine …

Crowding effect means that regions in your brain take on more than the task they're supposed to do, it being difficult for the brain sometimes, and so the original task might deteriorate because of it. Mine somehow could handle all of the extra tasks that were Augustine. Making Augustine even go beyond fucking neuroscience.

I hear my phone beep. I take it out and read the message.

Nemesis with Benefits: Come home, please, or at least tell me you are somewhere safe.

I ignore it, only to hear another beep. This time from the app.

Adam: If you feel more comfortable talking through this, then that certainly is an option.

I scoff. "Speaking of different shapes, he's playing dirty. Foul, evil man."

"What did he do?" Ji-hye asks.

"He texted me, and I ignored it, and now he's texting me through that app, knowing I won't be able to resist that. Since I'm 'in love' and all."

Eve: Well, "Adam," you know my situation all too well. What is it you think I should do?

Adam: You should give your husband a chance. If you had, you could have connected with him. And made the connection yourself. Can you love Augustine too? Please? The one who has been annoying you because it seemed to be the only way to make you notice him. To pay even a sliver of attention to him.

Adam: I'm yours. Will you finally be mine?

I can't help it, but seeing Adam and romantic words next to each other makes my heart flutter. Almost making me type *yes* in all caps, but I can't give in.

Eve: I can't just do that. There is so much that needs to be discussed.

Adam: Come outside, so we can start doing exactly that. Discuss, that is.

My heart sinks to my toes. I look up at Ji-hye, pure terror kissing my entire face.

"What?" she asks.

"He's here—I mean, he's outside."

Eve: How? How do you know where I am right now?

Adam: When you're anxious, you're unaware that you play with the beads of your ring. When you're sad, you're in your room, wiping away your tears with Lady. When you're happy, you go to that coffee shop next to our house with all your notebooks and books. And when you're confused or angry, you go to the pub to drink wine.

"Okay, I need you to let me use the back door," I tell her.

Adam: Don't even think about using the back door to run away from me again.

I turn my head left and right, scanning the place, but he isn't here. "What the actual fuck? Is he reading my mind as we speak?"

Ji-hye chortles loudly. "He probably thought about the whole thing to the extent of knowing your every move."

Well, he had a whole night to think about everything, and he said he enacted a million different outcomes, so she isn't wrong.

Adam: I can't read your mind. Believe me, I wish I could, but the truth is that I just know you too well. I always pay all my attention to you.

"Are you sure this place isn't bugged?" I ask her.

She reads what's on my screen. "Not anymore." And then she says, "Straight out of a K-drama, I bet he's wearing a suit."

"I love K-dramas! He always wears something that resembles a suit, but maybe he's wearing an entire suit now though."

Adam: I don't want to come inside. I want you to come to me. However, I'm getting very impatient, especially if you ignore me.

Eve: Not ignoring you, just finding you creepy.

Adam: Can you find me creepy while standing in front of me?

Eve: That would be *too* creepy. I like the distance we have now.

Adam: Distance has always been our problem, love. Without it, we wouldn't be in this situation right now.

Adam: *Tu me manques*, Eve, in more ways than one. I wish you would stop running away from me, so I could finally have you once and for all. I will be so good to you. Let me be good to you.

I turn to Ji-hye. "Do you happen to know French?"

"Oui, un petit peu."

"Huh?"

She smiles. "A little."

I show her my screen, and she starts reading. "Literally translated, it means *you are missing from me*. But it just means *I miss you*."

God, he has always had a way with words. Since I'm Eve, he means from his ribs. Since I'm Kristina, he wants to see me.

"Go to the man you love and talk it out. It's time," she urges.

Reluctantly, I get up and hand her my card.

"It's on the house since you're being courageous now."

I try to suppress my smile, failing miserably. "Thank you for everything. You truly are an angel."

"And you are too. Time to spread your wings. But if you ever want to talk again, don't hesitate flying back to me."

I say goodbye to her and start making my way to the door to leave.

I see Augustine leaning on his car between the front and back door. Wearing a three-piece suit, as predicted. Gray. Holding a bouquet of red roses. Twelve.

And then a clap of thunder follows the lightning strike. And when it does, so does the realization.

I might not know French, but I do know what *coup de foudre* is—overwhelming love at first sight. And since *at first sight* has never been our strong suit, at the millionth sight—under a different light, the darkness of the night.

Now that I see him, I realize I'm in love with him. Or rather, all of him.

You gorgeous man, was I truly that blind? You were right in front of me all this time. Of course it's you. How can it not be?

I walk toward him. "Ha, Gustav, what's the big idea?"

"Funny you should mention that again."

Funny you should mention that phrase again since Adam used it when I asked him what I could give you on the day you were born. Of course, you found that funny. It was Adam's birthday too.

I point at the bouquet. "Flowers?"

He corrects me, "Roses, since you seem to understand their meaning alone."

"What do you mean?"

"When I proposed to you, I asked you if you would want me to keep buying you flowers. *Yes* left your lips before no did. Duly noted, I told you. So I ended up buying you flowers every few days. I've been trying to talk to you through them for the longest time. It was the only way I could.

"When I gave you gardenias, I meant, secret love. When I gave you clovenlip toadflax flowers, I meant, *please notice my feelings for you.* When I gave you yellow hyacinths, I meant, *I'm jealous of the peasant.* And when I give you this"—he hands me the bouquet—"I mean, *be mine, my love.*" He gets down on one knee. "I'm going to propose to you again. For the love of God, put me out of my misery. Will you be my faux nothing?"

I drop to the ground myself, resting on my knees and putting the flowers down next to me. "How ... how do you possibly see this working? Do you realize that we fell in love with different versions of each other?"

"I don't have that problem. This is the best thing that could have happened to me. It's only logical that you are her. It only confirms that you would captivate me in any form you take. I would always choose you. Whether there are two screens between us or only my restraint, I would find you and fall in love with you."

"Wait. What do you mean, captivate you in any form?"

"I'd always liked Eve. I just fell for you harder. And when I realized that, it just felt wrong, talking to her. As if I was committing infidelity, not being true to you. So I continued to talk to her while keeping a certain distance. And when she confessed, I rejected her. To stay true to you."

You prick. That distance and rejection really took a toll on me. It even made me sleep with you.

"I don't believe you. You're just saying this so I give in," I tell him.

"Then let me prove myself to you. But in order to do that, you have to come with me to my office. I promise I won't do anything other than show you what I want to show you. And if you still want to leave afterward and sleep somewhere else tonight, I will respect that choice, even though I dislike it."

He grabs the bouquet and my hand, lifting us up. Then he walks around the car, opens the door for me, and I get in. He gets in himself and starts driving to his office. We don't talk during the ride, like words are being spared for when he shows me what he wants to show me.

We arrive in front of his office door, and he unlocks it. I see our reflection in it, reminding me of the very first time we met. It started here, only for us to end up here.

I go inside, and he closes the door behind us, locking it. The first time I was here, I practically yelled for him not to close the door. Now, I don't mind it at all. I even like the privacy. Things have drastically changed in the span of months.

He gestures for me to sit on the chair behind his desk—his chair. I do, and he unlocks the drawer underneath the desk, rummaging through it. He pulls out a journal and hands it to me, with the back facing me.

Then he leans against the edge of his desk, next to me, with crossed arms and feet.

Before I can turn the journal over to open it, my attention shifts to the wall. Specifically, to a painting. One that is very hard to miss, one that wasn't here the first time I was in this office.

Almost the entire painting is gold, except for the woman painted on it and the patterns on her dress. She has long, curly brown hair and brown eyes ...

She looks *too* familiar.

I point at it. "Who ... is that?"

He doesn't turn around; he keeps looking at me instead. "That is you, love."

"You painted that?"

"I did."

I knew he painted, but I'd never seen his work before. He's so ... incredibly talented. I would immediately believe it if someone were to tell me that this was normally displayed in a museum.

"What inspired it?" I ask.

"You, actually. It's why I found it funny that you mentioned the name Gustav again. The *Portrait of Adele Bloch-Bauer I*, also known as *The Woman in Gold* or *The Lady in Gold*, was painted by Gustav Klimt."

God, that accent. That is so hot—no. Focus.

"I have to thank that name for everything. If it wasn't for that day at the pub, when you were all tipsy and called me Gustav, you wouldn't have vented. We wouldn't be here. This painting is also a constant reminder that every occurrence in my life—no matter how bad—has led me to that one defining moment ... to you. I wouldn't trade that for the world," he says. "I thank fate that out of all the times you and I could have been born, we were born in the same era. But that wouldn't have been enough. What I'm truly grateful for is that all my choices and all your choices have led us to one another."

Adam, Augustine. I've said it before. I've thought of it before. Addressing it to you, to both of you. That out of all the random epochs, the more possibilities that we wouldn't have met than the ones we would, we found each other twice? I love that silly thing we cling on to as fate. I fucking adore it.

I'm too deep in thought still, which makes him fill the room with his voice. "When I realized my feelings for you, I wanted to see you all the time. You living with me wasn't enough. Even when we were apart, I wanted to see you. Hence, I painted you."

"And when exactly did this realization hit you?" I finally say.

"The moment you brought Lady home and I asked if I could hug you. But even before."

Even before? That's—that's like from the beginning.

He exhales. "And now, to prove my love for all of you, turn the journal over."

As he's still leaning against the edge of his desk, I shoot him a last look before turning it over. Only to find *Eve* in Arabic carved into the leather of the journal.

"Read everything I highlighted," he urges.

I skim through it and see dates from before I met Augustine highlighted. And certain passages.

You are the first person I have ever felt a genuine connection with.

I want to be with the real you.

Your words mean everything to me. I wish I could hear you say them.

The man manifested me.

I skim some more until I come across a section where Kristina and the date of the first time we met is noted down, with a lot written underneath. There are even more pages filled behind it.

I need to read that.

He yanks the journal out of my hands and laughs tensely. "I already proved that part, didn't I? I give you a finger, and you want my whole hand."

The feeling of him being inside of me. I want to feel it again. I want to feel it *now*.

"I would like just two fingers then, inside of me. Now."

"As much as I want to, I promised to just talk. Let me do that before I break my promise."

"Fine. You're right. You love both versions of me. Doesn't it bother you I didn't mention your Augustine side to you?"

"No, because I already know you have feelings for me. And if you don't, so be it. I'm not going to let anything get in the way of us finally being together. Not even unrequited love."

"But it is requited!" I say.

"I know, love. You never had to convince me, only yourself. I just wanted to hear you say it. It feels so good to finally hear you say it."

"How could you have assumed it when I just figured it out myself?"

"If you didn't feel anything for me, you wouldn't've been able to have sex with me. Since you couldn't go through with your hookup."

I gasp, stealing all the air in his office. "You knew about that?!"

"I had a hunch, which was why I was hell-bent on stopping you from going. I waited for you, sleeping on the couch. I woke up when you came back, and you returned way too early for it to have been a hookup. And you confirmed my hunch when we slept together. I'm glad you didn't, and I don't even want to know how far you actually went or else I'll find him and rip him to shreds."

So, he was fake sleeping. I can't really blame him. I also fake slept. We're even.

And why is everyone using that embarrassing hookup against me to prove a point? So I turned out to be demisexual. So freaking what?

He reaches for my hand. "Now that all of that is discussed and every possible combination of us loving each other has been met, will you finally let me profess my love for you without interrupting me? Without denying me? I need you to accept once and for all that I love you, Kristina, more than you can possibly begin to fathom."

"I will."

"Will you be my girlfriend?"

"I will be."

"My wife, willingly?"

"I am."

"Finally. Took you long enough. But patience is key, they say."

"It appears I have lost mine. Lend me yours to unlock me? I know for a fact that yours would fit perfectly, like lock and key."

He shakes his head, grinning. "Not yet."

He squeezes my hand for me to pay attention to his next words. "I need to hear you say it, not just accept my words."

"I'm your woman, and I'm so consumingly in love with you," I tell him. "So? Can you finally start giving me a key? Fingers? You know what? Because you made me wait for it, I want both hands now. One holding me here"—I point at my throat—"and the other entering me there." Then at my center. "Just like the first time, I want you to make love to me for a third time after all, since it's a charm and all."

A deep groan escapes the back of his throat. "You make me lose my morals. I'm a man of my word, but never when it comes to you. I get greedy when it involves you. Even if I promised I wouldn't touch you and that we would just talk, I wouldn't be able to resist you. I never could. But especially not when you offer yourself to me so willingly." He pauses. "Ha ... what should I do with you?"

"Me! You can do me, with me," I say, as if pitching this fine new product. Wanting him to invest in it, to buy it. Have a patent on it.

The corner of his mouth slightly lifts, then he turns around and slides everything on his desk away with one sweep of his arm, letting everything fall to the ground. Banging. Hopefully, I'll be next.

He gently taps his desk twice. "Sit and let me do you."

I sit on his desk, and he grabs my face to ask, "May I put my lips on yours?"

"Y—"

I guess any letter but *n* is good enough for him. He kisses me. So fiercely, as if he wanted to do this the minute he saw me. We start taking off each other's clothes. Me ending up in just my socks, underwear, and bra. Him ending up shirtless and with his pants resting on his waist.

We continue kissing, and he brings his hand inside my underwear, stimulating me.

Feels too good.

"Now, your other lips." He slides my underwear down to my knees and kisses my other lips.

And then I hear knocking, making me turn to the door immediately, and Augustine stand up straight. I see his assistant in the glass of the door.

"Mr. Elias?! I heard a crash and came as soon as I could. Are you okay?"

I whisper, "Oh my God, what if he can see?"

He strokes through my hair and whispers back, "It's one-way glass, love, remember? He can only see himself, exactly like you could."

I somehow feel more embarrassed now about checking myself out the first time I was here than I'd felt back then. You really get to see everything the other person does. His assistant just looks so … lost.

He brings one finger inside of me, places his hand on my mouth, and rests his chin on my shoulder. "All good. Thanks for asking. You may leave, Virat. I'm busy making love to my wife."

I gasp against his hand. I thought he covered my mouth so we wouldn't get caught, and now, he just plainly confesses what's going on?!

"I, uh … okay … I'm going then," Virat says.

"Also, Virat? Clear my schedule for tomorrow." He kisses my temple. "And the day after that." He kisses my earlobe. "For the rest of the year." My jaw. "You know what? I quit."

"Augustine … I can't do that, and you can't do that. I will clear it for the rest of the week. See you."

Virat finally leaves.

I slap his shoulder. "How could you say that to him?!"

He removes his chin from my shoulder to look at me. "I only covered your mouth because I didn't want anyone to hear your moans besides me. You're my woman. Your body, your voice—it's all for me and me alone. But no one gets to interrupt us. I'm just so happy right now. I want to shout it from the rooftops, share it with the world, that you are finally, officially, willingly mine," he says. "Let's make a new contract, being that there isn't one. I will begin stamping."

He gives small kisses across my whole body. My face, my neck, my breasts, my stomach, my legs—between them.

"Now, you have to stamp my version again," he says.

I kiss his cheek and shoulder.

He points at his crotch. "A stamp on every page."

I roll my eyes at him, tugging at the waistband of his underwear to hold it down and kiss it.

He inserts his fingers inside of me again. "Come on my fingers for now. Then, let's go home, so you can come on my cock instead. I will make us food and pour us a glass of wine, and then we can make love until the sun comes up. We can even pause to see the sunrise again and make love afterward," he pitches this time.

I whimper and say, "That must be uncomfortable, considering all the sand."

"I will bring a tent, my love. I would pick every grain of sand to make you feel comfortable, in a heartbeat."

Why do I have the feeling that he would do exactly that if I were to ask such a thing?

I'm all here for symbolism, though. The sunrise. Us meeting here. We met here, being further apart than ever from each other, and now he's inside of me. A full-circle kind of thing.

I can't help but love it *fully*.

CHAPTER TWENTY-FIVE

Adam: Kristina, I wonder, how much is too much?

Eve: Augustine. For the love of God, stop texting me through this and come downstairs. We have to go. It's time to confess our sins. Also, you are having too much fun with this newly acquired knowledge.

Adam: I can't help but love fate being on my side. And our names next to our faux ones? It makes it all the more real.

I'm sitting on the couch, and I hear footsteps descending. Even if we slept together—in all the ways two can—I woke up much earlier than he did. Actually, I didn't get a wink of sleep. I've been waiting for him to wake up because I realized that there was one thing, in particular, we hadn't discussed. Something I need to get off my chest before we start living out this little heartfelt fairy tale of ours.

He's holding two somewhat-small canvases against his chest, hugging them. "Good morning, love."

"Morning. We have to talk," I say sternly.

My tone makes him look tense. Maybe I should've added *good* to the *morning* this time.

"Talk? I swear, Kristina, if you break up with me right now, I might actually start crying. One day? That is too cruel, even for you."

Wouldn't it be divorcing you, though? I don't think he's completely aware I'm more his wife than his girlfriend.

I frown at him. "What? No. I just want to discuss something we haven't yet, so we don't leave anything unsaid."

Relaxation takes over his demeanor again. "Good." He sits next to me. "In that case, happy one day anniversary." And he hands me the two canvases.

On the first one, I see the beach and myself in my wedding dress. The moment I finally got to see the sunrise—*captured*.

On the second one, I see Lady and myself again, sleeping on the gray rug in the living room. The thing we used to do a lot when we just moved here—*showed*.

They look like printed-out pictures. His eyes being the lens, capturing moments, and his hands the nozzles, printing them.

He's amazing.

"Is this why your paintings are stacked facing the wall? Are they all of me?" I ask.

"Not all. Some are of Lady. She's a great muse."

And then another realization hits me. There's a lot of art on the walls here too, similar to what was in my scrapbook. The one he somehow also has, and since he's an artist …

I point at the artwork on the walls. "Wait. Everything on the walls … was made by you?"

He nods. "I drew most of it."

You drew it for me even though I was such a brat to you all this time.

Which is why I want to talk. Why I need to talk. Why I couldn't sleep.

I put the paintings next to me. "Augustine, we need to talk."

He places his hand on my leg for me to go on. To say what I want to say.

"I used you. You told me yesterday that the whole reason you were on that app in the first place was to form a genuine connection, that people honored you with their lips and not their hearts. I—how is what I did any different?"

"And I, you. It is different—"

I cut in on him. "It really isn't though?"

"It is. You were honest about your intentions with me. No one ever was. They told me they cared for me when, in reality, they cared about what I could give them. You told me you hated me the minute we met. You told me you wanted freedom and that I was a pawn to get there. What I wanted all along was honesty. You gave me that and so much more."

"But I wanted to manipulate you the first time we met, exactly like they did."

He chuckles. "You didn't exactly succeed, now did you, love?"

"No … but I could have."

"But you couldn't have. I didn't even give in when I saw how beautiful you turned out to be." He sighs. "At least we have the peasant to thank for being too incompetent to take care of his own affairs."

I can understand his jealousy of João when he thought I was in love with him. Now, I'm starting to think that Augustine just hates João.

"Since you had something you wanted to get off your chest … I do too," he confesses.

"Which is?"

"When did you realize you loved me?"

"You mean, Adam."

He shakes his head, disapproving of my words. "I mean, me."

"Uh ... well, during my 'hookup,' I found myself thinking about him."

He looks at me, warning me to try again with other words.

"Thinking about you. While I was kiss—"

He puts his fingers on my lips, closes his eyes, and shakes his head again. "No. I don't want to hear the second thing I somehow have to thank. It's too much to ask of me. Too much."

I thought you were just wondering about how much too much was. Well, there's your answer, love.

He removes his fingers. "You said it's time to confess our sins. What are we waiting for? I'm dying to get to heaven."

"You mean, to sleep with me."

"You knowing me so well? It never ceases to amaze me, love."

"Come in!" my mother exclaims.

We enter the house and greet her and Delano, and then they all sit on the couch. Except for me. I take my place behind the coffee table, placing my feet on the print of them. My old stage since I went on tour. And now? I'm back for one last performance—or rather, a speech. A life-changing speech about a life that has been changed *tremendously.*

"Augustinus, *habibi,* I made basboesa. Here, have some." My mother takes the plate that was already on the coffee table and puts two pieces for us on it.

Basboesa, which I like to call Egyptian semolina cake, is soaked in a very sweet syrup since the syrup that gets poured on it is quite literally sugar in water. Sugarcoated. Thus, too sweet, which makes it too delicious.

He devours what is his piece until he looks at me. I'm frowning at him for why he thinks confessing is a one-woman job.

He catches on and comes to stand next to me.

"I brought a guest star with me today." I drag Augustine from his sleeve to stand closer to me, making him almost lose balance.

I draw in air, only to draw out words. "Forgive me, Mother, for we have sinned."

She looks at us, bewildered. "What do you mean, you have sinned?"

"We married each other without loving each other."

Delivering bad news 101: announce that you're about to deliver bad news, avoid putting off delivering the bad news, and lastly, don't *ever* sugarcoat it. It's not basboesa to be sweet, just drop the bomb as bitter as it is, even though this one will turn out to be bittersweet, eventually.

Delano's mouth immediately falls open, and he shifts his attention from me to Augustine a few times.

And my mother, she seems ... *furious.* "What do you mean, you don't love each other?" Her voice increases in volume. "Why would you marry him if you didn't?!"

Now, shit really is about to go down.

I gently push Augustine to be a part of the audience again since the second act is about to begin, and its scenes are played by only one of the main characters—me.

As I push him away, with his eyes, he asks me, *Are you sure?*

With mine, I assure him that I am.

He sits next to Delano because when he walked to sit next to her, she looked pissed. It probably scared him off. I don't blame him. She's scary when she's mad. And now, she's exactly that. Mad. Furious. Pissed. Waiting for me to talk.

And yet I'm not as intimidated as I used to be. *Why is that?* I wonder. It certainly is a good thing because now, I'm going to confess to my heart's content. I can't wait to reach heaven after this in Augustine's embrace.

"I wondered, Mama, what it would take for you to see me as a woman—no, a human being."

She rises to her feet. Delano and Augustine are still sitting down, watching us.

"What are you talking about?" she asks.

"Exactly this. You asking me about my thoughts, wanting to have this conversation with me in the first place," I say. "To answer your question as to why I married him if I don't love him? Simple. I wanted responsibility. It felt as if you would always perceive me as this incompetent child. Suddenly, when a woman gets married, she's a real woman, an adult," I say and sigh. "I just needed more. I needed to feel independent. And the only way I could gain independence was to pretend to depend on someone else—him."

She holds both her temples with one hand, eyes closed. "Kristina, you can't marry someone just because you want to be independent. You have gone too far this time. You crossed the line!"

"Did I? See, I know it's wrong, marriage being sacred and all. And that almost stopped me from going through with it. Until I realized that in this godforsaken culture—because, yes, it's miserable, and even God didn't want to be part of it, why he created religion—it's more than common for people to get married without even having had a proper conversation before. The reason being that the man is a doctor, a lawyer, or an engineer. Does the cost of the degree dictate the degree of love? How ironic."

Augustine leans a little into Delano. "I love it when she plays with words. Twice in one passage? She never ceases to amaze me."

Delano whispers, "So, you do love her? I'm fucking confused, bro."

"Call me bro-in-law. And I'm not about to spoil the thing. Keep watching for the plot twist to happen. It's my favorite part," Augustine tells him.

I continue, "It took the guilt away and fueled the feeling that what I was about to do was more than fair. After all, I was just following the cultural norms. The ones you love so much, the ones I hate *too* much."

She's listening. She isn't interrupting me, telling me to stop. Nothing. She's actually letting me speak for once. Seemingly wanting me to continue. Or maybe I'm completely wrong, and I've traumatized the poor woman. Either way, it works out for me. I get to say more.

"There's just so much I disagree with, and it doesn't make me a bad person in the eyes of God. It makes me an autonomous person for once. It only makes me a bad person in the eyes of the people who're part of our culture. Jesus, it's like a cult. And frankly, I couldn't care less about them." I take a deep breath. "I'm living this life for myself, and I'm struggling already. I can't live it for them too."

Augustine attempts to secretly take a picture of me.

"Are you taking a picture of me right now?" I ask him.

He flinches and smiles. "I'm your number one fan, love. I just adore it when you speak. Breathe even." He holds his heart. "Your fierceness enchants me."

I giggle. He's such a flirt. *I love him.*

Delano and my mother face each other, more confused than I have ever seen them in my twenty-five years on this earth.

But I decide to confuse them even more. "It felt unfair that people younger than me could go alone on vacation, come home when they wanted, while I had a curfew still. You do realize that I did exactly those things once I got married, right? And all of a sudden, you wouldn't call me all the time, asking where I was anymore. I'm fine with that, but it's like you gave up all control."

"Because your husband fulfilled that role," she finally says.

Augustine whispers to Delano again, "God, I love being called her husband. And I tried, but she wouldn't let me be involved in her life."

"Bro ... what the fuck? Do you love her or not?"

Augustine ignores him and looks at me again through his screen. Actually being Adam right now.

"Did he? He's not supposed to replace my mother," I tell my mother. "Speaking of my husband, when I used to ask you about sex, you would get mad at me or tell me to drop it. And once I was married, you were the one to ask me the question right away. Making me lie since I hadn't had sex. Do you see why all of it is so frustrating? Do a mother and daughter only get to get close when they live apart?"

Delano now whispers to Augustine, "Wait? You guys never ..."

As he puts away his phone, Augustine says, "Of course we did. Rounds and rounds—"

Delano exhales deeply. "This shit is getting more confusing with each passing second. And stop. I don't want to know that."

"Then, don't ask."

"And this very moment, it proves my point. You never listened to me until now. If you had, I wouldn't have done it. But you only started listening to me after I got married, when it was already too late. You started treating me as an actual person rather than a project that had to be perfect, as if being graded by your society. And you, Mama, you are a perfectionist. Making me unable to ever make mistakes, but I did make mistakes. You weren't able to shield me from the things you wanted to shield me most from. Your control made me lose mine," I say, voice breaking. Because this confession will never not hurt.

Augustine's eyes immediately drop. Mentioning my past seems to hurt him more than it hurts me now.

"Do you realize what you have done?" she asks me.

"Do you realize what you made me do?" I ask her.

"Kristina—"

"Mama, I'm not done yet. Let me speak," I plead with her. "We do love each other now."

Saying that makes her calm down a little, but it makes Delano anything *but* calm. It even makes him jump up. "This was the plot twist?!"

"One of them," Augustine says while getting on his feet.

"You guys love each other *now*. Since when?" Delano asks.

"Depends on how you look at it, since yesterday or since the beginning," I say.

"You fell in love ... just yesterday?!" my mother snarls.

"No, I fell in love around our wedding," Augustine tells her.

"I did, too, around that time," I tell her. Wait a second. We fell in love around the same time? The irony.

"Yeah, with Adam," Augustine mumbles, rolling his eyes, as if disgusted by the name.

I narrow my eyes at him. "Are you seriously jealous of yourself right now? Seriously?"

Delano face-palms himself. "Adam? Who the f—I think it's just best if you guys stop talking, leave, and we pretend this never happened. Because the more you're supposed to clear up, the more it gets unclear."

The slap shook up his brain somehow because he's about to conclude everything to make sure he understands my speech.

"What the fuck? So, it was all fake. And now? It isn't. Just like that? Now that you mention it, you never looked in love. What changed?"

"Delano, your language!" my mother screams.

"Seriously, Mama? Not right now."

"Our secret identities got revealed," Augustine and I sing in sync.

"Your what now?" Delano asks.

I smile. "It's a long story. Maybe you should read the book."

"The what now?" Delano continues to ask.

"I'm going to write a book about it. Screw not being allowed to be artistic."

"Go, my love," Augustine cheers.

Delano grimaces. "I'm so glad we don't live together anymore. You've officially gone off the rails, Kristina. You're completely crazy."

Did he just use a figure of speech? *Miskien*, I must've really fried his brain if he had to resort to *that*.

"I love railing—" Augustine clears his throat. "I love completely crazy. Thank you for handing her to me at the altar."

"My pleasure entirely, bro."

Marriage of convenience? Enemies turned lovers? Forced proximity? All my favorite tropes in books. And now, in real life too. Besides, why not write a novel and turn us into a book? It's not as if anyone would stop me from chasing my dream. My husband certainly wouldn't. He's artistic himself. In fact, he encourages me to reach for the sun. To be it, to shine. After all, Augustine appears to be my number one fan.

My mom intervenes. "Augustinus, you were in on all this too?"

"I apologize, *tant* Diana, but I promise you, my intentions were pure from the start."

She exhales sharply. "I don't understand anything. All I know is that you should be glad that you ended up loving each other. What if you hadn't?"

"Well then, we just wouldn't have. I would've lived the rest of my life like I have the past half year," I say.

Now, Augustine intervenes. "I would have made sure that we had. *Trust me.*"

Delano and my mother start talking with each other, trying to meet each other somewhere in the maze I've put them in to get out of it together. To make sense of it all.

As they're finding a route, I grab Augustine's wrist and take him with me to my old bedroom.

I make him enter first and close the door behind me. I see his behind and impulsively pinch it, which makes him turn around, appalled, and guard it.

"Sorry ... I acted on my intrusive thought there."

"Your intrusive thought was groping my behind?"

"Yeah ..."

"Quid pro quo, my love." He grabs my wrist now, twirls me to face the door, and pinches mine.

I already knew he knew Latin since our very first encounter. I used to hate him for it, but now I find it hot. I might be sapiosexual too.

Speaking about realizations. A man? In my room? With the door closed? How is this even possible?

"Never, not in my deranged imagination, did I imagine I would bring a boy in here," I tell him.

He sits on the edge of my bed. "Want to do more than just bring a boy in here?"

I press my lips together and bob my head.

He lies down on his side, and I lie in front of him on mine. He wraps his arms around me and holds my hands, playing with my fingers. The familiar embrace I love so much. Somewhat spooning each other, mostly hugging.

"You must really like holding hands. I used to hate you touching my hand in the beginning," I say while playing with his fingers now.

"It was the only subtle way to feel your touch against mine. I sometimes wasn't even aware that I was acting on my impulses, especially in the beginning. And this one I couldn't inhibit."

Believe me, I noticed you couldn't. I even noticed you being surprised yourself that you were touching me sometimes.

I rub my hand against my sheets. "Most of the conversations I had with you, I was lying here, on this exact bed."

He holds me tighter. "Consider me to have passed through the screen."

"There are just so many things I wondered about and wanted to ask you as Adam."

"And I will answer many things. You want to take a trip down memory lane, Eve? Let's start with your first question."

"I want to go down on you, but I'll save that trip for later." I feel his inaudible laugh in his moving chest.

I slightly turn my head to say something more serious. "Why did you love the Garden of Eden so much?"

"Because if we—or, well, them—had stayed there, evil wouldn't have befallen the world. Abuse, pain, suffering, it wouldn't be here. The world would have been heaven quite literally on earth."

I love that. I take him up on his offer to answer many things and formulate my second question. "What kind of books do you read? I'm wondering because you always hide the spines of your books. Why do you do that?"

"Letting people know what kind of books you read, it gives them immediate access to your mind. Knowledge is power. I wanted mine to belong to me alone. But with you, I share everything." He pauses. "Anything really, but an author I particularly like is Osamu Dazai, a Japanese author."

"Do you ... want to annotate books and exchange them? Then we can have immediate access to each other's minds."

"I always annotate, so I'll give you one when we get home. Hand me yours when you're ready," he says. "But I can tell you what it is I'm thinking."

"Which is?"

"*Ana bahebik*. That's what I'm thinking, feeling. All the time. For the past half year now."

"*W ana bahebak*, Augustinus."

He kisses my temple.

"Would you read the book if I were to actually write it?" I ask him.

"An immediate insight into your innermost thoughts about me? That's the grand prize, my love. It can't possibly get better than that."

I grin like the idiot I am. "You know what I realized last night? We were chasing each other while running away from one another in a circle. We were basically rejecting each other and then comforting one another." Then, I say, "I guess you could say that we *requited unrequited love*."

"I'm tired, love. Let's never do that again, please," he puffs out.

I kiss his arm. Indicating that I completely agree. *Let's never run from each other again. Let us only chase one another when we face hurdles in the future.*

"We all have our demons to face, but I'm glad I faced mine with you by my side," I tell him.

His lips graze my ear. "I feel the same way, my love. With you, I feel comfort. You comfort me. Seeing you, I feel like all my problems and fears ... I feel like I can handle them and that everything will be all right. You have that effect on me. You are the thing that keeps me going, the oxygen that I need," he says. "Sometimes, it feels as if God created you just for me. Like my own personal drug. And I never want to get clean."

He did, Adam. I was made for you. And I hope you build tolerance, Augustine. I hope you will always want more because I want to give you myself entirely.

I used to relate addiction to love because I feared it. But now, everything has changed. If it's about true, genuine, unharming love, you can be addicted to wanting to see the other at their best, to having them reach their full potential.

I sigh. "There's just so much I don't know about you, things I will never know. Your first achievements, your little milestones."

He squeezes my hand. "But we have the future. Let's make the most of it together. But first? Let's go on a damn honeymoon."

"Where do you want to go?"

He laughs a little. "I want to keep showing you that the things you hate at first, you will come to love eventually. I want to keep changing your life—for the better."

"Huh?" I ask.

"We're going to Egypt, love, for our honeymoon. *Egieren*."

TWO PAINED SOULS HELPED EACH OTHER HEAL. SHE PROVED TO HIM THAT HE COULD LOVE A WOMAN AND TREAT HER RIGHT. HE PROVED TO HER THAT SHE COULD LOVE A MAN AND BE TREATED RIGHT.

The End

Epilogue

Six Years Later

Egypt, Sharm el-Sheikh

I'm lying on a beach bed, under a straw beach umbrella, with palm trees surrounding me. The warm sun caresses my skin, and the cool breeze touches it. I can hear birds chirping and the waves of the vast sea crashing against the coast. It's quiet and peaceful because the sun has just risen.

"Samia, be careful and don't walk away from your *baba*!" I shout.

I wish I could dance with them, but I'm too pregnant to even stand up, let alone participate. Besides, I have to guard the juices we just bought, which are in small bags with straws inside of them. We're in Egypt now, and juice is a necessity rather than a luxury here.

Exactly where Augustine wanted me all those years ago—at a juice bar. I can't even count how many times we went.

We're now at the beach. It's summer, so it's especially hot. Augustine and Samia—our three-year-old daughter—are dancing on the shoreline. She's standing on his toes, and he twirls her around like the princess she is. All three of us are wearing white *galabeyas*.

Thank you, Samia, for letting my dream become a reality. To dance with one's father. To live all my dreams through you. It looks like so much fun.

He lifts her up and walks toward me.

"*Ay*," I say, holding my stomach.

"You okay, Mrs. Elias?" Mr. Elias asks.

I smile at him. "I am, my love."

"I want a sandcastle, *Baba*!" Samia yells.

Augustine grabs the buckets he just bought and fills them with sand.

Her name is Samia, after Augustine's mother. She looks exactly like Augustine—green eyes and pitch-black hair. Her father's daughter. *Perfection.*

He has Samia Elias on his chest for both his mother and daughter. And the little fella in my stomach—who can't stop kicking me, probably jealous that he isn't drinking juice directly—his name is going to be Kyrollos, after my father. Maybe I should put Elias on my collarbone because I'm not sure Kyrollos Elias is going to appreciate Kyrollos Armanious on it when Samia Elias gets a whole chest. I think Augustine and I have to discuss that.

This way, his mother and my father are with us again through our children.

And my name? Well, it turned out that I accepted the offer of his last name after all. Because the man was too stubborn to let not having the same last name go. So, I ended up changing it to Elias. Kristina Elias.

Which made us go back to how we addressed each other at the beginning, only this time, it's different, of course.

Much is different, like how we obviously slept together again to make our loving children. The first two times were supposed to be the last, and yet there was a third time, but after that, in the past five years? I can't even begin to count how many times we have. Since we still like to do our rounds.

Let's see ... Augustine watched every Disney movie in existence, and it made me love him even more.

I started wearing my ring always too. Not just in front of others, like I used to. That made him love me even more since he used to be the only one to wear it all the time.

And Samia is best friends with everyone—with Marina and her husband,

Alex and Senait, Delano and Farah. And especially with Lady.

They start building the sandcastle next to me.

He kisses her head. "A castle for my princess." He then kisses my stomach. "For my prince." And then kisses me. "And my beautiful queen. How about we add one more heir? We can call them Adam or Eve," he says.

This is his way of telling me he wants to sleep with me.

"Augustine, I'm not having sex with you. I'm eight months pregnant. Give me a break."

"I have no breaks to give, love. How about after you deliver?"

"I'll have to check my schedule, but I'll probably be too busy birthing out a placenta."

"How about after delivering everything you'll be delivering?"

I cup his cheek. "Then I will make love to you until the sun comes up. And then some."

"Fine. Kiss me."

I do, and he licks his lips. "You taste like mine. Give me more."

"What's sex?" Samia asks.

I immediately let go of him and gasp.

Augustine gasps too. "That's a naughty word!"

She giggles, as she does best. "But Mama said it!"

"Mama is a naughty woman!"

I grab my slipper and hit his shoulder with it. "Augustine!"

"Teen!" He grabs some sand and throws it at me.

"Stop throwing sand on me when I'm wearing white!" I shout while rubbing it all off.

Samia points at my thighs, which are bare. "Mama! Your beauties are showing!"

Another thing that changed: I started wearing dresses. I came to love the summers too, not just the sun. And we taught Samia that if she ever sees someone with marks on their skin, whether it be freckles, moles, birthmarks, stretch marks, scars, or anything that makes skin not even, to call them their beauties. Like beauty marks. That it's a form of art, just like the tattoos Augustine and I have. There to stay, there to be embraced.

She's such a good girl.

The things I lacked, I get to have them through my daughter. And Augustine? I can't even put into words what he means to me. Both of them have healed me and continue to do so every day.

Augustine kisses my beauties. "Beautiful, exactly like the person who has them."

I beam at his words.

He holds up the towel that was underneath my feet to hide my face from other people. "I want to be the only one to see that smile. Don't make me tie you up in a tower, Rapunzel, the brunette one."

"It's fine. I would probably develop Stockholm syndrome."

When two people have been together for a while, social psychology suggests that passionate love gradually turns into companionate love. A deep connection. We have that, but we're just as passionate as we were five years ago. We're somehow still in our honeymoon phase. As if these last five years went by in a flash and we're still in Egypt for our honeymoon, not having returned here four times already. Maybe we're still in it because we postponed it for the longest time?

But one thing is for sure: even though we've seen the Pyramids of Giza a dozen times already, they still amaze us when we see them in the flesh, which is why we visit them every year. Soon, Kyrollos can see them too.

Augustine and I set up a foundation to aid anyone who's a victim of any kind of abuse and domestic violence. We give them the professional help they need to get them out of their situations and guide them in healing since it's a cause close to our hearts. And with every victim turned into a survivor, the more blessed I feel to be a part of their journey.

We made visiting our parents' graves a tradition as well. I give my father nine blue roses, and Augustine gives his mother eight dark pink roses, symbolizing his gratitude to and admiration for her. When we're at their graves, we always share stories of them. I mostly share the stories I heard about my father, and Augustine shares stories about his mother, letting me get to know her better, that it isn't too late for that. I love it when we go there and share stories. It's very intimate, and it always brings us closer after a long week of being separated from each other because of our daily duties.

Also, my mother and I found common ground. And have built a very deep bond. We're closer now than we were in my twenty-five years at home. She apologized even when we discussed everything in more depth, alone. We understood each other and forgave one another. I love the woman. Sincerely.

I actually wrote a novel. It's called *Requited Unrequited Love* and is based on Augustine and me. I used our journals as notes, meaning I finally got my hands on his journal to write specific passages from his perspective. I practically copied and pasted our conversations from the app, and we reenacted every little incident so I could get inspired while writing. He also drew the cover. It sure was a journey, but my loving husband was there for me every step of the way.

I have two passions. I love anything that is related to writing, and I love psychology. I wanted to share both passions through the book. I wanted to show others how anything you thought you couldn't seem to describe had words, after all. Who says you can't do both? Society maybe. I say let them deny you and do exactly what they deny you. You decide what your full potential is. You decide the limit. And please, let it be the horizon. No, let it be beyond the horizon. Let it be the *sky*. Not reaching your greatest potential because they said you couldn't? Let *us* deny them that.

I published it too. Some people loved it, while others hated it completely. Which is fine. It's a part of life. It's being unique, being human. Imagine everyone being alike. That would be awful—especially for personality psychology.

I got to tell my story, and I'm proud. Because I wanted to leave an imprint of myself in this world, not just behind my coffee table. So, even if it isn't for everyone, it's for a few. And that's all that counts because the few count for all.

And, of course, I'm feeling better now too. I would even say, feeling my best.

There was a time when I felt too much and didn't want to feel anything at all. I won't ever forget that, but it *can* get better.

It so can.

We finish our juices and throw them away in the bin next to us.

"Let's go get some sleep before the day actually starts," I say.

Augustine helps me stand up, and we both hold Samia's hand. In his other hand, he holds the buckets he just bought her, and I hold my slippers in mine.

I look at them as we walk next to the shore, leaving the beach. "Let's watch it tomorrow too."

"Forever, till my last breath," my loving husband answers.

"I requite that!" my loving daughter yells.

With the sun almost setting now, having achieved what was meant to be achieved today, I'm going to enjoy the remains of it with my little family of four, involving a lot of strawberries. Enjoying the ending, only to enjoy a new beginning tomorrow.

Laptop drop.

I didn't actually drop it. It's closed. I just wanted to stay true to the saying.

Oh, you get what I mean.

Kristina out.

Acknowledgments

I can't believe I've actually made it to this page. So first of all, thank you, me. Thank you for seeing this through to the very end, even when you were so insecure. Because you truly appreciate not giving up once you reach your goal. My whole life, I've been surrounded by people with talent and passion for music, sports, arts and crafts. Occupations that took their energy, but in return, gave them more, and purpose. I never had that, but I wanted it badly. You could even say that I was jealous of those who had. Never in my life did I have something that I could call my talent, my passion. I searched for it almost everywhere; I bought a keyboard, but didn't make music. I bought art supplies, but didn't make art. I bought and bought and bought, and did nothing. All I did was get older, poorer, but not more creative. I could never find that thing that was *mine* and eventually, I gave up looking. Then I got into a car accident, which forced me not to participate in life for almost a year. I hated the world, I hated how unfair life could be, and I hated being stuck in my own body. I wanted to escape the world. But all I really needed was to escape the depressive spiral, because I didn't want it to swallow me whole.

Somehow, the concussion I hated with every fiber of my being shook up my brain in a way for me to craft this entire new world. To escape to it. So, thank you, car accident, because without you, I wouldn't have written this story. I wouldn't have found, after all these years, the thing that's my passion.

Because discovering yourself doesn't happen in the timeframe society has set for you. Your teens might be about discovering yourself, but so are your twenties, thirties, forties, and even fifties. Discovering yourself happens until you are gone forever.

The cup is half full. I was lucky to have survived an accident when many don't. And knowing that you've been lucky, makes you want to milk that fortune for all its worth.

But I didn't do it alone, because it took a village, and I want to knock on each and every resident's door to thank them.

My dearest reader, thank you. Thank you for reading the first sentence, and thank you for reading the last. Thank you for believing in me, because for the longest time, I didn't. And sometimes, I still don't. I'm a work in progress. And words cannot describe how grateful I am to share my (first) discovery with the world, but most importantly, with you. It means the world to me, and you mean the world to me. So, if anything, I hope I could have meant anything to you as well. I hope that I have taught you something, even if it's small. I hope I made an impact on you, because that was the goal. Chase after what you want endlessly. Live this life selfishly. And love fiercely. And who knows? Maybe I'll see you at the next one, if you'll have me again, of course.

Mama. Thank you for encouraging me to do this when you saw that this was the only thing that painted a smile on my face in a long time, instead of telling me not to, which I think you would have done if you actually knew what's written in these pages—thank God you're far from fluent in English. Since this whole project began with having Adam and Eve in mind, you probably thought, 'Oh, Genesis, religion!' Well, yes, Mama, it is, but it also *really* isn't. I'll just keep showing you the cover and summarize every scene for you—and leave the ones where they touch, *untouched*.

V. The best sister in the world (and brother, father, mother) you're like everyone rolled in one. Thank you for taking this project seriously from the start, and for, instead of letting me feel like I'm going to be burned by reaching for the sun, bringing me its warmth by listening when I would ramble on and on about the plot and these characters. Fueling me to keep traveling this road. Sharing your experiences with me to write certain characters. You're actually the biggest inspiration for many scenes, and I think it would only be fair to consider you the co-author of this book. You made me believe the statement that the sky's the limit, and that I should go after what I want. I will, and I hope you do the same. I hope you won't let anything limit your creativity, because it's so out of this world, that I think it should be shared with it.

My Lady. Well, my Lady is a man, so I shall call him Mr. Whiskers. Mr Whiskers, I got you because it has been scientifically proven that cats are good for our mental health. (Dear reader, remember when Kristina made a powerpoint presentation to adopt a cat? Yes, you guessed right, that's non-fiction. I quite literally did that). You were born on the 26th of December and you changed my life for the better. I look at you and think to myself, I would face my worst fears just to keep you safe. You're not only my writing buddy, but also my baby and my savior (I'm not comparing you to Jesus, but since you were born on the 26th, you kind of are. I don't make the rules, okay?). I love you furrever. And dear reader, Mr. Whiskers urges you to stay pawsitive.

My therapists. I met you when I was at the lowest point of my life, and you brought down a ladder, extended your hand, and told me it was time to climb up again. You told me that it's okay to want to escape when things are rough and when I don't like the world. You encouraged me to create a new one. Thank you for helping me, but also helping me write. Thank you for being my therapists, but also my friends. A. I hope you get to finish writing your own book, because I want to read it. M. I hope you meet a man who sweeps you right off your feet, because you deserve it.

A. Thank you for always being there, but especially for when I need you the most. I think it's safe to say that in these past years, you became your true self. And I love you all the more for it. I can't wait for you to continue becoming your true self, and for you to do what you're meant to do in this world: make it better. I know times have been rough, but your smile never fades, and it's empowering. It empowers me, too.

C. Thank you for symbolizing women's empowerment, and for being a woman I strive to be. But because you work so hard, it's high time you relax. Although I can safely say that you're the one who taught me what resilience is. You're stronger than you give yourself credit for. And I'm waiting for your office romance to unfold. Even though you're denying it, my trope-heart is about to burst out of my chest. Because denial makes the best love stories. And you deserve nothing but the best.

Z. I just have one question for you: when are you getting cuffed? I hope this book made you realize it's time to look for a wife. And if you want me to be a matchmaker, just say the word. I have women lined up for you. You just have to promise that you will leave your bubble. And that you will put yourself out there. It's time.

S. You know the freckles the heroine has? Yes, inspired by you. You always try to keep yourself together alone, but I know you long for someone to hold your pieces together. So, I hope you get to experience a love story as intense as I tried to write this one. Because you deserve the kind of love you give others—which is genuine.

A. I hope you got the discovery you needed. Because it's time to put yourself and the things you actually want, first. And you're well on your way. I hope we will get to keep accompanying each other and root for each other on our journeys to ourselves. If not giving up could take on a human form, it would be you.

S. How are we both into books, but almost never discuss them? We should really change that. And I think now would be the perfect moment. It's funny, but I think we broke the ice between us before we even met each other. I've always felt like you were someone familiar, someone I know. But I think I understand why, because you're the epitome of peace and comfort. And I adore you for it.

Jovana. Thank you for working your magic by turning my very messy (*very* messy, it was to cry for) manuscript, into a novel. It wouldn't be the same without you.

Marla. Thank you for your kindness and patience with me. And I appreciate everything you've done for me. Your work truly is the icing on the cake.

P. I know what you must be thinking, 'You didn't tell me about this project for months, and now you're putting me last? Really?' But my love, I told you about the recency effect, didn't I? People will remember this and forget about the middle. I remember when I first told you about this project (the primacy effect, the first piece of information on something is remembered well, too) and you supported me. You even beta-read the first chapter when you don't actually read books. You gave such good feedback that I thought to myself, 'maybe he should consider becoming an editor?' So, if you're up for it, how about you beta-read all my work from now on? With your support, I think I can share the stories I have up my sleeves. They're heavy, so carry them with me? You're my punchline, en ik houd wel van jou, mijn lief.

About Author

Mina Ramzy is a daughter of Egyptian immigrant parents, born and raised in the Netherlands. With a passion for psychology and storytelling, she decided to combine them into books. She loves creating worlds, and she loves creating characters who have things to work with or through. Her goal is to raise awareness on important topics, but also to show the strength of human relationships. And to try and let everyone feel represented in her work.

In her free time, she can be found in the gym (well, this is the goal, she can usually only be found there when she remembers she has a membership). But what she *really* can be found doing is enjoying her me time, learning something new, planning her life, cleaning and organizing her environment, daydreaming, cuddling with her cat, eating loads of chocolate, and consuming stories. Or, plotting her next one.

She hopes that her stories make you feel something (pun-intended), your heart flutters, aches, and everything in between. And she hopes that she can teach you something new. Because at the end of the day, us readers *are* intellectual beings.

Printed in Great Britain
by Amazon